LIES
in the
DARK

A HEART OF THE INFERNO NOVEL

NICOLE FANNING

Nicole
FANNING
DELICIOUSLY DARK AND ABSOLUTELY THRILLING

LIES IN THE DARK

First Edition

Paperback ISBN: 979-8-9881623-2-2
Hardback ISBN: 979-8-9881623-1-5

Cover by: Charly @ Designs By Charly
Interior Artwork by: Charly @ Designs By Charly
Editing by Charly Jade
Proof read by Mikayla Christy
Formatting by Charly @ Designs By Charly

This book is for all the hearts in the world who feel a little broken, a little lost, or a little unlovable. You are perfect the way you are, and you are enough. Always.

PROLOGUE

Rachel

SEVEN YEARS AGO

The gun is heavy in my hand.

My dealer said it would be. He also said it's *quiet*. And it is.

So quiet, in fact, that in the silent room I can barely hear the safety click off.

I stand on Jaxon's side of the bed, aiming it directly at his head. I've been standing here for nearly ten minutes, just thinking. About everything.

Fuck him for looking so beautiful right now, honestly.

The dark gray silk sheets are wrapped indiscreetly around his body. His eyelids twitch, and his chiseled jaw tenses against the pillow, his well-defined abs rising and falling gently with every breath he takes.

Suddenly he shifts on the bed.

I breathe in sharply, but manage to keep the barrel of the gun still pointed at him. He mumbles something indecipherable in his sleep, and his brow furrows. I hold my breath as he rolls onto his

CHAPTER ONE
Rachel

"Come on, you little shit, open!"

It's been a while since I've broken into a hotel room and unfortunately, I'm a bit rusty.

Thick lake-effect snow falls around me and I can see my breath in the air as I stand on the slippery second-floor balcony of a sketchy motel on the south side of the city.

Chicago Lakeview Premier Extended Motel is an amusing contradiction. One, it has too many words in its name. Two, it is certainly not *premier*, as the building is at least forty years old and near condemnable; and three, the only *view* it has is the noisy freeway where cars whiz past sloshing the cold sleet beneath their tires.

I slide a credit card between the frame and the lock. It's an old trick I learned from a friend of mine. It doesn't work all the time, and especially not at high-tech new hotels, like the Jefferson. However, older motels like Lakeview can barely afford to keep the lights and heat on, let alone upgrade their security with the low fares they charge.

But this is good for me, because I finally feel the latch click.

Hell yes, I've still got it.

If the man staying here had any regard for his personal safety, he would've at least used the deadbolt. But when the door finally pushes open into the dark musty room it's clear he didn't.

Of course, he fucking didn't. Why would he?

After all, Adam Westwood is a cocky FBI agent who isn't afraid of criminals or murderers, or pretty much anything that goes bump in the night.

The room is dark, but warm. And since I just walked a mile from the bus stop in this awful weather, my clothes are soaked and I'm desperate to get out of the cold. I quickly step into the room and close the door behind me, flicking the light switch on the wall.

But it doesn't turn on.

Yeah, some Premier hotel, alright.

I feel around in the dark, hoping to find the lamp at the edge of the bed. But instead, my knee smashes hard into a wooden table leg, nearly sending me tumbling to the floor.

"Ow!" I shout, reaching the nightstand and flicking on the lamp. "What the actual fuck?"

"You took the words right out of my mouth," Adam's voice suddenly sounds behind me.

"Jesus!" I jump, whirling around to face him. "You scared the hell out of me."

He sits facing the door in the only semi-comfy chair in the room, a bottle of *Jack Daniels* beside him.

"Now see, *that's* funny. You break into *my* hotel room, and your brother is Michael Valentine, and your baby daddy is that insufferable prick Jaxon Pace. By all accounts, I should be the one who is scared," he says, pulling his gun out from beneath the cushion. "Coincidentally, I'm not."

I stare at the weapon in his hands, my heart starting to pound. He's angry. But I've learned that with dangerous men like him you can't show you're afraid…even if you *are*.

"You're right," I say, taking a deep breath. "But as you just said, my brother *is* Michael Valentine, and my baby daddy *is* that insufferable prick Jaxon Pace."

I take a step towards him, stopping only when I hear the safety click off.

"Your point?" He growls.

"If you want to intimidate me, Adam," I say with a smirk.

8

"You'll have to do a lot better than threatening to shoot me, as I'm far too used to it at this point."

He stares at me, his dark brown eyes emotionlessly scanning my soul.

Finally, the safety clicks back on.

"I never wanted to intimidate you, Ann—" he sighs. "I mean, *Rachel*."

I don't know what's more uncomfortable, the frustration in his voice or the look of disappointment in his eyes.

"Why are you sitting in the dark?"

"How about I'll tell you that after you tell me, what the fuck you're doing in my room?" He spits.

"Well, I didn't see your car outside, so I didn't think you'd be here," I say, scanning his face. "If I'm honest—"

"Honest?!" He suddenly snaps, making me jump. "You haven't been honest from day one! And here I am, risking my neck running all over the city, looking for *you*."

He stands to his feet and stomps across the room.

"I'm sorry, I don't remember ever asking you to do that for me," I fire back. "How was I supposed to know you were worried about me?"

"Of course, I was fucking worried! I mean, do you have any idea the kind of sick thugs that are—"

He stops, putting his hands on his hips and laughing sarcastically.

"But of course you do," he says quietly. "Because you're *in* with them."

"I'm not."

"Yes, you are!"

"Okay, yes, I am," I laugh, darkly. "But not in the way you think."

"The way I *think*?!" He thunders. "Please, tell me, how this is so fucking funny? Or how this could be viewed any other way? I know you're just a whore and all, but fuck! You're literally in bed with the enemy!"

"I am not a whore!" I shout back.

He stares at me, completely dumbfounded.

I mean, to be fair, that's how we met.

"I might make a little cash here and there taking clients," I sigh, defensively. "But that's not all I am. I'm a hell of a lot more

9

than that."

He laughs, swiping the bottle of Jack off the table and walking over to the dirty window.

"Naturally," he whispers. "What a fool I am. Here I am thinking there was something *real* between us. And you're... you're..."

He hangs his head.

"I'm what, Adam?" I snap angrily. "What am I?"

"You're just..." His voice trails off. "You're not what I thought you were."

"You know, that goes both ways," I say, locking eyes with him. "Let's not forget you've lied to me too, *Robert*."

"Don't call me that," he whispers lethally without turning around. "I stopped going by Robert a long time ago."

"Why?"

"That's none of your fucking business."

"Look," I say, my own frustration building. "I'm not even supposed to be here right now. Jaxon has me under house arrest, with half a dozen big ass bodyguards standing guard. But I snuck out, took a long uncomfortable bus ride, walked a mile in the snow, just to be here to talk to you because I thought you deserved an explanation."

"I have nothing to say," he says bitterly.

"You clearly have plenty to say," I fire back. "So be a man and just fucking say it with your whole chest."

He suddenly kicks the table in the room, sending it toppling on its side.

"Alright, fine! You want to talk, Rachel? Let's talk. How about we start with the fact that you're one of them!" He shouts, storming over to me. "And I'm sure that I'm just a joke to you, and your little criminal buddies."

"No!"

"Do you fuck them all too? Laugh about me while you're riding their dicks?"

"Fuck you!"

"Do you fuck *him* too? Jaxon?"

"Of course not!"

"Clearly you have in the past, as he's the *father* of your daughter," he says, narrowing his eyes at me as he grabs me by the shoulders and yanks me off the bed. "A daughter that you said you *lost* a long time ago. But that was all just a lie too, wasn't it Rachel?"

"Fuck you! I did lose her a long time ago!" I shout, shoving him off me. "You know nothing about me, Adam. You have no idea who I am or what I've been through, or what I've suffered because of this life! So do me a favor and don't try to profile me because I promise that your big head will get it wrong!"

I step past him heading for the door.

"You know, I did come here to talk to you. Why? Because even though you lied to me just as much as I lied to you, I thought you deserved that. I thought you were a good man," I say, the venom pouring from me. "You think you're so much better than us, but the truth is you're just as fucked, just as vicious and just as much a waste of my goddamn time!"

I yank the door open but just as I am about to leave Adam slams it closed, blocking my path.

Neither of us move, our rapid breathing the only sound in the room.

I should leave. I should shove his ass to the floor and walk out that door. But I just stand here, waiting for him to say something for what feels like an eternity.

"You're soaked," he finally says, his eyes only meeting mine for a moment.

Really? That's what you're going to lead with Adam?

Silently he walks over to the dresser in the small motel room and pulls out a sweater. He stares down at it in his hands as he turns to face me.

"Answer me this," he says quietly. "Was *any* of it true?"

His eyes find mine and suddenly I cannot move. He looks so…broken.

Maybe it *was* real for him.

It takes me a moment, but eventually I regain my faculties and take the shirt from him.

"It was real,"" I say, walking over to the bed. "A lot of it actually."

I steal another glance at him, before pulling my soaking thin shirt over my shoulders. But when I reach for the sweater, Adam suddenly grabs my arm.

"If you're going to stay, I need to know you're not wearing a wire."

Now I immediately understand: He wants me to undress… in *front* of him.

I can't blame him actually. It's a smart move.

I reach behind me and undo my bra, tossing it on the bed. Wrapping my arms around my shivering body I spin around.

"See? No wire."

"All of it," he nods to my jeans as well.

I snort, shaking my head.

"Yeah, we must've had something really *special*, huh?" I say sarcastically. "Although. I guess to be fair, it's not as if you haven't seen it all before."

He glares at me, then pulls out his wallet and throws two hundred-dollar bills on the bed.

Oh, that's how this fucker wants to play it, huh?

"Alright then if that's how it's going to be," I snap irritably.

I sit down and unzip my boots, tossing them on the floor before peeling my wet jeans from my body. Within moments I stand before FBI Agent Adam Westwood in nothing but my underwear.

"Satisfied? Bet the Bureau would love to hear about this."

He glances at me briefly before reaching into the drawer and pulling out a pair of sweatpants.

"Go take a shower. There's a fresh towel in there I haven't used. You'll warm up, and dry off," he says quietly, tossing the pants on the bed. "I'll order takeout. There's a Chinese food place with delivery that's somewhat palatable."

I realize in this moment I have a choice.

I could tell him to go fuck himself, put my clothes back on and walk out that door, and vow to never see him again.

…Or I can stay and see where this goes.

Fuck it. Let's take a walk on the wild side.

I grab the clothes off the bed, deliberately leaving the money where it lies.

"Chicken lo mein, with an eggroll," I call back to him, walking toward the bathroom. "And don't forget my fucking plum sauce."

CHAPTER TWO

ADAM

She's here.

I lean back in my chair, covertly sneaking a glance into the bathroom, where a very gorgeous, and very *naked*, woman steps into the shower.

She's actually here.

I wish I could say I'm completely surprised, but I'm not. Once I knew for sure that she hadn't been kidnapped or murdered, and finally learned the truth, I knew she would come find me. Why? Because she wants answers.

As do I.

For months I've been in this wretched city trying to find my dead partner's niece, whom I suspect has been kidnapped and sold into the sex trade. It's been a slow-moving investigation, mostly because I'm technically suspended with the Bureau, but also because billionaire Jaxon Pace has decided to throw every possible red-tape roadblock in my way. But, despite all of that, I must admit I've made decent progress.

I *know* there's a trafficking ring in this city. I'm so close to proving it and once I can prove it, I can find the girl I'm looking for, and I'll return to Langley a hero.

Then again…most *heroes* don't fuck prostitutes.

And even if they do, those heroes certainly aren't stupid enough fuck prostitutes who turn out to be the sister of the very man suspected of *running* the trafficking ring the hero is bringing down.

But how the hell was I supposed to know that?

I've been seeing 'Annie' on a pretty regular basis. Yes, she was a welcome distraction. And yes, I realize it's a bit hypocritical of me to be balls-deep in a hooker, while also trying to end sexual exploitation. But I treated her well, and paid her generously for our sessions. The ones she *let* me pay for, anyway. For the last few weeks, she stopped taking my money, and it felt as if we were actually starting to be something more.

It's unwise to think that after all of these revelations, any of my interactions with *Annie* were real.

"For a crappy motel, at least the water pressure is good," she calls from down the hall.

I snort to myself, shaking my head.

Unbelievable. She's seriously acting like everything is normal. It's not normal. It's beyond fucked. Why? Because practically everything we've said to each other for the last few months has basically been a lie.

I told her I was a private investigator looking for a missing girl, and she told me she was just an escort, who knew Michael Valentine.

And while some of that is true, none of it is normal.

What really grinds my gears, is the fact that I still *want* her. Badly. It's taking every ounce of my self-restraint not to walk down that hallway, rip open the curtain, grab her hair and fuck her hard, right there bent over the tub in the bathroom.

I can't.

I don't know if it's the fact that she lied to me, or the fact that I lied to her, but something about us feels…broken. I don't know if we can fix this, and at this point, I don't even know if I want to. Perhaps I over exaggerated this, and maybe there really wasn't a connection between us at all and it was just something I told myself to justify all the times we've gotten naked with each other.

…But I know it's not.

Because if I really didn't have feelings for her, it would be a hell of a lot easier to just walk away right now.

Fuck.

I just don't know how to feel right now. As an FBI Profiler, it's my job to remain detached. But I'm not, and I know I'm not, and I hate it.

Whenever I started to feel guilty about fucking Annie, I thought of myself as just a foot soldier gathering intel into Chicago's criminal enterprise. I told myself it was research. She didn't usually like to talk about work, but when she did, she gave me valuable information about my target Michael Valentine.

Information such as how Michael refused to hire girls from big extended families.

Annie didn't make the connection, but I did. He picked girls who were alone in the world because they were easier to manage. Friends can be bought or intimidated into silence, but relatives are a bit more persistent when their loved one goes missing. And they are especially ruthless when they turn up *dead*.

Historically, the most prolific serial killers in the world prey on a particular type: the *loners*. They often chose victims who were orphaned or abandoned. The runaways, the drifters, anyone who had few people in their life who would notice their absence, and raise the alarm.

It's clear to me now that's exactly how Michael is selecting his girls. He's intentionally cultivating women who were largely marginalized and forgotten.

And I can't stand for that.

…Even if I have to stand alone.

I still can't believe the fucking Bureau suspended me. Dicks.

Originally, I had the support of my superiors at headquarters for this mission. But when my second partner, Benjamin Minamoto, was killed running an undercover operative, I was devastated. And then some stupid head shrink suggested I undergo a psych evaluation. When I refused, I got slapped with a suspension. Apparently, they were concerned that I might be emotionally compromised, and that it might have become personal for me.

They were right. It *was* fucking personal.

And if you ask me, good investigative work *needs* to be personal. There has to be a fire, a motivation, some insatiable desire for justice…or justice falls short.

It was personal for Benjamin too.

He'd taken a special interest in this case, as it also allowed him to search for anything connected to the disappearance of his favorite niece several years ago. After my first partner, Scarlett, died in an unrelated car accident, I was reassigned to with Benjamin, who had also lost his partner. It took us a minute to readjust, but we soon became good friends. So when he told me about his niece, I vowed to help him with his mission. And I've kept that promise even after his death.

I *will* find her, and at the very least provide some closure for their family.

And, with Annie's help, I felt like I was making some progress. It was just an added bonus that things between us had developed past being just a transactional arrangement. Perhaps foolishly, we had blurred the line between profession and pleasure, and although neither of us were talking about it, we both knew it.

That was clear the moment Annie started *choosing* to spend the night with me without being paid. That's also where I could get her to talk, just a little, about what was going on in the shadows of Michael's budding criminal empire.

"I assume asking for conditioner is out of the question?" Rachel's voice echoes down the hall.

I say nothing but steal a glance into the mirror, which is conveniently positioned in such a way that I am immediately met with the reflection of her ass.

Holy shit.

Seeing her wet, naked body, just feet away from me, causes my cock to throb in my pants.

No. You can't get distracted, Adam. Not this time.

That's exactly what had happened before.

It had been a long time since I had enjoyed the feeling of a woman in my arms. And Annie, well she just fit perfectly. So many nights I'd watch her as she slept, curled up against my chest. It felt like she belonged there, with me.

Sure, she had a bit of a checkered past, but realistically, who didn't? It's not like anyone is truly innocent anymore. We're all a bit fucked, one way or another. And she just felt…right.

The problem was that obviously I couldn't *tell* her I was an undercover federal officer sent to investigate Michael Valentine. So, I went with the private investigator bit. And while it might not have been the entire truth, it wasn't exactly a lie either.

I thought it was clever.

I convinced her to ask around a bit and see if she could dig up anything amongst the cast of shadowy characters she associated with under Michael's employ.

Then everything came crashing down.

The night of the bombing at the opera house I arrested Jaxon Pace, and took him to an old warehouse where I had fucked Annie a few times. The interrogation was going fairly routine, until Jaxon brought up my sons, who were dead. Shocked that he knew this information, when it had been confidentially sealed, I snapped. I'll admit, I might've killed him. But at the very last second, who should walk through the door? *Annie*. Along with Jaxon's wife, and entire entourage in tow.

Annie stopped me from killing Jaxon.

Turns out, "Annie" was actually short for Rachel *Anne* Valentine, and she was far more embedded in this situation than I previously thought.

In my emotional entanglement with *Rachel*, I had made the fatal mistake of *assuming* she was just a low-level escort who just worked for Michael Valentine. I never once considered she could've been his presumed-dead sister because all of our official records on Rachel Valentine confirmed she was exactly that: *dead*.

I glance up at her again, watching the hot water snake around her breasts and hips as she smoothes her long dark hair, I can confirm she is very much *alive*.

…And very naked in my shower.

But now I don't honestly know how to feel. At the end of the day, she's still a *Valentine*. She's a fucking mafia princess. And on top of her sharing a child with that fuckhead Jaxon Pace, her older brother is the very psychopathic serial murderer and sex trafficker I'm after.

We've both lied to each other. A lot.

Now that the truth is on the table, the question is: has *everything* between us been a lie?

I don't know.

But I'm sure as hell going to find out.

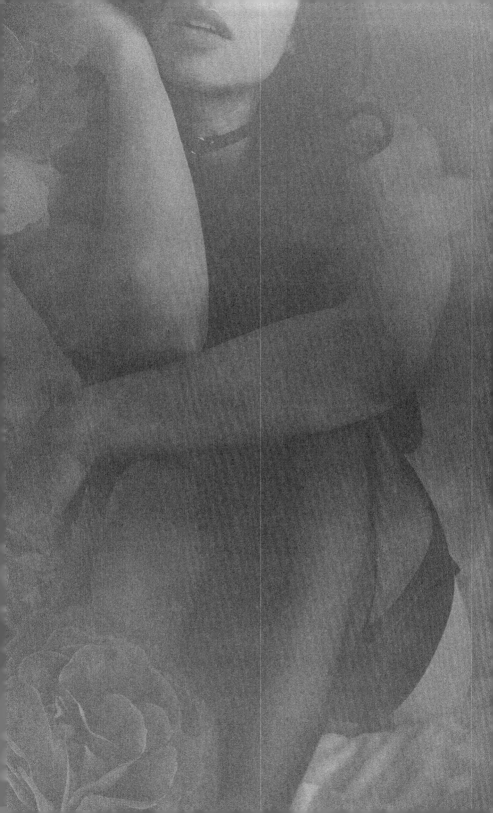

CHAPTER THREE

Rachel

"So where did you go to school?"

"No, no, no. Don't do the small talk thing," I say, cutting him off. "I'd say we're well past that now."

I take a sip of my beer and set it back down on the rickety old nightstand that sits between the two queen beds in the room.

"Plus, it's boring as fuck."

Adam clicks his tongue.

"While I don't disagree that it's boring," he says, as if he is barely holding back his rage. "As of right now, I don't know who you really are. Nor do I trust you. So unfortunately, that means you're going to have to give me something or you're going to have to leave. I really don't have time for any bullshit."

Fuck.

I take a deep breath.

This is going to be a long night.

Deciding the only way I'll be able to stomach this is with more alcohol I silently stand and make my way over to the small fridge in the room and grab another beer.

"I didn't go to school," I say, popping the lid off the bottle. "At least past the eighth grade."

"What?"

"Or maybe it was the ninth grade. I can't remember when I stopped."

"You're from the Valentine family," Adam scoffs. "Aren't you some Mafia princess or some shit."

"Some *shit* is more like it."

"I mean I thought you came from money?"

"No, my *name* is from money, honey," I say sitting down on the bed. "My reality is something very different."

"I don't—"

"Look, this isn't some fucking Hollywood movie, okay?" I snap, irritably. "It isn't some fairytale. In my world, everything is about legacy and propagation. It's cold and brutal, and in that frigid world I landed the unfortunate hand of being born a girl, which meant my needs, wants or dreams meant nothing to anyone. I wasn't a princess; I was a burden. And my shithead father took every opportunity to remind me of that every fucking day."

I take another drink, trying to hide the fact my hands are shaking, but I notice Adam's gaze stalking my movements.

Who am I kidding? He's probably already noticed.

"To add to my misery, the older I got the more I looked like my mother, which was a reminder that he was forced to marry the bitch. The man resented my very existence from the moment I took my first breath. And since my dear old mum decided to leave and save *herself* from the abuse, it was only natural that it fell instead to me. So no, I was *nobody's* princess. I don't have glorious childhood memories; I only have trauma and nightmares."

"I'm sorry," he says quietly.

"Aw shit, don't do that," I scoff, rolling my eyes. "I hate that. I don't need your pity. You wanted my story, *this* is my story. If you're going to need me to whimper, and cry, and say the world is unfair, and act like a victim then I will walk out that door!"

"I never said that."

"Right, but—"

"You say you don't want to be a victim, but yet you're acting like one," he suddenly snaps. "I simply said I was sorry, for fucks sake!"

He sighs and runs his hand over his head.

NICOLE FANNING

"Jesus Christ," he whispers. "This is like trying to have a conversation with a feral fucking mountain lion."

"Good," I grin. "Maybe we *are* getting somewhere."

"Fucking hell," he sighs, pouring himself a drink.

He closes his eyes and waves his hand, motioning me to continue with my story.

"So, you stopped going to school. How did your father get away with that? Taking you out of school and all?"

"He didn't take me out, exactly. Most aristocratic Mafia families in the syndicate hire private tutors for their kids. I mean, it's not like they can risk sending them to public school, and even private schools aren't much safer."

"Why?"

"Easier to lift them," I shrug. "Children of Mafia Dons are always liabilities, at least until they are old enough to defend themselves, anyway."

I take another drink.

Though Jaxon Pace gave me a run for my money when I tried to have someone lift Jessica from The Jefferson.

Well, I guess technically Natalie did.

"…Most Mafia Dons anyway."

Adam locks eyes with me.

"So if you had a private tutor then—"

"*Had* is the operative word," I say, swallowing hard. "I had a great tutor…until my father killed him."

"What for?"

I play with the disintegrating tag on the bottle in my hand.

"If I tell you, you're going to have to promise that you won't go all empathetic fru-fru on me."

"Try me."

"My brother and I had different teachers. Mine was named Professor Wyatt," I say with a sigh. "I had him from third to eighth grade. Or ninth or whatever. Point is, I liked him a lot. He was a good professor because he loved teaching, and he loved children."

Noticing the way Adam raises his brow at me as he takes a swig of his beer, I roll my eyes.

"And no, before you ask," I say, glaring at him. "He wasn't some secret pervert or anything like that."

"I never said that," he snorts.

23

"Yeah but your face–"

"Maybe you should just tell your story," he snaps back, interrupting me. "And not attempt to infer meaning from my face or put words in my mouth."

"*Anyway*," I hiss. "He was good to me. Better than my own piece of shit father was. He used to tell me how proud he was of me when I did well at something, and didn't yell or scold me when I failed. You know, all those warm fatherly vibes I imagine most children get from their *actual* fathers."

I swallow hard, looking down at the bottle in my hands.

"Looking back, I guess I should've known that was a death sentence in our world…"

I have to admit, it's been awhile since I've felt *this* good. But ever since Professor Wyatt told me this morning that I actually earned a perfect score on my latest Algebra test, I've been feeling pretty invincible.

And Michael never gets perfect scores. In anything.

I have just finished boiling the water for my lunch of macaroni and cheese, when my father's enforcer, Barry, stumbles into the kitchen, drunk.

"Well, look who it is," he teases. "The little fuck trophy."

"What?"

"Fuck trophy!" He laughs, clapping his hands together. "What? Are you too stupid to figure out what that means?"

I try to just ignore him, tearing the little packet of powdered cheese open and setting it next to the sink.

"You're filling out nicely though."

Suddenly he's behind me, the smell of his heavy aftershave, tobacco and booze lingering on him makes my stomach twist.

"Get out of my way," I say, taking the boiling hot water to the sink.

"What did you just say to me?"

"I said get out of my way," I demand, trying to sound confident while my heart starts to pound. "This pot is hot."

"Fuck the pot," he says, yanking the pot from my hands and knocking it to the floor.

Flecks of boiling water hit my leg, burning my skin.

24

"Ow! What the hell?!"

I shove him hard, making him stumble backwards. I move to clean up the mess on the floor, but suddenly his hand is in my hair, and he yanks me backwards. Then his body is on me, his fat stomach pins me against the counter as his hands slide up my sides.

"Get your fucking hands off me!"

Panic rises in my throat but despite my struggling I am no match for the large man holding me hostage.

"Help! Please!"

"Go on, scream your head off, it's not like your father gives a shit. You wanna look like a little woman," he growls in my ear. "Then I'll treat you like one, you bitch."

"You will do no such thing!"

Professor Wyatt's voice sounds from the doorway, as does the distinct sound of a gun cocking.

"Get your hands off that child immediately," he demands authoritatively. "Or I will shoot you right here."

"This doesn't concern you, old timer," Barry growls, still gripping my hair tightly. "So I suggest you go back to your books."

Two shots ring through the air, the sound echoing loudly in the kitchen. And down goes Barry. He gurgles as blood bubbles from his lips, adding to the giant puddle slowly pooling on the kitchen floor.

Oh my God!

Even though I've grown up around guns, I've never seen a man get shot before, so all I can do is stand here shaking.

"Are you alright, young lady?" Professor Wyatt asks, approaching me slowly. "Did he…hurt you?"

I shake my head, unable to speak. Instead I instantly make a beeline for him, burying my face against his jacket and bursting into tears.

"It's alright, Miss Valentine," he says calmly, wrapping his arms around me and patting my back. "You're safe now."

"What on earth is all that racket?" I hear my father say as he steps into the kitchen. "You're ruining my fucking nap."

His eyes scan the room, barely glancing at me before staring at the dead man laying in the puddle of blood on his expensive Italian tile.

"What the fuck is this?"

"Mr. Valentine," Professor Wyatt says calmly. "This man assaulted your daughter and I…I shot him."

"You mean to tell me that you just shot one of my best men?" my father asks, his voice no louder than a whisper.

Oh no…

My stomach drops, as I know that tone in my father's voice, and having experienced his lightning quick temper go from 0-100 in the blink of an eye many times myself, I shiver.

Immediately the tension in the room intensifies, like the heavy static electricity and eerie calm you feel just before a nasty storm rolls into town.

"Father, it was my fault," I say, trying to defend Professor Wyatt, hoping to save him from my father's wrath.

"No, it was not," Professor Wyatt counters, putting me behind him. "Your daughter was making lunch when this man walked in here and—"

"*This* man?! This man is fucking dead!" My father snaps, making me jump.

"Perhaps you didn't hear me, Sir," Professor Wyatt says calmly, but firmly. "But the man assaulted your daughter. I told him to stop, but he refused. So I shot him."

"Are you a hitman, Wyatt? Or a bodyguard?" My father asks icily, taking a step toward us. "Did I hire you for that?"

"No, Sir, I am a professor," Professor Wyatt replies, holding his ground as my father approaches. "Believe me, I never intended to shoot anyone today. I'm an educated man that you hired to educate your daughter."

"And so I suppose that you think that education of yours means you're smarter than the rest of us? Smart enough to start making the decisions of who gets to live or die around here?"

My heart starts pounding in my chest as my father takes another step toward us. Perhaps feeling the same impending anxiety, Professor Wyatt peels my arms from around him and gently pushes me away from him.

"Sir, I don't think you understand what I'm saying to you," he says. "This man was putting his hands on your daughter in an inappropriate manner."

"What I understand, Professor, is that Barry here was one of my best men," My father growls, staring at him coldly. "And now he is dead. Because of *you*."

I never saw my father pull his gun.

Perhaps I was looking at all the men standing behind him.

But I distinctly remember the spray of blood hitting my face when my father pulled the trigger and blew Professor Wyatt's head off right there in the kitchen.

Somehow I feel my body screaming before I hear it.

"Nooo!" I wail, my voice cracking as the limp body of my Professor slumps lifelessly to the floor. "Oh my God!"

"Take note. That's what happens when people think they know everything," my father says viciously to me. "Your little Professor here had a big head. So I blew it off."

I sob, kneeling next to Professor Wyatt's corpse.

"Shut the fuck up or you're next!" My father bellows. "You did this, you little bitch. I suggest you remember that the next time you go letting other people meddle in my business."

And without another word he turns and walks back out of the kitchen, leaving me sitting in a puddle of blood, alone with two dead bodies.

"Professor," I whisper, my entire body wracked with silent sobs as I lean over his chest. "I'm so sorry."

I wasn't sure what I should do, or what was going to become of me now that Professor Wyatt wasn't around to protect me anymore. But what I was sure of, was the fact that I was responsible for the death of perhaps the only man who had ever loved and cared about me.

And as long as I live, I would never forgive myself for that.

CHAPTER FOUR

ADAM

"That was the last time I was in school," she says quietly. "After that, I didn't dare ask my father for another tutor. The professor's death was my fault, and another one would be too much of a liability."

"Jesus."

"Hey," she snaps, pointing at me. "You promised not to go all soft on me."

"I'm not. But how the hell am I supposed to react to that, Rachel? That's terrible story."

"Meh," she shrugs, taking another swig of her beer. "I have way worse stories than that. Trust me."

How can she be so...okay with this? How could anyone?

But then I remember that I can no longer afford to have my guard down with Rachel. I have to treat her like everyone else I interview. Like a suspect.

My work brain takes over and instantly I notice Rachel's tells.

The way her foot is tapping rapidly on the bed, and the way she seems to be chewing on her lip, are all signs of someone who is trying to mask her true feelings.

So either she's hiding something, or she's afraid to tell me.

"What did you do?" I ask. "Like, what was the aftermath?"

"I just stayed out of the way. That was easier. Eventually when I saw the opportunity, I ran away and made my way into the city. Found a job clearing tables at some restaurant. That's where I met my best friend, Jessica. Well, ex-best friend."

"Ex-best friend?"

"She died," Rachel replies, taking another sip of her beer.

"Ah, I see," I nod. "How old were you when you left?"

"I dunno," she shrugs nonchalantly. "Probably seventeen?"

"What did your father have to say about it?"

"Hah, I don't even think he noticed. For a while anyway. Probably a year. And by that point, it didn't matter."

"What?" I ask.

"…Because then he was dead."

The callous way she says this is a bit unnerving, but I try my best to control the look I'm sure is written on my face.

"Come on Adam," Rachel says, narrowing her eyes at me, a sly grin on her face. "You were the one who told me that we weren't going to lie to each other, remember? Don't be coy, you already know all this."

I smile.

There she is.

Every time I think I have Rachel Valentine figured out, she throws a curveball my way. However, it's clear that she knows her naivety is disarming for men, especially men like me. She has learned how to utilize that to her advantage, like all smart girls do.

Rachel is far more observant. And I find that strangely hot.

But I can't let *her* know that.

"You're right," I smirk. "I knew he was dead. He was murdered in the cartel war."

I sigh, sitting back on the bed. "Him and his new wife, Penny."

"Slut."

"What?"

"Oh, I said *slut*," Rachel says, with a cocky grin on her face. "She was just another bitch who couldn't keep her legs closed, and he met at some club he owned. Same as my mother. Basically, a rinse and repeat scenario. Except at least this bitch was smart."

"Smart?"

"She snagged him by telling him she was pregnant, then after

30

they were married, wouldn't you know she *lost* the baby?"

"You think she did that on purpose?"

"I know she did," Rachel snorts. "She had her tubes tied when she had an unplanned abortion at 16. It was required in whatever podunk state she grew up in. But she'd get drunk and run her mouth. So, maybe not so smart, I guess."

I shake my head.

She raises her eyebrows at me.

"Excuse me while I have a human reaction to a ridiculous sentence that you said so nonchalantly. I can't help that," I say as she crosses her arms again and glares at me.

"Try, Adam. Otherwise, we will never make it through this story."

This girl...

I swear, there's something about her bitchy little attitude that frustrates the hell out of me. It makes me just want to bend her over my knee and spank it out of her.

But, she'd probably like that.

Hell, maybe I would too.

"Anyway, the lady who owned the restaurant was nice. She gave me a room upstairs. I worked hard for her, kept the restaurant tidy, and of course I always kept an eye out for her, to let her know when the cops were coming by."

"Cops?"

"Yeah," I smile. "You don't think she could afford downtown rent prices by selling soup and noodles, do you? Nah, she sold meth out the back of her shop."

I cough.

"One of her runners, that is one of the girls that delivered to the dealer, was a girl about my age. Jessica. Naturally, once I had proven I was trustworthy and hardworking, I became a runner too, and me and Jessica became friends. We would deliver the bigger packages together. No one questions two teenage girls walking around the city together."

"How long did this lady get away with this?"

"A few years. The trouble was, with me out running product, she didn't have anyone to give her the heads-up when the cops popped by anymore. They were on to her at that point."

"I assumed you guys had the police in your pocket."

"The Pace Family did," Rachel says, tilting her head and

31

pointing her finger at me. "They could keep the police distracted elsewhere when they wanted to. But this little old lady was stubborn and refused to pay tribute. So, they let them lift her. Jess and I knew we had to find something else to do."

"So, then what did you do?"

"Well, she had an uncle, well, actually I think it was a friend of her uncle or something. I can't remember exactly. Anyway, his name was Freddy Mack. He owned a strip club, and he gave us a job."

"Wait, wait, wait," Adam says, holding up his hand. "How old were you?"

She hesitates.

"Eighteen."

"Really?"

"Well, technically I turned eighteen a few months after I started working there," she shrugs. "But we didn't just get to walk in and start dancing. We bussed tables, barbacked, that kind of thing for a year anyway. But we spent so much time around the dancers that we picked up on a few things."

"That's just..." Adam shakes his head. "Exploitation."

"Maybe so. But for us, at the time, it was survival," she says, taking another drink.

"That's why it's exploitation," I sigh.

"Look, I get that you have your cop principles and all—"

"I'm not a cop."

"...But if you want me to say that I regret dancing, then you're going to be disappointed," She says, locking eyes with me and crossing her arms "My entire life up until that point had been one where I was exploited and ogled without my consent. Dancing actually gave me my power back. No one forced me on the stage, I just loved it up there."

I clear my throat.

Despite hearing about her shady start into stripping, images of Rachel in sexy lingerie, pole dancing flood my brain, and it suddenly feels a bit harder to breathe.

"My life changed once I started dancing. I didn't need anyone to pay my bills, I wasn't in debt to anyone, and I wasn't an inconvenience. I had my own power, and no one could tell me what to do."

"But..." I start to say, but then realize she's never going to agree with me on this topic. "Never mind. When did you meet Jaxon Pace? I assume since your daughter is seven that it was at least seven years ago, right?"

"Well, I had known him since we were kids. When we were really little our parents used to let us play together. But then everything kind of blew up between my parents, and after that Michael and I weren't allowed to see him anymore," she says, taking another drink. "And then I moved to the city, met Jess and kind of grew up on my own. I didn't see him again until about nine years ago."

"Tell me that story," I say.

As much as I don't want to talk about Jaxon Pace, I need more information for the profile I am making of Rachel in my head. This is strictly business and I need to treat it that way.

"You sure?" She winks at me, biting that lip of hers. "You don't need to change your tampon first, princess?"

"Fuck off," I growl. "Keep talking."

"Well," she says. "The first time I saw Jaxon Pace again was at this party my friend Jess dragged me too…"

CHAPTER FIVE
Rachel

"Jess, are you sure about this?" I ask, wrapping my coat around me as we get out of the cab. "I mean, Crissy and Ness said that taking marks from uptown was dangerous. Ness said they get too aggressive."

"That's what the coke is for love," Jess grins, pinching her nose. "Besides, Eamon is a regular of mine, and he said that he would have *goodies* for us."

She pulls the doors to the lobby of an expensive apartment building in the financial district.

"Great," I say, rolling my eyes. "Knowing there's drugs here makes everything better."

"I know right?"

"I was being sarcastic."

"Hello," Jess says with a smile to the doorman in the lobby. "We're here for Eamon West in 2103."

"Elevators are at the end of the hall," the elderly bellman says without looking up from his crossword. "I just sent your friends up there too."

"Friends?"

"Yeah, a blonde with a southern accent, and a brunette who

likes to pop her chewing gum," he says, now looking up over the top of his glasses. "I assume they were friends of yours."

He looks Jess up and down with a judgey stare that makes her smile quickly disappear.

She pulls the top of her dress, barely containing her giant tits up and turns on her heel toward the elevator.

"Fucking prick," she says, deliberately before the doors close. "And also, what the fuck? Crissy and Ness are here too? What are they trying to do, steal our score?"

"Seems like it."

"I told you we shouldn't have told those bitches about it," she says, now pulling her dress back down. "You're too fucking trusting."

"How was I supposed to know they'd find a way here?"

"Pull your tits out Rach," she says, now fussing with my dress. "Remember we need to make enough tonight to pay rent, or the landlord is going to kick us out."

"I got it," I say, slapping her hand away. "Do you still have that red lipstick on you?"

"Always," she says as she fishes it out and hands it to me along with a pocket mirror.

"So, who is here tonight?"

"Just Eamon and a few of his friends. You know, all those rich boy toys that come into the club and ask for private dances."

"And they expect us to do what, exactly?"

Jess says nothing but looks at me in a way that confirms what I already know:

Everything. They expect us to do everything.

"Sure you don't want a bump?" She asks just before the elevator doors open.

"On second thought," I say, biting my lip and trying to resign myself to the night's unofficial setlist. "Sure."

The apartment building is so nice that there's a small sitting area outside the doors of the elevator with chairs and a small table with fresh flowers. Jess walks over to the small table and pushes the flowers aside. She pulls out the little rubber-lined tin that she keeps in her purse and pours a bit on the table, using her credit card to cut it before lining it up in a line.

She uses what she refers to as her *back-up cash*, which is just a hundred-dollar bill she has rolled up tightly to snort half of it before handing it to me.

"You know we have to make tonight work," she says, as I take my turn, feeling my nose start to tingle the minute I snort the fine white powder.

"I know."

"Then why do you look so nervous?"

"Because I *am* nervous," I say, wiping my nose. "I don't know if I can really have sex for money."

"It's just sex, Rachel. You've had sex right?"

"Of course I have but—"

"And how was it?"

"What?"

"It was lousy, I know."

"How the fuck would you know that?" I scoff. "You weren't there."

"Might as well have been," she teases. "The walls in our apartment are thin as fuck."

"Okay, well, since you're a creep who listens to me have sex with men, you should know I had a great time."

"If you had, I'd have known that too."

"Oh my God!"

"My point is," Jess continues. "When that mediocre experience was over, you couldn't get that time back, could you?"

"Well, no."

Jess waves her finger around the pristine 21st floor lobby.

"Let me tell you something the business boys in these swanky apartments have figured out: time is money, babe. They hole up in their offices, with their diplomas and 401ks and billing hours and charging consulting fees just to sit behind a desk with a dick in their hands, watching SportsCenter and fucking over little people like us. And when they want to get their rocks off, they don't think twice about tossing a couple grand at pretty girls who moan on cue and smear red lipstick on their cock while sucking them off."

"Jesus, Jess!"

"My point here is that if you're going to get fucked and have mediocre sex either way, you might as well do it with someone who can at least pay the rent."

Fuck, I can't actually argue with that.

She wipes the table off with her hand and looks up at me.

"Look Rach, I'd never force you to do this," she says, taking my hands in hers. "If you really don't want to then we'll figure something else out, okay?"

I take a deep breath.

"But if you go in there, and we do this, then you *own* it. You hear me? We might be having sex with them, but we don't let them take anything from us. We take it from them. The choice and the power is always *ours*."

I nod.

"Alright, let's do this."

"Attagirl!" Jess says with a grin.

We make our way down the hall and knock on the door of 2103. A very good-looking man with jet black hair answers the door.

"Eamon," Jess says, her voice sultry smooth.

"Hello sexy," Eamon replies, looking her up and down. "Love the dress. Come on in, we've been waiting for you."

As he takes her coat his eyes find mine and he bites his lip.

"Who's this little lamb?"

"This is Rachel," Jess says. "You told me to bring a friend. But it seems as if you've already invited a few yourself."

"This is Bryan and Rodney," Eamon says, putting a hand on the shoulders of the men seated on the couch. "That's Tyler with Crissy behind the bar. You know Crissy, don't ya love?"

"Of course I do," Jess smiles coldly at Crissy, who is looking a bit guilty as we step into the living room. "Didn't think I'd be seeing her *here* though."

"Yeah, I caught her on the way out of the club tonight, she volunteered," Eamon says, as if he's proud of himself.

Then again, rumor has it that Eamon has always been that way.

"I heard there were going to be a few more gentlemen tonight," Crissy says, stepping forward and gently hugging Jess. "I didn't think you'd mind."

"Mmm," Jess smiles, narrowing her eyes at her. "I suppose some of that is true at least."

Yeah, the "I didn't think" part...

I can tell Jess isn't happy about Crissy and Ness being here. She would call it poaching, but she's doing her best to try and hide it. Jess has been taking private clients like this for a while and one of the first rules she told me was that you never make a scene at a client's place.

Knowing Jess, she will just save "the scene" until we're all back at the club tomorrow night, so she can make an example of Crissy and Ness, and show the rest of the girls what happens when you step on her territory.

It's why everyone is afraid of her.

Suddenly the door to the patio opens and a man steps inside.

Chestnut brown hair, tan skin, and piercing blue eyes, he's so beautiful that my entire body freezes in place and my heart starts pounding in my chest.

"Jackie! Look, the rest of the girls have arrived!" Eamon says, handing Jess a glass of wine and wrapping his arm firmly around her. "Maybe one of these will strike your fancy? Ladies, may I introduce you to the infamous and inappropriately loaded Jaxon Pace."

Part of me thinks that name sounds familiar, as the man named Jaxon smirks and shakes his head, walking over to the bar.

"Jaxon over here just got back in town, and it seems he is a bit picky this evening," he says, as Jess giggles, throwing her hand on his chest. "He's already turned down the chubby one, which is surprising because usually he likes 'em with a little more meat on the bones than I do. But he turned Crissy down too."

Crissy smiles but stiffens uncomfortably, sitting down silently on the armrest of the couch. She glances up at Jaxon eagerly, but then back down at the glass of wine in her hand.

I guess not being chosen sucks.

"Sweetheart, just sit on the couch," Eamon says, suddenly snapping his fingers at Crissy. "Or on the ottoman, or the chair. Literally dozens of actual *seats* for you to sit on. I don't need you and your fat ass breaking my armrests, that couch is worth more than you."

Crissy turns beat red, and immediately relocates.

"Now, now Eamon," Jess teases playfully. "Everyone likes what they like. There's no need to be an asshole."

"*Asshole* is just Eamon's default setting," Jaxon says, walking back into the room. "But you know what they say, you are what you eat."

Everyone laughs, including me.

Hmm, and he's funny too.

39

His eyes catch mine and suddenly I cannot move.

"Well, if you don't want her, I'll—" Rodney starts to say looking at me licking his lips, but then Jaxon smacks him hard in the chest.

"No, I'm taking *her*," he says without taking his eyes off me.

"Oh. Alright, brother," Rodney says defensively. "You get first dibs, I know that. She's all yours."

"I guess me and Bryan can share the other one," Rodney laughs.

Jaxon stares at me for a moment before his attention is diverted when Eamon makes yet another joke about Ness, like the asshole he is. Jaxon smiles politely, but it doesn't reach his eyes. He seems bored of this entire scenario, but even his smile is sexy.

What is happening to me?

"Where did the chubby one go? What's her name again?"

"It's *Ness*," Crissy says, tucking a strand of hair behind her ear. "And be nice. She's in the bathroom."

"She better not be getting fucked up in there," Eamon shouts down the hall. "Ness! Yo, Ness! Hurry the fuck up! I didn't pay you to decorate my guest bathroom."

"Hahah!" Tyler laughs. "Yeah, the powder goes *in* your nose, Sweetheart, not on it."

"Speaking of," Jess says, biting her lip and squeezing Eamon's arm. "You got something for me?"

"Don't you worry darling," he growls, grabbing her neck and kissing her hard. "I've got plenty for you."

The door opens and Ness stumbles back out into the living room. I can't help but notice she looks a little messed up already.

"Rach, you're here," she says, with a smile. "That's nice."

"Well, now that everyone is here, how about we get started?" Eamon shouts, clapping his hands together.

"So, what do you want me to do for you?" I ask.

He chuckles.

Why the fuck is he laughing?

"You've clearly never done this before, have you?"

"Of course I have!" I say defensively, feeling my cheeks heat.

"Uh huh," he smiles smugly. "Has anyone ever told you that you're a terrible liar?"

"No, they usually think I'm pretty good actually," I snap, now somewhat angry that he could accurately identify this is indeed my first time as an escort.

But my pride refuses to let this dickhead have the satisfaction.

"Seems to me that you just don't know what you want," I say, raising my nose to him.

This time he laughs, something that seems so out of place given the mercurial pout he's been sporting all night.

"Fair enough," he looks at me over the top of his drink. "Why don't you pick something then?"

"M...Me?" I stutter nervously.

"Yes, you," Jaxon grins arrogantly. "Since you're so experienced and all."

"I could dance for you?"

"Is that supposed to be a question?"

"Motherfu—" I start to mutter under my breath.

"What was that?"

"Nothing," I quip, realizing how quickly that backfired.

"You seem confused," Jaxon says, still fucking smiling.

It's not lost on me that the only thing that's made this arrogant prick smile this evening is watching me stumble around this process. He's looking at me like a predator that enjoys playing with his prey.

"I'm not confused," I fire back. "It's just a little hard to dance without music."

Without saying a word, and without breaking eye contact, he reaches on to the table in front of him and grabs a controller. He presses a button and suddenly music erupts on the patio. He presses a second button which makes the tiki torches lining the patio light up.

"Do you live here?"

"Not exactly."

"Not exactly?"

"Let's just say I'm here enough to know how to operate the radio."

"Oh, so you do this...a lot?"

"Ya know, that's a lot of questions, but not a lot of dancing."

Fuck, he's right. He's a mark. He's just here to help me pay the rent. Why the fuck should I care what the mercurial Mr. Pace does in his spare time...or *who*.

Also, I deal with cocky fucks like him day in and day out at the club, so I refuse to treat him any differently.

I start to find the rhythm in the soft R&B music playing on the balcony, and pull some moves from my favorite pole routine. Every move I make, Jaxon's eyes are glued to me.

He...likes this.

The confidence I'd forgotten before comes flooding back to me. I lock eyes with him as I step over to him, and straddle his lap. His hands are instinctively on my thighs, and I shudder.

Fuck, why does he have such an effect on me?

I grind myself against him, feeling his arousal against my pussy. His cologne is intoxicating, as is the look in his eye when I softly run my fingers through his hair. As his hands snake up my back to the zipper of my dress, I hear him breathe in deeply. He presses his lips to my neck, and collarbone, making me moan.

I continue working my hips against him, and bring my face close to his. I want to kiss him, but some part of me needs him to do it first. Jaxon Pace is a beautiful man, and suddenly I'm excited at the prospect of fucking him tonight.

Kiss me. Come on, kiss me.

I'd have done it already if he was anyone else. But for some reason, some part of me needs him to do it first. I need to feel his desperation, his burning desire to have me, to truly believe a man this beautiful wants me.

I grind myself against him harder, as he presses his face close to mine.

This is it, he's going to do it.

But then, the fucking door opens and Tyler starts to step out. "Hey Pace, do you—"

"Hey, asshole, I'm dancing here!" I shout back, angrily.

"Jesus, sorry," Tyler says as he retreats back into the building. When I turn back around to face Jaxon he's laughing.

"What?"

"That was," he says, between laughs. "Amazing."

Well there goes that idea.

"Fuck you," I say, trying to get up.

But Jaxon holds me fast.

"No, no," he says, still trying to stifle his annoying amusement.

"Don't go anywhere."

"I think the moment has passed," I snap, trying to get up again. But again he holds me firmly.

"Stop," he growls, with a grin. "You're feisty. I like that."

"No, I—"

I'm mid-sentence when Jaxon threads his hand up into my hair and presses his lips against mine.

Time stops entirely.

The smell of him, the taste of him, completely overtake my being. I kiss him back, feeling his tongue push into mine.

When I pull away, I can feel my racing heart.

"So is now a good time to tell you I've never done this before?" I whisper quietly.

He chuckles again, before kissing me again.

"I know."

"...But I," I say, trying to find my words, feeling my cheeks heating again. "I still want to fuck you."

"I know that too."

"Cocky prick," I giggle back.

He grins, as if I've truly seen him for who he is.

"Where were we?" he asks, kissing me again. He reaches up the back of my dress and my breath hitches.

Slowly I feel him unzip it all the way down my back. He reaches up and pulls down the strap on my left shoulder, kissing the base of my neck and slowly down my chest.

I don't know how I scored Jaxon Pace as my first client, but instead of being nervous, I'm anxious. I actually *want* to fuck him. Maybe more than once.

I close my eyes and grind my hips against his erection, knowing that within seconds his mouth is going to be around my nipple.

But nothing happens.

I look up, but instead of feeling the intense desire lingering in his eyes, I see something different: shock. And reservation.

"What?" I ask, acutely aware that he is looking directly at the tattoo on my left shoulder.

"Your tattoo…"

"You don't like tattoos?"

"What did you say your name was again?"

"Rachel?" I snort, incredulously.

"No, your *last* name."

Immediately I freeze.

"I…didn't."

"It wouldn't be *Valentine*…would it?"

Fuck.

I immediately yank my dress back up and stand up.

"I knew it," he mutters to himself. "Fuck."

"You knew what?" I snap, irritably. "You don't know me."

"I do though," he sighs, running his hand through his hair.

My heart starts pounding in my chest.

"You don't know shit," I whisper, my voice shaking. "Fuck this, I'm leaving."

"That tattoo covers a scar," Jaxon says behind me, making me freeze in my tracks. "Your brother shot you with an arrow. I remember, I was there."

Suddenly it all comes flooding back to me. The memory of playing at the sprawling Pace Manor, my brother hunting me in the forest and actually shooting me with his toy bow and arrow. It was Jaxon who had taken it away from him and ran to get his mother.

"Oh my God…" I whisper.

"I'm sorry," he says, adjusting himself and standing to his feet.

"Sorry? Why are you sorry?"

"Because I didn't know."

"Didn't know what?" I snap, a bit loudly.

"You're a Valentine."

"So what, is that some untouchable peasant name to the great Jaxon Pace? What the fuck dude? My name is irrelevant."

"No, it's incredibly relevant," Jaxon says, confused. "You're a Valentine. It's one of the older Mafia families. There's protocol for this…sort of thing."

"This isn't anything!"

"But what I don't understand is why you're here," he says, motioning between him and myself. "Doing…this."

"Trust me, *this* is over! And for the record, I don't have a family. I left a long time ago, and from what I understand they are all dead anyway."

"No, your brother is still alive."

"Well good for him."

"No, you don't understand, he's got men out looking for you."
This makes my blood grow cold.

To any other orphan alone in the world, news that their brother
is actually alive would be incredible news. But it isn't to me. In
fact, it's the opposite. While my brother might've been a few
years older than me, and possessed a much quieter personality
than my father, he still had a cold and vicious streak like he did. I
can't even imagine what being in close proximity to that monster
every day was like. And given that I had taken the brunt of my
father's abuse for all those years, I can only expect that he turned
his mean streak on my brother the moment I walked out that door.

"Whatever they said I did," I say, feeling my body shake. "It's
a lie. I...I didn't do anything."

"What? Of course you didn't," Jaxon asks, now confused.
"They just have been looking for you. You know, to bring you
home."

"I'm good, thanks anyway," I say, walking toward the door.

But Jaxon suddenly blocks my path.

"Stay, I'll have my men take you home."

"You're not understanding, junior," I say, frustrated. "I don't
want to go home."

"You're right. I don't understand," Jaxon says, still blocking
my path. "Why on earth would you not want to be reunited with
your family? You're a Valentine. That name means something,
and it's one of the oldest and most prestigious families in the
syndicate. Why on earth are you here, selling sex for money?"

I sigh, trying to mask my growing panic and immediate desire
to just be off this patio, and far away from this building and this
conversation entirely.

However, given that I can't scale tall buildings, and Jaxon
Pace, who is coincidentally built like a brick house, is blocking
the only exit from the patio, I realize I'm trapped.

"My family name does mean something," I say, crossing my
arms tightly across my body. "Misery. Nothing but misery. I left
because my father was an abusive alcoholic who loved to torture
me any chance he got, okay? And the syndicate looked the other
way. So I did the only thing I could do, and ran away. I built a life
for myself, and I'm happy with it."

"You're happy selling your body?"

"Not all of us were born in the west wing of Pace Manor,

Jaxon. We don't all have trust funds or tons of disposable cash lying around," I spit. "Some of us do what we have to do to survive, and we have to pay rent, and up until this moment, it seemed this was going to be a mutually beneficial way to do that. But now it's fucked. So, I want to leave, and there's nothing you can do to stop me."

"I have six men in the lobby that would argue that point," Jaxon says, his face now serious. "And even by some miracle you make it past them, your brother has dozens more out looking for you."

Shit.

"I mean, you're not even using an alias, Rachel. Chicago might be a big place but the areas that we exist in are quite small. It's realistically only a matter of time before one of his men find you, and this little ruse of yours comes to an end."

"It isn't a ruse!" I shout back at him. "I thought they were all dead! And in case you didn't notice, I'm a big girl and I can provide for myself."

"By doing escort work?"

"Hey, before you go all rich-boy judgey on me, you're the one who hired me, remember? And for your information I want to be here."

"No, you don't."

"Yes, I fucking do!"

"Sweetheart, I've had more than my fair share of whores and I can assure you, you're not one."

"Fuck you dude! You don't know me!"

"I know your friend, and I know she *is* cut out for this work. Same with your two little buddies in there. But you? No."

"I'm sure I don't know what you—"

However, before I can finish my sentence, there is a loud thud, and we both look up to see Jessica's naked ass pressed up against a sliding glass door leading to Eamon's bedroom.

"Oh yeah! Fuck me baby!" Jessica moans.

"Jaxon! Hey Jaxon!" Eamon laughs, using the window as leverage to balance Jessica as he continues thrusting up into her. "Look at this shit, eh?!"

My jaw drops watching the ridiculous scene before us before Eamon shifts and moves Jessica back to the bed, out of our immediate eyesight.

There is a moment of silence between us before Jaxon snorts. Despite being frustrated with him only moments before, I can't stop myself from giggling a little.

"You were saying?" he chuckles.

"You know," I say, still giggling. "You can go to hell."

"Most likely, but that's beside the point."

He curses under his breath about how Eamon is a horndog, and then we both start laughing.

"But, in all seriousness," he says, turning back to me. "I can't just let you leave, Rachel. I know your brother."

"Are you...friends?"

Jaxon snorts again.

"No, definitely not."

"Enemies?"

He shakes his head.

"Again, it's just protocol. If anyone connected to the syndicate let it slip that you were here tonight with me, and I didn't immediately bring you back to your brother, it would cause... ripples."

"Ripples?" I ask sarcastically. "You're afraid of ripples?"

"No, more like I've caused enough of them lately and I'm trying to avoid causing more."

"Ripples," I giggle to myself.

"Fuck off," he says rolling his eyes. "But look, you know how this works, we came from the same world."

"I promise we really didn't."

He stares at me, his bright blue eyes scanning mine.

"You're going to have to explain, Rachel."

"Explain what?"

"Well, what *are* you doing here?"

"We needed to pay rent," I shrug. "You're right, Jessica does this all the time, and I guess Eamon is a regular client of hers or something, and he told her to bring a friend. For you."

Jaxon nods.

"And you would rather do this than—"

"Watch it," I snap.

"I'm not looking down on your choice of profession," he says defensively. "I'm just saying that you have options. Resources. People who want to help you. I mean your family is practically royalty in the syndicate, which makes you a Mafia princess."

"I promise you I'm not," I sigh, I look off over the balcony of the now snowy Chicago night sky.

"You see," Jaxon says, taking his drink off the table and sitting back against the chair. "How this whole explanation thing works is you actually have to give me something."

"Look, My father, well, he was an asshole, and I'm not sorry he's dead," I say, trying to keep my frustration at bay. "My mother left after years of abuse, and the moment she did my father started taking his anger out on me. Everything I did was always wrong."

Jaxon lowers his gaze and sighs.

"I was never going to be anyone's princess. So, I became the villain."

"Villain? What do you mean?"

"When I was younger, the most I could do was stay out of his way. But, as I got older I started finding little ways of fighting back. I mean, I was just a kid, so my knowledge of the world was limited, and so were my options. But I'd take all the bullets out of his guns, and hide them. Replace all his ice cubes in his office bar with ones made from toilet water, put Nair in his shampoo, that sort of thing."

"So, you just...*pranked* your father?"

"I guess you could say that," I say, biting my lip. "It was my way of trying to get back at him, you know? When I was just a teenager, he literally killed someone right in front of me. I knew then that he was actually a monster. After that I just avoided being around him as much as I could. Thankfully he met my stepmom and diverted his attention to her. But one night we got into it really bad. I ran away, and I never looked back. I found work in the city, I met Jess, and the two of us just made our own way. A few years ago I heard the cartel took over the Valentine house and killed everyone. I've got to be honest; I didn't weep for any of them."

"Not even your brother?" Jaxon asks.

I shift uncomfortably.

"For him I did," I say quietly. "A little. But you have to understand he's always been..."

"Difficult," Jaxon finishes for me, staring down at his hands.

"Yeah, that's a good word. He might have been my father's legacy, and worthy of his attention, but I'm sure like me, sometimes he wished he didn't get that attention if you know what I mean. My father was a nasty drunk, and he kind of took out his aggression on whomever or whatever was closest."

"I wouldn't call Michael the most empathetic human I've ever met," Jaxon shrugs, pursing his lips. "But I will say he's been trying to find you for quite some time. Ever since he got out of therapy and—"

"Therapy?"

Jaxon's face is suddenly blanketed with a complicated expression. One that seems to say "I've said too much," while simultaneously saying nothing at all. But before I can ask what he means by that, the sliding door to the living room slides open again and a visibly distraught Chrissy comes pouring out on the balcony.

"Rachel! Oh my God, it's *Ness*," Chrissy says, trying to pull a t-shirt over her naked frame. "I…I don't know what happened but she…she…"

"Chrissy, use your words," I say firmly. "What's the matter?"

"She's…she's not breathing!" Chrissy sobs. "I can't get her to wake up. Oh God, oh God!"

"What?!"

I look up at Jaxon but he's already walking through the door into the living room.

An unresponsive Ness lays on her back, her face is purple and her eyes rolled back into her skull.

"What the fuck happened?" Jaxon snaps, shoving Tyler up against the bookshelves.

"I don't know man! I swear! One minute we were just goin' at it doggy style, and the next she just fell the fuck over man!"

I kneel down beside her, trying to feel a pulse, and noticing the marks on the crease of her arm.

"What did you give her?!" Jaxon demands.

"She had some of Eamon's Ecstasy," Tyler says. "And…"

"And?!" Jaxon says again, slamming Tyler into the shelves again.

"And she said she wanted a little dope, so I gave her a little from my stash. But you know, I think she was a little fucked up before hand, she was in the bathroom for a while."

"You fucking idiot!" Jaxon snaps, slamming him for a third time into the end table next to the couch.

Between the sound of the vase and lamp on the table that just broke Tyler's fall, crashing to the floor, and Chrissy pounding on Eamon's door, eventually it opens.

"What the fuck is going on out here?!" Eamon shouts angrily. "I'm wasting a good high on all this screamin' and hollerin'!"

Jaxon has released Tyler, sending him crumpling to the floor. He immediately pulls out his phone and starts texting someone furiously.

"Oh, fuck, what the fuck is this shit,"

"It's Ness," Chrissy sobs, grabbing his arm.

"Get the fuck off me, slut!" Eamon recoils.

"What the hell?" Jessica says, appearing in the door, having quickly covered herself with Eamon's shirt.

"Ness…she…she…oh God, I think she's OD'd!"

"Fuck!" Eamon shouts.

"Ness, can you hear me?" I say, trying to shake her gently. "Come on, girl, don't do this."

"I'll call paramedics!" Jessica says, quickly running over to her purse and fishing out her phone.

"Fuck no you won't," Eamon thunders, yanking her phone away.

"Hey!"

"You're not calling anyone!" Eamon shouts at her.

"This isn't a joke, Eamon, she could die!"

"And by the time paramedics will get here the only thing they will do is cause a shit ton of problems for me!"

"Dude…" Tyler says, shocked at the callousness of Eamon's response.

"We need to get her medical attention!" Jessica shouts.

"Oh my God! Oh my God!" Chrissy sobs.

"Will someone shut that bitch up and let me think?!"

I search the room for Jaxon but he's nowhere to be found.

What the fuck? Did he just leave?!

But just as I am thinking the worst of the future Don Supreme of the Chicago crime syndicate he appears back at the door, carrying a black leather bag.

"We need to get her out of this apartment," Eamon says, his eyes wild. "I think we can roll her in the rug, right?"

"What the hell?!"

"Bro you're not serious?!" Rodney snorts.

"I know I'm not seriously going to jail for some stupid fucked-up slut dying on my apartment floor!"

"No one dying yet," Jaxon says, kneeling down next to Jessica, he turns to me. "Cradle her head."

I watch as he pulls what appears to be some sort of triangular syringe out of the bag. He pops the packaging off and pushes it up her nose.

"What is that?" I ask, feeling my hands shaking.

"Narcan," Jaxon says unemotionally. "Now we just have to pray it works."

CHAPTER SIX

ADAM

"And did the Narcan work?" I ask.

Rachel nods.

"Lifestyles of the rich and famous I guess." I mutter under my breath. "So, what happened?"

"Well, it's kind of a blur, but the short version is everyone quickly dispersed, Jaxon had some men take Ness to the hospital and she lived. Happily ever after."

"Yeah…just what I was thinking," I say sarcastically. "Where did Jaxon get his hands on Narcan?"

Rachel shifts herself on the bed and crosses her arms across her chest, chuckling to herself.

"The one benefit of being a party boy Mafia-Don-in-training with a drug habit, is that your security squad is required to always have it on hand. Among other reversal drugs. And always be somewhere in the immediate vicinity."

I snort.

"You're kidding?"

"Not a bit."

"What do you mean 'Mafia-Don-in-training?' I ask. "I thought Jaxon was the Don?"

She grins.

"Not at that point. His father was still the Don. But of course with Jaxon, being the heir, he had twice the security."

"Why?"

"Because a Mafia Don's legacy is more important."

"More important than what?"

"Almost everything," Rachel smirks, pulling her legs up under her body. "A Don's number one priority is to maintain power. After all, power is the only way he can protect the ones he loves. But what good is power if it leaves the people you love vulnerable after *you're* gone?"

I sit back in my chair, as Rachel reaches for her purse.

Instinctively, my hand twitches to my gun belt hanging from my shoulder.

"Relax," she says, pulling out a copper metal cigarette case.

Shit.

She pulls one out and lights it.

At first I thought about trying to stop her, since I doubt the hotel will like that, but then again, it's not as if they give a shit. From the look of the lobby alone, I assume as long as someone doesn't get murdered in one of their rooms, they're satisfied.

"The Mafia has a long history and an even longer memory. And a concern for any Don is how that history will remember him," Rachel continues, taking a swig of her beer.

"Your father was a Don, wasn't he?"

"Sure was," she snorts. "And let me tell you, that history doesn't remember much of him. And what it does remember, isn't very flattering."

She takes a long drag.

"It's like…my one consolation for how shitty he treated me."

Realizing it's too hard to resist the smell of her cigarette I walk over to the window and crack it, before pulling out my own pack and lighting one.

"Anyway, where was I?" she continues, sitting back against the headboard. "Oh yeah, Jaxon. The men assigned with protecting an heir have the most important job of any in the syndicate. They're trained to protect him against any threat. Including himself. If he gets himself in trouble, they get him out of it. Period."

I snort.

"What?" She asks.

"Nothing, it's just comical the way you're talking about it."

"How is it funny?"

I take another drag of my cigarette.

"Because you talk about it as if the Don is the most important powerful person on earth. Like he's the President of the United States or something."

Rachel chuckles.

"Depending on the Don, he could be *more* powerful than the President."

"Is that so?"

"And more terrifying too."

"I dunno about that," I shrug, folding my arms across my body. "I'd say having access to nuclear codes makes a man pretty terrifying. And powerful."

"I wouldn't disagree," Rachel says, flicking her hand. "But at least the President has people specifically in place to check his impulses. A Mafia Don does not. A fair majority of them are power hungry psychopaths that you do not want to cross."

"I'll remember that," I say, rolling my eyes.

"I'm sorry, do we offend you?"

"Yes," I nod, flicking the cigarette butt out of a massive hole in the window screen. "No one has any fear of breaking the law. Probably because you have no respect for it. And why would you, I guess. You people have no laws. No rules."

"Oh we have plenty of laws, and rules."

I snort.

"Yeah right."

"No," her tone is immediately serious. "There *are* rules."

"Criminals with codes, is that what you're saying?"

"That's exactly it. And whether or not you want to hear it or accept it, there's actually a benefit to it."

I laugh out loud.

"Enlighten me," I snort, grabbing another beer. "Tell me what benefit the Mafia could possibly have?"

"We can go places you can't."

I stare at her.

"Think of it this way," she says, sitting up on the bed and looking at me. "You joined the FBI, I assume because you want to help people, yes?"

"Yes."

"But," she says, holding up her finger. "Let's say you catch a bad guy."

"Like your ex-boyfriend?"

"No, I'm not talking about some snobby asshat like Jaxon. I mean, a *really* bad guy. Someone who has an insatiable bloodlust, who hurts people for sport and just wants to watch the world burn."

"So…like your *brother*," I say quietly, watching her face.

She swallows hard before looking down at the aged old mattress, fiddling with the shoddy comforter.

"Yeah," she says, biting her lip. "I guess more like him."

The disappointment in her voice makes me feel immediately defensive, like maybe I went too far.

"I wasn't trying to—"

"Anyway, yes, let's use Michael as an example," she interrupts, finally looking back up at me. "He got away with killing your partner, did he not?"

"He will pay for that," I growl. "If it's the last thing I do."

"But that's just it, Adam," she says, with a sigh. "He *won't*."

What the hell is she talking about?

"Even if you catch him—"

"I *will* fucking catch him," I snap irritably, my blood already boiling.

"Okay, well even if you catch him, you're not an idiot."

"Excuse me?" I whisper lethally.

"You know as well as I do, there's absolutely no chance of him ever cooperating with you."

"At this point, his cooperation means very little to me," I grumble.

"Well, now, he has all of Black's money and resources, and blackmail on important people."

"Again, that wouldn't make a lot of—"

"…People in power, Adam. I'm talking about government officials. The kind of people who could stall hearings…set up a jailbreak."

My blood immediately runs cold.

"If you know of any government officials who are compromised Rachel, then you need to tell me."

She swallows hard.

"Maybe."

"Maybe?" I snap, feeling my frustration bubbling. "Rachel this isn't a fucking joke, Rachel!"

"I'm not fucking saying it is!" she snaps back defensively.

"If you knowingly withhold evidence, that makes you an accomplice, or at the very least an accessory," I say, pointing at her. "Something that could land you in jail!"

"And being a narc, or sharing evidence, with someone I don't fully trust could land me at the bottom of the river!" She shouts at me, jumping to her feet. "My psychopathic brother is a monster, Adam. He's far more dangerous than you realize. And he has eyes and ears and dirty cops everywhere. So perhaps you need to remember that you're not the only one who has reasons to be suspicious, okay?"

Her words stun me to my core. Mostly because she's not wrong. I guess somewhere in my frustration about *her* lying to *me*, and trying to separate myself from these convoluted emotions I feel for her, I forgot that I haven't exactly been a model of honesty with her either.

So how can I honestly expect her to trust me, when I've lied to her for our entire relationship?

…Or whatever, *this* was.

But now she's shaking.

Suddenly my profiler instinct takes over once again.

Rachel's small frame is trembling before me, her chest heaving. Her face is pale, and she's chewing on her lip again.

Conclusion? She's clearly more terrified of Michael than of anyone or anything else in the world, including incarceration.

But despite her fear, she *still* came here. To see me.

That has to mean something…right?

"You're right," I say quietly. "Please, continue."

She takes a deep breath and then tucks her hair behind her ear, before sitting back down on the bed.

"Anyway, all I was saying is that now he has…connections. Some of them I know, and some he deliberately keeps secret, even from me."

She shoots me a pointed glance.

"And a few of those connections have the power to undo all of your hard work to catch him."

"Not to be dismissive, but even the state has ways of manipulating him," I say quietly. "Believe me, they can be quite persuasive."

"But that's what I'm trying to tell you, Adam," Rachel says pleadingly. "There's no way you could control him, he's not afraid of anything you could threaten him with."

"Well, I didn't necessarily say *threaten*, but—"

"...And there's no prison that could hold him. At least not without it ending in a bloody riot every single day."

I shift, uncomfortable at the truth in her words.

"I mean, he was already granted an insanity plea," she whispers quietly. "And he *wasn't* insane."

"Yes he is."

"Okay, yes, he is. But he knew exactly what he was doing. He literally got away with murder. Several, actually."

I can feel my blood pressure rising.

"You talk about following rules and the law, like you're taking some invisible high road. But what you don't seem to understand is that you're limited by what the law allows you to do. But Michael understands it. And since he knows your hands are tied, there's nothing you can do to scare him."

I stare at her.

"You're saying your brother isn't afraid of anything?"

"There's only one thing my brother is afraid of," Rachel says, swallowing hard.

"And that is?"

"Jaxon Pace," she says, her eyes locking on mine.

I snort.

"Rachel, every single rich asshole thinks because they have money they are somehow above the law. It's hardly original. But eventually they learn the hard way that the rules apply to everyone. Even someone like Jaxon Pace."

"No, Adam," Rachel says, shaking her head. "They don't."

"Oh," I growl, my blood boiling. "I assure you, they do."

Rachel sighs.

"Jaxon can go places you *can't*, Adam. Because of *who* he is, and who he knows."

"Yeah, I'm sure the aristocracy is quite a resource," I say sarcastically.

"I'm not talking about the fucking aristocracy," Rachel says, firmly. "Jaxon's biggest asset is that he employs skilled people. *Smart* people, who know how to get him access to places that even the President himself would struggle to get into."

"Oh, I'm aware of exactly *who* he employs." I say through gritted teeth. "I'll admit I was a bit slow on the uptake but Jaxon let a few things slip."

She rolls her eyes.

"I'm not just referring your friend from the Bureau—"

"He's *not* my friend," I whisper venomously.

"Well, whoever or whatever that guy is. He's not Jaxon's *only* resource. He has an army of men who are all ex-military or mercenaries, all of whom would die for him in a heartbeat. He has bankers keeping him rich, doctors keeping him alive, researchers keeping him informed, and engineers building him bunkers in his backyard. He's got spies all over the world, feeding him information and between facilitators like Ethan and the slew of attorneys managing his affairs, he's always within an arm's reach of some meticulously crafted contingency plan, at all times. And if all that wasn't enough," She continues. "Jaxon knows people, who are just as connected to those resources, and the *underworld*, as he is."

Shifting in my chair, I scratch the five o'clock shadow on my chin.

During my interrogation with Jaxon at the warehouse I figured out that Jaxon had employed *Ghostrider*, my nemesis from my early days at the Bureau.

Being a tech genius, and an incredibly proficient hacker, Ghostrider was dangerous enough on his own, having hacked a number of personnel files, some of which were incredibly personal, and confidential.

Like *mine*.

So, the thought that Jaxon essentially has an army of men that are skilled and dangerous in his employ, is incredibly unsettling, for more than one reason.

"Forgive me, but it almost sounds as if you admire him," I say, pursing my lips together.

She sighs heavily and scratches her head.

"It's complicated."

"Right," I snap, unable to contain the clear venom in my voice this time. "Well, I hope you two will be very happy together."

"Excuse me?" She looks up at me, and suddenly I realize that I have made a grave mistake.

CHAPTER SEVEN

Rachel

*H*e really did not just say that to me...
My heart immediately starts pounding and I feel my rage bubbling in my veins.

"What?" he asks, albeit a bit nervously.

"I know you're not sitting here, actually suggesting to me that I still have *feelings* for Jaxon Pace."

"Well, I mean you did just give me a list of benefits of being with him so—"

"No, *asshole*," I snap angrily. "I gave you a list of reasons that my brother fears him. And why *you* should too."

Adam opens his mouth to say something, but I immediately cut him off.

"Let me explain something to you, because you don't seem to be getting it," I whisper lethally. "Michael fears Jaxon because Jaxon will *never* take the high road. Definitely not when it comes to war, and especially not when it comes to vengeance. And unlike *you*, who is bound by the government you serve, Jaxon's hands are not tied. Additionally, he has enough money, power and influence to never see a single consequence for any of his actions."

I lean forward on my knees and narrow my eyes at him, making sure I have his full attention.

"And I, of all people, know better than anyone how vicious Jaxon Pace can be," I growl, but to add to my frustration, my anger has reached a fever pitch and causes my voice to tremble.

I fucking hate when that happens.

But I'm not finished with Adam. Not by a long shot.

"Make no mistake, Agent Westwood, Jaxon is a true Don. He's just as disruptive, just as dangerous, and can be just as depraved and unhinged as Michael can be. And when you've crossed him, he will stop at absolutely nothing to destroy you."

The composed and calculated Adam Westwood's face looks pale, clearly stunned by what I have just told him.

Good. I need him to be.

I need to drive this point through his thick fucking skull once and for all.

"Yes, we had a relationship. Yes, we have a child together. But that bridge was burned a long fucking time ago, and you have no idea what being with Jaxon Pace did to me," I say darkly. "So unless you want me to walk out that door and never come back, don't you ever imply that I still have feelings for him!"

"I didn't know that's how you felt," he says quietly, shifting in his seat.

"Well now you fucking do. That man has caused me more pain and misery than you could ever know. He's the reason I moved across the country, the reason I faked my own death, and the reason I…"

I pause, my heart rate skyrocketing and my cheeks heating as my rage explodes within my chest.

"That bastard is the reason I don't have a fucking relationship with my own daughter. Do you understand?"

"Rachel, I—"

"I said," I snap loudly. "Do you fucking understand?!"

His face darkens, and he glares at me. His eyes fall to the floor, and he clicks his tongue in his mouth, something he seems to do whenever he's angry but trying to control it.

Wait just a fucking minute…He's angry?!

Perhaps I was a bit angry and forceful with my tone, but that's only because *he* pissed *me* off!

I could disregard him being mad at me for lying to him, or

even his snippy little comments about me being an escort. But the fact that he would imply that I would risk sneaking out of house arrest and coming all the way down here to see him, while still harboring feelings for the married Jaxon Pace, who made my life a miserable purgatory for so many years, instantly infuriates me.

And the sheer audacity of this man, to sit here and get annoyed with *my* anger, or *my* tone is the last straw.

"Actually, you know what," I say, slapping my thighs. "Fuck this. I'm done."

"What?" he asks.

But I've already stood up and am grabbing my sweater and my pants from where they are currently drying off on the small little room furnace.

"Wait…" he says, standing to his feet and walking over to me as I shake out my pants. "What are you doing?"

Shit, they are still wet, and freezing.

But I don't care.

I hate feeling vulnerable, and that's all I've felt this entire time I've been here, sharing these unflattering parts of my past. Vulnerable. Exposed. Naked.

"Rachel, what are you doing?" He asks as I start to pull his sweater off of my body.

"I'm giving you your clothes back," I snap, tossing it on the bed. "Because I'm leaving."

"What?" he gasps. "No. You're not."

"Oh yes the fuck I am," I say, pulling my wet sweater back on my body, feeling like the wind is knocked out of me the moment the icy cold fabric touches my torso.

"No, you can't," he says, grabbing his sweater off the bed. "Your…Your clothes are still wet. You'll get hypothermia."

"Good, at least it will save me from getting murdered by one of Jaxon's bodyguards the minute the catch me trying to sneak back on to the property."

I reach for my leggings, but Adam snatches them off the furnace before I can.

"Give me my pants, Adam."

"No," he snaps. "They are still wet!"

"Fine then, I'm keeping yours."

"That's fine," he says with a mildly satisfied smirk pulling at the corners of his lips.

"...But I'm still leaving," I say, smiling at him.

His smirk fades.

Good.

I step past him and start packing up my cigarette case and lighter back into my purse.

"No, you're not leaving," he says firmly, locking the deadbolt. "Don't be ridiculous. It's still snowing, and you've been drinking."

"Good thing I don't have a car and I took the bus," I say, throwing my purse over my shoulder. "Pretty sure those are still running unless it's an actual blizzard."

"You're not going anywhere," he says, now blocking my path to the door. "You're overreacting."

"Fuck you!" I shout at him. "Get out of my way!"

"Rachel," he tries to reason with me.

"Don't you *Rachel* me!" I snap, trying to walk past him. "Fuck you and fuck this conversation that is clearly just been a waste of my time!"

"You're not leaving."

He puts his hands out to stop me.

With his hands outstretched I see my opportunity and hit him hard in the stomach.

"Watch me!"

He falls onto the bed, and I squeeze past him.

However, the deadbolt is old and heavy so it takes me a few extra seconds to get it open and pull the door open. And as soon as I do, a blast of cold wet sleet sprays me in the face, knocking the wind out of my lungs.

Holy shit, that's cold.

But just as I go to take a step outside, I feel Adam's hands around my waist, pulling me back inside the hotel room.

"What are you doing?!" I shout, pounding against his hands with mine. "Put me down!"

I try to grab the door frame to stop him from pulling me inside but slip as it's completely coated in snow and ice.

"Adam Westwood! Put me down!" I shout. "I'm leaving!"

"No, you're not"," he says, carrying me back into the room, despite me trying to scratch and slap his hands.

He dumps me back on to the bed before quickly shutting and

locking the door behind him.

"Just wait a minute, Rachel."

"I'm done waiting, and I've already wasted enough time here this evening!" I scream at him angrily, rolling off the bed and lunging toward the door. "I want to go home!"

"No, you don't," he says, blocking me.

"Yes, I do! And you can't keep me here!" I shout reaching past him trying to unlock the door.

"Keep your voice down," he snaps. "You'll wake the whole complex."

"Oh really?!" I snap angrily. "Help! Help! Somebody, please!"

"Rachel, stop it!"

"Help!"

"Rachel, will you knock it off?" He hisses, angrily. "I'm just trying to have a conversation with you!"

"Help! Please!" I shout, feigning emergency. "This crazy man is holding me hostage! He's got a gun and he's going to kill me! Please! Heeeeeellllllllp!"

"That's enough!" He suddenly shouts at me, so forcefully it makes jump and stumble backwards, falling down onto the bed. "You're acting like fucking child!"

Oh no he didn't....

"Fuck you!" I shout at him, jumping to my feet again and lunging straight for the door.

Reaching around him I try desperately to unlock the deadbolt. But Adam blocks my path, his hands pushing mine away every time I reach for the lock.

"How dare you call me a child!" I scream at him, slapping at him with all my rage. "You pompous fucking asshole! You have no right to—"

In one quick motion, Adam grabs my hand and spins me around so that he's holding me tightly, pinning my back against his chest.

"Rachel, I'm sorry!" He says, his voice a strange mixture of frustration and fear. "I'm sorry, okay? I shouldn't have said that."

For a moment, I continue to struggle against him, but almost by design my body relents to the feeling of his strong arms around me, and the scent of his body so close to me nearly disarms me completely.

"I'm sorry," he repeats into the crease of my neck, his voice almost a whisper. "You're right, I had no right making that comment because I don't know your story yet. Especially with Jaxon."

I push back against him with my elbow once again but he holds me tightly.

"...But maybe that's just my *own* fear talking."

I stop struggling.

My heart continues thundering in my chest, no longer from rage, but from the unfamiliar safety I suddenly feel, tangled up here in Adam's arms.

Even if I kinda hate him for it.

"Look, I can't force you to stay, Rachel," he says, still holding me firmly. "That's not what this is."

"And what exactly would you call this?"

"I...I don't know," he whispers into my hair. "I just...well, I just couldn't let you leave. Not like that."

"Not like that..."

His words affect me more than they should, warmth flooding my veins.

Why do I love hearing him so desperate for me to stay?

"I'm going to let you go now," he whispers.

No. Don't. Not yet.

But I know, I cannot let him *see* the effect he has on me. Instead, I inhale his scent one last time, hearing him sigh deeply, his breath shuddering. Slowly he releases his grip on me.

"You're right, I can't stop you from leaving," he says quietly, with my back still to him. "I mean...I *won't* stop you."

Even though I am free, I don't move.

His touch was like electricity in my bones. My mind instantly races through every single memory where his body was wrapped around mine. Every night I spent here at this hotel, or other hotels around the city, wrapped up in his arms.

I miss it. I miss *all* of it.

Turning around slowly, I find he hasn't moved an inch. His brown eyes find mine and it is then I see the look of resigned fear written on his face.

Adam won't stop me because that goes against his principles.

...But he doesn't want me to leave either.

It might not mean much, but it means *something.* So, without thinking I cup Agent Westwood's face, and kiss him.

CHAPTER EIGHT

ADAM

Her lips are on mine and instinctively my hand snakes up her face. I slam her into the wall next to the door, slipping my hands under the back of her shirt and feeling her smooth skin. I bury my face in her neck, savoring the taste of her and pressing my erection against her.

My pull to her is magnetic. Her body is my familiar and most favorite drug, and all I want is more of her.

"Yes, Adam…" She moans.

But when I pull back to look at her, two things hit me at the same time.

First, that she is, quite possibly, the most beautiful woman I have ever seen.

It's the second thing that hits me like a big yellow school bus. And that is that I have no idea *who* she really is.

For months this beautiful woman has told me things about her, and her life, that weren't the truth. Or at the very least weren't the *whole* truth. And so even though my body craves her like the very oxygen it needs to survive, I fear all of this could just be an act. Some I either she was told to play, or one she chose to become.

"Annie, I…" I start to say, catching myself lost in my own

confusion. "I mean, Rachel, I…I…can't do this."

Her brown eyes burrow into my soul, a crippling mixture of disappointment and desperation that nearly shatters me where I stand.

"Why?" She whispers, her breathing rapid and erratic. "This is hardly our first time, Adam."

"I know," I swallow hard, trying feebly to reign in my desire to ravage her. "I…I don't *know* you."

"Yes, you do," Rachel whispers, cupping my face in her hand.

"No, I don't. You told me things about you, and I thought I knew who you were…and who we were."

She drops her hand and suddenly her face becomes angry as she steps toward me.

"But you…you lied to me just the same!" Rachel snaps, defensively. "You're just as guilty. You told me your name was Robert and that—"

"I know what I told you, Rachel," I sigh. "That's the problem. There's just so many lies. And I just…don't know what's real, and what's not between us."

Silence settles over the room, but neither of us move. Her eyes find mine and suddenly I cannot move.

How does she do this to me?

"Okay, yes," she says as she takes a step toward me, tucking a strand of hair behind her ear. "We weren't exactly truthful with each other."

"That's an understatement," I snort.

"But," she snaps, glaring at me. "It wasn't malicious. That's what you're missing, Adam. And perhaps the reason I can see past it, is because I know the difference between a lie that is intended to hurt, and a lie that was simply *survival*. That's what this was."

"Even still, it doesn't change the situation."

"It could," she argues. "But we're not there yet."

She takes another step toward me.

"This was simple before. We were just two people who liked to fuck, fucking. It just got all complicated somehow."

"Yeah, again, understatement," I sigh, tearing my eyes away from hers, knowing I don't have much restraint left in me to resist her. "Believe me, I had no idea how complicated this would become."

"Well, what if we *uncomplicate* it?" she says, swallowing hard and pressing her hand to my chest. "What if we forget all of this, and pretend it's simple again. If only just for a moment."

"What?" I ask, my heart rate skyrocketing again.

Gently she slides her hand up my chest, pulling on my shirt collar.

"What I'm saying is," she whispers. "What if, for just a second, we take a time out from all this heavy shit, and we go back to being those two people who just like to fuck."

"What?"

I realize I've repeated my question and am still just as confused.

"What if we just fuck, Adam?"

Surely, I must've misheard her. Because she can't really be suggesting that we just...

"I mean, when you met me and we started doing...whatever *this* is," she continues, a coy smile on her face. "It was strictly a business arrangement."

"Rachel, we're well past all that and—"

"Will you just shut the fuck up and stop overthinking this for one second?" She snaps, suddenly.

I am too stunned by her aggression to even respond.

"You want me, Adam. I know you do, I can *feel* it," without warning, she reaches forward and grabs my cock.

Oh fuck.

I shudder, feeling her hands on me, stroking me.

"And you know what?" She whispers, leaning in and kissing my neck. "I want you too. Badly."

Game. Fucking. Over.

The moment these words leave her lips, something in my brain snaps. I instantly push her against the wall, pinning her by her throat.

She gasps, but not as if she is afraid. But as if she *enjoys* it.

I chuckle to myself.

"Now I know you're not suggesting that I just fuck you like a client," I whisper, running my thumb against her soft bottom lip. "Are you, Rachel?"

I can hear her breath trembling, but she lifts her nose at me.

"And what if I *was*?"

"Oh, I don't think it would be safe," I growl. "For *you*."

71

"Why the hell not?"

I squeeze her throat tightly.

"Because that sassy little mouth of yours has been pissing me off since you walked through that door. And trust me, sweetheart, I have more than a few things I could do with it."

I watch as her eyes drift south my mouth. She bites her bottom lip and looks quickly back up at me.

"Well, I mean technically you've already *paid* me," she whispers, an irritating smile skating across her face. "So, what if I just want to fuck?"

"I'm warning you, Rachel," I whisper, my voice low and lethal. "Don't tempt me."

"I said," She repeats, slowly. "What if I *want* to fuck?"

I smile.

My mind is racing, hearing her rapid breathing and seeing the desperate longing on her face. Finally, I lean in. Her eyes widen and her body tenses but all I do is kiss her cheek softly, bringing my lips up to her ear.

"Then I'm going to *fuck* you, Rachel," I whisper, darkly. "Really, really, fucking hard."

I pull back, finding her eyes locked on mine. I can practically see the wheels turning in her head, as I glare down at her, my heart starting to pound.

Finally, she grins, and tilts her head back against the wall.

"Prove. It."

The filthy irreverence of her two-worded proposal, and her cocky defiance shatters what remains of my resolve.

Alright, Ms. Valentine, if that's how you want to play it...

With my free hand I yank open my belt buckle and unzip my fly, pulling my now rock hard erection out of my pants.

"Go on then," I growl, biting her earlobe. "Get on your fucking knees and earn your money, like a good whore."

She hesitates a moment before dropping to the floor. Then she takes me in her hand and begins to rub my cock back and forth against her lips, tantalizingly slow.

Sweet Mary Mother and Joseph...

Her eyes find mine again and wraps her mouth around me and swallows my cock deep into her throat. I must admit, I've always been impressed by her skills. She nearly takes my entire length down her throat before she pulls back and does it again.

And then again, each time her soft lips squeezing the head of my cock tightly. It feels so incredible that my knees almost buckle beneath me and I have to lean one hand against the wall just to steady myself.

But when I see the bratty little smile across her face, I chuckle, because it's then that I realize she thinks that *she's* the one somehow controlling this situation.

Oh no, no, no. That's not how this is going to go.

Without hesitation I grip the back of her hair and shove her head down hard, making her choke. I pull out only to ram my cock back down her throat several more times before letting her up for air. She coughs, and I watch with satisfaction as the drool drips off her slutty lips.

I let her breathe for a moment before I lean down and grab her chin, pulling her face up to look at me.

"Now, when you're done choking, I want you to answer me. Are you sure you want to do this, *princess?*"

This word elicits the exact effect I anticipate, and she immediately glares up at me before grabbing my erection and aggressively stroking me.

"Don't flatter yourself, Agent Westwood. You couldn't choke anyone with this tiny cock."

I grin.

There's the sassy bitch I know.

With one motion I pick her up and toss her over my shoulder, carrying her just a few steps across the small room and dropping her on the bed.

"Stay on your fucking back, and put your head over the edge."

"Yes, Sir," she laughs, sarcastically.

I chuckle to myself as I yank my shirt off and toss it on the bed before grabbing her face again. I kiss her hard, biting her lip.

"You know Rachel, if you keep taunting me with this cocky mouth of yours, I'm going to have to assume that just means you want me to *fuck* it."

Holding her head firmly off the bed, I shove my cock back down her throat, as she groans, squeezing her thighs together.

"You like that, slut?"

She mumbles something with her lips around my cock, and I thrust in again, making her gag.

"I'm sorry, I can't hear you," I tease, pumping in and out

73

mercilessly. "Come on, princess, speak up."

"Fuck you!" she gurgles in between my thrusts.

When her face starts turning red, I finally let her up for air, and she immediately coughs and gasps, a tiny groan escaping her swollen lips. Her eyes have started watering at this point and are now streaming down her cheeks.

"Aw, your mascara is running, honey," I laugh.

I wipe her eyes, rubbing the black smudges into her cheek before smacking it gently, watching her jump.

"You seem a little out of breath, eh? Have you had enough yet?"

"Not. Even. Close," she spits at me defiantly.

God, why do I love her stubborn sass so much?

"Good, now show me what I paid for."

I reach forward and yank her sweatpants down, revealing her smooth bare pussy. But the moment I do, I nearly cave.

Goddamn...it's beautiful.

But I'm not stupid enough to tell her that. Not right now.

Rachel has at least always been direct in what she wants. And what she wants tonight is nothing more than just a good hard fuck, without frills and without attachment.

So that's exactly what I'm going to give her.

"Don't get comfortable, I'm not done using that sassy mouth yet," I say, grabbing her face again. "Spread your legs and rub that dirty pussy for me."

She obeys, opening her legs and rubbing her long slender fingers against her clit. I swallow hard, feeling as if the entire room has gotten warmer. This might be a horrible idea, but I can't deny her perfect body looks so hot, splayed out like this.

"Open," I command as I thrust into her mouth again, fucking it hard and fast until she chokes again. When I pull out, she coughs and I smile with satisfaction as more spit dribbles down her cheek.

"Oh god," she gasps.

"Yeah, you take a breath," I laugh, yanking her shirt over her head. "In the meantime, I'm going to fuck these juicy tits of yours."

"Fuck!" She moans as I grab her nipples, pulling on them quickly before letting go. I repeat the process several times and then squeeze her breasts together as I straddle her face.

74

"Go on then, slut, suck on my balls. But just know if you do a shitty job, I'm going to go right back to fucking your face, do you understand?"

She says nothing, but I feel her tongue on my taint as she grips the back of my legs, taking both of my balls in her mouth.

"I said," I thunder, squeezing her nipples hard. "Do you fucking understand?"

"Yes!" She yelps. "Oh God, yes!"

She presses her tongue to my taint and starts sucking.

Jesus Christ...that feels amazing.

I squeeze her tits together, rubbing her swollen sore nipples under my thumbs as I pump against her chest, deliberately rubbing my balls on her face.

"Did I say you could stop rubbing that pussy?"

Immediately she reaches her hand down and rubs her fingers against her pussy lips. I watch as her fingers, with her signature black nail polish, rhythmically move in circles, stroking her clit and it's all I can do to keep from busting my load right here on her stomach.

No, not yet.

Despite me manhandling her like I *don't* care about her right now, I know deep down that's not true.

Which is the root of my problem.

I wish I didn't care about Rachel, as it would make my life a hell of a lot easier...but I fucking do. I know I do. However, I also know that no matter what we say to each other tonight, we might not be able to fix this.

So, if this is last time I ever get to fuck this girl, then damnit I'm at least going to make it *memorable.*

And that's when I see something that gives me an idea. A really, really, *filthy* idea.

One perfect for my filthy little Mafia slut.

Letting go of her tits, I step back, and push her by her shoulders back up on the bed.

"Sit up, and turn around," I say as I start walking away, but I quickly turn back to point at her. "But don't you dare stop rubbing that pussy."

"Yes, Sir," she says, clearly a little dizzy.

I walk over to sink in the room and flick on the light. I stare at my naked reflection in the mirror, admiring Rachel's spit still glistening on my cock. I run my right hand instinctively over the tattoos scattered across my chest. The cold fluorescent light makes my abs and arms look even more defined; However, my pale skin doesn't hide faint bruising still visible from nearly a month prior. Bruising that was a souvenir from the night I got jumped and kidnapped at her brother Michael's club.

I still don't know how I made it out of his custody, only to wake up on the other side of the city with a hangover. But hey, maybe I'll get an answer for that later from Rachel.

…After I'm done fucking her into a coma.

I turn the water on and grab something off the counter, washing it completely before yanking the towel off the wall and wrapping the item up inside.

I take one more look at myself and smile, before walking back over to the gorgeous naked woman on the bed.

She lays there on her back, one arm over her head, one rubbing her pussy as instructed.

"Good girl," I whisper, licking my lips. "Now come here."

Without warning, I grab both her ankles and pull her down, all the way to the edge of the bed. Lifting her legs I push them back.

"Sit up and hold them."

I kneel down in front of her, pressing down on the backs of her thighs and siding my tongue up along her slit.

"Holy fuckkkkk," she moans, throwing her head back.

"Let me see," I say, using my thumbs to open her up, revealing the bright pink flesh of her tight little cunt. Silently I admire how fucking gorgeous it is before going back to dragging my tongue up and down between the lips. I bury my face in her pussy and start sucking on her clit aggressively.

"Yessss!" She moans loudly. "Fuck you could do that forever."

Her deep brown eyes catch mine, and for a moment, my plan to remain the cocky asshole about to rage fuck her nearly derails completely. There's no denying it. Rachel Valentine is stunningly beautiful. So beautiful it hurts.

Don't Adam. Don't feel, just fuck.

I stare her down as I spit directly on her pussy.

"This is disappointing," I lie, reaching my finger deep inside of her. "Because you are not nearly wet enough,"

"Oh my God…" she whispers, closing her eyes.

Yeah, that's how she always liked it.

76

She loved my long fingers, working in and out of her tight pussy. I take my time before slowly working another finger in and rubbing them hard against her G-Spot.

"What are you tonight?" I ask, moving them faster.

"I'm...I'm..." she moans, her jaw slagging open.

"Hey," I snap, slapping the back of her smooth thigh hard. "Stay focused, princess."

"Don't call me a princess!" She snaps at me.

I yank my fingers out of her and grab her chin hard, pulling her head forward toward me.

"Now you listen to me, slut. Tonight I'll call you whatever the fuck I want to call you, because tonight you're my whore." I whisper against her lips. "Got it?"

She glares at me but eventually she nods. I release her, and shove my fingers back inside her. And despite her little temper tantrum, within seconds she's melting in my hands again and I can hear her breathing instantly quicken.

"Now, tell me what you are."

"I'm your whore," she moans, trying desperately to fight her own resignation.

"That's right. But this whore's pussy isn't nearly ready for me."

"That...that feels so good," she whimpers, as I continue moving my fingers around inside her.

"Hey, remember, you're *my* whore tonight. So if I decide to let you cum, it will be when I say you can cum, and it will be only if you earn that privilege, understand?"

"Yes."

"Yes what?" I snap.

"Yes, Sir."

"Fortunately, I have something that can help with that."

I grab the empty beer bottle from the towel on the floor.

"You should be grateful, I was even nice. I went and washed it for you."

"What the fuck is that for?"

"Oh you know the answer to that already," I grin. "I'm going to fuck you with it."

"Adam!" She gasps.

"I think you misunderstand...This isn't for *your* enjoyment," I say, gently pressing the tip of the glass bottle inside of her and pulling it out again. "It's for mine. I'm the paying customer, remember? And I want to fuck you with this bottle, because I want watch you get wet from it…like the whore you are."

Her jaw drops…just like I expected it would.

But what I *didn't* expect is the wicked smile that slowly and suddenly starts spreading across her face.

"You're a fucking pervert, you know that?" she whispers, narrowing her eyes at me. "But, at least that just means you're not as vanilla as I thought you were, that's a relief."

Now I have to stop my *own* jaw from dropping.

Well that certainly backfired.

I can't say what frustrates me more: her utter indifference, or that bratty attitude of hers. All I know is that I can't let her see her catty response get a rise out of me, or the game is over.

"I see," I say, continuing to gently work the neck of the bottle in and out. "So you're just a whore who is so desperate to get fucked she'd enjoy putting anything inside this filthy hole?"

"Ye…yes, Sir," She whimpers, holding her legs tightly and throwing her head back. "Oh Goddd."

Her pussy starts dripping down the bottle as keep working it in and out of her, her moans growing louder, and breathing heavier.

I swallow hard, grabbing my throbbing cock and rubbing it hard with my free hand.

"If you keep doing that," she whispers, as her legs start to shake. "I will cum."

Fuck that.

"No," I growl. "You won't."

I pull the bottle out of her, and yank her up on her feet, spinning her around. Grabbing her left breast aggressively in my hand, I bury my face in her neck and bite her, sucking on the spot hard before kissing all the way up to her ear.

"*I'm* going to cum," I whisper forcefully, nibbling on her earlobe as she moans. "And if you want to cum, you only get to do it *on* my cock."

Leaning over, I reach into the bedside drawer to grab a condom.

That's when I hear Rachel snort.

"What was that? About us being well past this?"

That's when I notice it.

The way her eyes divert from mine. The disappointment in her sigh. Her sarcasm is just a deflection from one simple truth:

Me using a condom, after months of not using condoms, *bothers* her.

But even if my profiler's assessment pings a reaction from me, I know I can't let it deter me from using common sense. So I simply smile, clicking my tongue against my cheek.

I cup her face with my hand, kissing her softly.

"No honey, what I said was, I don't fucking *know* you," I whisper against her lips, a false softness in my voice holding back my obvious frustration. "We agreed this is a transaction, remember? Nothing more."

For a second I see something flash in Rachel's eyes, but she lowers them to the floor. But as quickly as it appeared, she snaps out of it and smiles up at me.

"Of course. Transactional only. As we agreed."

Before I have time to process what that's all about, she takes the condom in my hand, and without breaking eye contact, rolls it slowly over my cock.

"Go on then, Agent Westwood," she whispers against my lips. "Use what you paid for."

Holy fucking shit.

Her firm grip and the sultry tone in her voice make me forget about the awkward exchange, and instantly make my cock throb.

I grab the back of her head, pulling her lips to mine and kiss her again. This time it's deep and passionate, and I shove my tongue into her mouth. Then take her arm and turn her around pushing her down on her knees on the edge of the bed.

Without wasting anymore time with pomp and circumstance, I step up behind her, shove my cock inside of her, grip her hips tightly, and start to fuck her. Hard.

"Oh God yes!!" She shouts loudly. "Fuck me, Adam!"

My name is the last thing I hear her say before the world fades away.

Maybe I slapped her ass.

Maybe I pulled her hair.

Maybe I switched positions.

I don't know, I can't be sure.

What I do know, however, is that somewhere in there I finally let go and lost myself in the rhythm and the electric feeling of our bodies intertwined.

There's something beautiful about this moment. A euphoric simplicity in all the things deliberately left unsaid. There's no more words. No more complications. No roles. How we feel, or don't feel, doesn't matter.

Nothing matters, besides *this*.

Because, right here in this moment, we aren't a Mafia princess and a suspended federal agent trying to piece together the broken remains of our situationship.

We're just two people who like to fuck. Fucking.

And as Rachel cums hard on my cock, and I explode inside of her, I wonder if just maybe that's enough.

Rachel and I fucked. And then we fucked again. And again, and again until we both collapsed from exhaustion.

While I would never say I'm one of those guys with a ten inch cock, I know it's above average. And I also know, it never disappoints. Perhaps that's because it just so happens to stay hard after I cum. Or perhaps it's because as an FBI profiler, I know how to read a woman's body language. And in recent months, I have learned how to read Rachel's like the back of my hand.

When we both come up for air, we lay side by side in the bed, in silence. Both of us trying to catch our breath after one insane bacchanal of ecstasy.

But somewhere in the post-orgasm clarity, I can't escape the impending feeling of guilt that seems to be sitting on my chest.

"Tell me," I whisper quietly. "Do you regret doing that?"

She laughs, reaching over to the end table and grabbing her cigarette case and lighter.

"Of course not," she says, lighting one and inhaling deeply.

She runs her hand through her hair before passing me her cigarette.

"Do you?"

I appreciate the drag, as it gives me a moment to think of my response.

"No," I breathe. "But…"

"But?"

"But," I continue. "You're being honest with me, right?"

She laughs, taking the cigarette back from me.

"Well, I fucking hope so," she snorts. "Especially considering all the preaching you've done about how that's so important."

"Honesty *is* important, Rachel," I sigh, laying back against the pillows. "At least it is to me."

"But…why though?"

"Why? Because that's just what you do in a rela—" I cough loudly, clearing my throat as I catch myself.

Whoops.

I immediately try to find a different way to say what I'm trying to say.

"I guess honesty is just part of how I know what's real."

I sit up on my elbow and look at her, her perky nipples just barely covered by the thin sheet.

"Surely, you want to know that too?" I ask. "Especially after all the preaching *you* did about how all of this was feeling like a waste of your time?"

She puts the cigarette into a beer bottle and turns to look at me.

"I mean, how do you know that any of this is real, Rachel?"

Her eyes scan mine, and she stares at me for a really long moment, almost as if she wants to say something, but decides against it.

The quiet grows into a small silence lingering between us. And when she continues to stare at the sheets, not saying anything in response, I give up and lay back against the pillow.

Staring up at the ceiling I struggle with the battle raging within me. It's not that I didn't enjoy what we just did, more that it makes me wonder if sex is all Rachel and I are good at. And if that's the case, then maybe whatever this is between us, *is* a waste of time.

"Did you really come looking for me?"

Rachel's voice is quiet, but it breaks the heavy silence between us.

"You know, when I disappeared for a few weeks. When I was being held at the Pace Manor."

"Yes," I whisper, still staring at the ceiling. "I did."

"That's real enough to me, Adam," she whispers quietly.

81

She presses her hand to my chest, causing me to feel my pounding heart hammering away, and I turn to face her.

"It's the *effort*," she says quietly.

"What?"

"You asked me how I know that any of this is real, after all the lies we've told each other," she says. "It's the effort."

Her eyes fall from mine and her face twitches.

"What about it?"

"Let's just say I know what it feels like when someone doesn't care if you suddenly disappear."

Whoa.

She takes a deep breath.

"I don't care what your real name is, or what your actual job is. I don't care that you've lied to me," her voice trails off and she closes her eyes. "But I do care about you."

"Why?"

My question, barely above a whisper, echoes in the cold room. But when her eyes lock with mine, I instantly recognize the sincerity behind them.

"Because you make me feel...real." She says quietly.

I want to say something, but all of my words escape me. And before I can compose anything of value she just smiles and rolls over, collecting my clothes off the floor.

As she starts pulling them on, I scramble to think of something to say.

Do I ask her if she's leaving? But...what if she says yes?

She stands to her feet, and I realize my moment of opportunity is fleeting quickly, and I instantly sit up in the bed.

"Rachel—"

But suddenly she turns and faces me, her eyes closed.

"Look, Adam," she says softly. "I...I...don't know if I can actually give you what you want from me."

Shit.

"And, what is it that you think I want from you?"

"I don't know," she says quietly. "Hell, I don't even know what I want. All I know is I'm not a *good* girl, okay? Despite my last name, I don't have any class or connections. And you can forget about bringing me home to your parents."

She laughs, running her hand through her hair as she starts pacing at the end of the bed.

Fuck, she's panicking.

"I mean, I'm not girlfriend material," she scoffs nervously. "I don't like brunch, I hate interior decorating, and I don't even know how to boil water, for Christ's sake!"

She walks toward the bathroom, but then quickly turns back around, grabbing the box of condoms on the table next to me and tossing it on the bed.

"This is what I know, okay?" She says with another nervous laugh. "So, when you, Mr. Straight-and-Narrow, talk about honesty and not knowing what's real and what's not, and tell me you're afraid of my intentions, I get it! But I have absolutely no idea why you're with me because I have nothing to offer you."

Her voice cracks and instantly every wall I'm trying to install around my heart, crumbles into nothing. I am out of bed and by her side, just as she starts hyperventilating.

"Rachel," I say calmly. "Breathe, okay? Just, breathe."

"I'm...I'm fine," she says, taking a deep breath and pushing me away from her.

I raise my hands but refuse to leave her side. She takes a few more deep breaths before nodding.

"My story," she says slowly. "Is all I have to give you, and more importantly, it's all I *know* I can give you. But it's only going to get worse from here, and I understand if you're not interested in complicating your life any further by going deeper into mine. So I...Well, I can go if that's what you want."

I lock eyes with her, my mind immediately racing.

If I had my way, I would kiss her, and tell her how I really feel about her, and how I don't want her to go. At all. But something tells me that would send her bolting out the door.

And the thought of losing her, after worrying incessantly, and frantically combing the city for her for weeks, feels like a searing hot knife has been jammed straight into my chest.

What is this?

In all my years as a federal officer, I've never felt anything like *this* before. It makes absolutely no sense to feel such an intense pull to someone I barely know. And especially someone who has already broken trust with me.

But then again... I've broken Rachel's trust too.

And she wasn't wrong when she said the lies we told each other *weren't* out of any malicious intent. They were simply to preserve our identities in a world where every secret is a weapon.

I suppose if she can trust me, even just this amount, then perhaps I can trust her too. Or at least I can try.

"I'm going to take a shower," I say quietly. "Why don't you join me, and you can tell me what happens next."

"In what?"

"Your *story*."

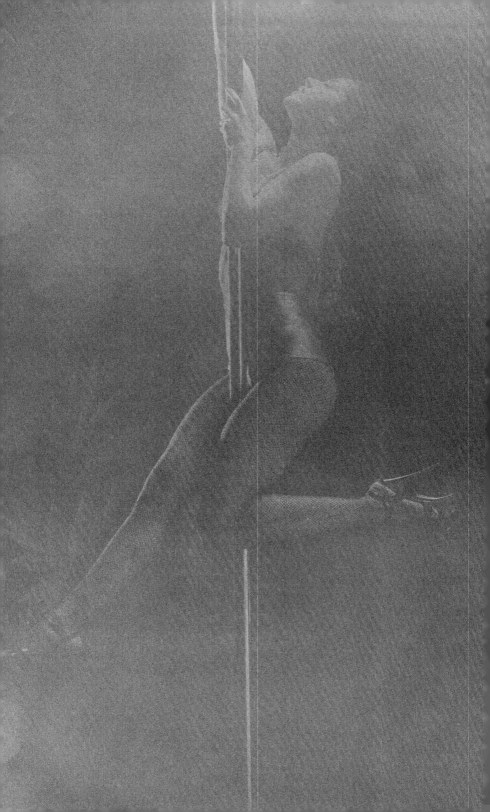

CHAPTER NINE

Rachel

The morning after Ness's overdose I am awakened by Jessica stumbling around in the kitchen.

I hear the cabinets banging around and then I hear her smash her head on something, followed by a dish smashing all over the hard kitchen floor.

"Goddamnit!"

"Oh my God" I groan. "Could you be any louder?"

She ignores me, and all I hear is the sound of more cabinets banging, and suddenly the baby starts crying from down the hall.

"Aw, shit!" Jess hisses.

"Well, now you've done it," I grumble, rolling over and covering my head with a pillow.

"Mandy? Mandy!" Jessica shouts, stepping into the hallway and pounding on a door. "Mandy, wake the hell up!"

"Oh my Goddd what?!" A sleepy teen girl calls from inside.

"Can you please go and change your sister?"

"Mom, come on! It's Saturday!"

"Girl don't give me attitude this morning," Jessica warns, but she sounds more exhausted than terrifying. "I need to know where the coffee is."

"We don't have any."

"Shit," she grunts, "Where's the rest of her formula?"

"We don't have any of that either." Mandy sighs.

"What?!" Jess groans. "Why didn't you tell me that?"

"I did. Last night." Mandy counters, rubbing her eyes.

"No you didn't," Jess scoffs.

"Yes, I did!"

"No, you really fucking didn't!"

Oh for fucks sake...

"She really did, Jess," I call from the couch. "You told her you'd get it on the way home, and then you forgot like a dumb bitch."

"So why didn't *you* remind me?" Jess snaps.

"Because," I chuckle. "I *also* forgot like a dumb bitch."

Jessica is quiet for a second then swears under her breath.

"Alright, fine. *I'll* change the baby," she says as she reaches for her purse, digging around inside it. "Mandy, you take this and go run to the corner and get some formula and coffee."

"This isn't enough for both," the teen says, clearly annoyed.

"Fine!" Jessica smashes more cash into Mandy's hand.

Without another word, the grumpy teenager groggily sulks over to the door, pulls on her sweater and storms out the door, slamming it behind her.

"That child—" Jessica sighs, rubbing her eyes.

"Is *just* like her mother," I chuckle. "She's not a morning person either."

The kettle goes off, forcing Jessica to silently make her way back into the kitchen and pull it off the stove.

"Are you sure we really don't have any coffee?"

"Well, I think there's some of that instant stuff you got from the food bank."

"Is that still good?"

"How would I know? I won't touch it. It looks like brown swamp water."

"I'd drink swamp water if it took away my headache. My head is throbbing."

"Your head?" I tease. "That's surprising."

"Surprising?"

"Yeah, I thought for sure it would be your coochie, after witnessing the way Eamon was trying to jack-hammer you through that glass door."

"Oh my God," she whines, covering her face with her hands. "I forgot about that."

"Oh I haven't," I laugh. "Don't think I ever will actually."

She fights a chuckle as she stirs her hot brown water walking back into the room and sitting down in the chair opposite me.

"Pretty sure the imprint of your ass will be permanently seared into my memory for all eternity. Hell, it's probably still imprinted on the glass this morning."

This time Jessica snorts into her cup and we both laugh.

"Stopppp!" She giggles collapsing back against the couch. "Laughing makes my head hurt."

But neither of us can help it.

"Fuck you," she chokes, still struggling to get her giggles under control. "You know what sucks, that asshole kicked us all out of his apartment, before he even paid me."

"Really?"

"Not a dime!" She says, suddenly annoyed. "And like, yeah, he didn't get to finish, but still, we did fuck! I feel like I'm at least owed for the time I put in."

"Send him a bill."

"I should!"

We start laughing again.

"Oh well," she sighs. "At least the drugs were fun. I mean until Ness had to go ruin it."

"Speaking of," I say, leaning back against the cushions. "Do you think we should go see Ness?"

"Fuck no," Jessica snorts. "That bitch knew that was *our* score, she and dipshit still decided to impose. If she didn't nearly die, I would've sent her to the hospital myself."

"Your compassion is overwhelming, Jess."

"It ruined my high!"

I stare at Jess, gauging her face, and remembering the way she and Eamon were talking to each other.

"Did he," I say quietly, choosing my words with care. "Give you something, *other* than the coke?"

She smiles but doesn't reply.

That's weird...

I know Jess has done coke for the last few years. And even though I'm not exactly keen on the idea, mostly due to the fact that she has kids, she's always insisted that's as far as it will ever go. And as strange as it might seem, I could accept that because she never does it in front of her kids, and because nearly everyone we know has a bump every now and then, so for us it's not that uncommon.

However, her behavior with Eamon last night was suspicious, as is her refusal to answer me right now.

Jess and I have never kept secrets from each other, and between the two of us, we have a lot of them. I'm the only one who knows about her *blackmail box* filled with pictures of some of her more ridiculous encounters. The idea behind the box is, if anyone ever tried to start trouble for her, or if she ever needed a favor, she'd have a wild card she could use.

Recently I've just had this sneaking feeling she has been experimenting with other stuff, and right now Jess doesn't seem interested in telling me about whatever Eamon gave her, or did *with* her privately.

But before I can pry into why, the baby kicks off again in the other room.

"I got her," I sigh, standing to my feet.

"You sure?"

"Yeah, I have to pee anyway."

In the tiny bedroom allotted to baby Ivy, I find the tearful seven-month-old wailing in her crib. Her face lights up the moment I reach for her and by the time I pull her into my arms, she has stopped screaming.

I change her, dress her, and give her lots of kisses before taking her into the bathroom with me. After relieving myself and washing my face, I carry the cooing infant out into the living room and hand her to her mother.

Thankfully, Mandy soon returns from the store with both formula and some actual ground coffee. She dumps it in front of her mother and retreats back into her poster-clad bedroom, which doubles as the teen girl's personal shrine in tribute to her favorite professional hockey player, James Matthews.

Even with a headache, I smile to myself.

Our tiny little apartment might be cramped, and always noisy, but it's home. Our own little safe haven from the outside world, and together, the four of us are a family.

The only real family I've ever had.

"Check the mailbox before you talk to Mr. Defeo!" Jessica calls from the door. "If Jeff mailed his child support, maybe we can use it to pay Mr. Defeo!"

"Okay."

"It's white with—"

"A blue label," I finish with a wink. "I'm usually the one that deposits them for you, remember?"

Jessica laughs.

"That's right. But if you're going down there to sweet talk him, at least pull out the girls," Jessica laughs, motioning to my chest. "He likes you better because of your tits."

"Maybe I will bust them out when I warm up," I laugh, closing the door behind me and wrapping my sweater around me. "But not before, or they might freeze."

While I did deliberately wear a sexy low cut top, the hallway in our poorly-heated building feels like the arctic circle. And because the elevator is broken, I have to walk down all five frigid flights of stairs to the first floor where the mailboxes are, to get to the apartment of our on-site landlord.

The first thing I do when I get there is check the mail like Jessica said. But unfortunately, when I open our slot, there's just miscellaneous bills and a few pieces of junk mail. No blue striped check from the courthouse.

Shit. Guess I am gonna have to use my boobs.

I pull up on my push up bra before knocking on his door.

He almost immediately answers.

"Mr. Defeo, hi. I just wanted to come by and—"

"Ahh, Miss Rachel!" He says, enthusiastically. "My favorite tenant! Thank you for your payment."

"Well, that's actually why I'm here," I smile pleadingly. "Look, I know we're a few weeks late on the rent, and I know we still owe you a little bit for last month, but I promise we're going to have it real soon and—"

"No, no, it's all settled!"

"What?"

"The nice gentleman came by this morning and paid for you. I've already gone and deposited it in the bank this morning."

"Um...what?" I repeat.

"The tall gentleman in the suit."

What is he talking about?

"Could you be more specific?"

"The uh," he says, holding up his finger. "Wait just a minute. I still have the receipt, I think."

He closes the door and I stand, utterly confused.

This has to be some sort of mistake?

Suddenly the door opens, and Mr. Defeo appears with a small piece of paper in his hand.

"Here, here!" he says, handing me the deposit slip.

And it is then that I notice two things:

It's a check for $20,000...with *Jaxon Pace's* family crest.

"This man came by and paid your balance for the entire year," Mr. Defeo says excitedly. "Including what was still left over from last month. So, you see, you're all set!"

"That's..." I say, my voice trailing off.

"Was there anything else?"

"Um...no?"

"Okay, well I'm going to get back to my shows then. Let me know if you ladies need anything, anything at all, okay? Remember Leo Defeo is at your service!"

"Heh, heh, that sounds...good," I say slowly, turning away.

By the time he says goodbye and closes the door I have stopped listening. I wander down the hallway like a zombie, completely lost in my spinning thoughts.

Jaxon Pace came here and paid for my rent. How did he even know where I live?

Silly question, his family runs the fucking city.

But...why? Why would he do that?

I'm nearly to the third floor when I notice that one of the other envelopes in my hand has the Pace Family crest as well.

What the...?

I tear it open and inside find a small note.

Sorry things got out of hand.
I never got to pay you for that dance.
-J

92

Holy shit.

That's when it hits me:

Jaxon Pace just bought a $20,000 lap dance.

"Wait, wait, wait, tell me again," Jess says excitedly as we get off the bus. "So like, our rent is paid for? All of it? For the rest of the year?"

I nod.

"Haha!" She says, clasping my arm and skipping in her steps along the downtown city street. "That's fucking amazing, especially considering you didn't actually *do* anything with him, right? You said you guys just talked?"

"That's literally all we did."

"Wow," she snorts. "Must've been some conversation."

You have no idea.

Although this immediately brings my mind back to that exact uncomfortable exchange Jaxon and I had atop Eamon's patio. The one about how my brother has apparently been searching for me, for months, and wants me to *come home.*

Home.

The word itself makes me shiver, and I wrap my coat tightly around my body.

The truth is, Valentine Manor is not my home anymore. And for very good reason. I have no interest in being anywhere near that creepy old house, and I have even less interest in accepting my brother's help.

I'm finally doing well for myself.

Well, maybe not *well*, considering we did just struggle to pay rent, and food is pretty scarce around our house as of late. But Jess and I have always figured it out, one way or another. I don't need anyone's pity. Or help.

Jaxon didn't really give me that choice in the matter.

And while his gesture is sweet, I don't really know how to react to him paying thousands of dollars at the drop of a hat for me. He barely even *knows* me.

I wonder why he did it?

93

Thankfully we reach the doors to the club before we completely freeze solid.

"Brrrr!" I shiver, stepping inside the darkened dance floor, immediately grateful for the warmth.

"At least this place is always warmer than our apartment." Jess sighs, adjusting her duffle bag as we head to the back.

"Yeah, because you keep the place set so low, we could practically hang meat from the ceiling," I snort.

"Heat is expensive here in the winter," she playfully hits my arm. "Hah, maybe you should get Jaxon Pace on the phone and see if he'll pay our heating bill too!"

"Shut up, Jess," I roll my eyes.

We step through the doors into the large dressing room. Not even half the girls are here right now, but the room is already bustling with activity and noise. Half-naked show girls are scattered throughout the room, chatting, stretching, dressing, and waxing.

The familiar scent of hair spray, nail polish, and floral body lotion fills the room and I inhale deeply.

This is my real home.

As strange as it may sound, this was the first place I ever truly felt safe and comfortable being myself. And although admittedly I'm closer with some of the girls more than others, these are my people. My family.

And they are the family I *chose*.

"Ah, ladies," the house mom Delavine, who most of the girls affectionately call "Ma" or "Del" for short, sighs. "So nice of you two to finally join us."

"Relax, Del, we're not necessarily late," Jess says.

"You're not necessarily *early* either," Del replies, shooting her a disapproving look. "Everyone else has been here for at least twenty minutes."

"That's because everyone else doesn't have to come as far as we do," Jess retorts playfully. "And we don't make the bus schedule. Take it up with the City Council."

"Or maybe take an earlier bus?" Del grunts back. "Have either of you heard from Ness or Crissy?"

Jess shoots me a look and then shrugs.

"I heard Ness was in the hospital. Overdose I think," she says, turning and heading for her locker. "Not sure about Crissy, though they are always together."

"Fuckin hell..." Del sighs, as she pulls a paper from her pocket and a roll of tape.

"Already girls, listen up. Reservations for private tables have been filled since Monday, so we will have a packed house tonight. This is the lineup for the evening," she says loudly. Sarah, Ria, Becca and Shaniya, you're up on the mainstage from 10-12 in half hour increments. And, since every time I make a clear schedule y'all end up bitching or switching it up anyway, I haven't made one this time, so you can decide amongst yourselves who takes what time slot."

She brushes her hair out of her face and ashes her cigarette before continuing.

"Where's the twins?" she asks, looking around the room.

"Here, Ma!" Maggie, usually also referred to as Mags, who is one of two gorgeous red-headed girls replies, stepping forward, followed quickly by her identical twin sister May.

"Good. You two along with Talia and Vivi, will take the right elite stage from 10-12. Mikayla and Dolly, Olive and Nila you have the left. Same thing goes for you lot—half hour increments, you can squabble amongst yourself to figure out who goes when but I don't want any gaps or lags, got it?

The girls nod.

"Repeat rotation from 1am-3am."

She then shoots a lovingly annoyed look at Jess and I.

"You two are on VIP," she winks. "Jess, you're on from 12-12:30 and Rachel you're on from 12:30-1. Alternate as you wish afterwards, just make sure the DJ has your song list. Oh, and Jess?"

"Yes, Mummy?" Jess teases with a wink.

"Be a dear and take a few requests from the other girls," she says, rolling her eyes. "You know I'm good with letting VIP call the playlist, but don't be completely selfish."

"It's not my fault their taste in music sucks," Jess sighs next to me, but I hit her quickly in the shoulder.

"You got it, Ma," I call back, peeling off my sweater.

Del nods, and then turns back to the rest of the girls.

"We have a busy night tonight ladies, so make sure you're on your game. If I look up, I better see your tits and bits and all times, got it?"

The girls chuckle and nod their agreement, always finding Del's signature line about 'tits and bits' mildly amusing.

"I think that covers it," Del finishes, taping the schedule to the lockers. "Any questions, before I go chat with the bar?"

"Yeah," Talia, the new transplant from Ohio asks, raising her hand. "When do the *rest* of us get a shot to be on VIP?"

"When you can bring in the money *we* do," Jess fires back, grinning at her.

"Well, that's my point" Talia sneers, crossing her arms and glaring at Jess. "If we never *get* the opportunity here, then how are we expected to bring in that kind of money?"

"And that's *my* point," Jess fires back, glaring at Talia. "No one here expects *you* to."

"Jess," Del sighs, rubbing her eyes.

"But," Talia snorts. "It's not fair!"

"It's not supposed to be," I smile, feigning politeness.

"Look honey," Jessica smiles, flipping her hair back behind her ear. "Just because you were semi-good at flashing your tits around some podunk farm-town strip club, doesn't mean you have *actual* dancing skills."

"Oooh!" A low murmur goes up amongst the girls in the quiet room. Several of them cover their mouths with their hands, desperately trying to stifle their laughter.

"I wasn't the *only* dancer at my club! I was the—"

"*Lead dancer,*" the rest of the girls suddenly erupt in unison, rolling their eyes. *"Blah, blah, blah!"*

Loud giggles now surface around the room, as everyone has clearly had enough of Talia's non-stop boasting over the last five weeks. Apparently, the delusional twit seems to think that because she was a highly prized piece of ass at her last club, she should get the same seniority here.

But that's not how this works.

Jess and I have made damn sure of that.

"This isn't cow country, sweetie." I say sweetly, batting my lashes and laying my head on Jess's shoulder. "And unlike other clubs in the city our clients aren't factory boys or day laborers."

"So?!" Talia snaps furiously.

"So," Jess snarls, wickedly. "Our high-end city boy clientele expect prime rib, not your scraggly-ass hamburger thighs."

"Hey! What the fuck!"

The giggles evolve instantly into howling laughter, as Talia turns a bright shade of red.

"Jess," Del snaps, clapping her hands together. "Can you just behave, for once?"

"No, Ma," I snort, opening my locker. "She really can't."

Talia looks at Del with an open shrug, silently demanding that Del punish Jessica and I in some way.

But there's absolutely no chance of that happening.

Jess and I are the most requested dancers, and for the most part, we run the place when Del isn't around. Over the last few years, we've earned the right to have the VIP section on the most crowded nights, and some of our regulars even expect it.

Del just throws her hands in the hand and walks out of the room, shaking her head. A fuming Talia storms after her, and the rest of the room returns to its regular conversation.

"God, why do I love getting under her skin so much?" Jess laughs, throwing her hair into a bun and grabbing our shower stuff.

"Because deep down, Jess," I giggle, pulling our towels out of my bag. "You're just a bitch."

"Facts."

Jess and I have hot water at our apartment, but it doesn't have the same water pressure as The Nyx. Once an old private gym that was converted into a private exotic dancing club, a lot of the little conveniences like the showers or giant locker rooms end up being a benefit to the dancers-having more space to get ready.

Since our clientele are some of the wealthiest men in the city, Del has strict rules about how all of her dancers prepare for the night.

We stretch, shower, wax, primp, paint and polish. Everything must be fresh and perfect, at all times. We're allowed to pick our own outfits, but she must approve them, making sure that even our shoes are in good condition.

Fridays and Saturdays are our biggest nights, and Jess and I nearly always work the VIP section on one of those two nights. No matter how good the money would be, we never work both, because if our regulars knew they could see us either night, they would only show up to one...and we want them desperate to see us.

While we wait for VIP to fill up, Jess and I help run drinks from the bar. We flirt, we tease, we smile, hoping we can earn a few good tips before we even get up on stage.

It's half past eleven when Jess signals me that she's heading backstage to get ready for her set.

"This is my last round," I say to the bartender, taking the two drinks from him. "Where are they going?"

"VIP," he winks at me. "They just got here. Rowdy bunch tonight."

I wade through the busy club, making my way over to the VIP section.

Suddenly, someone bumps into me, and I nearly dump both drinks everywhere.

"Hey, asshole! Watch where you're—"

But my words catch in my throat the moment his eyes find mine...because Jaxon Pace is standing in front of me.

"Rachel?"

I stare at him, aware that his eyes are canvassing my entire body, and also aware I'm not actually saying anything in response. But his commanding presence has made it impossible to think clearly.

"Um, hi," I finally manage to squeak out.

"What are you..." he says, tilting his head to the side and furrowing his brow. "Doing...*here*?"

"Hey! Waitress!" Someone calls from the VIP section behind me. "Are we actually going to get those drinks before the show starts or are you going to just stand around fucking talking all night while the ice melts, eh?"

"Shut it, Vic," Jaxon snaps, shooting him a look before turning back to me.

But now I feel incredibly awkward.

"Yes, sorry," I say, looking up at Jaxon for a moment before walking past him and into the section.

"Well, my, my, you're pretty," a good-looking young blonde man in a suit says as I set the drinks down. "Tell me, sweetheart, do you do private dances?"

His hand traces up my thigh, and even though I'm used to this, I can't help but cringe.

Is it just because Jaxon's watching?

"John," Jaxon suddenly snaps, smacking the man's hand off my leg. "Fuck off."

"Whoa man," The man named John responds, throwing his hands up. "Didn't know you'd already claimed her."

Jaxon takes my arm and pulls me out of the section.

"What the hell are you doing?" he demands, forcefully.

"Excuse me?" I snap back. "What do you think I'm doing?"

"Why are you here? At a place like this?"

"Because I work here, dummy! I'm a dancer!"

Jaxon shakes his head, as if he can't comprehend what I just said to him.

"I'm sorry, what?"

"I. Work. Here." I say, spelling it all out for him, crossing my arms across my body. "This is my job?"

"You shouldn't be here," he growls.

"And why the fuck not?!"

"Because it's…." he says, frustrated. "It's beneath you."

My jaw drops.

"Are you *serious*?!"

He glares at me, telling me that he is, in fact, serious.

"Oh, that's rich," I say, shoving past him. "Considering you're here too, are you not? What does that say about *you*?"

"Rachel," I hear him say, feeling him reach for me.

I avoid him, pushing his hand away and whipping my head back around to glare at him.

"Last I checked, I don't need Jaxon Pace's approval to do whatever the fuck I want with my time and life," I say, pointing hard to my chest. "So, save your breath and the life advice for someone who actually gives a shit."

"I'm just saying that someone of your…*stature* shouldn't be seen in a place like this." He scoffs, gesturing to the room.

I smile at him.

Oh, this cocky bastard.

"Enjoy the show, Mr. Pace," I say, batting my lashes at him.

And with that, I instantly turn on my heel and walk back into the dressing room.

No, not walk. I *ran*. All the way to Jessica's little vanity area where she was busy trying to button the top on her outfit.

"Jess, I need a favor!" I say, breathlessly.

"Oh God, who are we murdering?" Jess looks up angrily. "Is it Talia? I swear to fuckin God, I will beat that bitch if she—"

"No, no," I continue, immediately yanking my lingerie out of my locker. "I need to switch dances with you."

"Huh?"

"Jaxon Pace is here, and he—"

"What?!" Jess says excitedly. "Oh my God, did he come to see *you*? I bet he did! Holy shit, Rach!"

"Listen!" I snap, starting to undress. "He just gave me some pompous speech about how I shouldn't be in a "place like this," and he royally pissed me off."

"Um, yeah. Rude." Jess snorts, scrunching up her face.

"Well, he's in the VIP…"

"Oh, girl," she grins wickedly, as my words register in her eyes. "I got you."

She immediately stands to her feet and wraps her black silk robe around her body.

"Can I wear your light up heels?" I ask, throwing my makeup bag on the vanity.

"Of course!"

Like the trained professional I am, I quickly paint on my bright red lip stain, before edging the corners with my pencil.

"No, no, no, you can't wear this for Jaxon," she says, taking my violet teddy from the hook next to me and throwing it back in my open locker. "Wear *this*."

Reaching into her own locker she pulls out a stunningly gorgeous black lace open-cup caged bralette and G-string set.

"Oh no, Jess, I can't wear that," I say, pushing it back to her. "It's yours, you spent nearly half your paycheck on it."

"And, when we tried it on we both agreed it looked better on you, anyway," she says, shoving it back to me. "You're wearing it tonight. It's yours."

"But…it's brand new!"

"Even better, bitch," she says, ripping the tags off. "And for the record, I didn't *actually* buy it. I pinched it."

I giggle.

"Naughty girl."

"It has the garter and the fishnet stockings too. And look! The bralette even has a little rhinestone heart in the middle," she winks at me. "It's like it was made for you, *Valentine*."

"Jess…"

"Stop talking and start dressing!" she snaps, kicking off her heels and sprinting barefoot toward the door. "You only have ten minutes! I'll tell Donnie we're changing the songs, and I'll be right back to help you get ready! Heat up my hair wand!"

I look down at the gorgeous piece of tiny fabric in my hands and smile, gripping it tightly.

I'll fucking show you, Jaxon Pace.

"Gentlemen, I now present for you, tonight's main event. She's the thief of hearts, the bewitcher of minds, the sensual and seductive... *Salomé.*"

Donnie the Nyx DJ growls my name into the mic as the dance floor lights up and smoke fills the doorway.

As Heartbreaker by Pat Benatar starts to play, I start my routine. Watching as the loaded simps in the front row start to groan and gesture toward me. I grab the pole, swinging my leg around and pulling myself around.

The lights flash and I locate Jaxon still in the VIP section.

He looks positively livid.

Which just fuels my fire even more.

I release the pole and get down on my knees in front of one of the VIPs, the same blonde man who touched my thigh earlier. Reaching for the tie around his neck he grins at me hungrily as he stuffs hundred dollar bills in my G-string.

Deliberately I wink up at Jaxon before moving along to the man next to him, who practically empties his entire wallet on the stage. I trace my finger along the older man's chin and watch him lean in eagerly, thinking I'm going to kiss him.

But instead, I pull away, returning to my pole and twirling myself around again.

I shook a glance in the direction I last saw Jaxon, but he's nowhere to be found.

Whatever.

My point has been made. I belong here, on this stage. Watching these powerful, influential, and extremely wealthy men trip over themselves for an ounce of my attention.

This is where my power is.

I wind up to do my signature flip, listening as the screaming crowd turns feral and noticing all of the money pouring on to the stage in front of me.

But then suddenly the music stops and all the lights in the building go out.

What the actual fuck?!

"Everyone stay calm," Donnie calls forcefully. "It's just a brown out!"

But something in core tells me that it's not just a brown out.

No, I know, that somehow Jaxon had *something* to do with this convenient power outage.

Thankfully, the stage is lined with lights that illuminate in case of something like this, and combined with Jessica's light up heels I am able to find my way backstage. Jess and a handful of the other dancers have gathered to see what the hell is going on.

"Is this a bad joke?" Jessica snaps at Donnie, now fumbling around in the dark with just a small pen flashlight.

"When will the power come back on?" Another whines. "My hair isn't curled yet!"

"Ladies, please," Donnie sighs. "Just give it a minute. I'm sure we'll get it sorted out soon. We're working on it."

"How the hell does that happen? Don't we have a generator for this kind of thing?" Talia scoffs.

"Shut the fuck up, Talia," Jess snaps, rolling her eyes.

"We're still working on it. We don't know what happened."

Oh, I bet I fucking do.

I yank my robe off the wall, pulling my phone out of my pocket and turning on the flashlight app.

"Rach, where are you going?" I hear Jess call after me.

But I'm already storming down the hallway, my path illuminated by Jessica's flashing heels sending bright sparkling flashes up the blacked-out walls. Behind me I can hear the sounds of increasingly irritated customers, groaning and shouting their disapproval.

I make my way to the electrical room, where as expected I find Del and the club's owner, Victor Black standing in the hallway, with a bunch of burly men dressed all in black.

Along with Jaxon Pace.

"Jackie," Victor begs, "It's one of our biggest nights! You know I can't afford to just shut down the whole damn club! I have staff I have to pay."

"Please, Mr. Pace," Delvina pleads. "We have girls here that need to perform. It's their livelihood."

"I'll reimburse you," Jaxon says, refusing to remove his hand from the breaker.

"You!" I snap.

"Rachel, dear," Delvina sighs. "I'm sorry about your dance, we're working on it and—"

"You did this on purpose!" I spit, thundering toward him.

But before I reach his face to punch it, one of the giant men steps in front of me, blocking my path.

"Rachel!" Del shouts.

Jaxon smirks.

"You know what, Vic," he says, staring at me and narrowing his eyes. "I think I've changed my mind."

He flips the breaker back and suddenly light returns to the building. In the distance I can hear the elated customers cheering, along with the squeals of the dancers now echoing down the hall.

"What the hell?" Victor says, looking between me and Jaxon.

"Tell you what, I'll keep my hands off your breaker box if you can guarantee me that Miss *Salomé* here is *mine*," he says, pointing at me. "For the duration of the evening."

Everyone in our odd little circle falls silent, as all eyes suddenly turn to me.

"What?" Del, Victor, and myself all mutter at the same time.

Jaxon grins, which just infuriates me.

"Absolutely not!" I growl, throwing my hands on my hips.

"Fine. Have it your way," Jaxon shrugs.

He reaches back up to the breaker and immediately flips it back off, sending the club back into utter chaos.

"Now, wait just a minute," Victor pleads frantically, throwing his hands out between us. "Look, Jackie, I'm sure we can come to some sort of an agreement here. Can't we?"

Jaxon flips the breaker back on.

He crosses his arms and arrogantly smiles at me.

"I guess that's up to her."

My jaw drops.

"But...wait...what?"

Jaxon reaches *again* for the breaker, sending Del and Victor scrambling to stop him only to be stopped, *again*, by Jaxon's gigantic bodyguards.

"Stop!" I snap, and to my surprise, he does.

I stand there, panting, my heart racing in my chest.

If I don't agree to Jaxon's demands, everyone in the club is going to suffer. Our wealthy clients will start to leave soon if this doesn't get resolved, and the girls, who are my *family*, won't make the money we all rely upon just to get by.

With my hands balled into fists and wanting desperately to slap the smug little smile off his face, I finally relent.

"Fine," hiss through gritted teeth. "I'll do it."

"Oh, thank God!" Victor breathes, running his hand over his sweaty balding head.

"But I want double the private hour pay," I smile. "For every hour until closing. With *tip*."

"Done," Jaxon smiles, slamming the breaker box closed.

He reaches into his pocket and pulls out a wad of hundred dollar bills, grabbing half and handing it to me. "Tip included."

Still glaring at him, I snatch the money from him and shove it in my pocket.

Fucking asshole.

"Jesus, Jackie," Victor sighs heavily, shaking his head. "If you just wanted the girl you—"

"That will be all Black," Jaxon snaps suddenly, his icy tone making us all jump. "Go enjoy the show."

Delvina shoots a very confused look at me, and I gently shake my head, telling her silently that I also have absolutely no clue as to what the hell is going on.

The two of them make their way down the hallway, murmuring quietly about how they are going to get things back on track for the rest of the night.

"Gentlemen," Jaxon says, nodding to his men.

Without another word, all of his bodyguards turn and walk down the hallway after Del and Victor until they too are out of sight. I now stand, alone, in the hallway with Jaxon Pace.

"Do I have your attention now?" he grins, narrowing his eyes at me and sticking his hands in his pockets. "Little *heartbreaker*?"

Something inside me snaps. I step forward, a seductive smile on my face as I place my hands on Jaxon's shoulders.

…And knee him, hard, in the crotch.

"How dare you!" I snap, as he winces in pain, throwing his hand against the wall to steady himself.

"You had absolutely no right to interfere with my dance!" I shout at him.

Staring him down, I watch as he regains his composure, now glaring at me. Without warning, he grabs my arm and pulls me down the hallway and into one of the private rooms, shoving me into the large lounge chair and slamming the door.

For a moment, fear flashes in my brain, wondering what he plans to do to me.

"You don't seem to fucking get it, do you?" He snaps at me. "I'm only trying to protect you! You're parading around up there, nearly naked, for Christ's sake! People will talk, Rachel. They already fucking are!"

"And you don't seem to get that that's good for my fucking business Jaxon!"

"You don't mean that."

"And you don't know me well enough to know what I mean and what I don't!" I spit at him. "I like people looking at me!"

"Yeah? And what if your *brother* had been in the audience tonight? You know, the brother you're actively trying to avoid? How the fuck do you think that would go, eh?"

I gasp, my heart dropping into my stomach.

"Weren't you just telling me last night that you're trying to stay off his radar? How can you do that when you're up there on stage flashing your tits for half of Chicago?!" He roars, gesturing toward the club. "Jesus, Rachel, use your fucking brain and stop being so goddamn stubborn!"

"Fuck you!" I shout back at him, jumping to my feet. "I'll have you know that I don't answer to you, or anyone else, so you can take your protection and your snobbish judgment and shove it up your fucking ass!"

Suddenly he pushes me up against the wall and crushes his lips to mine. I freeze every thought evacuating my brain.

Well, for a *moment*, anyway.

"Jaxon," I whisper, my heart racing and my head spinning. "What are you doing?"

"You know Rachel," he breathes. "I have no fucking idea."

CHAPTER TEN

ADAM

"And?" I ask, as Rachel finishes her story.

"And what?" she replies, confused.

"Well, what happened?"

"We fucked," She sighs. "I didn't think you'd want me to spell that out for you in graphic detail."

"No," I say sarcastically. "I actually don't. Just give me the general details."

"The general details?" she laughs sarcastically as I stand up and walk to the window, lighting another cigarette. "It was good for a minute, and then we started fighting. A lot. And believe me, a lot of them got pretty heated."

"You know, Rach," I snort. "Somehow, I do find that really easy to believe. You're both hot-headed and impossibly stubborn. I'm sure that's a fantastic recipe for a great relationship."

She laughs.

"Yeah, no, it really wasn't."

"So then why did you," I say, clearing my throat. "...*Stay* with him?"

"Because it was the first time anyone had given me any kind of attention that wasn't...sexual."

"But," I say, scrunching up my face. "It *was* sexual?"

"Well, yeah, but like, not only sexual," she shrugged. "At first his overbearingness was sweet. But when he would go out with his friends, or go do whatever business Mafia-Dons-in-training do, while expecting me to just be waiting around for him, it got old. Quickly."

"Did he expect you to be waiting around for him?"

"Honestly, I don't know what he expected," she says, shifting uncomfortably. "But I could only sit around in my apartment for so long. I missed my nights at the club, with my friends. I missed how I felt on stage."

"He made you quit?"

"Well, again, not necessarily," she shrugs. "He didn't make me quit, but he had lots of opinions about it."

I flick the butt out the hole in the screen and close the window behind me.

"He wanted you to stop dancing," I say quietly, my eyes falling to the carpet. "Because he wanted to protect you."

"Well…yeah, actually."

Suddenly Rachel looks up at me.

"And let me guess," I continue, rubbing my thumb across my bottom lip with a sigh. "You resented him for it."

She nods.

The room is quiet for a moment, but Rachel's gaze says a thousand things.

"My wife was an exotic dancer when I met her," I say quietly. "I didn't mind it at first."

"But?" Rachel asks.

"At first I loved coming to see her. But the more involved we got emotionally, the harder it was for me to separate what we had versus what was just a performance for her clients."

Rachel pulls her knees up to her chest.

"Did you ask her to stop?"

"Yes."

"And did she?"

"Eventually," I sigh. "But only after she got pregnant with our first child."

"Your wife," she says, swallowing hard. "*Died*, didn't she?"

I smirk to myself.

Well, I knew we'd get here eventually.

"Yes," I say, with a nod before locking eyes with Rachel. "She did."

Her brown eyes hold mine, refusing to move.

"Tell me." She whispers quietly.

No. I can't.

I shake my head.

"No, I'd rather not."

"Well, too fucking bad, Adam," Rachel scoffs. "You think that I want to sit here, dumping all of my shitty past on you? No, of course not. But that's the only way this will work."

I stare at her, floored by her boldness. She pauses, only to flip her hair to one side. That's when her foot starts tapping again, and she folds her arms across her body.

It occurs to me that perhaps the reason she's pushing for this story isn't because she just wants to trade miseries with me.

…But maybe because she actually does want this to work.

However, as much as this revelation makes my stomach untwist just a bit, I know I'm not ready to talk about *that* yet.

Very few people know about what happened between my wife and I. But they've all reacted the same. There simply is *no* reaction. And maybe that's because what reaction could you possibly have to someone telling you outright that they…

Don't go there, Adam.

The memory of my wife, and what happened to my kids is the room in my house of memories that I refuse to visit.

In my time as a federal agent, I've come up against the worst of the worst. Killers, rapists, pedophiles. I've hunted them, fought them, and put most of them behind bars…and some of them in the ground. But none of them haunt my nightmares.

Not *anymore* anyway.

My eyes find hers and everything around me comes to a halt.

God damn, she's pretty.

A part of me wishes none of this was happening right now. I wish we weren't sitting here, just rehashing all of our sins, and exes and trauma. Because right now, all I want to do is kiss her.

She sighs.

"Adam, this is a two-way street," she says, her voice suddenly gentle. "I'm giving you what you asked for, the truth, in all its ugly, gory, detail. But you have to give me something in return, because, well…"

Her voice fades off as she suddenly lowers her eyes to her lap, apparently swallowing back whatever she was going to say.

She chickened out.

"Because?" I ask.

She shakes her head.

"No, what were you going to say?"

Again, her eyes find mine, and she looks at me sympathetically.

"Just say it."

"Because it just feels like that's unfair."

Well...shit. I can't argue with that logic.

It is unfair.

I stare at her a moment longer before leaning forward on my knees and running a hand over my head.

"Look, Rachel, I'm not saying I won't talk about her ever," I say, quietly. "I know we will need to at some point."

I swallow hard.

"But you need to know those memories...I'm just not ready to talk about them *yet*."

She looks at me, and then looks out the window, disappointment evident on her face.

I have to give her *something*.

"I tell you what," I say, trying to extend an olive branch. "If you ask me anything else about me, I promise I will tell you."

She looks back up at me, her face scanning mine.

"Okay," she says quietly. "What made you join the Bureau?"

Now that is a good question.

"My father."

"Was he an agent too?" She asks, laying down on her side, propping her head up on the pillow.

"No," I smirk to myself. "He was a serial killer."

Rachel's jaw drops. Exactly as I expected it to.

She immediately sits back up on the bed.

"Your father," she whispers. "Was a *serial killer*?"

I nod.

"Richard Maddox, the Springfield Shooter," I say, standing up and walking over to the fridge, grabbing the last two bottles of beer.

"Did he...I mean...what did..." Rachel just shakes her head, taking the bottle from me. "Sorry, hold on, let me get my thoughts in order."

I chuckle.

"It's fine," I grin. "It's a lot to take in."

I sit back on the bed opposite her, resting my head on the headboard.

"He came from a large conservative farming family in rural Pennsylvania, joined the army when he was eighteen, and was promoted as a sniper. When the war ended, and he came home, he got married and had two kids—me and my brother."

"Are you older or younger?"

"Older," I say, pressing the bottle to my lips. "I was ten and my brother was seven when dad first started going *hunting* on the weekends. At first my mom thought nothing of it. But then he started coming home from these trips with miscellaneous jewelry, or articles of women's clothing, like a leather jacket with silver stars and tassels. They weren't anything close to what she would wear, but my father gave them to her, saying they were gifts. That's when she started to get suspicious."

The wind howls outside, battering against the shoddy window as the tiny space heater struggles to keep the poorly insulated hotel room warm.

"I think she thought he was having an affair, or several. And when she finally bucked up the courage to confront him, that's when the abuse started. At first it was just a back-hand across the face, or shoving her into the wall, but then it started to get worse. Once my brother spilled a glass of milk from the table and my dad beat him twenty-nine times with a belt, leaving welts that lasted for days."

"Jesus…" Rachel whispers.

"Just breathing wrong in front of my father could warrant a beating, and so my mother stopped asking questions, and we did our best to stay out of his way, and looked forward to his weekend hunting trips."

I clear my throat, taking a large sip of beer before continuing.

I need all the liquid courage I can get.

"That's when they started finding the bodies," I say quietly. "Two, four, seven, twelve…they literally started piling up. Transient young women, raped and shot in the back of the head, covered in leaves and moss, dumped along the highways."

"Holy shit," Rachel says, biting the nail on her thumb.

"I was too young to really know what was going on, but when

they started posting the estimated dates of abduction and death on the television, I can only assume my mother started putting it all together."

Rachel looks up at me, her eyes wide.

"You can only assume…" She repeats quietly.

"…And then she saw one of the missing girl's pictures, wearing the same jacket as the one my father had given her."

Rachel's jaw drops, and I bite my bottom lip.

"Holy fucking hell…"

"The police showed up at our door one day, and asked to see my father. They questioned him, but for whatever reason, they never arrested him. But he knew that my mother had something to do with it."

"Oh no," Rachel gasps, crossing her legs.

I take another drink.

"The house was quiet all week. No one spoke. And then Friday night, my dad told us that we were *all* going on a camping trip in the morning," I say slowly. "I remember thinking it was odd, as it had been years since we had last gone camping as a family."

Rachel takes a sip, her eyes glued to me.

"The next morning, we drove deep into the Tolland National Forest, then got out and hiked even deeper. He told us he had the perfect campsite prepared for us."

Rachel pulls the blanket from off the bed and wraps it around her body, but her face is unemotional.

"When we finally reached the site, we set up camp. We pitched the tents, built a fire, and my brother and I went and caught frogs in the creek. Dinner was quiet, but there was no fighting. We toasted marshmallows and made smores before we all settled in for the night. And as I crawled into my sleeping bag in the cool night air, for just one brief moment I felt like this was the happiest I had been in a while," I say, looking down at my hands on the beer bottle. "…And then it all went straight to *hell*."

I awake in the darkness.

Insects chirping and the familiar sound of my little brother,

Tuck, snoring are all I can hear.

I'm confused, because my body feels tense, as if something has startled me, but yet everything seems calm.

Why am I awake?

"Richard...why? Why are you doing this?!" My mother's whispered sobs, and the sound of shuffling immediately answers this question. "Please...don't do this!"

Oh no...

My fight or flight response activates, and I want to go to her.

However, the last time I tried to get between my dad and my mom while they were fighting, I was taught a very painful lesson. That was the day my father slammed me into the glass coffee table and I ended up with thirty-seven stitches.

...And mom ended up in the hospital for two straight weeks.

"Wake the kids, Jen."

My father's gruff voice sounds different tonight.

"Richard...please..." My mother's tearful pleas are so visceral.

I hear him grunt, followed by her yelping in pain.

The dirt beneath my sleeping bag shakes, and even in the darkness, I distinctly see the faint shadow of her body crashing to the ground just on the other side of the thin tent wall, inches from my face.

"Wake. The. Kids."

Her labored breaths and whimpered cries, mixed softly with her muffled pleas, crawl slowly toward the tent zipper.

Terrified, I screw my eyes shut and pull my sleeping bag over my head.

Maybe this is just a nightmare.

My heart starts pounding in my chest as I slide down farther in my sleeping bag.

"Please...just leave them alone..." I hear my mother sob again. "They...they are just *kids*. They're innocent Richard. Please don't!"

I hear the distinct sickening thud of flesh hitting flesh.

Something wet sprays the tent wall.

"Wake them, Jen," my father growls. "*Now.*"

I am so terrified I nearly wet myself.

No! I can't! He was so furious about that last time!

But I nearly piss myself anyway when the tent zipper slowly

unzips, and my mother's bruised and bloody face comes into view.

Like most kids, I've always thought my mother is the most beautiful woman on earth. She has long dark brown hair, hazel eyes and a smattering of freckles across her nose that crinkle when she smiles.

But tonight, she *isn't* smiling.

Peeking through my lashes the woman I see before me has a busted lip, and a black eye so swollen her face looks physically deformed. Her pale blue night dress is covered in dark red stains, likely from her broken, crooked nose, that is still dripping wet blood. She is nearly unrecognizable.

It takes all of my restraint not to scream, because in the pale moonlight, this tattered shell of a woman looks nothing like my beautiful, freckled mother, and more like one of those undead zombie monsters from the movies.

But she isn't a monster.

No. My mother is the only thing *protecting* us from the monster.

And from the fingerprints around her neck, and the scratches, bruises, and bite marks on her arms and legs, it's clear that she has fought with everything she has to distract him from us, for as long as she could…but has *lost*.

"Boys…" my mother says tearfully, faking a smile as her shaking hands gently touch our sleeping bags. "Wa…wake up. Your father has…something he wants to tell us."

My little brother wipes his eyes sleepily, not registering the horrors I have just witnessed.

"Come on boys," my mother whispers, tears streaking down her dirty disheveled face. "It will be quick…and then we can all go back to sleep, okay?"

Even though I'm terrified, I know I need to do as she asks. Because I know that if I don't, the monster who stands outside, panting feverishly in the night air, will hurt her even more.

And I can't let that happen.

"Come on, Robbie," she says, reaching for me, plastering a smile on her face.

I take my mother's hand, my legs shaking beneath me.

"Tuck," she says, shaking my little brother's sleeping bag gently a second time. "I need you to get up buddy, okay?"

"Yes, Momma," Tuck yawns, unzipping his sleeping bag.

"Mom," I ask, swallowing hard. "Is...everything okay?"

"Yes, sweetie," she whispers, pulling me close and squeezing me so tight she nearly chokes all the wind from my lungs. "You know I love you, don't you, Robbie?"

"Yes, Mom," I whisper back, holding her tightly. "I love you too."

Something is different.

I don't know what, but I can feel it in the energy that lingers around us like a fog.

"Jen...get them moving," the monster grunts, grabbing the back of my mother's hair, and yanking her head back violently. "I'm getting impatient."

"They're coming, Richard," she gasps, masking her pain with quiet anger, and squeezing me even tighter against her chest.

He releases her head, and she nearly collapses, her breath trembling. My little brother now crawls toward her, still groggily unaware of the situation.

"I love you both so much," she whispers, cupping both our faces, exhaustion evident. "No matter what happens, I love you, forever."

Something is very wrong.

There is no hiding her pain now, the tears streaming down her face as she utters the same words she's said to us every night when she'd tuck us both in bed.

"I love you forever," my brother and I whisper back, squeezing her tightly.

"Jen!" My father snaps, making us all jump. "Now!"

My brother and I follow our mother out of the tent, stepping into the cold night air in nothing but our bare feet and our matching monster Buzz Lightyear pajamas.

Mother pushes us behind her, as my father stands in his thick cargo pants, and long sleeve thermal shirt, stained with my mother's blood...and holding his hunting rifle.

"Tonight, we're going to play a game," he growls.

He throws his head back and takes a last swig, before tossing the now empty bottle of whiskey into our makeshift fire pit, its embers still glowing softly from dinner.

The sound of the glass shattering makes us all jump.

"Richard..." My mother pleads. "Please...don't do this. Take me instead."

My father says nothing, instead glaring at her with a terrifyingly wicked grin spreading on his scruffy face.

"Don't you worry, I will get to you," he says loudly. "But first we're going to play hide and seek."

"Richard! Please!"

"Mommy?" My little brother says, tugging at her dress. "I'm…I'm scared."

"Well, *I'm* going to count to thirty," my father continues mockingly, the alcohol slurring his speech.

"No!" My mother wails, her voice cracking.

"And you're going to run off and hide," he laughs. "Got it?"

"Oh God…" My mother wails, her entire body shaking. "No! Please, don't do this!"

"Mommy!" My little brother cries, now utterly terrified.

"Starting right…" he says, turning around. "*Now!*"

"No! Please!"

"Thirty…Twenty-Nine…Twenty-Eight…Twenty-Seven…"

My father begins his countdown, and my mother suddenly grabs my shoulders, and quickly kneels down beside us.

"Robbie, Tuck," she pants. "Listen to me right now!"

"Twenty-five…twenty-four…twenty-three."

"You run as far into the forest as you can," she sobs, her eyes wide. "And you keep running, do you hear me?!"

"Twenty-two…twenty-one…"

"Mommy! No! I want to stay with you!"

"No, Tuck," she says, firmly, wet tears staining her cheeks. "You have to run as fast as you can. Right now!"

"Nineteen…Eighteen…Seventeen…"

"Mom?!" I say, my terrified voice cracking.

"Go now, Robbie!" She commands, turning us around and shoving us toward the forest. "Run and keep running! Don't stop! I will be right behind you!"

"Mommy!"

"Sixteen…Fifteen…"

"Go! Right now!"

She picks up the fire poker we used just a few hours ago to toast marshmallows, and suddenly time slows around us, and the world fades away.

For as long as I live, I will never forget the look on my

mother's face that night. Because I knew right then, it was the last time I would ever see it.

Her sad eyes meet mine, and without saying a single word, it's as if I can hear her speaking directly to me, telling me to take my brother's hand and…run for my *life*.

So that's what I did.

Barefoot and terrified, I pulled Tuck into the forest, and we ran as fast as we could away from our campsite, away from our mother, and away from him.

And when a single gunshot echoes loudly into the frigid forest air, I know my beautiful, loving, and incomparably brave mother has done the very last thing she can do to give us more time to get away: She sacrificed herself.

Because there, in the darkness, a monster was *hunting* us.

I chug the last of my beer, needing a moment to collect my thoughts before looking over at Rachel.

"Holy fucking shit," she whispers. "That's…"

"I know," I say, not needing her to finish that sentence. "Believe me, my therapist had a field day unpacking that one."

"So, your father was a serial killer," Rachel says quietly. "And he took you all out to the woods to…to kill you?"

I nod.

"Apparently that was where he liked to take them," I say quietly. "He knew those woods like the back of his hand. He would pick up hitchhikers, or sex workers from truck stops. He'd tie them up, drive them out to the middle of the woods, have his way with them, and then set them loose—"

"…So he could hunt them," Rachel whispers.

"Like animals," I say, staring at the drawers on the dresser. "That was the thrill for him. The ultimate big game."

"Wow," she says quietly. "So, how did you…"

Her voice trickles off, and I look up at her.

"Survive?" I snort, twisting the empty beer bottle in my hands. "My mother. She put up quite a fight, using the fire poker to whack and stab him as much as she possibly could before he got a shot off. She inflicted some serious damage. Enough that he was bleeding out as he was tracking my brother and I through the woods."

"Your brother," Rachel says quietly. "Did he make it too?"

I close my eyes, wanting so desperately to end the story here, and talk about anything else.

But I promised her the truth.

…And she needs to know.

"My father shot my brother," I whisper, my stomach twisting. "While I was holding his hand."

"Jesus Christ," Rachel says, covering her face with her hand.

"He went down, and I…well, I let go and kept running," I shake my head. "Like a fucking coward."

My chest swells with rage and I suddenly toss the empty bottle angrily across the room. It shatters against the wall, sending pieces of amber glass ricocheting everywhere. Running my hands over my head, I screw my jaw shut.

If I were her, this is the point I'd be leaving, and I fully expect her to bolt from this shitty motel like it was on fire.

But to my utter surprise, she doesn't. Instead, Rachel silently gets up and crosses the small space between the two hotel beds, sitting down next to me.

"I'm sorry, Adam."

"Don't," I snap, trying desperately to swallow back my bile. "I don't need your pity."

"Oh, shut the fuck up," she snaps.

What did she just say to me?!

I glare up at her, wondering if perhaps she is the bravest woman I've ever met.

"As you said to me, it's not pity," Rachel says defiantly. "It's simply me acknowledging the truth."

Looking away, I take a deep breath, my mind a twisted mess of emotions I had told myself I would never unpack.

"You were just a kid, Adam," she whispers. "You weren't a coward, You did everything you were told to do, and everything you could. You took your brother, and you ran. You witnessed something first hand, that you shouldn't have, and you simply didn't know how to process."

My breath is shaky as she takes my hand.

"Which is something I understand, completely."

The heartbreaking way she says this, and my recollection of her story about her tutor, instantly diffuses my rage.

I've seen doctors, and therapists, all try unsuccessfully to unpack my trauma. And then of course there was the media frenzy, and all of the people apologizing both personally and privately for my *experience*.

However, despite their best efforts, no one could really give me any comfort. Because no matter what they said, they didn't know what it was like to see someone you love die right in front of you.

But Rachel *does*.

The fact that she's listening to me, and just sitting with me in the gritty residue left behind by this horrific memory, resonates with me.

And the moment she takes my hand, she somehow yanks me back from the edge without even knowing it.

The understanding in her eyes silently urges me to continue, and I am able to resign myself to finish the story she asked to hear: the reason I joined the Bureau.

"We were right by a creek bed when Tuck was shot," I say quietly, clearing my throat. "I think that's the only reason I was saved. I ran up the river and found a tree with a hollowed-out base. I scrambled inside and just waited."

"Did he find you?"

"Almost," I sigh. "He was bleeding profusely at that point, and I could hear his footsteps crunching outside."

I close my eyes. The memory is so hauntingly visceral I can almost remember the smell of the rotted-out tree, the tickling of the spider webs on my neck, and the sound of the stream nearby.

"Fuck you," I whisper.

"Excuse me?" Rachel asks, letting go of my hand.

"That's the last thing he said," I continue. "And then I heard the gunshot go off."

"Oh..." Rachel whispers, pulling her legs up on the bed and turning to face me.

"When I heard it go off, I...well, I thought *I* was dead."

"But, the bullet didn't hit you?"

I shake my head. Leaning back up against the headboard I lower my eyes from hers, staring at the ugly floral pattern on the scratchy bed cover.

"He shot himself," I say quietly. "Nearly four feet from my tree. He must've known he was dying, and gave up, right there."

Rachel just shakes her head.

"I laid in that tree until the sun came up though. I was terrified he was outside, fucking with me, waiting for me to come out so he could shoot me too."

"But you climbed out," she says softly. "How did you make it out of the woods?"

"At some point in the night I drifted off to sleep, simply from sheer exhaustion," I continued. "I woke up the next day when some hikers just happened to pass by."

I click my tongue inside my mouth.

"They'd found Tuck's body first, you see, and they just started screaming," I chuckle sardonically. "So you can imagine, when I crawled out of some rotted old tree trunk, dirty and covered in my brother's blood, they just about pissed themselves."

Rachel nods.

"Anyway, they called the cops and the paramedics and whisked me off to some hospital, while they combed the forest. But when their cadaver dogs found more than just my family in that little stretch of woods, well, that's when shit just exploded. Total media frenzy, you know."

"I...I can't even imagine that," Rachel sighs, shaking her head. "What happened to *you*?"

"Oh I got shipped off to my grandparents' house," I reply. "And I know this is where you're probably expecting me to say that I was miserable and lonely, and turned into this dark tortured soul, intent on getting my retribution on the world."

"But?" Rachel asks, narrowing her eyes at me.

"I just wasn't," I shrug. "I wasn't much of anything. They were nice people. The farm was quiet. I was quiet. And the town they lived in was small and full of quiet small-town kids who didn't really have much to talk about. So, I just didn't talk about it."

I pull my cigarettes from my pocket and light one, taking a long drag. When I rest my hand on my thigh, Rachel reaches forward and takes it from me, taking a drag too before handing it back.

"What do you mean you didn't talk about it?"

"It's strange. It's like in some ways, my young brain just...

blocked it out," I say, shaking my head. "Because he killed himself and left a ton of evidence back in the garage, they didn't need me for much. The FBI was able to identify the majority of the bodies and they closed the case. Meanwhile I was with my maternal grandparents, who had my name changed to theirs to protect news reporters or anyone from tracking me down. The internet wasn't around back then, and they didn't have cable at the farm, so I didn't see much of what was happening on the news when it was happening."

I take another drag on my cigarette.

"I was right at that turning point in my life, you know, right before puberty and shit," I say, as Rachel takes it from me. "So hormones and girls had me distracted. And I joined a baseball team, and buried myself in my schoolwork. I started getting accolades and scholarships to some of the best schools."

"But you still remembered things," Rachel asks gently. "Like your mother, brother, and…"

I nod.

"I did, and I would occasionally have nightmares from PTSD. Night terrors, I think they call it," I say, running a hand over my head. "Still do sometimes."

I shiver, remembering just how often and how vivid some of those night terrors could be.

"But that's when the internet started making its debut," I say quietly as Rachel dumps the cigarette butt in her empty beer bottle. "And that's when I learned the truth about what my father had done, and how the FBI had uncovered the whole horrific double life my father had lived…with us."

Rachel nods.

"Something about that, registered with me," I say quietly. "I wanted to be one of the good guys, I wanted to help people."

I swallow hard.

"I'm sure that sounds incredibly cheesy, especially for a Mafia princ—"

"Don't say that fucking word, Adam," Rachel growls, grabbing the neck of the bottle. "Or I swear I will crack this over your fucking head."

This makes me laugh.

"Okay, okay, killer," I say, putting my hands up defensively. "Anyway, I made that my goal. To work for the people who tracked down these psychopaths and bring them to justice."

Biting my bottom lip, I tip my head to the side.

"…Or hopefully stop them before they kill anyone else."

"So," Rachel says, looking at me intently. "You're saying you just moved on completely? Like you never had any residual… issues from this whole ordeal?"

I grin.

"No," I whisper quietly, shaking my head. "I had plenty of issues. You don't see your entire family murdered and *not* acquire some issues. But that's another story. This is just the end of this one, and the answer to your question of why I joined the Bureau: to right the wrongs of my father."

She opens her mouth to say something, and my instincts tell me that she's disappointed that this is all I'm willing to confess right now.

But she doesn't say that. Instead, she thanks me.

"For what?" I snort.

"For making me feel like I'm not the only one who is a little fucked up."

Her irreverence in light of my horrific familial rap sheet, is oddly calming.

Glancing up at me briefly, a soft blush settles across her cheeks as tucks her hair behind her ear. She looks down at the bottle in her hands before smirking to herself.

"So, do you, uh," she winks. "Wanna smash this one too?"

I smile.

She's so fucking pretty, Jesus Christ.

"No," I say quietly. "But thank you."

And then, without a word, Rachel leans forward on the bed and kisses me. But it's not a soft, comforting kind of kiss. No, this kiss is deep, and passionate, and instantly incinerates whatever restraint I had, which was keeping me from doing the exact same thing.

But even as my hand wraps around her soft brown curls, and I flip her on her back on the bed, shoving my tongue into her mouth, some part of me wants to ask her *why*. Why on earth she would want to fuck me after hearing the shocking, terrible, and horrifically gruesome story of my past?

We have so much to sort through. So many stories still to hear, and much ground left to cover.

However, like it has so many times before, my desire for Rachel defies all logic. It overpowers my hesitance and resolves to just put a band aid on the gaping chest wound I just divulged, and simply fuck this gorgeous woman into oblivion.

Maybe this is her coping mechanism.

...And maybe she has a point.

CHAPTER ELEVEN

Rachel

After Adam and I finish fucking, again, we lay under the sheets, hearing the wind howling outside.

"As strange as it is," I laugh. "I think I'm warmer when we're naked than when I'm bundled up in sweatshirts and pants."

"That's not strange, it's science," Adam chuckles.

"Yay for science," I chuckle, as he shakes his head.

"So," he says softly, trailing his fingers down my arm. "Can I ask a question?"

"I sure as hell hope so," I chuckle. "You've already got me in bed with you."

"You said you and Jaxon weren't good for very long."

"That's not a question," I scoff.

"My question is," he says, smacking my ass somewhat playfully. "If it wasn't good, why did you stay?"

"Ahh, now that is a question. But one I don't necessarily have an answer for," I roll over, so that I'm looking at him. "The beginning was a whirlwind. We spent the better part of two weeks together, drunk on some island somewhere. I think he was trying to get me to realize what my life could be if I just quit dancing and jet set around the world with him."

"And that life wasn't at all appealing to you?"

"It was, for a minute. I don't know," I sigh. "It was like it was great when I was with him, but then we came back to reality. And while his reality had him very busy, mine had me sitting at home, waiting for him to come by. I got bored. Then I got angry. Then we'd fight. Then we'd make up."

I lay my hand on Adam's chest.

"Jaxon was always good at the make-up part," I say. "It was just the communication and fidelity parts he struggled with."

"So like…the *rest* of the relationship?'

"Exactly…"

"I'm so proud of you bitch!"

"What?" I laugh, opening my locker.

"Well," Jess says, yanking off the lacy brassiere she's sporting and rifling through her bag for her t-shirt. "You've been sitting around the apartment, moping, for weeks. It's nice to see you back on stage. You killed it!"

"Oh…" I say quietly, biting my bottom lip and pulling my jeans up over my hips.

"You were amazing up there, Rachel," she says, leaning in next to me. "You looked like a total badass."

"I don't know if badass is the appropriate term for a pole routine."

"Um, it is when you do it as well as you do," Jessica laughs, pulling on a pair of black leggings. "But I mean it, Rach. Tonight, you chose yourself, for the first time in a long time and I am proud of you."

She immediately walks over to our little vanity setup and starts packing up our makeup and beauty products.

"Well, thanks," I chuckle under my breath, sighing deeply. "But if I had to guess, I bet *he* wouldn't be very proud."

"Who fucking cares what Jaxon Pace thinks!" Jess snaps loudly, slamming the cap down hard on the bottle of hairspray. "He hasn't called in weeks. And like I totally respect that you tried to respect his wishes when you guys were together but you're not anymore and…"

She suddenly stops mid-sentence and looks up at me, with a look of embarrassment.

"Shit," she says, closing her eyes and shaking her head. "I didn't mean it like that."

"Yes, you did," I say softly, with a disappointed smile. "But it's okay. It's the truth so…"

She drops the stuff in her hands, walks over to me and immediately wraps her arms around my neck in a giant hug.

"I'm sorry," she whispers. "I shouldn't have said that."

"It's fine."

"No, it's not fine. You're going through a hard time, and you're getting over him and I just ran my stupid mouth like a stupid bitch."

I giggle, tapping her back in hopes she will let me up for air. But she refuses to let go.

"You're going to be fine," she whispers. "Each day will get a little easier."

I swallow hard and then pull away. I know there's truth in her words, but I'm just not prepared to deal with the emotions rising in my chest.

"Honestly, I'm fine," I say with the most convincing smile I can manage. "Fuck him."

"That's the spirit," Jessica smiles back, hitting me on the shoulder.

"Now come on, if we hurry, we can still make the party at The Garage."

"What?"

"The Garage," Jess grins. "That new grungy biker country bar. There's a late-night party going on there, and I want to go ride the mechanical bull!"

I shake my head.

"Jess, I love you, but I just finished my first night back on the floor in weeks. I don't have the energy for bikers, bulls and country music."

Jess grins.

"I've got something for that, you know."

"Coke can't always be the answer, Jess," I giggle, searching through my duffle bag. "Besides, I seem to have left my normal bra at home."

"Even better!" Jess laughs. "You'll have sparkly titties showing through your shirt all night!"

"For reals," I roll my eyes, buttoning up my shirt. "I'm tired, sore, and all I want is a hot shower and to go to bed."

"Don't be a grandma," Jess whines, rolling her eyes. "And don't leave me to go by myself!"

"Why are you so hell bent on going anyway?"

"Because Eamon is going," she says, zipping up her bag. "And he owes me for the other night."

"You want to see him again? How can you face him after leaving your ass print on his glass door?"

She laughs.

"He's my best client!"

"I mean, that much is true. He only ever asks for you."

"Which is just the way I like it," Jess grins, sticking out her tongue at me. "But the fucker owes me money! We are going!"

"No, *you* are going," I say, pulling my boots out of my locker. "I've got a date with my pillow and some Celine Dion infomercials."

Jess's face suddenly turns sympathetic.

"Rach, you're just going to go home and think about Jaxon Pace," she says, stepping up to me. "You need to forget him, and what a better way to do that than to come have some shots and party with me?"

"I'm sorry, did I hear someone mention Jaxon Pace?" A voice sounds from behind us.

I turn to see the twins, Mags and May, coming around the corner, their faces eager.

"Even if we did," Jess snaps. "I don't remember this conversation being open for discussion."

"You said he ghosted you?" Mags asks with a smile.

"I never said that."

"Well, something to that effect," she shrugs. "You should know honey, that's his MO."

"Excuse me?"

"He does that to everyone," May chimes in, crossing her arms. "He's slept with nearly half the girls here. In fact, he was with me and Mags a few months ago. At the same time."

"It was a great night though," Mags says to her sister.

"It really was," May blushes. "He's an incredible lover."

"Oh God yes, best oral I've ever had." Mags gushes.

"And his cock…." May says, shivering. "Mmm."

"He just ghosts afterwards," Mags says with a shrug. "He's a great lay, just not relationship material."

"I wouldn't take it personally, sweetie," May whispers, her eyes narrowed.

My cheeks heat and my blood boils, but before I can even react, Jessica pushes past me and grabs May by the throat, shoving her hard into the lockers.

"Ow!" May yelps loudly. "What the fuck?!"

"Jess!"

"You know what I wouldn't take personally, sweetie," Jessica sneers. "No one fucking asked for your opinion, so why don't you and your snobby little twin fuck off before I beat your ass?"

She releases May and the girl recoils, glaring at Jessica. For a second, I fear that a fight is about to break out. But most of the girls here wouldn't dare to challenge Jessica to a fight, as she is by far the scrappiest girl at the club, who isn't afraid to throw hands.

"Leave," Jess growls lethally.

Immediately, the two girls scramble away.

"Bitches," Jess breathes, shaking her head. "It's probably time I beat someone's ass for real around this place. They are getting far too fucking bold."

My heart is pounding.

I don't know what frustrates me more, the fact that these two girls would take it upon themselves to come and say this shit to me, or the fact that I know the shit they are saying is true. Jaxon does have a reputation around town for getting in and out of pussy like a taxi cab.

…I just thought I was different.

Famous last words, Rach.

"So," I say, taking a deep breath. "About that party…"

The Garage was one of the most unique bars in the city, mainly because it used to be, in fact, a garage.

Remodeled after a fire destroyed the original auto body repair shop, its foreign investors had converted the building into some strange hybrid of country western bar, with a techno vibe, and a lot of biker patrons.

Jess had given me a bit of the history on our bus ride downtown, but seeing it in person is an experience in itself. And, since the bouncer is a client as well as Jess's part time coke dealer, when we arrive we're able to skip the line and walk straight inside.

The place is massive, with an upstairs VIP loft, gigantic dance floor and a mechanical bull pit. And true to its namesake, the owners had decided to leave four of the eight original large garage doors that cars used to drive in for oil changes or repairs, all of which opened up to a heated patio area with fire pits and lounge chairs.

Inside the wrap-around bar is made of clear resin and spans three of its four walls. Its fifteen gorgeous female bartenders are dressed in glow-in the-dark bikini tops, denim shorts, and cowboy boots.

"Isn't it weird?" Jess snorts, waving her finger around.

"It's like the place is having an identity crisis." I say, still trying to take in the bizarre atmosphere and I.

She laughs.

"I think I heard someone say the owner runs an art gallery in Germany, or maybe it was Russia," she shrugs. "Maybe that's why it's so...*quirky*."

"Quirky is definitely the right way to describe this place."

"But like, in a cool way," Jess gushes. "It's modern and hip, but also gritty and—"

"...And *country*," I interrupt, glancing from the band on the stage to a group of men line dancing to some mashup of techno and bluegrass, in their leather vests and cowboy boots. "And if I'm going to have to listen to this horrific music all night you better put a drink in my hand. Several, actually."

"You got it lady," Jess snaps. "But first, what do you say we hit the bathroom for a little you-know-what, eh?"

I raise my brows at her and shake my head, knowing full well her little bathroom trip is just so she can take another bump of her coke.

But after we find the line for the bathroom could nearly wrap around the building, Jess calls in another favor from her bouncer friend and he lets us past the gold rope so we can use the VIP bathrooms upstairs.

"Pays to know people," Jess snorts, with her tongue out.

"...Or *blow* people," I laugh, and she joins in with me.

We reach the top of the stairs and slip into the VIP bathrooms unnoticed. Immediately Jess pulls out her little eye shadow container filled with coke. While she preps a line for herself, I reapply my bright red lipstick.

"You want any?" she asks, handing me the rolled up $100 bill. But I shake my head.

"Suit yourself," she shrugs.

Finishing off the little bit left, she pinches her nose closed.

"I am proud of you for coming out though," she says, throwing her head back and sniffling. "Admit it, babe, it has to feel good."

And as much as I hate to admit it, it does.

"It will feel better when you get me that drink you promised me," I wink at her.

We're both giggling as we exit the ladies' room, and I accidentally collide with a man walking past me.

"What the hell—" I start to say, but then am stunned by how handsome the man is.

The man is tall and lean, dressed in a perfectly tailored light gray suit and a tight black tee that clings tightly to his abs. His soft green eyes scan me up and down, his naturally bright blonde hair fading down to his well-trimmed beard that forms quickly into a smile.

"Well, hello there, beautiful," he says in a thick Russian accent. "Where are you heading off to?"

"Hi," I grin, feeling myself blush. "We were just headed down—"

"To see *you*," Jessica interrupts, shooting me a knowing look. "You looked lonely, honey."

"As a matter of fact," he says, motioning back to a group of men in the VIP area looking eagerly in our direction. "We were getting a little lonely, and a little bored. Waiting on our boss."

"Well, then it was fate," I grin, catching his eyes raking my body again. "We're anything but boring."

"Is that so?" He winks. "Well, it's nice to meet you, Miss Not-Boring. My name is Yuri."

I chuckle.

He's kinda cute.

"Hello Yuri, I'm Rachel," I smile at him, batting my lashes. "And this is my friend Jessica."

Several drinks, and at least three bottles of Grey Goose later, Jessica and I are being regaled with stories of Yuri and his friend's time in Russia.

Apparently, they work security for the owner of the bar, and while they don't go into much detail about the type of business their employer does, all four of the men have been working for him for the last few years.

We are just about to open our fourth bottle of vodka when the music cuts out.

"Alright y'all," a man with a comically thick southern accent calls over the speaker system. "It's about that time for our weekly "Buck Off" competition! We're warming up Ol' Billy the Bull, and we invite any daring young riders to come on down and test your skills!"

Laughter goes up from the dance floor, along with a few cheers.

"And as always, the cowboy or *cowgirl* that can stay on him the longest, will be the winner of this fine, authentic leather cowboy hat from Harper's Haberdashery!"

"Oh my God," Yuri laughs. "This is my favorite part."

"What?" I ask, taking a sip of my drink.

"Every Friday night, these drunk Americans pretend that they can ride fake bull."

His accent, and perhaps the alcohol makes his comment even funnier.

"If you would like to get in on this competition, just come on down and the ringleader, James, will get you signed up!" The DJ continues.

"It's so funny," Boris, one of Yuri's dark-haired friends, laughs. "They only last a few seconds before they all fall off."

"Yeah! Look at me! I'm strong cowboy!" Igor laughs.

The boys proceed to reenact the hilarious fails they have watched from their perch in VIP every week, making Jess and I laugh incredibly hard.

"I bet," Jessica says, taking a sip of her drink. "I bet a woman could do better than any of those men."

"Hah, you're crazy," Yuri laughs.

"Why am I crazy?"

"Because," Boris laughs, waving her off. "If strong man could not hold on, what makes you think tiny woman could?"

"Right!" Boris agrees.

"I think you've just not met the right woman," Jess argues, sitting back against the chair, a smug smile on her face. "Besides, we are used to riding!"

"Yeah, *cock* maybe, but not bull!" Igor laughs as the rest of the men join in.

Perhaps it's the vodka, but his comment stirs something in my bones, and suddenly I am overcome with a desire to prove him wrong.

"You know what," I say, pointing at the men at the table. "I think I'm going to go down there and I'm gonna win."

"Hahaha!" Boris laughs. "There's no way!"

I down the rest of my drink and slam my glass down hard on the table.

"Watch me."

Yuri looks up at me, a playful grin plastered across his face.

"Definitely not boring," he winks. "Alright, little girl. Let's go see what you've got."

He mutters something in Russian, and all four of the men stand to their feet, and Jess and I join them.

But when I stumble a little, and a small wave of dizziness hits me, my resolve falters. Jessica steps over to me and takes my arm, helping me keep my balance.

"Jess," I whisper. "Is this a stupid idea?"

"Probably," she shrugs, gripping my arm as we carefully start to walk down the steps. "But aren't those the best ideas?"

"Not always," I giggle. "Sometimes they result in me doing things that could end in serious injury!"

"Well, then don't let it end that way," she says, as we make our way across the dance floor, once again filled with the music and line-dancers.

By the time we reach the bullpit I have a knot in my stomach. *Shit. Maybe I was a little bit too bold for my own good.*

Yuri and his big burly friends shove their way past the handful of other potential riders, up to the front. A man in a plaid shirt, Levi Jeans, cowboy hat, sporting a glow-in-the-dark name tag with the name "James" stands holding a clipboard.

"Pretty girl would like to ride fake bull," Boris says, motioning me forward. "You will put her on."

"She can get in line," some frat-boy looking fucker says irritably from behind us.

But the moment Boris, who is built like the Sears Tower turns around and looks at him he puts his hands up and apologizes, without Boris needing to say a word.

"I'll need her ID," James says, smiling at me.

For a moment, I consider chickening out, but then I feel Jess squeezing my arm.

"Go on, Rach, you can do it," she says.

I bite my lip and make my way forward through the small crowd of people standing around the bull pit. James holds his hand out, as I quickly fish my ID from my wallet and hand it to him. He looks at it and writes something down on his clipboard before handing it back to me.

I make sure that Yuri and Jess are both out of earshot before leaning in to whisper in the man's ear.

"If it's okay," I smile timidly. "I'd like to watch a few people go before me."

He looks up at me, somewhat confused.

"I made a stupid bet with my friends that I could do it, and now I'm too afraid to back out. That Russian guy is scary."

He chuckles to himself.

"No worries, little lady," he grins, winking at me. "I'll put you near the end, so you can watch it go around a few times."

"Thank you!" I breathe.

When I make my way back to where Yuri and the group are, Jess returns from the bar with a bottle of water.

"Here," she says, opening it and handing it to me. "So, you can sober up a little."

Gratefully I take the water from her and chug a few sips.

"Alright, ladies and gents," James calls from behind me. "It's time to get started. First up, we have Kyle Conners! Hop on up

Kyle!"

From the crowd, the short frat-boy looking guy with a pink polo shirt appears. Obviously hammered, his face is beet red, and he stumbles a bit on the soft surface of the protective mats lining the floor.

"Go Kyle!" One of his friends standing on the sideline's cheers, raising his glass shakily in the air, spilling it on himself.

Kyle wobbles as he tries to climb on top of the mechanical bull, much to the entertainment of the crowd standing around. Eventually one of his buddies helps him up, and he gives a thumbs-up to James.

The bull starts to turn, before suddenly whipping back around the other direction...sending Kyle plummeting to the mat.

"Aw, bad luck, Kyle!" The announcer laughs. "Fortunately for the rest of the riders, 2.8 seconds is an easy time to beat!"

"Ha Ha! Idiot!" Boris laughs loudly, pointing at Kyle.

"That's not fair! My...my hand slipped!" Kyle whines, trying to plead his case as bullpit workers push him out of the ring.

"Oh well! Next up, Christopher Polk! Hop on Christopher!"

We watch as Christopher tries his hand at the bull, managing to stay on for a good seven seconds and change before being sent crashing into the mats as well. A handful of other riders try their luck, but none of them manage to stay on very long. That is until a dude in a cowboy hat somehow stays on for eight seconds.

"Well, it seems like Matthew was able to stay on a bit longer than Christopher, and a whole lot longer than poor Kyle, so unfortunately that means you're out boys."

"I already told you!" Kyle whines loudly, his face somehow even redder. "My hand slipped!"

"Yeah, that's what they all say buddy," James jokes, making the entire crowd laugh.

Everyone except Kyle that is.

"But you know what they say around here," James continues with a smile. "If you mess with the bull, you get the..."

He holds the microphone out to the crowd.

"*Horns!*" The audience cheers, with enthusiasm and laughter.

"That's right! Congratulations Matthew! You're the new time to beat! 8.4 seconds!"

I swallow hard, feeling my heartbeat in my ears, knowing that I am next.

"Well, gentlemen it seems we have a *lady* contender!"

"Woohoo! Hell yeah!" One of the drunk frat boy's hollers loudly, before being hit by the drunk and dejected Kyle Conners, still appearing to be nursing his wounded pride.

"Help me give a big ol' hearty Garage *yeehaw* to the beautiful, Miss, Rachel Vaaaaalentine!" James bellows loudly.

"Yeeeehawwww!" The crowd cheers.

Nervously, and kicking myself for letting the alcohol do my thinking, I make my way across the black gym mats that surround the bull, doing my best to stay vertical.

"Aw, and look, he's even a good sport," James teases, seeing Cowboy Matt waving me forward offering to help me up. "See, boys, that's what we call *chivalry*."

"Sit as high up as you can," he whispers, helping to guide my foot into the stirrup.

"What did you say?" I whisper back.

"Sit up as high as you can and grip it as tight as you can with your thighs," he says under his breath, clearly sensing the apprehension in my face. "Hold the rope with your stronger hand, but keep the other one free. Use it to help you balance."

"Thank you," I smile back politely.

"You got it, cutie," he winks, before walking away.

I lookup, expecting to find Jessica in the crowd, but she's no longer with Yuri. That's when I see that Eamon has just arrived, seeing the two of them talking over by the bar.

But before I can be a bit disappointed that she left me, I hear the whirring of the bull whirring to life beneath me.

I feel the first buck before it spins quickly to one side, nearly dumping me onto the mats. But remembering the advice Cowboy Matt just whispered to me, I quickly clench my thighs tightly and raise my hand in the air for balance.

But just as I do I feel two things happen at once:

First, the buttons on my blue button-up dress shirt pop open, exposing my sparkly champagne-colored bikini top.

And second, the crowd goes wild.

"Hell yeah, Rachel!" I hear Jess yell, apparently returned. "You can do it babe!"

"She's done it!" I hear the announcer say. "9.6 seconds and counting, Rachel Valentine is our new record holder!"

Even though I can't hear anything besides the roar of the

crowd, I feel the embarrassment of my busted shirt dissipate, and the rush of adrenaline and euphoria take over.

For just a moment I feel completely...free.

And then it all goes to shit.

BANG! BANG!

Gunshots ring out, followed by screaming and the sound of breaking glass as the lightbulbs overhead burst. I turn to look, but as I do, I lose my balance and am bucked off the bull, crashing down hard into the black mats.

"Ow!" I say, as my hand comes down hard on a large shard of glass, slicing it open.

"Turn that fucking thing off or I will shoot you right here!" A man shouts at James.

I turn to look and suddenly my blood runs cold.

Oh shit. I know who that is...

"I said turn the fucker off!"

"Okay! Okay!" James stammers nervously, as more panicked screams go up around the room. "I'm turning it off, okay?"

The bull comes to a halt as does the conversation around us, and before I know what's happening, the man has rushed across the mats toward me.

"What the fuck do you think you're doing...*sister*?!"

Michael Valentine, my brother, suddenly grabs me by the hair and starts pulling me across the ring.

"Ow! Let go of me!" I shout, trying to fight against him.

But as he slams me into the side of the ring, all of the air is forced from my lungs.

"I have been looking all over this fucking city for you," he spits at me angrily. "And *this* is where I find you?!"

Without warning, he hits me hard across the right side of my face.

"Do you think this is appropriate behavior?" He says, hitting me hard on my left cheek. "Riding bulls with your tits out like a whore!"

Instinctively, I throw my hands up to protect myself, and his slaps turn into punches, connecting with my forearm hard.

"Hey! Asshole!" Jessica's voice rings out on the other side of the ropes. "What the hell do you think you're doing?!"

"Michael, stop!" I shout, curling into a ball.

But he doesn't. He only hits me harder.

Suddenly something comes over me, and without thinking I lunge for the only thing I can think of—his legs. He crashes down on the mats and suddenly I am on top of him, punching him in the face with all my strength.

But my moment of superiority doesn't last long. He flips me over on my back and suddenly his hands are on my throat. I scratch at his hands, feeling the air choking from my lungs.

He's going to kill me!

"Get the fuck off of her, Asshole!"

Matthew, the nice man who helped me onto the bull, slams his shoulder into Michael, knocking him off me long enough.

"Don't you know better than to put your hands on a lady?"

I haven't seen my brother in a decade, but even still I can already anticipate his reaction before it happens. He whirls around punching Matthew in the throat, before cracking him hard across the jaw. Completely unprepared for Michael's attack, the poor man slumps to the ground.

"Stay. The. Fuck. Out. Of. My. Business." Michael snaps, kicking the man hard in the stomach with every word.

Matthew groans when Michael eventually stops and turns back to me, pulling his gun from his holster.

There is more screaming as people run terrified from the ring and out of the exit.

"You...are a *slut*," he hisses, walking back over to me.

I push myself up onto my elbows.

I hear a safety click off...but it is *not* Michael's gun.

Looking to my left I see that Yuri, Boris and the rest of the men Jessica and I were drinking with have hopped into the ring and are now standing directly behind me.

"No guns inside the building," Yuri says with a smirk. "Or fighting. We put it on sign, since you Americans are stupid and need things spelled out for you."

Michael runs his hand through his now sweaty hair and glares up at Yuri.

"I wasn't looking for trouble," He hisses at him.

"Well you'll find it," Yuri grins, completely unfazed. "If you don't leave now."

I pull my shirt closed around my exposed chest, tasting blood in my mouth from where my tooth cut my lip, scrambling quickly for the edge of the ring.

"This is a private family matter," Michael snaps, getting up in Yuri's face. "So, mind your business and fuck off!"

But Yuri just smiles, unfazed by Michael's temper.

"You make it our business when you come into our club, and cause trouble." Yuri says, opening his suit coat and flashing his gun. "Do you know who my boss is?"

Michael chuckles to himself.

"Yeah, dickhead, I know who your boss is," Michael sneers. "But even *he* doesn't get to tell me what I can and cannot do with my own sister."

"No, but *I* fucking do."

Another voice thunders behind me that I also instantly recognize, causing my stomach to drop through the floor.

I turn slightly to see Jaxon glaring at Michael as if he wants to rip his head from his body. He glances down at me briefly, before locking eyes with Michael again.

"And I say you're not going to touch her again."

What the fuck is he doing here?

"Rach," I hear Jess say quietly behind me, pulling at my shirt. I slip out behind the ropes of the ring and Jessica wraps me in a hug.

"Are you okay?" she whispers, wrapping the scarf she wore around my bleeding hand.

I nod, turning back to the ridiculous scene before me.

"What the fuck is going on down here?" another man with a thick Russian accent steps up beside Jaxon.

"Mr. Antonov, th..that man," James the announcer says nervously appearing out of the crowd and pointing at Michael. "He came up and shot the light and—"

"I wasn't fucking talking to *you*," The tall dark stranger snaps, glaring at James before turning to Yuri. "What are all these people doing standing around, huh?"

Yuri's demeanor instantly changes. Up until this point he has seemed so cocky and sure of himself, even willing to stand up to Michael with a gun in his hand. But somehow in the presence of this man, Mr. Antonov, he now looks small. And terrified.

"What the fuck do I pay you two idiots for?!" He starts speaking quickly in Russian, as Boris and Igor start nodding and pointing between me and Michael.

Whoever he is, he must be Yuri's boss.

A vein in the man's neck throbs as he continues yelling at Yuri and the men in Russian as they exit the pit. Yuri continues, what I can only assume is an apology based on his tone, as Mr. Antonov continues scolding him, waving his hand around angrily toward the growing crowd around us.

"Get the fucking music back on," Mr. Antonov growls, pushing Boris toward the stage. "And then make like a whore and get the fuck out of my sight."

Yuri takes a step toward me, but Mr. Antonov grabs him.

"Wet your cock on your own time!" He snaps, smacking him hard across the face.

Without another look in my direction, Yuri disappears into the crowd.

"Get him up," Mr. Antonov points at poor Cowboy Matt still holding his ribs. "This isn't good for business."

"Michael," Jaxon snaps angrily. "Go the fuck home. Now."

Michael glares at Jaxon, and then at me.

"I want to talk to my sis—"

"I don't give a shit what you want," Jaxon hisses venomously, cutting him off. "You've caused enough problems tonight, and you two can have your little family gathering on your own time. But if you don't walk out that door in the next ten seconds, you won't be walking ever again, do you understand me?"

Whoa.

Michael looks furious, but even from where I'm standing, I can tell there is a part of him that at least fears Jaxon is serious. He doesn't argue, and instead, he slips underneath the ropes, and storms off toward the door.

"I want him gone," Jaxon says to one of his men, a tall, handsome and ripped ginger man. "If I see his face anywhere in this zip code I will put a fucking bullet in his forehead, understood?"

The ginger man nods once before following Michael out to the parking lot.

The band starts playing their music again, and within seconds the atmosphere in the club has shifted back to normal, as if everything that just happened, never happened.

"Mr. Pace," The tall Russian man says, walking over to Jaxon. "I apologize for the inconvenience."

"If anyone needs to apologize, Roman, it's me," Jaxon says,

140

shaking his head. "Forgive me, but my commander seems to have forgotten his place this evening."

His commander?! Michael works for Jaxon?!

"I will pay for the damage to your ceiling."

The man named Roman waves him off.

"No, no, trust me it has seen worse," he says with a light chuckle. "I've learned things like this tend to happen where tits, dicks, and booze are involved."

Yuri returns to the group, nursing a cut on the side of his face from where Roman's massive rings connected with his cheek. He glances up at me briefly before taking his place by Roman's side and lowering his eyes to the floor.

"Men are...simple." Roman says, shooting a disapproving look over at Yuri.

Jaxon snorts, rubbing his chin.

"Well, I sincerely hope the actions of mine haven't soured your thoughts toward our proposal?"

Roman Antonov, the scary dark-haired Russian man smiles.

"On the contrary, it's only increased my interest. But perhaps we will leave the children at home next time."

"You have my word, he will be dealt with," Jaxon growls quietly. "Unfortunately, it's not the first time, and my father doesn't tolerate hotheads who get distracted from their duty. And neither do I."

"Well," Roman says, his eyes falling to me. "Mine seem to have gotten distracted as well."

Jaxon looks down at me, and then at Yuri.

Fuck. Is it that obvious? Or did Yuri tell this Roman guy?

"Shall we head upstairs and continue our business?"

"As much as I would like to, it is late, and it seems I have some other business that requires my...*attention*," Jaxon says with a sigh, glancing toward me. "Perhaps we can arrange another time?"

Roman nods, smiling politely.

"Of course," he says, extending his hand. "I will have my people contact your people in the morning."

Jaxon shakes it briskly before turning back to me. However, the frustrated look on his face immediately makes my heart start pounding.

Shit. He's not happy.

141

He whispers something to another one of his big burly bodyguards and the man runs off. Jaxon walks toward me, unbuttoning his jacket and wrapping it around my shoulders.

"Here," he says, his voice quiet but his tone frigid. "Did you check a jacket?"

"No, I—"

"Of course you fucking didn't," he mutters, under his breath before touching his ear. "Pull the car around."

He places his arm around me and immediately starts pulling me toward the door.

"Where are we going?"

"We're leaving."

"But, I—"

"Rachel," Jaxon whispers forcefully. "I will speak with you in the fucking car. But don't say anything right now with these people listening."

He's really pissed.

"Wait, no," I say, stopping firmly.

"Rachel," Jaxon growls.

"I came here with Jess, Jaxon," I say, breaking from him. "I can't just go leaving without—"

"Look," Jaxon snaps, turning me around and pointing over to Jess standing next to Eamon. "She's fine. Either Eamon will take her home, or my men will make sure that she gets a ride. Now for the love of God, let's go before you cause me any more trouble."

He resumes his hold around me and pulls me toward the exit, but this time I don't object. There is a car already waiting for us as we exit the building and as Jaxon unceremoniously opens the door for me, I can feel the tears streaking down my cheeks.

I know he's upset, and I can't blame him. Everything that just happened inside was a fucking nightmare.

"Give me the kit," Jaxon orders his driver as he steps into the car and slams the door behind him. "Take us to her apartment."

Jaxon's driver gets out and hands him the same black bag as he had the night of Ness's overdose.

"Give me your hand," he says, as he pulls bandages and ointment out of the bag.

Reluctantly I obey, and he examines the cut on my hand before applying ointment on it and wrapping it crudely in bandages.

"Drive," he commands.

But as the car pulls away, suddenly I feel myself get angry.

"Sure, Jaxon," I say sarcastically. "You *can* come over tonight. That works for me."

"Oh, I'm not coming over," he snaps back angrily, making me jump. "I'm dropping your ass off."

"Why so you can go fuck another one of your whores?!" I shout, my rage building. "Since I assume you have dozens of them all over the city!"

"What?!" He snaps angrily. "What whores?"

"Whatever piece of ass you've been sticking your dick in!"

"I don't have any whores! But what I do have is a giant you-sized problem that could've been avoided had you just listened to me in the first place!" He yells angrily. "I told you weeks ago about your brother looking for you, and all the drama it would cause if he found you flaunting your body for money!"

"I wasn't flaunting my body!"

"What the fuck do you call this?!" He seethes, flipping open the flap on his jacket, exposing my busted shirt.

"It was an accident!" I snap back at him, yanking his jacket closed. "I was having drinks with my friend, and I decided to ride the mechanical bull—"

"You know Rach," he snaps sarcastically. "I really don't fucking care for your excuses."

"It's not an excuse! I was having fun and my shirt popped open while I was riding the bull! That's all! I didn't do it on purpose!"

"Right," Jaxon snorts. "Of course. And yet, had your brother not seen you flailing about with your tits out—"

"Fuck you, Jaxon!" I shout back. "I didn't anticipate him being there tonight any more than I anticipated you being there, and not out with one of your whores!"

"Why do you keep saying that?!"

"Because you haven't called me in weeks!"

"So, because I didn't call that automatically means I'm out fucking someone else?!" He thunders. "How about I had shit to do that involved me traveling and I had neither the time nor the energy!"

"They still make phones, Jaxon!" I say, smacking the one in his hand and sending it tumbling to the floor. "You could have called and—"

"Sometimes some things take precedence!" He thunders.

"Yeah, like all the other *whores*."

"There are no fucking whores!" His voice is so loud it shakes the windows. "Believe it or not, I have bigger things on my mind than pussy! Things that have been under construction for years, things that are far more important than whatever drama is going on with you and your equally foolish hot-headed brother!"

"Speaking of my brother," I say, turning to face him.

"Ah, here we go," He chuckles sarcastically to himself, rubbing his chin.

"You keep saying you warned me about him."

"I did!"

"No, you didn't!" I shout, as loud as my lungs will allow. "You told me your *opinions* on my lifestyle, and my career choice and said it was unconducive to staying off Michael's radar—"

"...Exactly!"

"But you neglected to tell me that he *works* for you!"

My words ring in the tiny car that now goes as quiet as a tomb. Jaxon glares at me, panting, but says nothing.

The only sound is the sound of the silent driver's leather gloves gripping the steering wheel as he turns down my street, and suddenly I feel bad that these two men have witnessed our very loud argument.

"I...tried to warn you," Jaxon says, his voice now eerily quiet. "About your brother. And what he was like."

"How?" I scoff softly.

Jaxon stares at me, seemingly unable to reply.

"I mean, you told me he was looking for me," I continue. "But you told that Roman guy tonight, that he was a hothead, and it wasn't the first time he had flown off the handle."

"What's your point?"

"My point, Jaxon, is that all you told me was that *you* thought it was a bad idea for me to be stripping. But you never told me Michael was so...*violent*."

My voice trails off, and I can still taste the blood in my mouth from where Michael's slap had cut my lip.

The anger in Michael's eyes, the disgust in his tone, all of it had been so terrifying that I actually thought he was going to kill me...After not seeing me for years.

My brother had always been different. Never one for kindness, generosity, or caring. And certainly not for forgiveness. But he had never been that bad.

My heart is still pounding as Jaxon and I sit in the silence that envelops the car, until it comes to a stop outside my apartment building.

Quietly Jaxon clears his throat.

"You're right," he says quietly. "I was trying to protect you from the truth, without telling you the truth. I should've told you what he really...*is*."

Sighing heavily, I tuck my hair behind my ear and glance up at my darkened building, looking unbearably cold and vacant somehow in the late morning hours.

I'm still royally furious with Jaxon for having such little compassion, considering everything I just went through with my brother. But I can tell he at least feels some remorse for how he reacted.

...And I really don't want to be alone tonight.

"I've got time," I say, swallowing hard. "Do you want to come up?"

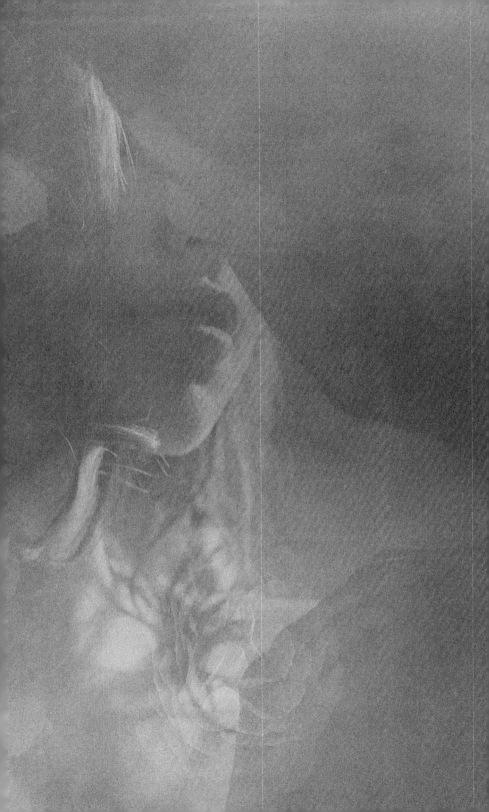

CHAPTER TWELVE

ADAM

"Anddd let me guess" I sigh. "You fucked him."

She lowers her gaze.

"You say that like it's a bad thing."

"Using sex in hopes solve an argument is—"

"Smart," Rachel says, cutting me off.

"No, Rachel," I shake my head, rubbing my eyes. "It's not."

"Yeah, *Adam*," she says sarcastically, crossing her arms. "It is. Because at the very least it diffuses the situation."

"What?"

"Think about it, when are you the least angry?" She says, waving her hand. "Immediately post orgasm, right? It's the olfactory period."

I stare at her, tilting my head to the side.

"Do you mean *refractory*?"

"Yeah, sure," she sighs, waving her hands around. "Whatever you want to call it."

I can't help but chuckle.

"Well, it's kind of a big distinction," I say, raising a brow at her. "The refractory period is the crash after an orgasm, while olfactory has to do with your sense of *smell*."

She stares at me, her lips pursed.

And then, from out of nowhere, something about her little flub makes me laugh. And I mean *really* laugh. Harder than I am ready for.

Perhaps it's the way she said it, or the fact that it was an innocent mistake, but there's something naively adorable about the way she blew it off. And to my surprise once I start laughing, Rachel starts giggling too.

"Way to go ya ass," she giggles, sardonically "Making fun of the poor rich girl who didn't graduate high school."

"Rachel," I plead, through my slight laughter. "That's not what I was doing…"

But the innocent slip of the tongue has at the very least diffused the mood between us. Something so simple and lighthearted that felt foreign to us, stuck in the middle of this heavy conversation right now.

"Anyways, what I was trying to say before I was rudely ridiculed," she says playfully, waving her hand. "Banging one out has benefits. It just takes all the unnecessary *emotions* out of the equation."

"I'm not completely disagreeing with you, but…it's still an argument even after you're done fucking."

"Right, but now it's manageable."

"What the fuck does that mean?"

"Ugh! What is so hard to understand?! You fuck, then you're both happy and you get to the…the…"

"…*Refractory* period?"

"Yeah, and then all those over excited emotions are gone. You're left with just the meat of the argument to sort out."

"Except that it doesn't actually work that way. It's just sticking a band aid on a bigger issue, which is the root cause of all those emotions."

"Emotions are unnecessary."

"No, Rachel, they are very necessary."

She scoffs.

"They are," I say firmly. "It's part of who you are. And the problem with having sex, when you're already emotionally compromised, is that it's bad for your psyche."

"Oh my God," she snorts, rolling her eyes. "People have makeup sex, Adam!"

148

"Right, but makeup sex is different," I argue. "Makeup sex is *after* you've worked it out. After you've compromised or apologized."

"I still don't get it," she sighs, throwing her hands in the hair. "I feel like we're saying the same thing."

The tone in her voice, and her closed body language tells me she's frustrated. It suddenly occurs to me that this might be a concept she really doesn't understand.

I have to find a better way to explain this.

Sitting up on the bed, I turn to face her.

"If you are arguing with someone, it's because one way or another, they have disappointed you. Whatever they said or did was something that hurt you, right?"

"Okay, yeah," she shrugs.

"So, on some level, you're *hurting*, right?"

She pauses for a second before nodding slowly. "Okay…"

"And if you're hurting, that is the moment when you are technically the most vulnerable," I say slowly. "So, making love, while fighting, is really just opening your heart up to the person who hurt you…*while* he's still hurting you."

She stares at me, and it's almost as if I can see the moment my words actually register with her.

Shifting on the bed, she tucks her hair behind her ear. Rachel might not realize it, but this is her biggest tell when I occasionally strike an emotional nerve that she isn't ready for.

"Well," she says, leaning back on the bed with her hands and bouncing her foot. "That little explanation was lovely, but I don't make love, Adam. I fuck."

"I mean, I think you're missing the point of what I'm saying here—"

"No, I haven't," she says defensively.

"Sure, okay, but circling back, you *have* made love before," I say as a question more than a statement.

She shakes her head.

"No, I haven't," she shrugs again. "And honestly, it's fine. I've never understood the appeal, and I have absolutely no interest in it."

Her words stun me.

But before I can react she glances at the clock and suddenly her face goes white.

149

"Oh shit," she says, jumping to her feet and running to the window.

"What? What is it?" I ask.

"It's quarter after five," she groans, running her hand through her hair. "Shit! I've missed the last bus until 7am, which will be way too late."

Immediately I'm on my feet.

Wait, she's…leaving? We were just getting somewhere.

"What do you mean the last bus?" I ask, approaching her as she frantically paces.

"Shit! I'm fucked!" she snaps angrily.

"Whoa," I say, putting my hands up defensively, alarmed at her tone and sudden frazzled behavior. "Calm down, princess, and use your words."

"Adam," she says irritably. "I'm under house arrest, remember?"

"Yeah, because of Jaxon," I growl, stomaching the bile that instantly fills my guts. "But clearly you're here so…?"

"Because I *snuck* out!" She says, frantically starting to pack up all of her stuff. "It's a long-complicated story, but I actually asked to be under house arrest."

"What?" I say, now completely confused. "What the fuck are you talking about? You asked to be under house arrest?"

She sighs heavily and stops shoving things in her purse to look at me.

"Look, we don't have time for the long version, but the short version is, I was a prisoner at the Pace Household while I was recovering from injuries I sustained in rescuing Ethan," her eyes finding mine briefly. "…And *you.*"

Suddenly memories start flooding back to me. Memories of being drugged, cuffed and beaten and thrown into a cage in a warehouse. There was a gunshot, a lot of yelling, and a fire.

And then I remember being hauled through the flames and shoved into the back of an SUV.

"Wait, Adam?!"

I distinctly remember hearing Rachel's voice as they pulled me into the car.

"You were *there* that night?"

"Yeah, it was a rescue attempt to get Ethan back," Rachel says shortly, pulling out her wallet.

150

I stare at her, completely lost.

"Ugh, okay, look, Michael kidnapped Ethan and was going to kill him. I went and told Natalie, who then told Jaxon. I gave Jaxon this perfect plan on how to rescue Ethan from the warehouse without a big fiasco, but as usual he didn't fucking listen to me or follow my plan. So when they didn't show when I told them to, I was worried Michael would kill Ethan, so I got him out myself and replaced Ethan in Michael's cell with some asshole who groped me in a bar one night."

"What?" This is all I can think to say.

"But then, it all went to shit. They caught you, and brought you to the warehouse. I got Ethan out, but then Jaxon got caught. And we were all about to die, before Jaxon's little fangirl Alpha Squad bros showed up and saved the day."

Rachel clears her throat.

"So, I guess, yeah," she says, awkwardly. "I *was* there when they rescued you too."

All I can do is stare at her.

On one hand, it certainly fills in some of the blanks that I had from that night, but the fact that she was there the night her brother kidnapped me and the story she just told me is so outlandishly ridiculous that I don't know what to say.

"All of that still doesn't explain you saying you asked to be under house arrest."

"Oh, yeah!" She says, chuckling at herself. "Well, anyway, Jaxon was a dick and kind of kidnapped me that night."

"What do you mean, 'kind of kidnapped,'" I say, narrowing my eyes at her, still confused. "Either you were kidnapped, or you weren't."

"Honey, in the Mafia, there's a handful of different ways to kidnap somebody. Sometimes it's a nice kidnapping, or it can be a malicious kidnapping, or it can be just to scare you."

I rub my eyes.

These people are fucking bonkers.

"And what was *this* kidnapping?"

"Of the nicer variety," she shrugs. "He didn't trust me, so he locked me in his bunker for a while. Then when I got really sick from some infection in my arm, I was moved upstairs and then when you arrested him at the opera house—"

"I didn't arrest him," I correct her, crossing my arms across my chest. "I interrogated him."

She stares at me blankly.

"In the FBI," I say, with a playful grin. "We have a bunch of different ways to *interrogate* somebody."

She smiles.

"Well, when you had him at the warehouse, interrogating him, Charlie, Ethan and Natalie came to me, explained the situation, and asked me if I might know where you would've taken him. I took them to that warehouse where we…"

Her voice trails off and she blushes, tucking her hair behind her ear.

I raise an eyebrow at her, but I know exactly what she is eluding too. That was the warehouse I brought her to so we could have some really dirty sex. And we had a very good time.

"Anyways," She says quietly, "after the interrogation, Jaxon told me I wasn't his prisoner anymore, and I was free to go. But since Michael had gone insane and blew up the opera, and might have suspected in my absence that I was working *with* Jaxon, I didn't feel safe being…alone."

I take a deep breath, tapping my finger on the dresser in the room.

"I mean," I say slowly, "You could've come with *me*."

I look up, and see her biting her bottom lip, crossing her arms tightly across her body.

"Yeah, well," she says, swallowing hard. "That was the night we both learned that we'd been lying to each other. And you didn't seem very keen on me at the moment."

I stare at her.

What she doesn't know, and what I can't *let* her know right now, is that nothing could be farther from the truth.

That was the night I learned that she was actually still alive, after fearing the worst. So, seeing her show up with Jaxon's people, had royally pissed me off. I didn't think she was sleeping with him, but a part of me worried if she'd been fucking me, and using me on his orders.

And I really hate that motherfucker.

When she left with them, it sent me into a spiral. A really, really, whiskey-fueled spiral, to a place where I thought everything between us had been a complete lie. And that nothing we had was real.

If I'm honest, I'm still unsure.

There's still at least the possibility that she is working for Jaxon or at least for Michael, and I am getting completely played.

But...some of Rachel's behaviors, and a smattering of things she's said, or accidentally said, have made me at least...*pause.*

She clears her throat.

"Anyway, that's when Jaxon and Natalie came up with the idea to put me up at my parent's mansion, but technically I'm still under house arrest."

"How was that *Jaxon's* decision?"

"Because he owns it," Rachel says, matter-of-factly.

She opens her mouth to say something, but looks at the clock again, and then instantly panics again.

"And I have to get back there."

"What?" I ask, heart rate immediately skyrocketing. "Why? If you *were* a prisoner, but now you're free, why would you choose to go back to being a prisoner?"

"Because I'm safe there, Adam," she says, biting her lip. "Do I want to be free? Yes, of course I do. But I guarantee Michael is looking for me, and if he finds me, he will kill me."

The way her face pales, and the fear that registers in her eyes, makes my stomach twist.

She really is terrified of him.

"Even though it is a prison, at least there I have protection *from* Michael," she whispers, her eyes falling to the floor. "Jaxon's men are standing guard, 24/7 to keep me inside the building."

"And they are clearly doing a fantastic job of it," I murmur under my breath, running my hand through my hair.

She shrugs with a smirk.

Unable to look at her, I lower my eyes to the floor.

"I know things about that house that even Jaxon Pace doesn't. I know how to get in and out without being seen. It's risky, but I..."

Her voice trails off and I look up, finding her staring at me.

"I just had to see you," she whispers, her voice so quiet I barely hear it over the sound of the furnace.

She had to see me.

The thought of her leaving, right now, after all the progress we've made, feels like acid being poured into my veins. I don't want her to leave. At all.

I just got her back.

And then there's the unsettling knowledge of the spiral that will commence the minute she leaves again.

I bite my lip, clearing my throat.

"You could stay," I say quietly, hearing my heart pounding in my ears. "Here, I mean, with me. I could protect you."

Her brown eyes burrow into mine, as if they want me to understand something left unsaid, before they fall to the floor.

"I want to," she says quietly. "I really do."

"But?" I whisper, the familiar pain seeping back in.

"I can't," she says apologetically.

"Of course," I say, trying to swallow my venom.

She has to do what she has to do. I have to understand that.

But I can't deny the disappointing combination of feelings that flood my body.

The panicked fear that something will happen to her, the dark insecurity that all of her *feelings* were just an act, and the ironically painful acceptance that the minute she walks out that door, I am going to be longing for her frustrating presence once again.

But Rachel doesn't need me. She doesn't need anyone.

Except Jaxon Pace's useless bodyguards apparently.

"But," she says quietly, her voice pulling me back from the brink of yet another whiskey-fueled nightmare. "You could come *with* me."

Instantly my eyes find hers.

"What?"

She tucks her hair behind her ear, slowly dragging her bare foot behind her right.

"Come with me," she repeats, looking up at me. "If you do exactly as I tell you, I could sneak us both into the manor, and we could continue…whatever it is we are doing."

She's joking, surely? Or is this an invitation to a trap?

I stare at her, observing all of her behaviors, because after all, that's what I'm trained to do.

The way she looks at me, and then nervously looks away.

The way she fidgets with the string on my sweatpants.

The way she keeps tucking her disobedient curls behind her ear.

No, it's not a joke. She wants me to come with her.

154

And even if it is a trap, if it keeps me by her side, at least I'll know she's safe, because I'll be *with* her.

Everything in my bones tells me that trusting Rachel Valentine is a risk. She is broken, and flawed, just like me. She is dangerous, a fire threatening to rage out of control at any moment.

…And I am her pyromaniac running enthusiastically into the flames.

"I'll need to pack a few things first."

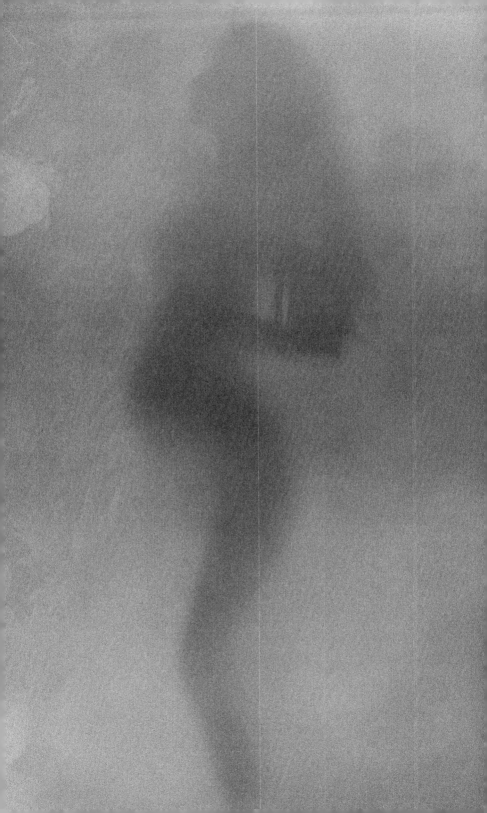

CHAPTER THIRTEEN

Rachel

*H*e's going to come with me.

As embarrassing as it is, my heart is soaring.

"While you're packing," I say gently, sitting down on the edge of the bed. "I suppose I could tell you more of my story. We're kind of at the important part now."

He chuckles to himself.

"I'm all ears…"

"So, tell me why we are lugging groceries for someone else, halfway across the city, when we don't even have food in our apartment?"

"Trust me," Jess smiles.

"Uh huh," I sigh, rolling Mandy whines. "Why can't we take the car?"

"Because cars take gas, and gas costs money," Jessica snaps. "And we have no money, remember?"

"Well, I think we could've sprung for a tank of gas," I snort. "Especially considering the money we earned last—"

But I stop when I see Jessica making a motion with her hand, telling me silently to stop talking, just as we finally reach the steps of a townhouse.

"We're broke, and we have no food left in the house," Jessica says, adjusting the sleeping infant on her chest. "Remember?"

She grabs Mandy's shoulder and glares at her, whispering forcefully.

"And I better not see that cell phone either, missy. Did you leave it at home like I said?"

"Yeah, Mom, God. I left it at home," Mandy fires back angrily, pulling away from her mother.

"And if she asks you anything about your father?"

"I tell her that we still haven't heard from him, and he's a deadbeat who hasn't sent any money."

Jess literally just got his money yesterday. Is she high?

Jessica reaches for her daughter's arm again, but the girl quickly avoids it.

"Mandy, I'm serious!"

"Jess, come on," I sigh, confused why she's being so hard on her daughter. "I think the kid gets it."

"And do not say anything about mommy's friends visiting the apartment."

"That should be easy," I snort, still confused why Jess is acting so bizarre. "You don't have any friends, hoe."

I wink at Mandy, who smiles momentarily but then suddenly looks past me, her eyes lighting up immediately.

"Hey GiGi!"

"My Dandy Mandy!" An elderly woman calls from inside a parka on the front steps of the townhome. "It's been far too long since I've seen you! My, you're getting so big!"

Mandy races up the steps, drops her bags of groceries and instantly wraps her in a hug. Jess and I follow up behind her.

"Sweetheart," Jess coos, faking a smile while addressing her daughter. "Please pick these up before Gram Gram's oranges roll all over the patio."

"Oh, don't worry about it," The woman smiles, cupping Mandy's face one more time before pulling her in for another hug. "They've probably been rolling around in pig shit before they got here! That's why you should always wash your fruit."

Mandy smiles, but does as her mother asks and picks up the oranges, stuffing them back into the plastic bags before heading inside the open door.

"Hi Grams," Jess says, giving the woman a hug. "You remember me telling you about my friend Rachel, right?"

"Why, yes!" The woman smiles. "How are your kids?"

"My *what*?" I ask, confused.

"You're the teacher, aren't you?" The elderly woman says.

"Um," I say looking over at Jess, who nods at me, her eyes wide. "Yes! That's me, alright. The teacher."

"I was a teacher once myself," The woman smiles. "I taught high school kids though, which is much different than teaching kindergarten. I bet you have a lot more fun than I did."

I chuckle, nodding nervously, wanting to kick Jess for apparently forgetting to tell me about the fictional career she seems to have gifted me.

"I'm Doreen," the woman says, extending her hand. "Or you can call me Grams or GiGi, whatever feels right! Please, come inside."

She ushers us inside and closes the door before immediately turning to Jessica.

"I made lasagna, since it's Mandy's favorite, and her birthday was last week. It will be done in a few," she says, reaching for baby Ivy. "Now, you best give me my great grandbaby before I explode!"

Jessica's grandma is quite possibly the nicest woman I've ever met. She kind of reminds me of Mrs. Chen, the elderly Chinese woman who I worked for when I left my family home and came into the city to make it on my own.

…Minus all the drug dealing.

"Jess, do you want some more?" She asks. "You're looking far too skinny these days."

"No, I'm good thank you, Grams," Jess says. "And don't worry, as a waitress I get a free meal while on my shift tonight."

"I'm so proud of you. I know it's hard being a single parent, working, and sneaking in college night classes on top of it?" Doreen sighs, shaking her head. "I don't know how you do it."

"Me either," I say, locking eyes with Jess across the table as I take a sip of my wine.

"It's sad that you don't have any help from…well, *you know*," she says, apparently deciding not to say the word *father* in front of Mandy. "That's just wrong."

Jess purses her lips and bats her eyelashes innocently as she nods in agreement.

It takes everything in my power to keep a straight face. While I can understand Jess not telling her grandma that she's a *stripper*, her over-commitment to these incredibly tall tales she's been telling her grandma, is almost making me nauseous.

In fact, it's *actually* making me nauseous.

Out of nowhere, I suddenly feel like my face gets really hot, and my teeth feel slimy, in that way you feel just before you're about to vomit.

Oh shit…

"Excuse me," I say quietly, "I just need to use the restroom."

I quickly make my way upstairs to Doreen's bathroom on the second floor, far away from the dinner table, and by some miracle I make it to the toilet just in time.

For the next ten minutes I am locked in a miserable dance of vomiting up all of Doreen's delicious lasagna, and flushing, before needing to do it all over again.

Finally, when I can't possibly have anything left in my stomach. I hear a knock at the door.

"Hey Rach, you okay?" Jess asks. "I'm coming in."

"No, I wouldn't—" I start to say, but it's no use, Jess walks in anyway, instantly covering her nose.

"Holy shit, bitch," she gags. "It smells like puke and air freshener!"

"That's because it is puke and air freshener," I say, leaning back against the tub. "I don't know what the hell came over me, but something did not agree with me. Maybe it was the wine."

"Aw, fuck babe," Jess says. "Give me one second, let me find you something to clean up with."

She leaves the room and comes back with a washcloth.

"Here," she says after running it under some cold water. "Put this on your forehead and your neck. It will help."

I do exactly as she says, and it does indeed help a little bit.

"Let me see if my grandma has something for that in here," Jess says as she opens up the medicine cabinet and grabs a big white bottle. "Ah, yes! Here we are."

She grabs a tiny plastic cup, filling it with water before handing it to me.

"Tylenol for you," she says, dumping a tablet into my hand.

I immediately toss it back, hoping to God, I can keep it down for more than five minutes.

"...And a Percocet for me," Jess laughs, yanking an orange prescription bottle from the cabinet. "I swear, old people get the good shit."

"Wait, what?" I ask. "Jess, why are you taking your grandma's medication?"

"Oh, don't get all bent out of shape. I know for a fact she doesn't take them all the time," she says dismissively. "I'm only taking a couple, and besides, it's not as if she can't get more. Docs give them to old people like candy."

She shakes some pills into her hand before screwing the cap back on and putting it back in the cupboard.

"Girl, do I need to be worried about you?" I ask, leaning my head back against the tub.

Jess snorts.

"Says the girl who just threw up a whole dinner my grandma made from scratch," she winks at me.

My stomach gurgles.

"Let's not talk about food," I say, putting the washcloth over my head. "Maybe ever again."

Jess laughs.

"Okay, well, I need you to feel better, and quick. Because Grams just offered to keep the kids for a couple of days, and I am dying for a night out!

"Yeah," I say, reaching for the toilet as another bout of nausea comes over me. "Let me get back to you on that."

161

Unfortunately, my condition didn't improve.

Jess's Grandma was kind enough to drive us home, so we didn't have to brave a city bus, with me having to throw up every ten minutes.

When we got home I made it to the couch, and crashed, hoping that since it was closer to the bathroom, I could get there in time if I needed to.

Thankfully, the sickness gave me a bit of a reprieve, but I woke the next morning with a migraine, feeling absolutely disgusting.

"Up you go hot stuff," she says after I manage to stomach a bit of tea and toast. "You're taking a shower."

"Jess, I—"

But she's determined, literally yanking me off the couch, and pushing me toward the bathroom.

As I start off down the hall, I hear my phone chime.

That *particular* chime that's dedicated to one particular person.

Jaxon Pace.

I turn back, but Jess has already grabbed my phone and is looking at the screen. She looks up at me and raises an eyebrow.

Shit. I knew texting him was a bad idea.

"I'm sorry I've been so distant, and I'm sorry you don't feel well, is there anything I can do for you?" She asks, reading his text aloud.

I walk over to her and take the phone from her hand, my cheeks turning red. I don't know why I feel guilty for texting the man I've been sleeping with for months, but suddenly I do.

"I thought you hadn't heard from him?" Jess asks.

"I hadn't," I say sheepishly. "Not for a few weeks. I thought perhaps a 'I'm sick' pity text might warrant a response."

"Apparently so," Jess says following me down the hall. "So, now what? You're going to just forget about him asking you to stop dancing, and put your life on hold for him again, only so he can disappear for weeks on end doing who knows what?"

"Jess," I snap, yanking a towel out of the closet. "Don't, okay? I'm just really not in the mood."

She bites her bottom lip and crosses her arms.

I roll my eyes and hand her the phone, knowing that it will be quicker to just let her go through my text messages.

"Oh…" she says quietly, as she scrolls back through the

sporadic and cryptic messages from Jaxon.

Messages about how he's apparently been working on a deal with some foreign investors, and some big *test* he was preparing for. But nothing of any real value to *us* or our relationship, which was honestly starting to feel a bit lonely.

"Yeah," I grunt, turning into the bathroom. "So, you can save your lecture."

I turn the hot water on full blast and rest my hands over the sink, staring at my haggard appearance in the mirror.

Slowly, as the cold room fills with hot steam the faint lines of the tic-tac-toe board start to appear on the mirror.

It's an ongoing game I taught Mandy when she was little. She's the X's and I'm the O's. Whenever one of us goes to take a shower, we take turns using a paint brush, soaked with soapy water, to trace the outline of our next move on the board on the mirror. When the next person showers, they let the room fill with steam, look at the board, and make their move.

The game has continued for nearly a decade, and so despite my shitty mood, I still pick up the paint brush and mark my O on the mirror.

"You're still playing that silly game with her?" Jessica says quietly, as she steps into the bathroom. "When will it end?"

"Whenever she stops wanting to play, I suppose," I shrug. "Kids grow up, and all the small silly stuff will lose its novelty. They stop wanting to play with you at some point, so I'm just cherishing the time I have while I have it."

Jessica nods.

"That's cute," she says, looking at the board on the mirror. "You know, you'd make a really good mom someday."

I snort.

"What?"

"Which reminds me," she says, producing a bright pink box from behind her back. "Before you shower, I'm going to need you to take one of these."

My jaw drops.

"A *pregnancy test?!*" I scoff. "What the hell? Why?!"

"Because as the mother of your 'unplanned' game partner, and a bonus kid," she says, opening the box and pushing the plastic stick into my hand. "I know the signs. Trust me."

"What signs?!"

"Your mysterious nausea for one," Jess says, counting on her fingers. "Yesterday wasn't the first time you have thrown up in the last week, Rach."

"That was because we had some Chinese food that didn't agree with me!" I say, laughing.

"Uh huh, a bit suspicious considering I had the same thing as you, and *I* didn't get sick," she says, listing another finger. "And then you've also been super tired lately,"

"I've been pulling double shifts behind the bar since I've not been dancing. You know this!"

"...And your tits are bigger," she says, raising a brow at me. "You were practically spilling out of your favorite top Friday night, you even mentioned it to me."

"I can't believe this!" I say, exasperated.

"...And," Jess says aggressively. "Your cycle is synced with mine, and *you* are late. By over two weeks."

I open my mouth to say something, but I can't.

She's...right.

My period *is* late.

Now that I think about it, I remember thinking it was late at the time, but shortly thereafter I got into a big fight with Jaxon, and he randomly whisked me away to his house in Texas for a week as an apology. And I just forgot.

Sitting down on the edge of the tub, I stare down at the test in my hand, which has now started to shake.

Holy. Shit.

"Just take it," Jess says softly. "It will probably be negative, but speaking from experience, you should at least *know*."

"Jess..." I whisper, absolutely terrified.

She kneels down in front of me and takes my hands in hers.

"Pee on the fucking stick," she says slowly, her voice gentle but firm. "I could be wrong, and you could just be late. But it's better just to have peace of mind, eh?"

I nod slowly.

She opens the package for me, and I do as instructed.

"Now, get in the shower," she commands.

"What? No, I have to wait for—" I start to say, but she spins me around and pushes me toward the tub.

"It will be waiting here, with your *negative* result, when you get out," Jess says encouragingly. "But right now, you're wasting all the hot water. Which as you know is a precious resource around here. Besides, it will definitely make you feel better."

"Finneee," I sigh, quickly stripping off my t-shirt and panties and stepping into the tub.

The moment the steaming hot water on my skin, I feel my body relax.

"So," Jess says, inquisitively, "You guys left off where?"

"Um, with me agreeing to bartend instead of dance," I say, running my hands through my hair.

"Does he at least have an explanation for why he keeps disappearing? Because it seems like he does it *a lot.*"

"Sometimes?" I say, yanking my shampoo bottle off the rack. "I mean this is what frustrates me! He's great when we are together, but then he's so quiet when we're not. And I get his dad is training him to take over as Don Supreme and all, but he's so vague and secretive. It's like his default setting."

"...And then add in the fact that he's slept with half the girls at the club isn't very flattering," Jess says. "I mean, the guy is a total manwhore."

"Very helpful, Jess," I grumble. "Thank you for that."

"Hey now, not trying to upset you," Jess says defensively. "You're a dancer, Rachel. You're a natural. Probably the best I've ever seen. And it's so sad, watching you pour drinks or wait tables when I know that you're better than all of us at the club and happiest up there on that fucking stage."

Turning to face the shower head, I brace myself against the wall, letting the water, and her words wash over me.

Again, Jess is right.

Being with Jaxon might have perks, and he might be an incredible lover and a lot of fun to be around.

But being with him has caused me to sacrifice a part of myself that has drained the joy from my existence. And on some level, I resent him for it.

"Look, Rachel," Jess sighs. "I support whatever makes you happy. And in the beginning, yeah, he made you happy. But now you're almost like a ghost, stuck on some residual loop, just floating from one day to the next. Your happiness is completely dependent on his happiness, or whether or not he decides to suddenly appear back in your life."

"I...I know," I mutter quietly.

"And I know you like him and all, but I think you're sacrificing far too much to be part of his world."

I throw my head back, staring at the condensation droplets on the paint that's peeling off the old ceiling.

"I mean, he's not a bad guy or anything—"

"Well," I chuckle. "He kind of is. He's in the Mafia. And eventually he will be the Don Supreme."

"Right, and do you think the Don Supreme would want his wife, stripping?"

"No," I snort. "But I'm *not* his wife."

"Not yet," Jess argues. "But you have to think this through. If you two stay together, you'll never dance again. This lonely, empty feeling you have right now will never go away. You'll be constantly waiting around for him to give you permission to live. And honestly, that sounds so sad."

Her words are harsh, cutting straight through my bones to unfortunate truths I've been mulling over, and avoiding, for weeks.

"I need to break it off," I whisper, standing under the flowing water.

"Hate to say it, but I really think you do, Babe," Jess agrees. "But, you'll never do if you keep making excuses for him—"

"I'm not making excuses for him!" I snap instantly, only to realize how ironic that sounds. "Let's pretend I said that without yelling."

"Sure thing," Jess snorts sarcastically. "Do you know when you're seeing him again?"

"No, I don't know," I sigh. "He told me the last time we talked that he was going to be busy with this deal with the Russians."

"The Russians?"

"I'm pretty sure it's the same guy who is the boss of those two guys we met at The Garage. You know, Yuri and Boris?"

"You mean, that scary-but-also good-looking guy?"

"Yeah, him," I laugh. "His name is Roman Antonov, I guess he's the Russian Mafia boss who runs New York."

"And that's Jaxon's competition?"

"No, I think it's more like he's a potential business partner."

"Oh," Jess mumbles quietly as I turn off the water. "Well, that's...*interesting*."

I turn off the water, grab my towel from the rack.

166

"You know," I say, my frustration building as I dry myself off. "You're right. You're absolutely fucking right. I've been in denial and I'm delaying the inevitable. Jaxon Pace and I aren't compatible. He needs some pretty little princess to sit at home and obey him, and that's just…not me. And I'm done sacrificing my happiness for someone else's comfort. So, screw him, dude. I'm done!"

By the time I yank back the shower curtain, I am fuming, and ready to call the elusive, cryptic future Don Supreme and tell him I never want to see him again.

But then I see Jess's face, and the two little pink lines on the pregnancy test in her hand and I realize two things at the same time:

I am pregnant.

And Jaxon Pace was here to *stay*.

CHAPTER FOURTEEN

ADAM

If I thought Virginia was cold, it has nothing on Chicago. While the thick lake-effect snow has finally stopped falling outside by the time Rachel and I leave the hotel, the bitter wind is still whipping through the buildings with such force it's hard to pull the passenger door open.

"Damn, Agent Westwood," Rachel says as she walks slowly toward me, trying not to slip on the ice. "You're holding the door? A gentleman still in the face of the elements?"

"Yeah, well, I'm only a gentleman for the next thirty seconds," I say, holding my jacket closed. "Because I'm losing feeling in my hands. So come on princess, hurry up."

"I'm coming, I'm coming," she says, hopping into the car. "And stop calling me princ—"

I slam the door closed, cutting her off and chuckling to myself as I quickly make my way around to the driver's side, tossing my duffle bag in the back seat and climbing in.

I can hear Rachel's teeth chattering over my own, and quickly start the car.

Well, I *try* to start the car, but when the engine still hasn't turned over by the third time, I get a little nervous.

"Oh God," Rachel laughs. "And here I thought we might die trying to drive in the weather, turns out we might just freeze to death in your car."

"Give the ol' girl a second," I say, turning the key again, and this time she fires up. "Aha! See!"

I smack the dash a few times with my hand.

"She hasn't failed me yet."

Rachel chuckles into my hoodie.

But when I go to turn on the wipers, they don't even move, having apparently frozen to the windshield.

"Fuck," I mumble to myself.

"Let me guess, you don't own a scraper, do you?"

"Well, I do," I sigh. "...at my house in Virginia."

"Perfect place to keep it, Agent Westwood," She snorts.

"It's fine. If we just give it a few minutes, it'll melt," I shrug, annoyed that she has a point.

"Yeah, except we don't *have* a few minutes."

Reaching into her purse, Rachel grabs something and then promptly gets out of the car.

"What are you..." I start to ask, stepping out with her. But I watch as she starts using a credit card to start scraping some of the ice off the windshield.

That's actually...brilliant.

"Holy shit," I say, shaking my head as the card removes the ice with ease. "Where did you learn to do that?"

"You'll find us Midwesterners are pretty resourceful," she says, walking over to my side and handing me the card. "But be a gentleman again, and do your own fucking side."

She climbs back inside as I quickly scrap off my half of the windshield as quickly as I can, the biting cold hurting the skin on my hands.

As I pull the door open to climb back inside, I glance down at the card in my hand.

"Here you are," I say, handing it back to her. "*Jessica Erikkson.*"

I stare at her.

"You look disappointed," she grins, putting the card back in her purse. "Don't worry, it's not another alias."

"Uh huh, so I can assume that Jessica doesn't *know* you use her credit card as a makeshift ice-scraper?"

"She doesn't."

"This is probably about the time that I should remind you that credit card theft is—"

"...Not really a problem if the person is *dead*," Rachel interrupts, reaching down and blasting the heat.

"Oh," I say quietly. "I didn't know."

"No, you just assumed."

Well shit. I walked into that one.

The moment that had felt a bit relaxed suddenly feels heavy, lingering in the cold little car.

"Rachel, I'm sorry I—" I start to say but she waves me off.

"It's fine, Adam," Rachel shrugs, seemingly unbothered. "I'm used to people assuming the worst about me."

And now I feel like even more of a dick.

"That's what I mean—"

"Jesus," she mutters, rolling her eyes. "You need to chill the fuck out and stop being so sanctimonious. For the record, it *was* stolen, just not in the way you think."

I stare at her, trying to wrap my head around that sentence.

"We have to get going though, we need to get to the manor while it's still dark out if we have any hope of getting in and it's at least a thirty-minute drive from here in good weather. It's going to take even longer in this sludge, so assume whatever you want, apologize if it makes you feel better, but for the love of God please start driving," she says firmly. "It'll probably be safer to take the interstate west than to take side roads, because those get plowed and salted first."

Without knowing what to say in response, I simply throw the old car into drive, and we slowly pull out of the parking lot.

Rachel Valentine is unlike anyone I've ever met.

She says exactly what she thinks, all the fucking time, and even though it's a bit crude or blunt, it's almost refreshing in a way. Because at least I never have to guess.

Well...sometimes I do.

The first bit of our drive is slow, and silent, the only sound is the sound of my reliable but clunky old car puttering down the mostly empty roads.

"I'm grateful you wanted to come with me," Rachel says quietly. "It at least made me feel like maybe you do like me. At least a little."

I can't explain why, but something about this statement just grinds my gears.

Is this entire thing just a joke to her?

I mean it's not as if she's openly come out and said what she actually *wants* out of this. I've only had bits and pieces of real authenticity from her, at least where her emotions are concerned.

"Tell me what you're thinking." She says. "Because your silence is loud as hell."

"You don't want to know."

"That bad, huh?" She chuckles sarcastically.

No. You know what? We're not going to play this game.

I'm not letting her out of this conversation.

"You really want to know what I'm thinking? I'm sitting here wondering what you want, Rachel," I sigh, shaking my head. "I mean, you haven't told me."

"Ever consider I don't know?"

"No, I think you *do* know, and you just don't want to say," I say a bit sharply. "And so, I'm left with no idea of what you want, or how to make you happy."

"But that's just it—I don't want you to make me happy," she says, throwing her hands up with a laugh. "God, what is this obsession with happiness?"

"What?"

"I mean why does everyone, always, feel the need to be happy all the fucking time?"

"Um, maybe because being miserable is miserable?" I snort, indignantly. "Of course people prefer to be happy, Rachel."

I flip the blinker on and slowly roll the car around a corner.

"...At least normal people, anyway."

She glares at me.

"Well, I'm not normal then."

"Understatement."

She wraps her arms tightly around her body and cocks her head to the side.

"Fine, but then you know what, Agent Westwood? Neither are you."

Her words sting, but not because they are wrong.

"Again, understatement."

"Constant happiness isn't reality."

"I don't disagree with you," I say, with a nod. "I'm just saying most people prefer to be happy as opposed to miserable."

"Yeah, because most people are weak as fuck," she says, glancing out the window. "They can't handle adversity."

"And you can?"

"Is that a real question?" She asks with a laugh.

"No," I say quietly. "I suppose not."

"I've lived my life in a constant state of adversity," she says with a sigh. "Jaxon made some comment to me a while back about how I'm not trustworthy."

I say nothing. I hate agreeing with Jaxon Pace on anything, but I do admit I'm finding it hard to trust Rachel. Especially considering all of the detailed lies she's told me so unapologetically over the last few months.

But then again, so have I. And I need to remember that.

"...And I get why he said it," she continues. "And why maybe you feel the same way."

Fuck.

"He said I only ever look out for myself, and will hang anyone out to dry if I have to."

I swallow hard, wishing I had anything to stay in response but internally battling with my own thoughts.

"But he's looking at isolated incidents where my back was against the wall, and I had no other choice. Yeah, I've had to make some tough decisions that perhaps screwed other people over. But I'm the only one who has ever looked out for me. I don't have people to watch my back or come running to my defense. So how is it fair for him to *put* me in situations where I have to fight for my own survival and then judge me for how I fucking survive it?"

"It's not," I say with a nod.

And I really do agree with her. It's clear she's had a harder life than most, and unfortunately has had to claw her way out of situations.

"And you know, I've had people, that I thought I could trust, fuck me over without so much as a second thought."

A familiar chill traces my bones, and I fiddle with the heater once again, hoping it will finally come back on.

"But," she says softly, rubbing her arms. "The truth is, I *am* actually very trustworthy. When I trust that person in return."

Hearing her say this pricks my heart. I don't know if it's the way she says it, but it sounds so foreign to her. As if trust is a concept that has eluded her.

"We've all had our trust broken before, Rachel," I say softly. "It never feels good. And it never gets easier."

"I never *meant* to lie to you, Adam," she says softly, biting her lower lip. "That's what I meant when I said it wasn't malicious. When we met you seemed like a nice guy, who didn't know anything about my...other life. And I was trying to protect you from that. Because as you've seen, it's pretty brutal."

I turn another corner, my heart starting to race.

"...And then things just evolved between us. I tried to tell you things about me, *true* things about me, but through the alias of someone who wasn't the sister of a psychopathic Mafia boss. Somehow, I thought that...well, that it might be easier for you."

"I know," I whisper quietly, unable to say anything else.

"I do want you to know the truth. All of it. Whatever you want to know."

For some reason, hearing her say this, lifts the burden of my suspicion ever so slightly.

"But I need you to know, before this goes further, that I'm not a *happy* person, Adam. Not usually. Just so that you're not trying to make me happy unsuccessfully. I'm a mess. I'm complicated and difficult, and sometimes I just want to be bad."

With my eyes firmly on the road I try my best to hide my smirk.

Fuck, why does that excite me so much?

"I understand that that might be a difficult concept for you," she says, shifting in her seat. "You know, as an FBI agent and all."

"Depends on how bad you want to be," I reply quietly.

"I don't know."

This time I smile.

"Yes, you do. You just don't know what you can tell *me*."

She is quiet for a minute.

Shit. I may have backed her into that corner.

"Tell me something you've done," I say, trying to sound as encouraging as possible.

"I've done it all," she whispers to herself.

"I guarantee you haven't," I say, shaking my head.

"You don't know me, Adam," she says, a little bite in her

voice. "As you keep so politely reminding me."

Fuck. Why do I already regret saying that to her?

I don't have to use my FBI profiling skills to figure out that my comment to her really hurt her feelings.

"I know you enough."

She laughs, crossing her arms tightly across her body.

"Look, I'm sorry if my comment offended you," I say quietly, without looking up from the road. "About not knowing you. It was—"

"True," Rachel says quietly, looking out the window.

"But we've both lied here," I continue, swallowing hard. "Which means I have some blame here too."

"Now that's an understatement," she mutters quietly.

"And knowing that some of what you told me about your life—"

"Most of it," Rachel says, turning back to look at me. "You know most of it. The only things I lied about were my real name and where I was from. Everything else was true."

She turns back to the window.

"Which is more than I can say for what I've told anyone else."

"Okay," I nod. "Well, that's the same for me. It was just the details that were a little murky."

Rachel snorts but says nothing.

"But my comment to you was unfair, and I'm sorry. Because at the very least, I know you're not your brother," I say quietly. "Otherwise, you'd be working with him, and not against him."

She bites her bottom lip.

"How do you know I'm not?"

I swallow hard, her words catching on a massive fear I have with her.

"Because," I whisper. "You saved Jaxon. And not only him, but you saved his entire team."

I clear my throat.

"…And, well, *me*."

She stares at me, without saying a word, before looking back out the window.

"Which is why," I sigh. "You are trustworthy. And as much as I hate to admit it, because I hate the guy, I assume even Jaxon feels the same way I do. Otherwise, he wouldn't have given you an entire house."

"Well, you haven't seen it. And he gave it to me as a *prison*."

"Trust me, Rachel," I say sarcastically. "I don't have to see it to know there are far worse prisons than some sprawling luxury estate."

She shrugs but says nothing.

"My point is," I continue. "You told me that Jaxon does what he wants, right? Well, if he thought you were just as dangerous as your brother, he wouldn't have hesitated to…"

My voice trails off, the thought strangling me in my chest.

"Don't look now, Agent Westwood," she scoffs to herself. "But you might be starting to respect him."

I laugh out loud.

"Yeah, that's never going to happen," I growl, switching lanes. "But my hatred for Jaxon Pace is a topic for another time. Now tell me why you want to be bad."

"You make it sound like I've gotten a thrill from stealing lipstick from the drug store," she laughs.

"Have you?"

"Yeah, but who hasn't?"

"I mean," I chuckle. "*My* teenage petty theft item of choice wasn't necessarily lipstick, but okay, fair point."

"But that's not really what I was talking about," she says, playing with the string on my sweatpants.

"Then enlighten me."

"I've kind of already said it, Adam. I'm just not a good girl."

"Yeah, you said that when you went on that tirade about how you don't know how to boil water, and you don't like brunch," I say with a smirk. "Which, I don't think makes you a bad person, Rachel."

"But I'm an escort."

"That also doesn't make you a bad person."

"No, I'm not saying *that*," she sighs, frustrated. "You're just not getting it."

"Well, maybe I would if you stopped trying to dress up what you want to say in the way you think I want to hear it?" I snap, now slightly frustrated.

"Okay fine, how about the fact I'm an escort you're a *cop*? How about that, Agent Asshole? Is that clear enough for you?" She suddenly snaps. "I love what I do, and I am not ashamed of it. I don't have a problem with being with you, but since *you* seem to get a hard on reminding me what's illegal, I can only assume *you* have a problem with it."

"Well, I don't, okay? So, you're wrong!" I snap back, my anger rising with hers. "You can let that go."

"No, I fucking can't!" She shouts back at me. "Because several people have said that to me before."

"Said what?"

"That they accepted me for who I was, or that my lifestyle or line of work didn't bother them," she says angrily. "But then at every turn tried to make me into something I'm not, and I'm sick of it!"

"I'm not Jaxon, and I'm not trying to change you!" I shout back at her. "I'm just trying to get to know the real you!"

"Well, here you go! This is who I really am!"

"Rachel, we are two adults having a conversation, in a small car," I growl. "And I'm warning you, I've had just about enough of you shouting and screaming at me."

"Good!" She laughs sarcastically. "Because, this is what I meant by me not being a good girl! Sometimes, I just want to be bad. I wanna steal a credit card, or break into your hotel room, or push all of your buttons or just scream at the top of my lungs because that's how I feel inside!"

She sighs, collapsing back against the seat, as I do my best to just keep my eyes focused on the road ahead, my hand gripping the tattered leather steering wheel.

"I want someone to *feel* all these emotions with me," She sighs, her voice fading off. "But you make me nervous as hell."

"I make *you* nervous?!" I laugh, exasperated.

"Yeah you do. Because you're practically a fucking saint."

"Rachel, I promise you," I snort indignantly. "I'm not."

"Well in my world, you are."

I shake my head, gritting my teeth together.

"But you know what?" She scoffs quietly to herself, biting her lip. "I guess in a way, it kind of makes sense."

"What makes sense?"

"My preferred form of masochism is going for men that I know I'm not compatible with," She laughs at herself. "And thinking that someone as good as you, would want someone as fucked up as me, is laughable. Because you deserve someone good, like you."

From the corner of my eye, I see her pull her legs up to her chest and run her thumb along her bottom lip.

"...Some *princess* of your own," she whispers quietly.

And right there, in my cold shitty car, another piece of the puzzle that is Rachel Valentine's falls into place.

And I finally understand.

"There it is," I say quietly.

"What?"

"What you want to say, but couldn't," I say quietly. "You're terrified of being vulnerable with me."

"Now wait a minute—"

"...And how it could hurt you," I say, cutting her off. "And you know Rachel, I know exactly how you feel."

"No one ever knows how I feel," she says quietly, shifting in her seat.

I smile to myself as I stare at the road.

"I know what it feels like when you've been hurt by people you trust. I know what it's like to fear losing the people you love. And I know what it's like to feel everything so deeply you feel like it's suffocating you, and you wish you could just feel nothing. And that whole tirade you just went on, isn't just hostility or defensiveness, even though you'd really like for me to think it is. It's preemptive *self-sabotage*. Because deep down, you don't actually think you're worthy of being loved. But not just by me, by anyone."

Rachel says nothing. Absolute silence descends over the car and it takes me a few minutes for me to even steal a glance over at her.

She stares out the windshield, playing with the string on my sweatpants.

"You're going to want to get off at the next exit," she finally says quietly. "And yeah, you're right. I *am* scared."

I take a deep breath.

"So am I," I whisper.

"I *have* done really bad things, Adam," she says quietly.

"So have I." I say quietly. "Trust me, Rachel, I've got a few stories of my own, and more than a few skeletons in my closet."

Literally.

I shift uncomfortably, my wife's face coming to mind.

No. Not yet.

178

"Yeah, well, I'm afraid I'm going to share part of who I am, or what I've done, and it's going to be too much for you. Because sometimes, it gets the best of *me*."

Yeah, I know how that feels too.

I grip the steering wheel tightly, shifting in my seat again.

"We've all done things we regret," I say gently. "And we all have to live with the weight of those consequences. But I've found that sometimes, it's about how you balance your ledger."

"What?"

I shake my head.

"I'll tell you another time," I say, pulling off the freeway.

"No," Rachel says defensively. "Explain."

Debating whether or not I should tell her this, I internally throw up my hands and decide why not.

"It's about the balance," I sigh.

"I don't understand."

"My job means that I do a lot of, well, *bad things*, as you said," I say, looking up at her briefly. "I've had to kill people. Bad people, mind you, but they were still people. And that never really leaves you."

"The guilt?"

I nod.

"For a while it was completely debilitating," I say, quietly, remembering, just for a moment the darkness and the countless days I spent isolated in bed, reeling from my first kill in the line of duty. "I tried medications, therapy, but none of that did much for the crippling guilt I felt. The only thing I found that helped a little, was the feeling I got when I *helped* people. When I saved someone, or made a difference in their life. Selfless acts of kindness and sacrifice."

"At the end of the road, turn right," Rachel says. "But continue."

"I started trying to live my life by that *code*, if you will. If I took a life in the line of duty, or hurt someone, or did anything that weighed negatively on my conscience, I would make sure to lighten it by doing something *good*."

"You balanced the scales," she says, shifting to face me.

"Exactly," I nod. "And it's allowed me to sleep at night."

She settles back against the seat, silence enveloping the car.

"What if you've done something, really, really bad?" she asks

179

quietly. "Or, maybe you helped someone else do something bad. Something…unforgivable?"

"Nothing is unforgivable. You just might have to really work at it, and do a lot to make up for it," I shrug.

"But what if the person you did it to," she whispers, looking down at her hands. "Refuses to forgive you for it?"

I glance over at her, seeing her pained face looking out the window.

Suddenly I'm reminded of what Jaxon told me, about Michael kidnapping his wife, Natalie.

I wonder if that's what she's referring to?

Instinctively I pick up on her tight body language, the way she chews on her lip and the way she's fidgeting with the string. She's edgy and uncomfortable, telling me that whatever she's thinking about, clearly bothers her. Deeply.

My own body tenses just thinking about that asshole, Jaxon Pace, and the idea that Rachel could be talking about him. I debate saying anything at all, because fuck that guy.

And yet…

I suppose it would be significantly hypocritical of me to be sitting here talking about redemption, forgiveness, and 'doing the right thing,' and let some rich dickhead make me act selfish and get the better of *me*.

Fucking hell.

"Again, all you can do is try to make it right by doing what's right," I say, swallowing my own unflattering thoughts of Mr. Pace. "As long as you do all you can do, and you know that, then peace will follow."

She stares at me before nodding slowly and glancing out the window again.

I clear my throat.

"From my experience, when it comes to remorse and regret, our actions define who you are, and the peace you will have or the burden you will carry," I continue softly. "If you've apologized sincerely, and done all you can do, and if he refuses to forgive you, then you have done all you can do. Then it's on him, and it's *his* own burden to carry. He will have to live with the fact that he refused forgiveness."

She immediately turns to look at me.

"He?" she asks, her eyes wide. "Who is he?"

"No one," I say with a smile. "Just a figure of speech."

"Oh, you're going to want to turn left at the light," she says. "We're almost there."

"Good," I say, suddenly pulling the car over on the side of the street.

"Wha…what are you doing?" She asks, sitting up, confused.

I put the car in park, but leave it running. Turning to face her I put my hand on the back of her seat.

"Rachel," I say quietly, doing my best to appear calm while my heart pounds in my chest. "I need you to *tell* me what you want from this. Truly."

"What do you mean?" She asks, her eyes wide.

"You know exactly what I mean," I say, my tone firm. "How far are we taking this, and why?"

"Adam," she laughs nervously. "I don't know what you—"

"No, Rachel," I say, cutting her off. "Don't be coy. Not this time. Not right now. Before I go any further, I need you to tell me what you really want…from *me*. And just know that if you lie to me, I will know."

She smiles and opens her mouth to say something, but upon seeing the serious look in my eye, decides against it. She stares at me for a minute, before taking a deep breath.

"I want you to come with me," she says slowly.

"Why?"

"Because I want to continue this conversation."

"But *why*, Rachel?"

"Because I want the truth," she fires back, her face now serious too. "Which, as I understand, is exactly what you want from me, is it not? To know if whatever this is…is real?"

It takes everything in my power to maintain my stoic face, because hearing her say this, out loud, is everything I was selfishly hoping she'd say.

I notice the way her leg is bouncing, and the nervous way she wrings her hands.

She's being honest.

"Well?" She asks, reminding me that I haven't responded.

I swallow hard and nod.

"Yes, Rachel," I say quietly. "I do want the truth. All of it."

My eyes fall from hers for a moment, and I sigh deeply.

"Because even if this doesn't end up working out, or if I can't give you what you want, at least you'll know you got all of my honesty. And hopefully that will be enough."

She smiles gently, and for a moment, my composure falters. I suddenly find myself lost in the beauty that is Rachel Valentine.

Even here, in my oversized pants and sweater, she looks like a goddess. Her long dark hair, still slightly messy, and its natural curls, the result of me not having a hair dryer at the hotel, frame her face perfectly. Her flawless porcelain skin is dotted only by the small beauty mark below her lip, and the soft dimples in her cheeks, that appear at the slightest of smirks.

But what has always been my weakness, are her *eyes*. Dark brown with flecks of gold and amber, they pull me under her spell every time and it takes all of my self-control to regain my composure.

So, when she reaches over and places her hand on mine, it nearly pushes me over the edge completely.

"Look, Adam," she says softly. "I don't need you to promise me anything right now. The only thing I really want from you is the grace to feel like a human being. One who is allowed to be messy and chaotic sometimes."

Her eyes close for a moment, and she sighs, shaking her head.

"I'm working through a lot on my own too, and if anything, I'm just sick of feeling like I'm some empty specter that hovers at the edge of my own existence. I want to feel. And I want to feel Everything."

Her words stun me, and for a minute I am speechless.

For perhaps the very first time, Rachel is not only being honest with me, but also vulnerable.

…And isn't screaming about it.

"Left at the light, you said?"

"Pull in that driveway," Rachel says, pointing.

"Wait what?" I ask, placing my foot on the break and staring at her. "I thought you said we needed to *sneak* into this place? Now you're telling me to just pull up the driveway?"

"We are, but not at my house," she grins. "It's easier to get on the property from next door, as there's only a big tree line. And I doubt you want to sneak up the driveway from the road in this cold, considering it's like an eighth of a mile long."

"Oh…"

"Also, your car would definitely get towed."

"Why?!"

"Because you're in *Snobsville* now Adam," she snorts. "And I'm sorry but your car is an eyesore. The neighborhood watch wouldn't even hesitate."

"Some people just can't appreciate good taste in motor vehicles," I joke.

She chuckles softly.

"What's your plan for that?" I say, pointing at the eight-foot rod-iron gate that blocks the path.

But before I can even look over at Rachel, she's jumped out of the car and is punching in numbers on the keypad.

"Okay, that's impressive," I nod as she hops back in the car, rubbing her cold hands together. "But considering it's just past five a.m., aren't these rich old farts going to notice people coming up the driveway?"

"Relax," Rachel says, rolling her eyes. "No one has lived here in like eight years."

"Bad housing market?" I ask, as we approach the gigantic, darkened house. "No one wants to buy an old, dilapidated mansion?"

"More like the fact that six people were murdered here."

"*What?*"

"Irish Mafia family. Descendants of the same family who helped the cartel kill my father." Rachel shrugs, pointing towards the garage. "Pull the car up to that door, you can park it in there for now. I know that one is empty, and there's a window where we can watch the Pace Patrol."

"I don't…I mean…" I say, throwing the car in park and feeling a bit shocked that she could say it so cavalierly. "What family? What murder?"

"*Murders*. As in plural. And you'll probably need to lift the door," she says. "It's too heavy for me. Try not to make too much noise though, the property line isn't that far from the Valentine Manor, and Jaxon's men will get suspicious if you start randomly banging shit around, as they know this old house is vacant."

I stare at her for a second, unable to comprehend all the information she just sputtered off at me.

Instead, I get out and jimmy the garage door open, trying to make as little noise as possible. The inside is dark, with the exception of moonlight filtering through a window on the back wall opposite us.

"Alright, now what?" I ask, getting back in the car.

"Well, since there's going to be a changing of my guard soon, I figure we can just hang out here for a minute, in the heat, until they're finished. Then we'll sneak in along the tree line while they're distracted."

Rachel says, settling in against the seat.

"And while we wait, you'll tell me about the Irish family that was murdered here?"

"No."

"What? Why not?"

"Because it's *boring*," Rachel says, rolling her eyes. "They were bad people. They got what was coming to them. Blah blah blah. No one cares. The End."

I can't help but laugh,

"Forgive me, but I find the description of *bad people* mildly ironic coming from a mafia princess."

"I am not a Mafia princess!" She snaps at me. "Basically they wanted in the mafia, the Pace's told them no. So they joined up with the cartel. They bought this house, and befriended my dumbass alcoholic dad, and when he least expected, allowed the cartel access to the property."

"Jesus," I breathe. "So they were responsible for what—"

"Happened to Michael. Yes," Rachel says, rolling her eyes. "But when the Pace Family found out, they slaughtered them all. Mercilessly. The end. Are you happy now?"

"Well, *happy* is the wrong word..."

"Anyway," she sighs, folding her arms across her chest. "I thought you cared about *my* story, not the story of some shitbag family that used to live next door?"

Sensing this is certainly a soft spot, I throw my hands up defensively.

"Fair enough, Miss Valentine," I say apologetically. "By all means, continue..."

CHAPTER FIFTEEN

Rachel

I don't remember much of the afternoon after I found out I was pregnant.

I know there was a lot of screaming. A lot of panicking. And a lot of tears. Once I had calmed down enough to at least stop hyperventilating, Jessica wrapped me in a blanket, gave me some more tea, and gently discussed my options.

But there wasn't much *to* discuss.

Those two pink lines meant that I was carrying the *heir* of a Mafia Don. And not just *any* Don. The heir of the future Don Supreme…the future head of our entire syndicate.

And, thanks to my mother, I knew better than most that there was *only* one way this was going to go.

I *was* having this baby.

I'd be lying if I said a tiny part of me, in the back of my brain, didn't at least consider going down to that *clinic* the girls at the club talked about.

Perhaps to some that might seem heartless, but at that point I was more concerned with uncomplicating an immediately complicated situation. The one with the depressing scenario Jess described, where my life would be permanently yoked to the orbit of Jaxon Pace.

So on some level, the idea of being *not*-pregnant at the end of a simple appointment, was attractive.

But in the end…I couldn't.

And surprisingly it wasn't because of Jaxon. And it wasn't because I was religious or saintly. I didn't feel guilty, because I learned a long time ago to shut off all those pesky emotions. I was responsible for myself, and to myself, and I always had to prioritize my needs above everything and everyone else. Because no one else would.

I decided to keep my baby, because…I *wanted* to.

Now I had someone to prioritize. Someone I *was* responsible for. And even though I had not met them yet, it didn't matter. I still cared, immediately, and more than I ever thought I could.

After I had made my decision, Jess and I had another good cry, and like a true friend, she vowed to help me as much as she could. We then set about deciding how I should *tell* the future Don Supreme that I was carrying his baby.

But I knew I needed to tell him in person.

So, after a few text messages, and a phone call to a mutual friend of Eamon's, Jess was able to find out that Jaxon Pace was going to be at The Garage that night.

So that's where we went too.

And even though I might now be a knocked-up Mafia baby mama, I went all out. I got my favorite metallic sequined dress, and heels that lace up my calves. I wanted Jaxon Pace to know that I was going to have his baby, but he *wasn't* going to take my spirit and put it on a trophy in his mansion.

And even though I had been sicker than a dog earlier that day, I was feeling like a million dollars the moment we stepped through that door.

"Let's get a drink" Jess says as we step up to the bar. "We can have a scan around the room, see where everyone is. I'll have a gin and tonic and what do you want?"

"You forget," I laugh, pointing to my stomach. "Pregnant, remember?"

"Oh yeah, shit," Jess says, smacking her forehead. "Gin and tonic for me and cranberry water for her."

I glance up to the VIP loft, seeing it packed to the brim with giant bodyguard-looking dudes.

"You said he's here?" I ask Jess, unable to see the tables or lounge chairs over the tops of the giant men.

"Tyler said they all would be here," Jess says, scanning the crowd.

"Wait, Jess," I say nervously, grabbing her arm. "What if Tyler said something to Eamon or Jaxon. Like what if he warned them and they decided to go somewhere else?"

Jess grins wickedly.

"I swore to him to secrecy on the *blackmail box*," she winks at me, before leaning back against the bar and taking another covert look around the room. "So, unless he wants the pictures I have of him high out of his mind and spraying his load everywhere, leaked out into the world, he wouldn't have said shit to anyone."

Suddenly she turns back around quickly.

"Fuck," she whispers, grabbing her drink off the bar. "I just spotted Eamon, and I think he's coming over here."

She nudges me playfully and leans in to whisper in my ear.

"Pretend to be saying something really funny to me."

"What?"

"Ha ha ha!" Jess laughs, grabbing my shoulder and taking a sip of her drink. "That's so funny, Rach!"

"Jesus Christ," I roll my eyes, taking a sip of my disappointing cran-water.

"Jess? Is that you?" Eamon's deep voice comes from behind us and we both turn around to face him. "Holy shit! It is!"

"Oh my God," Jess purrs, "Eamon, what are you doing here?"

"Ty and I came here with Jaxon," Eamon says, kissing her cheek. "But he's fucked off playing poker upstairs with that Russian guy and Ty's off hitting the slopes in the bathroom, if you know what I mean."

His eyes slowly scan Jess's body up and down.

"Wow, you look great, babe."

His eyes find mine and canvas my body just the same.

"You *both* look great."

Ew. No thank you.

Trying to hide my cringe, I smile politely, and turn to look at the loft again. But my stomach twists when I see a group of six young girls, wearing the smallest scraps of fabric, being let into the VIP elevator.

They must've been invited.

"You should've told me you were coming out tonight, and maybe we could have come together," Jess grins, running her hand up his chest before leaning into his ear. "Maybe we still can."

Oh God, why do I feel immediately nauseous again?

Eamon laughs nervously.

"Heh, I'm sorry babe," he says, running his hand over his greasy head. "I had no idea you'd be free tonight, otherwise I wouldn't have—"

"There you are!" Suddenly another female voice appears beside us, wrapping herself around Eamon. "I came back from the bathroom, and I couldn't find you on the—"

But then she stops, and her face goes white.

"Maggie?" Jess says, her tone instantly cold. "What are *you* doing here?"

She glares at Eamon, and then at Maggie, all four of us already knowing the answer to that question.

Maggie swallows hard and shifts uncomfortably, stepping slightly behind Eamon.

Out of the corner of my eye I see the elevator door open to the loft, and the giggling girls being let into the VIP area.

"Eamon," I say, sensing that this evening is likely going to disintegrate quickly, and not wanting to leave without telling Jaxon what I came here specifically to say. "You said Jaxon was upstairs?"

He nods, looking nervously between a furious Jessica and a very uncomfortable looking Maggie.

"Jess, are you—"

"Go talk to Jaxon, babe," Jess says sweetly, while glaring icily at Maggie. "You probably won't want to see this anyway."

Not needing to be told twice, I set my drink down and grab my purse. As I cross the dance floor, I see the two giant bouncers stationed outside the elevator door. Realizing I don't have Jessica's *inside connection* like last time, I have to find a way up there on my own.

But I've always been good at getting men to do what I want.

Quickly I hike my dress up a little and plaster my most innocent smile on my face as I pull out my phone and send myself a text message. Once it chimes through, I pretend to bury myself in my phone and head straight for the elevator.

I am stopped when a gigantic bouncer bicep blocks my path.
…But I was expecting this.

"Whoa there sweet thing," the man says firmly. "I know you're a bit distracted there, but this elevator is just for VIP."

"Hiya, Sugar," I giggle. "I know, I was meeting some friends here, but I think they already went up without me."

He pulls up his clipboard.

"What was the name under?"

I giggle again.

"Well, I actually don't know."

"You don't know?" He asks, looking at me suspiciously. "I thought you said they were your friends?"

"Well technically they are my *coworkers*," I say, winking at him. "I've never met them before. See our *agency* sent us over. At the request of Mr. Roman Antonov."

I hold up my phone showing him the text I just sent myself, with the address and instructions of what to wear.

"Oh, I see, so you work for one of those escor—"

"*Companionship* businesses, Sugar," I say, batting my lashes at him, and touching his giant arm gently. "We don't say the other word anymore."

I press my finger to my lips and wink at him.

"Oh right of course," he chuckles, pressing the button for the elevator. "Go right on up, miss."

"Thank you so much."

And within seconds I am alone and on my way up in the VIP elevator feeling pretty fucking sure of myself.

When I step onto the floor, I am met with a dozen intimidating men, all standing around casually. I hear their whispered little compliments and crude comments as I walk past, ignoring them.

There does seem to be a lot of men here…

And when I come around the corner I can see why.

In the back section of the VIP area, there sits an even more exclusive section with an elevated poker table. A handful of well-dressed men sit, including Mr. Roman Antonov and my baby-daddy, Jaxon Pace. The man I came to see.

But the moment I see him, my heart sinks through the floor.

Because standing directly behind him, running her hand down his chest, is a gorgeous blonde in a skimpy black dress and bright red lipstick.

191

Whatever power I felt walking in this club, or stepping off that elevator, evaporates in seconds.

And when I watch her wrap her arms around his neck, and whisper something in his ear, making him smile, I feel like I have just been hit in the stomach with a baseball bat.

He's here...with a girl.

I don't know how long I stood there and stared at him, but when one of the other men seated at the table smashes his hands down angrily on the green felt, I am finally shaken from my trance.

I need to get out of here. Immediately.

Quickly I turn on my heel and head straight into the VIP bathrooms, which are thankfully empty. I slip into one of the stalls and have to steady myself against the wall as my heart starts pounding in my chest.

My fear was correct. Everyone was correct.

Jaxon *is* seeing someone else.

I pull out my phone to text Jessica, but when my shaking hands go to send the text, I realize I have absolutely no service.

Fuck!

I lean back against the wall, closing my eyes, but the images of this beautiful woman with her hands all over Jaxon play behind my eyes. I want to cry. Or scream. Or both.

But I can't do it here.

No, I need to be as far away from this club as I can possibly be before I allow myself to cry. So, gathering my courage, I walk out of the bathroom and straight back onto the elevator.

Shit what if the bouncer questions me?!

I pull out my phone, intending on faking an important phone call. But when the elevator doors open, I find no bouncers. In fact, I find no one.

Instead, there is some sort of a commotion happening over by the bar and on closer inspection I realize that that commotion is Jessica...fighting with Maggie!

What the actual fuck is going on?!

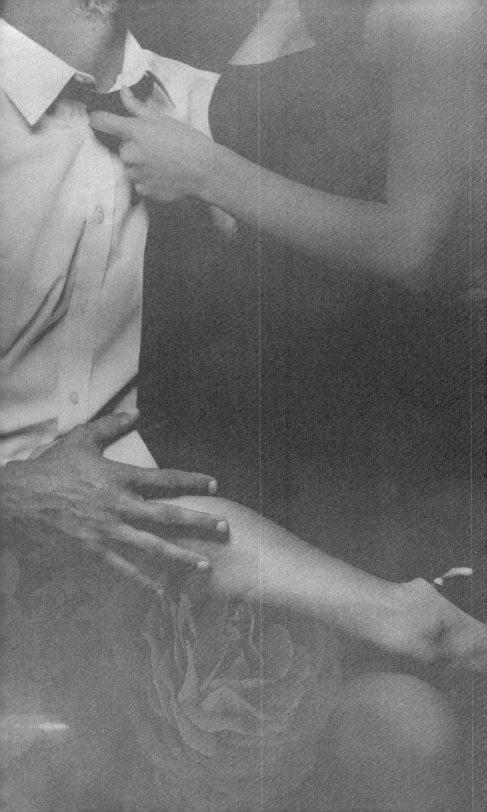

CHAPTER SIXTEEN

ADAM

Sneaking into the Valentine Estate was actually easier than I thought it would be.

After waiting for the guard change, Rachel and I make our way along the relatively dense tree line that separates the two properties. Backing up to the trees, in the far-right corner, sits a little alcove of tall thick hedges surrounding a small reflective pool and the family's century-old mausoleum.

A very thin door, hidden from sight by the hedge, allows us access to the back of the marble building.

While it looks as if the mausoleum was meticulously maintained for decades, it appears to have recently fallen into a state of neglect. The wicks of the dozens of dusty candles have all but disintegrated, and the sound of crunching leaves and dead insects under our feet echoes loudly in the cold room.

"Looks like this place could use a good sweep," I say, setting my duffle bag on the floor and quietly closing the door behind me.

"Why?" Rachel asks sarcastically, pulling a flashlight from under a moth-eaten velvet altar cloth. "It's not as if the dead give a shit. Most of them were asses in life, now they're all ashes in death."

"That is how the old saying goes, isn't it?" I say, brushing a giant cobweb out of the way. "*Asses to ashes*."

"Shh, do you hear that?" She suddenly says, putting her hand to her ear, trying to listen.

"Hear what?"

Instinctively I pull my gun, moving quickly to the small window in the stone tomb and scanning for any movement.

"That's the sound of all my dead ancestors," Rachel winks at me. "*Not* laughing."

Wow…You walked right into that, Adam. Dumbass.

"Gotcha," Rachel says, clicking her tongue.

I roll my eyes, pursing my lips together as she chuckles quietly to herself, flicking on the flashlight.

"Good one," I say sarcastically. "I'm sure your relatives are positively rolling over in their graves."

"That would be quite a feat, considering we cremate all of our dead," she says, slapping her hand against one of the names carved in stone on the wall.

"Cremation, huh? Thought for sure you guys would go with the whole decapitation route," I say, pointing to the large-than-life statue of St. Valentine erected in the middle of the floor. "You know, in honor of your patron saint. Lack of a head would at least make for smaller caskets."

"Well, you should see how small they get when you fry the fuckers," Rachel grins. "Takes up way less real estate."

"While I'm not shitting on your family home," I say, looking around. "I doubt Jaxon is so much of a sadist as to put you up in here. So it feels like I'm missing something."

"That's alright, most men are usually pretty *clueless*," Rachel winks at me, walking up to the giant statue. "Do watch your feet, Agent Westwood."

She pushes a gem on one of the statue's rings and to my amazement, the large marble tile I'm standing on starts to lower into the ground. I hop off quickly as it drops a few inches below the surface, and then starts to slide underneath the tile next to it revealing a staircase.

…And an entrance to a *tunnel*.

"Okay, now that's just cool," I say, throwing my hands up defensively. "I can't even think of anything funny to say to that."

Rachel smirks before starting down the stairs.

"Before his dissent into his crippling alcohol addiction, my father was once a good friend of Dimitris and Ismena Pace. One day Dimitris gave him a rare gift: a tour of the underground tunnel system at Pace Manor. "

"Pace as in, *Jaxon Pace*?"

"The one and only," Rachel nods.

Yeah, the one and only dickhead.

"My father was so impressed by what he saw, and after considering how convenient a secret tunnel would be if he ever needed a quick exit, he decided he needed one of his own," Rachel says, as I climb down into the tunnel with her.

"I take it that even though he was *in* the Mafia, your father was still paranoid about getting murdered by the Mafia?"

"Honey, in the Mafia, you're always worried about getting murdered by the Mafia," she winks at me. "But no, he was more worried about the *feds*."

"Bet he would have *loved* one coming up into his secret tunnel," but when I dust the dirt off my pants I hear Rachel snort, and start to giggle, and it's then that I realize what I just said.

"Whoops," I chuckle. "I didn't mean it like…"

"Now *that* was funny," she laughs, and I join in with her.

Pressing a button on the wall the tile slowly and silently slides back in place. We are instantly plunged into darkness.

Rachel turns on her flashlight and uses it to find a light switch on the wall. She flicks it on, and there is a soft buzzing sound, however, nothing happens.

"I mean, I'm not ragging on the secret escape tunnel, but this seems like a bit of a design flaw."

"Just give it a second," Rachel whispers in the dark.

And sure enough, after a few more seconds a dull fluorescent bulb flicks on above us, then another one about ten feet in front of us, and another in front of that, illuminating the long concrete tunnel stretching into the distance.

"The lights will only work if the tunnel entrance is completely sealed and locked from the inside. That way if you're hiding inside, you don't have to worry about light seeping through the cracks and giving away your position. Also so that you know from the other side if the other entrance is open already."

"Why?"

"Well, in case someone is waiting for you," Rachel replies. "It's set up so you'd see light at the end of the tunnel, or flashlight, or hear the sound of someone moving in the dark. It's meant so that no one can surprise you."

Smart, actually.

We continue quietly down the long concrete tunnel to the other side. When we reach the end, she repeats the process of shutting off the lights, disengaging the lock and turning on her flashlight. Using the beam, she finds the handle on a large wooden door and slowly pushes it open.

As it swings open, I realize that this is not *just* a door, but instead a large painting on hinges. We step into what appears to be a small library or study, with floor to ceiling bookcases, a large desk sitting in the corner, and a baby grand piano.

"That's impressive," I say, as Rachel closes the painting door behind us.

"It's not real."

"What?"

"The painting," Rachel says, pointing at the frame. "It's not an original, obviously. It's far too big."

"Oh, I was actually talking about the secret tunnel," I say, pointing to the painting. "But the painting is nice too."

"If you say so," Rachel shrugs. "My grandfather had it commissioned by some impressionist artist in Florence. Apparently, it's a replica of—"

"Twelve Sunflowers in a Vase," I say, finishing for her. "By Vincent Van Gogh."

I look up to find her staring at me.

"My mother took me to an exhibit one time when it came by the capital. She loved Van Gogh."

Rachel says nothing, but she stares at me.

The hairs on the back of my neck stand up, as I notice the sad look that suddenly blankets her face. However, even with my instincts, it's hard to determine why.

Perhaps she feels bad for me, knowing about my mother. But then again, maybe it's because she never *had* experiences like that, given the fact that her mother left when she was little, and her father was a piece of shit. I sincerely doubt that awful man ever did anything like that with his daughter.

And now suddenly I feel bad for *her*.

She sighs deeply.

"Do you want a tour?" she says, looking up at me. "Or can it wait til the morning? I don't know about you, but I'm wiped."

I smirk.

Of course she'd say that.

For Rachel, slipping past half a dozen armed bodyguards and sneaking into the Valentine Estate via a secret tunnel is nothing but a regular Tuesday. Meanwhile my adrenaline is still coursing through my veins, and my heart's still pounding.

"The tour can wait," I say, nodding to the couch in the study. "Where are we sleeping? Because that couch over there that looks like it will only fit one of us, and it also looks pretty uncomfy."

Rachel bites her bottom lip before tucking her hair behind her ear.

"Well, I mean you're welcome to sleep in here if you like. Might be dusty though."

She looks away from me, and then I understand:

Rachel wants me to sleep with her but doesn't want to say it.

I assume because actually *asking* me for something will make her feel vulnerable if I say no. And I'm learning, quickly, that the one thing Rachel Valentine hates more than anything else in the world is vulnerability.

I smirk to myself.

For a girl that has no problem speaking her mind and acts so tough and disenfranchised when it comes to typical human emotions, it's kind of ironic how uncomfortable she feels when she actually wants something.

It's also kinda cute, though.

However, she did buck up and *ask* me to come with her tonight. And she also asked me to be patient with her. Which is something I am trying to do.

I set my bag on the ground, and without another word, I walk toward her and gently cup her face in my hand.

She nearly destroys me when she looks up at me with her big brown eyes. My thumb brushes her cheek as I lean in and kiss her slowly, taking care to be gentle and tender, instead of shoving my tongue down her throat like usual.

"I said," I whisper against her lips. "Where are *we* sleeping?"

Immediately I see her eyes light up, and feel her heart start racing beneath my fingertips, gently brushing her neck.

"Upstairs," she says quietly, her voice trembling.

I nod, winking at her softly.

"Lead the way, Miss Valentine" I say, kissing her again.

I slowly pull away and I can see the soft blush settling on her cheeks. She clears her throat and turns for the door. Grabbing my bag off the floor I follow after her.

"Do we need to lock up or anything?" I ask as I step into the massive marble foyer.

"I guess you can if it makes you feel better," Rachel shrugs, starting up the stairs.

"What?" I ask, confused.

"You have your gun right, Agent Westwood?" She says, stopping briefly, her hand on the banister.

"Um…yes?"

"Well, Jaxon's men have theirs," she sighs, tilting to the side. "They also have a key to the house. The one benefit to being under house arrest is that no one really wants to get in, they only really want to get *out*."

The simple truth in her statement stuns me, but I continue after her. Convinced that for every mystery I unlock to Rachel Valentine, there's probably a hundred left to discover.

CHAPTER SEVENTEEN

Rachel

My head is pounding and my phone is ringing. But the sun is blasting through the window, directly into my eyeballs, so I have to cover my face just to look at the screen.

A random 312 area code? What the hell?

I don't usually answer calls I don't recognize, and just let them go to voicemail. However, something in my gut prompts me to answer this call.

And it's a good thing I do.

"Holy shit, Rach," Jess says frantically on the other end of the line. "Thank God! I was worried you wouldn't answer!"

"Jess?" I ask, sleepily. "Why are you calling me from an unknown number? Where are you?"

"I'm downtown," she says, her voice trembling. "At the State Street Central *Jail*."

"You're in *jail*?!" I ask sitting up in bed.

"Who's in jail?"

A deep man's voice says suddenly next to me, and I scream,

nearly falling out of bed when I look over and see Yuri laying in bed next to me.

"Um, ow," Jess says, a bit annoyed. "Thanks for breaking my eardrum. But, yeah, I thought you knew that?"

What the hell is Yuri doing here?!

My jaw is hanging open as I stare at the very sleepy, and very naked Russian man currently rubbing his eyes next to me.

"I mean, the whole club saw me beat..." she pauses. "Well, let's just say it was a bit of a spectacle. I guess I just assumed you saw it too."

Spectacle is the right fucking word!

"No, I didn't," I ramble off, staring at Yuri.

Shit. Shit. Shit.

As I scramble out of bed and realize that I too am completely naked.

Oh God...that means we definitely fucked.

"Are you...Are you okay?" I ask Jess.

"No, Rach," Jess snaps. "I'm in fucking jail. And I'm kind of in a bit of a situation here, okay? I only get one non-collect call, and you're it, so I need you to wake up and actually fucking help me here!"

Shit. She's right.

Despite my utter shock at everything in my life right now, I somehow remind myself that Jess is in a far worse position than I am at the moment, and she needs me. Yuri and everything else can wait. It has to.

"I'm here, I'm here," I yank my robe from the pile of clean clothes I never put away and throw it over my shoulders. "What can I do? What do you need?"

"It doesn't sound like I am going to get arraigned until Monday morning at the earliest," Jess says with a sigh. "But when I am, I need bail money."

"Should I call your grand—"

"Absolutely not," Jess says firmly. "In fact, I need you to buy me some time with the kids. So, call her tomorrow afternoon, and tell her that I came down with whatever stomach bug you had and ask her if she will keep the kids a few more days. Just in case I don't get seen on Monday. But I need you to promise me that you will not tell her anything about this. Promise me, Rach."

"I promise!" I say, walking into the kitchen.

"And then I need you to call Eamon."

"What?!" I gasp. "You're joking right? I mean isn't he the reason you're in there in the first place?"

"Which is exactly *why* he should be motivated to help me," Jess says confidently. "And, after all, he still owes me, anyway."

"I don't know about that—"

"Rachel!" Jess snaps. "I don't have a lot of time. His number should be in my bedroom, in *The Box*."

She means her Blackmail Box.

"If that doesn't work then maybe—" suddenly Jess cuts out.

"Jess? Jess?" I ask, but the loud dial tone tells me that Jess's one phone call is over.

Holy. Fucking. Hell.

I sit down on the couch, in our empty living room, and force myself to start processing all of the ridiculous information that was just thrust into my face all before nine am.

Last night, I went to a club to tell a Mafia Don I am pregnant with his baby but chickened out when I saw him with another woman.

My best friend ended up in jail for fighting over some douchebag guy, only to call me this morning and say she needs me to call and guilt that douchebag guy into posting her bail money.

All while some naked Russian random fuckboy I apparently hooked up with last night snores loudly from my bedroom.

Jess and I are officially the steamiest shit show on earth.

But I can't dwell on that because Jess needs me. So, after double checking the naked Russian is still sleeping, I make my way across the hall to Jess's room.

Quietly pulling back her bed, I am able to locate the loose floorboard under which she keeps her famous Blackmail Box. I pull it out and dump its entire contents on the bed.

A repository of everything Jess might potentially have use for at some point or another comes tumbling out. Pictures, letters, receipts, and polaroid's, each labeled with a name, number, address, and date, and each one more graphic than the next.

Eventually I find Eamon's name and contact info, along with several photos of him doing cocaine…with *Jaxon*.

My heart stops at the sight of him.

The man I've been involved with for the last few months, who is also the father of the unborn child in my womb. And suddenly I feel incredibly nervous.

Is this really the man I want to have a baby with?

As far as entitled, spoiled, selfish rich kids go, Jaxon Pace is certainly not the worst of the worst. And not nearly as sexist, or generally awful as Eamon West is. But at the same time, could he grow up and get his shit together enough to be a father? And further still, could he do all that maturing in *nine months*?

I am terrified of doing this by myself, but perhaps it's an option I have to consider. Because there is also the knowledge that the sex of our child could further complicate things for me.

If I have this baby with Jaxon, and it turns out to be a girl, she would be treasured, adored, and spoiled.

However, if it's a boy, everything would be different.

A boy born to the Don Supreme would become the *heir apparent*. He would begin training to fight from the moment he takes his first steps, and be expected to follow in his father's footsteps, to one day take over the Pace Family Mafia.

The thought of anything happening to my sweet, innocent, baby makes my entire body tense, and my heart starts to race erratically as a dark thought creeps in.

Maybe deciding not to tell him last night...was a blessing.

Because if I don't tell him, I never have to worry about anything besides raising my little boy or girl into a decent human being, and not about what horrors could befall them under the guidance of our Mafia life.

But none of this is my priority at the moment.

Jess is my priority.

I pick up my phone and dial Eamon's number on the back of the sticky note on the photo.

"Hello?" He answers, groggily. "Who is this? And what the fuck do you want?"

"Hello Eamon," I say, swallowing hard. "It's Rachel, Jess's best friend and roommate?"

"Yeah, and I repeat, what do you want?"

Um, okay, rude.

"Well, I'm calling because last night Jess got herself into a bit of trouble. I don't know if you know this, but she got arrested last night for her fight with Maggie."

There is silence on the other end of the line.

The skeeze ball doesn't want to admit involvement.

"Well, anyway, she called me this morning and said that she's not getting arraigned until Monday, and she was hoping that you could, you know...*help*."

I swear I hear a faint chuckle.

"And how the hell do you suppose I do that?"

"She needs bail money," I continue. "And she said you owe her."

The faint chuckle turns into a cold, and merciless laugh.

"She says I owe *her*?" Eamon snorts. "She must've got hit real hard in the head then, because if anything she owes *me*."

"What?"

"She ruined my night, for the second time in a row," Eamon says arrogantly. "I'd already paid for Maggie, and for her drinks. Then Jess goes and has a bitch fit, and puts the bitch in an ambulance. So yeah, if anything Jess owes me for all the money, and coke, I wasted."

Is this asshole serious?!

"However," his voice is suddenly coy. "Perhaps if *you* wanted to work something out with me, *privately*, I might be moved to help your friend."

"What the hell are you talking about?" I snap.

"Well, you were looking pretty good in that dress last night, and it would definitely piss off Jaxon, which would honestly just increase the whole experience for me," he chuckles into the phone. "But you'd have to lose that tone of yours. And fast."

"Go fuck yourself, Eamon!"

"Nah babe, I don't need to," He sneers. "But if you ask nicely, I'll give you the opportunity."

"Eat shit and die!" I shout into the phone before snapping it closed and slamming it down on the bed.

"Fucking pig!" I grunt.

I run my hands through my hair feeling frustrated, defeated and royally anxious about what I am going to do about Jess's bail money.

What a scumbag!

It takes everything in my power not to immediately call Jaxon and tell him what one of his *best friends* just said to me. But considering he's probably laying in bed next to that trashy blonde bimbo he was with last night, I change my mind.

But when I pull up my text messages, I notice the text I sent him last night.

Me
3:37am: I hope she was worth it. Fuck you.

And the text he sent me in reply…that I'm just now seeing for the first time.

Jaxon
4:02am: I'm going to assume we need to talk.

Somehow his response infuriates me.
"Rachel?"
Yuri's voice rings down the hallway.
Shit…I forgot about him.
Slamming all of the shit back into Jess's Blackmail Box, I put it back under the floorboard and move the bed back.
But just as I finagle the bed back in place, I hear a thud, like something has fallen onto the floor, under the bed. Kneeling down, I pull up the comforter and see that on the floor, is a small pink pen case that looks like it fell out of the mattress frame.
That's odd?
I pick it up, and unzip it, and that's when my heart stops. It's a needle, a spoon, and a lighter.
Holy hell. It's a fucking meth kit.
Back before Jess had her daughter, she had briefly been into this shit. But she swore when Mandy was born that she had given it all up. However, never to this horrific little kit, is a small white bag of powder, which tells me that Jess has used this. Recently too.
Furious I grab the kit, and close the door and walk back down the hallway to the living room.
She's *using it again.* After she promised she wouldn't. I knew something had been up with her the other day. Despite what she said, or how she tried to play it off, I just fucking knew.
You know what? Maybe her ass should sit in jail a few days.
"Rachel?"
Yuri calls my name a second time, reminding me once again of his stupid existence, and also coincidentally reminding me of

my own poor decisions, effectively knocking me down a few pegs off my high horse.

Taking a deep breath I make my way back down the hallway and find him sitting up in my bed, grinning, his bright blonde hair a mess. I stop off in my closet, managing to tuck Jess's drug kit into the side pocket of an old duffle bag, deciding that I will dispose of it with the next trash run and never tell Jess about finding it.

"Good morning pretty girl," Yuri says in his thick Russian accent. "Did you sleep good?"

"Morning," I say quietly, crossing my arms tightly across my body.

I feel icky and guilty, but more annoyed that I feel icky and guilty. Especially since Jaxon had some other woman all over him last night, there's no reason for me to feel bad for having slept with Yuri. I don't owe Jaxon my loyalty, since apparently, he doesn't owe me any either.

Yuri stares at me for a moment before leaning back against the wall.

"This is the part where you tell me you regret what we did last night."

I do. I really, really do.

"No," I lie. "Not necessarily."

It's more the fact that I don't *remember* much about what happened last night, and how we even ended up here.

I didn't drink. Nor did I do anything *recreational*.

Did Yuri give me something?

Nothing in my gut, or in his behavior, gives me any cause to think that's what happened. But not knowing is what's driving me crazy.

"But before anything else, I have questions, Yuri," I say, sitting down on the bed. "And I need you to answer them."

Yuri spends the next hour filling in the blanks I was missing from the evening.

Apparently when I came downstairs in the VIP elevator,

Jess had finally lost her cool, and attacked Maggie. Naturally, I went to help her, but before I could get to her, I was accidentally rammed by some large biker man and knocked to the floor.

…Where I hit my head.

Thankfully, Yuri had been sent to see what was going on, but saw me unconscious. He picked me up, and pulled me out of the mob and into the storeroom. By the time I came to, Jess had already been hauled off by police, and Maggie was in an ambulance on the way to the hospital.

From what Yuri told me, Jess had actually *stabbed* Maggie in the neck with her stiletto.

As he recounts the story to me, bits and pieces of it come back to me. I remember him walking me up to our apartment, and volunteering to stay with me. I also remember that at some point I broke down and told him that I was pregnant, and I saw the baby's father with another man at the club that night.

…Which is apparently what led to a good old-fashioned revenge fuck.

I had hoped hearing the truth of what happened would make me feel better, but it doesn't. If anything, it just makes me feel worse. My present situation feels chaotic and terrifying and I'm obviously making very poor choices as a result.

The whole night feels like some sort of bad nightmare.

But it isn't.

Jaxon really had been at the club with another girl, Maggie was really in the hospital, and Jess was really sitting in a jail cell until Monday.

And I still haven't sorted out her bail.

I did, however, call *Del.*

While Yuri took a shower, I rang her and walked her through the entire situation. I was nervous at first, as I didn't want to make things worse, but I know Del has a zero tolerance policy for no-call, no-shows, and Jess was scheduled to work tonight.

Which is definitely not going to happen.

It was a good thing I did though, because Maggie's twin May had already done the same, and had given Del her side of the story, which could have cost Jess her job at Nyx entirely.

By the time Yuri got out of the shower, and got dressed, Jess still had a job, but was sitting on probation.

"I don't know what to say," Yuri says as I walk him to the door.

"Last night was fun. I would definitely do it again sometime."

Yeah, definitely not going to happen.

"Yeah, it was fun," I lie. "I'm sure I'll see you around. But please, remember what I said about keeping what we did last night a secret."

I really don't need Jaxon hearing about this.

"Don't worry," he smiles, opening the door. "My lips are sealed. I won't tell anyone."

"Thank y—" I start to say, but instantly I freeze.

Because standing there, in the door…is my brother.

Oh. My. God.

"Oh," Yuri grins, looking at Michael arrogantly. "Nice to see you again, buddy."

My heart immediately starts pounding in my chest. Part of me doesn't want Yuri to leave, but another part of me knows if he doesn't there will certainly be a bloodbath.

"Michael," I say nervously. "What are…what are you doing here? I didn't know you were coming."

"I was just stopping by," he says to me, without taking his icy glare off the Russian man standing next to me.

Yuri nods goodbye to me and walks past him and down the stairs.

I breathe a momentary sigh of relief, but it evaporates quickly when I realize that I am now standing with Michael Valentine, the very man who attacked me, publicly and violently just a few weeks ago. And I'm alone.

Is he here to hurt me?

The thought makes my hands shake and I smile at him politely.

No. He can't. Because of Jaxon.

Technically he still reports to Jaxon, and even if I am furious with him for being a manwhore, I know that Michael knows, he cannot touch me.

…At least I think he does.

"Do you," I say, swallowing hard. "Want to come in?"

I step back, motioning for Michael to come inside. He stares at me for a moment, and then silently follows me into the apartment.

"Give me just a second," I say, faking a smile. "I'll go get dressed."

Michael says nothing, staring at me with his blank expressionless face.

I feel as if I am locked in a cage with a wild tiger.

"Excuse me," I say as I walk quickly into my bedroom.

Closing the door, I take a few deep breaths to try and calm myself as I grab an outfit from the dresser.

And then an idea comes to me. It's not a great idea, and definitely not what I had in mind. But it just might work.

Zipping my jeans, I immediately grab my phone off the bed and do the only thing I can think of.

Me:
3:37am: I hope she was worth it. Fuck you.

Jaxon
4:02am: I'm going to assume we need to talk.

Me:
10:02am: Yeah, we do. Because I'm pregnant. It's yours.

Am I really doing this? Once I do, there's no going back.

I press send, but my hand is shaking so badly as I stand there debating that I drop the phone. I try to catch it but instead it tumbles loudly to the floor.

Shit!

I snatch it up and stand upright, listening for signs that Michael is still in the kitchen where I left him.

"Everything okay in there?" His voice suddenly sounds on the other side of the door, making me jump.

"Heh, yes," I say nervously, straightening my outfit. "Everything is fine, I'll be right out!"

I glance down at the text thread and notice it was sent.

…And *read*.

Well…that's that then. It's done. Jaxon knows.

I breathe an anxious sigh, shove the phone in my pocket, and throw the door open, finding Michael standing there in the hallway, waiting for me.

I'm immediately aware of how tight the little hallway is.

"Are you hungry?" I ask, stepping past him and walking into the living room.

"What was that man doing here?" He asks darkly.

I stare at him, realizing that he looks just as scary and

212

intimidating as he did the night he yanked me off the mechanical bull.

And then I remember, there's a gun in the kitchen.

It's unloaded, and I don't even have any bullets for the thing, but still, a bluff is better than nothing.

"Oh, I just needed a ride home," I say, walking into the kitchen. "Are you sure you don't want anything to drink?"

"Rachel," he growls, his footsteps approaching me.

"That's literally all it was, Michael," I say, yanking open one of the drawers. "And it's actually none of your business."

Thank God, it's still there.

"Don't lie to me," he appears in the doorway.

"I'm not."

I reach into the cabinet above me with one hand, leaving the drawer open...just in case he makes a move toward me.

"He was in your house," Michael says, stepping into the kitchen. "First thing in the morning that seems a bit suspic—"

I yank the gun from the drawer and point it at him.

"He drove me home," I hiss angrily. "Jess and I went to the club, she got into a scuffle and got herself arrested. I needed a ride home and Yuri volunteered. End of story."

Michael takes another step toward me, but I click the safety off of the gun.

"I'm not lying to you, but let's also get one thing clear," I growl. "I don't answer to you, and I don't owe you a goddamn thing. I've made my own life here, and you don't get to show up and have opinions about how I live it. And I don't care if you're my brother, my friend, or fucking Santa Clause. If you think us sharing a set of genetics will stop me from pulling this trigger, then you're in for a rude awakening. Got it, brother of mine?"

I glare at him, hoping this is enough, but also knowing that in truth, there is nothing I can actually *do* with this gun. I silently debate how quickly I could toss it and make it to the staircase.

But then he lowers his hands, and grins.

"Now you're speaking my language," he nods, relaxing and leaning back against the counter. "Got any beer?"

I stare at him before slowly lowering the gun.

Holy shit. It...worked.

Keeping my eyes locked on him, to make sure he isn't bluffing, I pull a beer from the fridge and toss it to him.

"Why are you here?" I ask, still holding the gun.

"Heard a rumor or two going around about you," he says, cracking the can open. "But I had to see for myself."

"Had to see what?"

"If you were all bark and no bite," he says, taking a drink. "Gun in the kitchen? Now that's some baller shit."

"You still haven't answered my question," I say, feeling my phone vibrating in my pocket. "So, I'm going to need you to do that now."

"Straight to business," he says, tilting his head with a grin.

"Yeah well, as fun as this little family reunion is, I actually do have shit to do today."

He chuckles.

"Well, family is exactly why I'm here," he says, turning and walking into the living room.

Rolling my eyes, I bite my bottom lip. My phone vibrates again, but I ignore it. I keep the empty gun in my hand but follow him out into the living room. I find him sitting on the armrest of the sofa, looking at a picture of Jess and I last summer.

"What about family?"

"Our bitch mother is alive," he says without looking up at me. "She's been trying to keep a low profile, but Victor Black tracked her down."

"Oh…" I say softly.

What the fuck? I don't give a shit about her.

"According to him, she's been at some medical rehab facility in Wisconsin," he says, picking up another picture frame. "Funny, because as I understood it, she wanted out, but she was supposed to leave everything behind. But apparently, she was granted some alimony."

"Okay, and?" I snort sarcastically. "Forgive me, Michael, but why the fuck should I care about—"

"Because she has our money!" He suddenly shouts, his head snapping up to glare at me and his eyes black and terrifying. "*All* of our money. *All* of the Valentine Estate, all the accounts, all of the inheritance that should be rightfully ours, is in her name, while we starve to death, barely scraping by!"

He beats his chest violently, leaving red marks on his chest, visible under his unbuttoned shirt.

"So yeah, you *should* care, because that fucking cunt is going to milk the whole thing dry and leave us with nothing!"

What the flying fuck is going on?

I haven't seen Michael in ages. We may be related but we aren't close, and we never were.

My name has never been a source of pride for me. Only pain and misery.

When the cartel executed their hit on my family, I had already ran away from home. However, my brother, my father, his slutty wife Penny, and my baby half-brother Cameron from a different woman, were all at home. The only one to survive that encounter was Michael, and from what I've overheard he suffered, death itself would have been less horrific.

After it happened, everyone in town was talking about the *tragedy* at the Valentine Estate. My brother was rescued by the Pace's, and after therapy attempts failed, sent to a facility for severe trauma victims.

And even as just a runaway teen. I knew that I had to keep my mouth shut. I did my best to just disappear into oblivion, and for a while it worked. In time the world seemed to forget Malcolm Valentine had a daughter.

I never *felt* like a Valentine, and I still don't.

So why the hell should I start now? Especially for him.

After all, the first time Michael saw me, in nearly a decade he physically attacked me. Now, just weeks later he's showing up at my door, trying to talk to me about our family legacy and estate?

Why?

My phone vibrates in my pocket again, and again I ignore it.

"Michael," I sigh, "What is it you want from me?"

He smiles, the act itself seeming to rebel against the muscles in his face, making him look distorted.

"When mother left, the Pace's negotiated an annuity for her, likely to keep her quiet. Well, when dad kicked the bucket, the estate should have passed to you and me. But you were gone, and I was sent to the asylum."

"I still don't—"

"Let me fucking finish!" He shouts angrily.

"Okay, okay!" I throw my hands up in the air defensively.

He runs a hand through his hair.

"Anyway," he hisses glaring at me. "When that all happened, they didn't know if there would be any heirs to pass it down to so the Pace's put the entire estate under mom's name. And now that whore has everything."

I nod, feeling my phone vibrating in my pocket.

"I mean," I say slowly, trying to choose my words carefully. "That's awful, but what can we do about it? Is there a way we can get it back from her?"

"Not we, little sister," Michael grins. "*You.*"

"Me?"

He nods.

"Because of my...history," he pauses. "I'm not eligible to be in charge of the estate. But you can. So, you have to go visit this bitch, and get her to change the will."

My jaw literally drops.

"You're joking," I whisper. "You can't be serious."

"I am serious," he says darkly. "It's the only way."

"Michael, I...I can't," I snort, standing to my feet.

"You have to, Rachel. It's the only way."

"It's not that I don't want to help you, but I haven't seen or talked to this woman since I was five."

"What the fuck does that matter?" He asks stubbornly. "I will give you the paperwork, you visit her and make her sign it. Simple and easy."

"It's never that easy, Michael!" I laugh, pacing across the floor toward the window. "And if you only knew the shit I have going on right now. I have other things on my plate right now that need my attention more than this and-"

But in an instant, his hand is on my throat, choking me.

"Mich..." I try to scream, scratching at his hand as he slams me hard into the wall.

"I tried asking nicely," he growls, his face turning red as he squeezes my windpipe.

I gasp for air, my lungs burning.

"This isn't a fucking request little sister," He hisses as my vision starts to blur. "I'm not letting you filthy fucking whores cheat me out of what is rightfully mine and so if you—"

BANG!

Just as I am fading from consciousness, I hear the front door suddenly smash open and seconds later, Michael is forced to release my throat as he is thrown across the room into the coffee table, which splinters into pieces.

I hear shouting, and the sound of more furniture breaking.

My consciousness returns just as Michael is led from the room by some big burly bodyguards.

Jaxon Pace's bodyguards.

He came. Exactly like I hoped he would.

CHAPTER EIGHTEEN

ADAM

The well-lit bedroom at Valentine Manor looks and feels as if it's been modernized recently. The smell of fresh paint still lingers on the walls, and the bed and furniture are obviously new as well.

Rachel throws her purse on the giant bed and walks over to a large black wood dresser, and starts rifling through one of the drawers.

"Word of advice, avoid the windows," Rachel says as I stand in the doorway. "Jaxon's men are clueless, but they aren't stupid. And if one of them sees a man in the house, they'd assume the worst, and we'd likely be in for a blood bath."

"Noted," I nod.

"Thank God there's actually *normal* clothes," she says to herself. "If all there was to wear to bed was silk pajamas, I'd think I was stuck in a romance novel or something."

She thumbs through a stack of neatly folded t-shirts in one of the drawers.

"This is nice," I say, clearing my throat. "Did, uh…*Jaxon* do this?"

She snorts.

"Please, Jaxon doesn't *do* anything Adam. He leaves shit like this to Ethan to handle, because he has more class. Or at least the stomach for this kind of...thing."

"But I mean Jaxon still," I say, trying to stifle my jealousy. "Well, I mean, he bought you all of this stuff."

She turns to face me.

"Does that bother you?"

I don't know how to reply. What kind of question is that?

Of course it fucking bothers me.

She smirks to herself before selecting a shirt and grabbing a pair of black pajama pants from the drawer.

"Yes, Jaxon bought all this stuff. But don't worry, it isn't for me at all," she smiles. "It's just to ease his conscience for the time being. Or maybe Natalie's."

"What do you mean?"

"I think it's safe to say that if he had to keep me hostage at his house, or somewhere else, he's going to choose somewhere else," Rachel says, pulling her shirt over her head. "I mean, to be fair, it would be a tad awkward for a married man to have his wife and his ex-girlfriend under the same roof."

I swallow hard, feeling slightly uncomfortable at the thought of the man I hate, spoiling the woman I care about, whatever the reason.

"So, to answer your question, no, it was never *for* me. It was just a place to *put* me," Rachel continues. "And, no, I don't think the clothes were Jaxon's idea. I'm sure they were Natalie's."

"Why do you say that?"

"Because they're too...accurate."

"Accurate for what?"

"*Me*," she smirks to herself. "I went through them all earlier. There's t-shirts, jeans, slippers, sweaters. You know, the kind of clothes I'd *actually* wear as opposed to the crap one of his inflated stylists would've chosen for me when they weren't main-lining granola and matcha lattes."

"Natalie, huh?" I say with a sigh, trying to be polite. "Well, that was certainly thoughtful of her."

"Yeah," Rachel says, rolling her eyes. "She's kind of annoying like that."

I smirk, leaning against the doorframe.

"It's strange though," she says quietly, looking thoughtfully around the room.

"What is?"

"I was born in this house. Pretty sure in this very room in fact. And even though it's my family house, and they're all dead, and every inch of this place has been dusted, scrubbed and remodeled, I *still* feel like an outsider."

She's not wrong.

Rachel's purse sits beside her on the massive bed, and I can't help but feel as if she looks so small in the giant room. So out of place.

"All that being said, I am grateful that Jaxon updated the house," she says to herself. "At least it doesn't smell like my father's cigars anymore. I'd never be able to be here if it still felt and smelled like that old crusty bastard."

She takes another moment to look around the room before looking back up at me.

"Are you going to come in, Agent Westwood?" She asks. "Or are you planning to stand there until the sun comes up?"

I nod, and step into the room. Walking over to the couch, I take a seat and set my bag down beside me. I reach down to start to untie my shoes, when out of the corner of my eye I see a topless Rachel bend over and slip out of my sweatpants.

Holy shit.

My mouth instantly goes dry and my cock swells in my pants. There's no denying it, Rachel is by far the sexiest woman I have ever seen naked.

And I've seen more than my fair share of them naked.

Fuck me, I want her though. I want her badly.

Her deep brown eyes catch mine and I quickly look back to my shoes, my frazzled brain struggling to remember how to untie a simple knot.

"So, uh," I say, trying to recall what we had just been talking about. "He put you here, but gave you access to the whole house. Does that mean the grounds too?"

"Nope," Rachel chuckles. "Pretty sure he said something about telling his men to shoot me if I set a foot out the front door. I guess he thinks I'm a flight risk or something."

"I wonder why," I chuckle. "But I'm curious, how did Jaxon end up with this estate in the first place?"

As if on purpose, Rachel walks casually across the room to the ensuite bathroom, carrying her t-shirt but wearing nothing but her panties.

Well, now I know she's teasing me…

"Now that's a good story. It kind of ties back to the deal my father struck with the Pace's in regards to my mother," she calls from the bathroom. "The Pace's were more concerned with keeping Valerie happy, and silent. And you know the best way to do that."

"Money," I nod, staring at the glowing fireplace.

"Bingo. Well they were put in charge of the arrangements and so by default, when Michael was declared criminally insane, and I was missing and assumed dead, the estate reverted to Jaxon Pace."

"How much money does one guy need?" I snort, shaking my head.

"He settled the accounts, but he kept the house. For Jessica," Rachel says, brushing her teeth. "It's technically part of *her* inheritance. But I assume because it's nearly a century old, he's probably only invested in remodeling this shit hole so it will turn a better profit if and when they sell it."

I yawn.

Damn, maybe I am more tired than I anticipated.

Considering the fact that I've been up for nearly thirty-six hours straight, sitting on this couch is causing my eyes to feel as if they weigh a thousand pounds.

But the moment Rachel appears in the bathroom doorway, now wearing just a t-shirt and panties, I immediately wake back up.

It is then that I notice for the very first time tonight, a subtle yet playful smile across her face.

And I am done for.

So much of what we've discussed tonight has been *heavy*.

But, right now, here in this moment, she looks more relaxed than I have ever seen her. And it's absolutely breathtaking.

"Did you fall asleep on me, Agent?" She asks. "Have I bored you to death with tales of murders, betrayals and real estate transactions?"

I shake my head slowly.

Fuck me, she's gorgeous.

Flipping her long dark hair to one side, she walks over to me, and straddles me. Instinctively my hands snake up her smooth thighs.

"Thank you," she whispers.

"For what?"

"For coming with me," she says pressing her forehead to mine. "I…"

She opens her mouth to say something, but then stops, smiling politely, her eyes dropping from mine.

"What is it?" I ask.

But Rachel just shakes her head.

Gently I take the back of my index finger and lift her chin, forcing her to look at me.

"We agreed no more secrets," I say, softly. "The only way this works is if you tell me what's on your mind."

She bites her bottom lip.

"I just can't believe you came with me," she says, her eyes falling from me once again.

"Of course I did," I say, almost without thinking. "You asked me to."

Whoa…where did that come from, cowboy?

I try to corral my emotions into more clear and concise thoughts, but when she looks back up at me, her captivating eyes burrowing into my soul, they explode inside my chest.

"I, uh," I say, clearing my throat. "Gather that asking for things isn't something you enjoy doing, is it?"

She shakes her head.

"That's because in my experience, Adam, asking only ends in *wanting*," Rachel whispers. "And wanting, for me, has only ever ended in disappointment."

If I had a heart, it would shatter all over these ancient floors in the Valentine Estate.

I am stunned, to my core.

On the surface, Rachel Valentine appears cold and strong. But it's clear to me now that those qualities are simply crudely fashioned default defense mechanisms of a battered heart protecting a very soft, and very fragile center.

"I'm sorry," she says quietly. "I know I'm not very good at this whole relationship thing."

Holy shit…She just called it a relationship.

223

However, I know that if I acknowledge this, or tell her how I really feel, she could very well panic. And then everything we've done up until this point could be for nothing.

"Why do you think you're not good at it?"

"Because I'm not used to having someone around I can rely on. You have to understand, Adam, I've just been on my own so long that the only person I trust is myself," she shrugs. "I just have a hard time believing when people make promises, because I've had so many of them broken."

She clears her throat softly.

"This is just new for me. And I just hope I can give you what you want."

I smile, cupping her face with my hand.

"Rachel," I say softly, running my thumb along her cheek. "I know this is new, for both of us. But, I never want you to hesitate to ask me things. I promise I will never ignore your requests, and will always do my best to give you whatever it is."

"I know that, Adam, I just—" she starts to say, but I lean in and cut her off with a kiss.

"No, please," I say quietly. "I just need to say this. I realize that I asked you to tell me in the car what your intentions were before we got here, but I never actually told you *mine*."

She nods slowly.

I take a deep breath, and decide to jump right off the dock.

"Now, I wish I could tell you definitively how we're meant to sort through all this, or what we need to do to fix it. But I don't know. And honestly, I don't think anyone does." I wink at her. "All I know is, I want to be here. Because *here* is where *you* are."

Rachel blushes, and tucks a strand of her disobedient hair behind her ear.

"I also know," I continue softly. "Because of your past, and your trauma, you probably don't believe me when I say these things to you. And why should you? After all, you're used to people telling you lies in the dark, and then stabbing you in the back when your love no longer suits their needs."

Her eyes fall from mine, and she bites her bottom lip.

"But I'm not *them*, Rachel."

Slowly she looks back up at me, and I take a moment, relishing the magnetic pull I feel, lost in her eyes.

"I'm not a complicated man. I hold myself to a code, and I

try to keep my life simple. I also don't have the time or energy to waste on things I'm not serious about. So, you best believe, I wouldn't be here, driving in blizzards, risking bodily harm from oblivious bodyguards, and just generally over complicating the shit outta my life, if I wasn't serious about this. About *you*."

She chuckles softly, that adorable soft smile returning to her face again and threatening to derail me completely.

Stay focused, Adam.

"And while I'm fairly confident that I'm at least marginally a better man than the men that have tried to be with you, I'm not going to sit here and promise you the sun, moon and stars. Not because I don't think you deserve them, but because realistically, I'll never be able to give them to you."

She sits back on my lap, and my hands trace up her thighs once more.

"But I'm not here because I want to promise things to you," I say, looking deep into her eyes. "I'm here because I want to *prove* things to you."

Her breath trembles, and I see the way her lips part as my words register with her.

"I want to prove to you that a relationship can feel safe. I want to prove to you that you can rely on me to be there when you need me. I want to prove to you that I'm not scared of your bad girl days, and I can handle whatever is on your wild, crazy, chaotic little heart." I say, my hand gently cupping her face. "What do I want from you? All I *want* is to be the reason you smile like this, every damn day. And I hope that's enough."

I watch as her eyes scan mine and her lip trembles. She leans in and kisses me, deeply.

"It's enough, Adam," Rachel says softly. "It's more than enough.

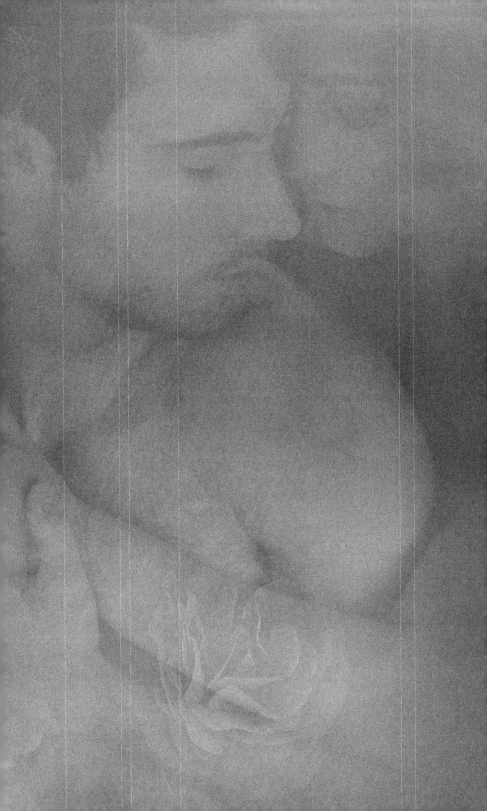

CHAPTER NINETEEN

Rachel

I kiss him and he immediately shoves his tongue down my throat.

Fuck being tired. I want him. Right now.

Pressing my tits against him, I wrap my legs around him, as his hands snake up my back. I can feel his throbbing erection against my thin panties.

He wants me too.

"Rachel," he groans as I grind myself against him. "I thought we were meant to be going to sleep."

"We can sleep after we fuck," I whisper urgently against his lips. "I need to feel you inside me."

That does it.

He hesitates no longer and wraps his arms around my back, lifting me up and carrying me to the large bed. He lays me down, and I immediately pull at his t-shirt, yanking it off his body.

God he's so fucking gorgeous.

He's leaner than Jaxon was, but definitely not skinny. Every inch of his body is pure muscle as this is a man who has clearly spent the better part of his life crafting his body into a work of art. I run my hand down his chiseled abs, all the way to that deep "V" of his pelvic muscles. His strong arms, which are pinning me to the mattress, are brilliantly defined in the soft glow of the fireplace.

I gasp as his hand slips between my legs and rubs my clit through my panties, but he silences me with a deep kiss.

"I don't know what you do to me, woman," he whispers, trailing kisses down my neck. "You're more dangerous than a drug. Hell, maybe you are one."

"I am," I grin, arching my back as he grips my breasts and sucks hard on my nipples. "So go on, take another hit, baby."

"Yes, Ma'am," he growls.

Adam yanks my panties down my body and presses my thighs back against my stomach before burying his face in my pussy.

"Oh my fucking God!" I moan.

"You taste so fucking good," he says, flicking my clit with his tongue.

He uses one arm to hold both of my legs open and slips the fingers on his free hand inside of me.

"Adam," I groan, his long fingers pressing deep inside of me and rubbing my g spot.

"God, I love the way your body responds to me," he says, swirling his tongue on my clit. "You get so fucking wet for me, you're practically soaking the sheets."

"Oh fuck!" I groan.

He presses deeper inside of me, and I blush, feeling my cum dripping from my pussy but unable to stop it. My legs start shaking as his relentless onslaught of my clit continues, building to my climax.

"I...I..." I moan, unable to form any cognitive thoughts.

My whole body twitches compulsively, each flick of his tongue or movement of his fingers inside my pussy feeling like electricity in my bones.

"That's it, Miss Valentine," He growls deeply. "Give in to me, and let me taste you."

Fuck me...

He sucks my clit and strums his fingers inside of me harder and suddenly I feel it happening. Adam forces me over the edge of ecstasy and my orgasm smashes into me like a freight train.

"Oh my God!" I shout, throwing my head back.

"Good girl," he purrs, his smile evident in his voice as he works his fingers even harder and sucking hard on my clit. "Give it all to me."

Shuddering I melt into the mattress, feeling the waves of pleasure crash over me.

"That…was amazing."

I breathe heavily as he pulls his hand from me, kissing my neck and nibbling on my ear lobe.

And without warning I feel him press his cock inside of me.

"Shiiiit…" I groan, feeling his entire length thrust up into me.

"Oh baby," Adam grins, "I hope you didn't plan on sleeping, because we are just getting started."

I have no idea what time it is, but I do know that the sun has just started to peek through the curtains when the two of us finally crawl under the covers.

"You said I could ask you anything," I say softly, laying with my head on his chest. "Right?"

I feel him nod, and kiss my forehead.

"Do you have any…reservations about us?"

He doesn't respond but I do feel his heartbeat start to beat faster in his chest.

Or maybe it's my own.

The truth is, I've been dying to ask this question and it feels as if it is eating me alive.

"I mean like, do you have any fears? About me, or about us and our…you know, *this*."

"Yeah, of course I do."

"What are they?"

I feel his fingers in my hair.

"Well, first, that you struggle to say what *this* is."

"No, I don't!" I say defensively, trying to sit up.

"You do," he replies, holding me fast. "But I've noticed it's only when you're thinking too hard on it."

"What?"

"Well, I hate to break it to you, but you *have* already called this a relationship when you weren't overthinking it."

Wait...I have?!

"And granted it was probably by accident, but that's my point. When you're being real with me, I can tell. Because it's the moment you let those walls down for just a fraction of a second and I get to see *you*."

I bite my lip, realizing that on some level, he's right. I place my hand on his chest, feeling the heat radiating from his body.

"I don't know who I am without my walls, Adam," I say softly. "They have served as my protection since the day I ran away from home. There was a time in my life that I couldn't let anyone know who I truly was, and over time, I got really good at just being whatever people needed or expected me to be."

He says, stroking my hair, laying another soft kiss on my forehead.

"I just don't know what I'm doing," I say softly. "I'm afraid I'm going to do it wrong."

Adam chuckles.

"None of us know what we're doing when we get into a relationship with another person, Rach," he says, adjusting himself on the pillow. "I mean think about it, relationships are two people who are attracted to each other, trying to merge their individual lives. Of course there's going to be bumps in the road, or differences of opinion, or that messy chaotic trial and error that comes whenever you're emotionally invested in the outcome. But, people choose to endure all that bullshit because they believe that being with that particular person is better than being alone."

The smell of his cologne and the calmness in his voice are oddly soothing.

"And that's the crux of it," he says, rubbing his hand up my arm. "You have to believe that being with that person will make your life better too."

Something about this sentence pricks my heart. But as I lay here in the darkness, cuddled in the warmth of his arm around me, I feel my anxiety rear its ugly head.

Because even though I know I'm safe with Adam, and even though I'm touched that he *was* willing to brave the danger to come back to the house with me, his dedication doesn't bring me any comfort. No, if anything it just terrifies me more.

Because it's *disarming.*

What he doesn't know, and what I can't bring myself to tell him, is that he makes me *want* to tear down my walls, brick by brick, and let him see all of me.

Because what if he doesn't like what he sees?

There are so many skeletons hiding in my closets, I've lost count of them all.

I assume most people regret something they've done in their life, but I don't just have *one* thing. I have an entire scroll of sins that would make the devil himself blush.

What would he say if he knew all the things I've done?

"I can hear you thinking," he says softly. "Why don't you just talk to me."

But I can't. My fear is literally suffocating the air from my lungs, and there's no way I can unpack all of this for him right now.

"It can wait til the morning," I say, squeezing him tightly, doing my best to try and mask my internal panic.

I hear him yawn, and his breathing deepens as I feel his heart rate slow, and then finally Agent Adam Westwood falls asleep.

The sound of a vacuum whirring in the hallway wakes me.

"What...The...Actual...Fuck?" I hiss sleepily.

"They've been here for an hour," Adam whispers next to me, without opening his eyes. "I think there's three of them."

"You know, for an FBI Agent incognito, you seem pretty unconcerned with getting discovered inside a place you're definitely not supposed to be." I whisper back.

"Don't worry, Babe," he says, trying to wrap his arms around me. "I locked the door."

"Oh, great. Problem solved," I say sarcastically, pushing him off me as I climb out of the bed.

Grabbing the pair of black pajama pants that I never got around to wearing last night, I pull them on and head for the door.

"Go get 'em, killer," Adam groans, pulling the covers over

his head. "And if you're going to the kitchen, you should know, I like my eggs over easy."

Rolling my eyes, I grab my pillow and whack him with it. "Ow!"

I head to the door, careful to slip out without revealing the man hiding in my bedroom.

There's an older woman in the hallway, running her vacuum just a few doors down from my bedroom. Without saying a word, I storm over to her, yanking the power cord from the wall.

"Oh!" She jumps, turning around to face me. "Miss Valentine. Did I disturb you? I apologize I—"

But I don't even let her finish her sentence.

Instead, I tear the giant vacuum from her hands and walk directly over to the balcony.

"Oh my God!" she gasps, immediately understanding my unspoken intentions. "Wait! Miss Valentine! No!!"

But without hesitation, I hoist the fucker over the banister and drop it, sending it crashing down to the foyer tile below. It instantly shatters into a hundred pieces, the collision echoing loudly against the walls.

"Get the fuck out of my house!" I shout at her.

The woman doesn't need to be told twice and immediately bolts for the stairs.

But I have to make *sure* she actually leaves, so I follow after her, chasing her down into the foyer.

"Ahhh!" She shrieks in terror. "Margie! Heather! Let's go, this woman is crazy!"

Crazy? Oh honey…I can give you crazy.

I pick up the nearest small object, some random ugly porcelain figurine on the nearest credenza and chuck it against the wall, smashing it to bits.

"You're damn right! I'm fucking crazy!" I shout, grabbing the vase on the table. "All of you, get the hell out! Now!"

The terrified woman runs screaming into the kitchen followed quickly by two other cleaners, who instantly appear from the study and ballroom.

Using my arm, I swipe everything off the top of another nearby shelf sending it all crashing to the floor.

As I swing the kitchen door open, I find all three of the cleaners, as well as a fourth woman in a chef's jacket, frantically scooping their buckets, baskets and belongings off the kitchen table.

"Are you deaf?! I said now!" I roar, grabbing a giant butcher knife from the block. "If you're not out of my house in thirty seconds I will kill all of you!"

However, it only takes ten for them to scramble out the door, and the bowels of the Valentine Estate to be emptied.

Adam and I are alone once again.

I smile to myself.

My God, that was...fun.

After doing a quick sweep of the downstairs to confirm there are not brave lingerers, I decide that I should probably lock the doors to the house.

Because even if Jaxon's men have a key, I doubt anyone but the Don Supreme himself would dare set foot in a house with a vacuum-tossing crazy lady wielding a butcher knife.

Stepping past the broken porcelain and pottery, I giggle to myself as I throw on the front door deadbolt.

But as I turn back to the staircase, I find a shirtless Adam Westwood standing at the top of the balcony, leaning his elbows on the banister.

God, he looks so fucking good.

"I take it that's mission accomplished, you bad little girl?" He says with a mischievous grin.

I smile up at him.

"Eggs over easy you said?"

"For a girl who claims she doesn't know how to boil water, you do make a mean scrambled egg." Adam says, sitting at the kitchen table, taking a bite of toast.

"That's a culinary skill you cultivate when you're poor," I shrug. "Because eggs are cheap. Well, they used to be anyway."

"What skill?"

"That if you screw them up, just mix them all together, sprinkle cheese on it and call it a scramble."

He chuckles.

233

"Yeah, looking back, we definitely ate a lot of eggs growing up," he says with a smile. "My mom never let us know the struggles we were actually facing."

He glances out the window for a moment, as if suddenly his mind is transported somewhere else.

"Sounds like your mother did her best to protect you from how ugly the world really is," I say softly.

He looks back at me.

"I'm almost jealous."

His eyes fall from mine, and he grabs his coffee mug.

"I want to tell you that I'm sorry you didn't have anyone to protect you," he says with a sigh, tilting his head to the side. "But I have this sneaking suspicion that if I do, you'll probably break this plate over my head. And then your delicious egg scramble will be all over the floor."

I chuckle.

"You would be correct there, sir," I say, picking up my coffee cup. "But to be fair, there's shit all over the floor now."

"And you scared off all the maids so I assume we need to find out if Valentine Estate has a golden-plated broom and diamond-encrusted dustpan somewhere."

This makes me laugh, and Adam too. But then slowly, silence settles back over the table.

"So," he says, finally breaking the silence. "What was it that you wanted to say to me last night?"

Fuck me...he remembered.

I immediately open my mouth to deflect, preparing to tell him that I don't remember, but before I can he puts his hand up and stops me.

"And," he says firmly, his eyes scanning me intently. "I'd like to remind you that we agreed, no *lies*."

My stomach sinks through the floor.

In truth, I do remember. Vividly. I laid in bed last night agonizing over all the terrible things I have yet to tell Adam about me and my past. Things that could potentially be too much for him to stomach or accept.

Adam leans in across the table.

"Rachel," he says softly, "this only works if you *talk* to me."

"But that's just it," I say softly. "I'm terrified this won't work, and I don't know how to tell you that."

I watch as the look on his face transitions from expectant, to disappointed. The room is silent for a moment, but then he gently clears his throat.

"Well," he says quietly. "I think you just did."

He shifts uncomfortably in his chair, tapping his fingers on his mug, and clicking his tongue in his cheek.

Shit, he took that the wrong way and thinks it's about him.

"Fine," I snap, finally giving in to the cache of explosives lying just below my surface. "Yes, I'm afraid."

"Alright," he breathes softly.

"And no, it's not because of anything you've said or done, but because of what *I've* done," I say sharply, pounding my hand to my chest as my heart starts racing. "Is that what you want to know? Are you happy now?"

"It's a start," he says calmly. "What are you afraid of?"

"Everything," I whisper, feeling my hand shaking as I run it through my hair. "Like, sure, I've told you a few gnarly stories so far, but as I said yesterday, they are only the beginning, and they are only going to get worse from here."

"I'm okay with that," he says. "I'm ready for it, and I want to hear your story."

"But It's not just my story, Adam!" I groan, my chest heaving. "It's…it's…me. All of this is part of me."

"I know that, Rachel," He says calmly. "That's what I want."

"And what if you change your mind?!" I suddenly snap, slamming my hand on the table. "You're asking me to break down my walls for you and be vulnerable, which is great for you, but that's my *only* protection!"

I laugh nervously, licking my bottom lip.

"Vulnerability is great when it doesn't cost you anything, Adam! And while you're asking me to lay my sins bare, I'm lying in bed with you, just waiting for the ax to fall on my neck. Not knowing what story is going to finally be the story that sends you running!"

"Rachel—"

"And before you say you won't run, please know they all run, Adam. No one can be bothered to stick around long enough not even my bullshit fucking parents!"

I reach for my coffee but realize that my hand is shaking.

"Shit," I mutter to myself, placing my other hand on top of it to try and hide it.

Well, now you did it. Self-sabotage implosion complete.

I want to run. Straight out the kitchen, out the front door, and as far away from this house and all these bullshit memories as possible. Getting taken out by Jaxon's prison guards seems more appealing than masochistically waiting for Adam's rejection.

But before I can move, Adam reaches forward and puts his hand on mine, squeezing it gently. The two of us sit like this, in silence, for what feels like an eternity.

"You're not going to believe me," he finally says quietly. "But you need to know, I'm afraid of the exact same thing."

"You're right," I scoff, shaking my head. "I don't believe that. Because you're the good guy, and my brother is the bad guy, and I'm not sure that your life could be better with me."

There. I said it. I actually fucking said it.

He stares at me before taking my hand and bringing it to his lips, kissing it softly. He then scoots over to me and takes both my hands in his.

"That's fine, because I *am* sure it could be better," he says softly. "And if I have to believe for the both of us, until you can believe it too, then that's what I'll fucking do."

Oh my God...

My jaw nearly drops into my lap, and all I can hear is the sound of my heart pounding in my ears.

"And you know what, Rachel," he says softly. "You're right."

"I...I am?"

Adam nods.

"I owe you an apology."

"Wait...what?" I ask confused. "What do you owe me an apology for?"

"Because I did this all wrong."

"I don't understand, what do you—"

"When you first came to my hotel," He says, leaning forward and running his hand over his head. "I was excited to see you, but I was angry. For a lot of reasons. But mostly because I felt like I'd been played. Like I'd been betrayed."

I bite my lower lip.

"...And I know you felt the same."

He's not wrong, but I don't know where he's going with this.

"And any betrayal, no matter how small or even how justified

236

it is, still makes you feel like the rug has been ripped out from under you. You feel vulnerable and exposed, and it might surprise you to know that I also hate that feeling. Because in my line of work, exposure equals death. Plain and simple."

"I mean, that's dark," I say quietly. "But it makes sense."

"Well, the only remedy I could think of to quell the chaos I felt the night you showed up was for you to explain your story. But in my anger I didn't *ask* you to tell me, I *demanded* you tell me."

I stare at him, feeling my heart thumping in my chest. He looks at me, a pained expression written across his face.

"So, yes, I owe you an apology, Rachel," he says. "Because I had no right demanding vulnerability from you, especially considering that I had violated your trust just the same."

"It's fine, Adam, I—"

"No, it's not," he says firmly. "Because I can't claim that I want to protect you, while making you terrified at the same time. That isn't…fair."

Holy shit.

His words strike a chord with me, and I have to bite my lip to keep it from trembling.

"And don't get me wrong, I want you to trust me with your story, and your fears, and your anxieties, and all the broken parts of you that need protecting," Adam says, his eyes burrowing into mine. "But I can't force that, it has to come from you. Otherwise I'm not giving you anything, I'm only taking. And that's not the way you build trust."

I am stunned, I cannot believe that this man is sitting here, saying these things to me.

"So, I want to fix it," he says, his eyes falling from mine. "I want everything and anything you tell me, from this point forward, to be only things you *want* to tell me, do you understand?"

I nod slowly.

"And, to prove to you that I'm just as invested, I'm going to get in the trenches with you."

"What do you mean?"

He takes a deep breath.

"I'm going to tell you my story," he says softly. "The parts I've been afraid to tell *you*."

"Why?" I ask. "Why are you afraid?"

He looks down at the table and takes a deep breath.

"Because I'm worried that they will ruin the image you have of me," he says, his voice almost a whisper. "And considering your ex is some powerful billionaire Mafia Don, who can give you million-dollar houses and buy you entire wardrobes, it's really easy to feel a bit…inadequate. So, I've been selfishly holding on to the small victories."

"You're not inadequate, Adam," I say, firmly. "Especially compared to Jaxon Pace. You're a good man. Far better than he is, I'll tell you that."

He smiles to himself, closing his eyes and licking his bottom lip.

"I'm not as good as you think I am Rachel," he whispers.

"What do you mean?"

"I've made mistakes too," he says gravely. "And I'm not talking about little mistakes here or there. I'm talking about big mistakes. Ones that hurt people. And ones that got people hurt."

There's no way for Adam to know, but his words chill me to the bone, his fears somehow matching my own.

"It's not flattering, and definitely not as interesting as yours, but it's part of who I am," he says, rubbing his thumb across the back of my hand. "But I've got a few skeletons in my closet too."

I nod slowly.

"I know vulnerability isn't easy. Especially for you. And I want you to know, and believe, that I'm willing to share my sins with you, and be vulnerable too."

He stares at me, and it's then I understand that he is waiting for me to decide whether or not I want to hear this story.

"Okay, Adam," I say, standing up from my chair. "Let's go."

"What?" he asks, clearly confused. "Go where?"

"Well, if we're getting to the really uncomfortable parts, we should probably relocate to the living room," I say with a sigh. "Because these kitchen chairs are uncomfortable enough as it is, and I'm not doubling up."

"Um, Okay?" He says, standing up. "But I guess if we're moving elsewhere, perhaps you could throw in a tour?"

"Why not," I shrug. "I need to find that old diamond-encrusted dustpan anyway."

CHAPTER TWENTY

ADAM

I am given the fastest walking tour one could possibly take of a 15,000 square foot mansion.

At least it came with entertainment, as I am blessed with apathetic commentary from a disaffected Mafia princess, who is utterly unimpressed with family as well as her heritage.

During our appraisal of the sprawling property, I am treated to such gems such as:

"This is the ballroom, where we might've hosted a ball. You know, if my father had *not* been a paranoid asshole with few friends he trusted not to steal the silver."

"These are all the bedrooms. There's a bunch of them. I don't care enough to do an inventory, but I'm pretty sure each room has pictures of ugly people or at least some useless antique trinkets some asshole in my family owned. I should have a garage sale. I bet the neighborhood watch would love that,"

"This is the pool. It's a pool."

Then again, Rachel Valentine was never one for words.

Or sentimentality.

From the tiny glimpse I've been granted of her life, these people might've been related, but they weren't her family, and they had all royally fucked her over.

And she still hadn't forgiven them. *Any* of them.

"...And that's why I don't clean the fucking mausoleum," she says with a smile as we settle on the couches in the study with fresh cups of coffee.

"Asses to ashes," I snort. "Makes sense actually."

"Alright spill," she says.

Oh shit...she's just jumping right in here.

I chuckle to myself, crossing one leg over the other.

"I take it you want me to just jump right in, eh?"

"Well, I want you to quit stalling," she says, rolling her eyes. "I've fed you, fucked you, and gave you a tour. Now it's your turn to give me the dirty laundry you promised me."

I chuckle to myself.

"Alright, how about we start with my ledger."

"Your *what*?" Rachel asks, scrunching her nose.

"My ledger," I repeat. "You asked me last night in the car about how I deal with guilt, well, I'm going to explain it to you. But it's a long and complicated story."

"At the risk of sounding ungrateful," Rachel says sarcastically. "Is this just going to be some boring story about your job?"

"Do you want me to tell you or not?"

"I do but I want to make sure this isn't you telling me about your work drama. I want actual dirt not some—"

"I cheated on my wife," I snap, interrupting her. "How about that? Is that *dirty* enough for you?"

Rachel goes completely silent, the shock on her face evident. And I instantly regret what I just said.

Fuck. This is exactly what I was afraid of.

"I told you," I say, quietly, wringing my hands tightly. "I'm not as good as you think I am."

Her eyes fall from mine to the coffee cup in her hands.

"I don't know the entirety of what happened with you and Jaxon," I say softly. "But from where you left off in the story, I was getting the impression that *this* might hit a soft spot."

The room falls silent, the sound almost deafening.

"Which is why I, uh," I say, swallowing hard. "Well, that's why

I've been nervous to tell you. As I said, it's not very flattering."

"Good thing I'm more than familiar with unflattering," she says softly, finally looking back up at me. "So go on, Agent Westwood, the floor is yours."

Taking a deep breath, I settle back against the couch.

"It's been a while since I've talked to anyone about my wife," I say softly. "I'd gone up to pay a visit to my grandma. She'd moved in with her sister in New York after my grandpa passed, and I wanted to tell her about completing my interview process with the FBI. The screening process and boot camp had been pretty rigorous, but I had passed with flying colors."

"I bet your grandma was proud," Rachel says.

"Oh ecstatic. Before I left town, however, one of my friends from high school lived over in the Bronx and invited me out to celebrate. Feeling pretty high on life, the two of us bar hopped a bit before we stumbled into this shitty little dive bar."

"The best kind," Rachel snorts, toasting her cup.

"It was a shithole," I laugh, "But when Candace Bell walked out on stage it was like time itself stopped. Striking long red hair, rosy cheeks, and bright green eyes, the moment her eyes met mine, I was completely smitten. I forced my friend to stay around until closing, hoping I could have a chance to talk to her."

"And did you?"

"I did," I grin. "But I was just aimlessly flirting, and eventually it was an hour past closing and he wanted to go home so he just flat out told her that *I* wanted her number."

Rachel chuckles.

"That's one way to do it. Did it work though?"

"It definitely worked. We spent a very passionate few weeks together before I got the call about my acceptance into the Bureau. That call changed everything."

"What do you mean?"

"Well, for starters, it caused our very first *real* fight about our future, and what we were doing."

"You did mention that you wanted her to quit dancing," Rachel says with a sigh, leaning back against the couch across from me.

I nod.

"As our relationship bloomed, so did my reservations about her dancing. At first, I loved watching her perform and that every other guy in that room wanted to be with her. Because she was *mine*," I say, leaning forward on my knees. "But, it was like the closer Candace and I became, the more I started to hate her dancing, *because* she was mine."

Rachel takes a drink of her coffee, and then places the mug in her lap, playing with the edges with her fingers.

"The thought of her grinding and dancing on other men, or sticking their money in her panties…" I say, my voice trailing off, the same feelings of rage still twisting in my stomach. "It equally infuriated and disgusted me. I wanted her to give it up and settle down with me. I wanted to have a family with her, all of it. And I didn't understand why she was so hesitant."

"Sometimes," Rachel whispers, without looking up at me. "It's not that easy."

I bite my lower lip, unable to think of anything to say.

"I don't know how your wife felt," she continues. "But I know for me, the only place I ever felt like I had power, or even any minute control over my life was on the stage. And Jaxon asking me to give that up was—"

"*Suffocating*," I finish for her.

She nods, her eyes finding mine.

"That's what Candace said too," I say quietly, placing my arm on the back of my chair. "And, being the young and stupid headstrong little prick I was, I made the mistake of giving her an ultimatum: me or the dancing."

"Let me guess," Rachel says as a knowing smirk settles softly on her cheeks. "She chose the dancing."

I run my hand across my chin.

"You know, if it hadn't been for the baby, I don't know if she ever would have called me again," I say quietly. "I'd been such an asshole. Said some shit I didn't mean, just because I was mad. You know how it goes."

"Yes, actually I do," Rachel whispers.

"Anyway," I say, clearing my throat. "I'd been trying to find a way to come up and surprise her, hoping we could try, and sort shit out. But I'd only been at my job a couple of weeks, and they were running me ragged already. I wasn't expecting her to call, and I definitely wasn't expecting her to tell me she was *pregnant*."

I take a deep breath.

"We were just kids having *kids*," I whisper softly. "We didn't know what we were doing."

"None of us do," Rachel nods quietly, playing with the fringe on the pillow in her lap. "What did you do?"

"Well, first I apologized then I proposed, and within a month we were married and moving into our first house together."

"Not to burst your bubble, Agent Westwood," Rachel says, pulling her knees up on the couch with her. "But this is all sounding pretty vanilla. And pretty happy."

I chuckle, taking a sip of my coffee.

"To be honest, we *were* pretty vanilla and happy, for a few years," I say as I set it back down on the table. "But when it went downhill, it went downhill quickly."

"Looking forward to it," Rachel says, winking at me.

I snort, shaking my head at her complete irreverence and apparent apathy for my feelings.

But really though, what else was I expecting?

"Anyway, the Bureau had me on a different assignment every other week. Some months where I'd be lucky if I had a total of five days at home with my family. We started fighting a lot. I couldn't understand why she was upset. After all, I might not have been making big money, but it was definitely enough to provide for us. New clothes, new furniture, and I was even able to buy her a car, which was something she had never had before."

"...All that white picket fence stuff you men *assume* we women want," Rachel snorts, rolling her eyes. "When the truth is staring you in the face."

I stare at her, her words oddly on point.

"Yeah," I say, clearing my throat again. "I missed that."

"Even as an FBI Profiler," Rachel says, shaking her head. "Yeah, this is what I meant by men are clueless."

I clear my throat, feeling the old familiar frustration rising in me, having recognized the irony myself.

"Yeah, well I didn't understand how lonely she was. And it wasn't like she ever came out and told me. So, I thought I was *doing* everything I was supposed to be doing as a husband and father," I say, clicking my tongue inside my cheek. "I loved her, provided for her, and I was faithful."

Rachel looks at me confused.

"I thought you just said—"

"...For a time," I say, interrupting her. "Remember this is

going to be a long story. But I promise we will get to that part."

"Fair enough."

"Anyway, that's when I started taking the harder cases."

"What do you mean?"

"Serial killers," I continue. "My supervisor told me I had a knack for breaking down the less than obvious cases. The ones that didn't actually follow a known or typical profile."

"…Because of your father," Rachel says softly.

I nod, slowly, rubbing my chin.

"I don't know if it was true, or if they just wanted me to believe it to be true, but I did have substantial success with those cases."

I take a sip of my coffee.

"But I *was* really fucking good with it…"

"You wanted to see me, Sir?" I ask, knocking on the door to my boss's office.

"Westwood," He grumbles, waving me in. "Come in, close the door, and sit down."

"Yes, Sir."

I do as instructed and take a seat in one of the worn out leather chairs in Special Agent Roger Weatherstone's office, the room smelling of cigarettes, black coffee, and some cheap ass plug-in air freshener.

Roger tosses a file across the desk.

"What is this, Sir?"

"A pain in my fucking ass," he sighs, running his hand over his balding head. "My advanced team was assigned this case, but those idiots have gotten nowhere with it and now I have two more victims and another fucking headache. "

I open the file, immediately greeted with a naked, decomposing body of a male, his arms and legs outstretched and nailed across two trees in the middle of a forest.

Behind it, another photo, this of a dead woman, sitting on her knees and her palms upright.

"The Alphabet Killer," I say softly, flipping the pages.

Roger says nothing, staring me down across his messy desk.

"But I don't understand, Sir, why are you giving this to *me*?"

"Because I don't have anyone else, and I've reached a dead end," he says flatly. "Thought perhaps you could take a look at it. Since you seem to have a good brain for it."

"Good brain for it..." Right. *That's why you're involving me.*

I nod, flipping the page to see another photo of a body, this one of a woman. She is also naked and in the woods this one positioned on her hands and knees.

"Toxicology says there's a number of drugs present, and there's evidence of ligature marks around the neck," Roger grunts, taking a sip of the black sludge in his Styrofoam cup. "Still waiting on a coroner's report."

"I heard he wraps wire around the bodies."

"Where did you hear that?" Roger asks me, raising a brow.

"Your advanced team talks too much on the mats," I smirk. "And those walls in the gym are very acoustically generous."

"Is that a fact..." he says, rolling his eyes. "Well, I'll have to have a chat with them about that."

"He doesn't use the wire to kill them though," I say, looking at yet another photo.

"No, he doesn't," Roger says quietly.

"...He's using it to *position* them," I say, looking at another photo, this of another man, on his back, legs straight up in the air and open. "You know, until rigor mortis sets in anyway."

"No shit," he whispers.

"Do we know if there was sexual activity?"

"Unfortunately, yes," Roger sighs. "But only one set of DNA is present. So, he's a serial rapist and murderer, who works alone, but seems to swing both ways. And who enjoys fucking with us."

I shake my head.

"You're wrong."

"Excuse me?" Roger says, snapping back to attention and shooting a glare in my direction.

"I said you're wrong," I repeat. "He's not fucking with you."

"Oh yes he is!" Roger says loudly. "Why the hell else would this sicko be leaving the bodies in those fucked up positions?!"

Jesus, someone is grumpy today.

"Answer me this," I say, ignoring him as I pull four of the photos of the deceased out of the file and slide it across the table toward him. "You call him the Alphabet Killer, why?"

"Because he's positioning the bodies in the shape of letters of the alphabet. We think he's spelling out a message." Roger says gruffly, pulling out his cigarettes. "I take it you didn't pick *that* part up from the mat sessions in the gym?"

Definitely grumpy. Wonder when was the last time he slept?

"Hey, don't be mad at me," I say with a smirk. "It's *your* team that's loose-lipped."

"Now wait just a minute—"

"But," I continue. "That's not accurate either. This has nothing to do with the alphabet, and this isn't a message."

Roger's face turns a bright shade of red.

"Son, I'm—"

"It's *art*."

The redness instantly disappears, and a look of complete shock skates across it instead.

"*What?*" he whispers.

"Sir," I say, taking a deep breath. "The range of possible motivations for serial killers are extensive and nearly impossible to pin down. But we do know that the vast majority of them focus on three things: availability, vulnerability, and desirability. You said that the first day I sat in your class, Sir."

He just continues to stare at me.

"And, yes, some of them want a message conveyed to the world. They want their story told."

He opens his mouth to say something, but I continue on.

"But the idea that he would take the time to position his victim's bodies in a way to give you one letter of the alphabet at a time, well, that would be a significant waste of time. And a risk for what would be his primary goal—*notoriety*. That takes time a killer can't guarantee he will have. And, if he's caught, at any point, he could risk not getting to tell his story."

Roger sits back in his chair.

"Go on," he says quietly.

"This isn't the alphabet, Sir," I say leaning over the desk. "It's art. These are BDSM poses."

I grab the photo of the man nailed in an X shape across two trees.

"The *Falcon* pose," I say, grabbing the photo of the woman, sitting on her knees. "The one you thought was an A? This is *Nadu*."

I grab a handful of the other photos.

"And the one you thought was a Y? That's the *Humble* position. N is *Table*, and the I is *Attention*," I say listing them off as I lay the photos back on the desk.

He stares at all the pictures and then collapses back against his chair, staring at me, his jaw slightly ajar.

"And there's more, Sir," I say, picking up the man in the X shape. "This man here? This is Alvin Marion. He's the son of the primary real estate developer for Central Park. And the woman here, in *Nadu*, is Desiree North, she's the daughter of a prominent Wall Street investor."

"Aw come on!" He laughs, waving me off. "And how the hell do you know that?!"

"Because, Sir, you currently have me working missing person's cases, and these families hire pushy people to call and harass us daily until we solve their cases. So, I'm used to fielding their phone calls. Specifically, from these two families."

"Oh my fucking God."

"I think you're looking for a killer who is connected to the BDSM community, as well as the aristocracy," I say, flipping back through the pages. "I'd be willing to bet, he's a trust-fund baby whose trust ran out of money. So now he has to work some insignificant, grunt-work job that has a polarity to the lifestyle he grew up around. So maybe check out some of the less-frequented art galleries, or residencies of college professors for contemporary art."

"Two of the victims had fake New York IDs in their belongings," Roger says, rubbing his chin. "And the concierge at the hotel Alvin Marion was staying at said that he checked in under that name," he says, raising a brow at me. "That's why I was surprised you knew that name. We just got his real identification back this morning. I'm surprised we didn't make that connection sooner."

"Don't feel bad, Sir," I say, shaking my head. "These are wealthy people who enjoy particular fetishes, and who will go to great lengths to enjoy those particular fetishes without risk to their reputation. They don't want to be discovered. But that's your confirmation that at least two of the victims knew each other."

"And how the hell do you know so much about this?"

I shift uncomfortably.

"I, uh," I say, clearing my throat. "I was involved with a bit of that community myself for a time."

"So," Roger says, rubbing his chin. "We need to get in touch with someone who heads up this...what did you call it? Kink thing."

"With all due respect, Sir," I say cautiously. "That's not going to happen."

"And why the hell not?"

"It's not exactly something I can explain to you in a simple briefing, Sir. But what I can tell you, is that privacy and anonymity is of the utmost concern. And will be even more so with a group that caters directly to the elite."

"What are you talking about?" Roger says, incredulously. "What are these people into here?"

I snort, clicking my tongue inside my check.

"As I said, Sir, it's not that simple. There's lots of groups and subfactions, some of which involve anonymous, casual sex. Others still can involve degradation, role-playing, humiliation, punishments, bondage, or Shibari, all of which is safer in the hands of someone who knows what they're doing. And that's how I think our perp has marketed himself, as a professional."

"You're saying he's a prostitute?" Roger says, folding his arms.

"No sir, that's not what I'm saying" I say, staring him down. "BDSM doesn't equal prostitution."

I sigh, leaning forward and rubbing my eyes.

How do I explain BDSM to a square like Weatherstone?

"Think of it like a club, Sir," I say, carefully. "For the recreational enjoyment of sexual fetishes by *consenting* adults. And sometimes, depending on the fetish, seeking out a trained professional is the safest way to enjoy it without injury."

"I mean, that's weird, but okay," Weatherstone snorts.

"Right there," I say, pointing at him. "For you, as a straight and narrow, God-fearing man from Virginia, the fact that some people *enjoy* that kind of recreational activity is simply weird and bizarre. It can come with an unfriendly stigma, and the fact *prostitution* was your immediate assumption, combined with the fact that sex work is illegal in most of the continental US, is exactly why some of these subfactions operate largely in anonymity. People like to keep their sexual preferences, whatever they may be, private for their reputations and safety."

"Right, but if it's not safe—"

"It *is* safe," I say firmly. "The community has safeguards and watchtowers of their own that prevent predators from thriving and getting this sort of thing, and I can assure you, that this one lone dissenter does not speak for the whole."

"So then," Roger asks. "How is he getting away with it?"

"Because he isn't working *alone*."

Roger nearly drops his coffee.

"He has an accomplice," I say with a nod, narrowing my eyes. "I guarantee it. And I'd be willing to be, it's likely a female. And the two of them are counting on the community's prioritization of privacy to protect them."

"Well, if we can't get anyone to speak to us," Roger says, shaking his head. "It will protect them, but leave lots of other people vulnerable."

I smile.

"I said *you* couldn't get anyone to talk to you, Sir," I grin. "I never said anything about *me*."

CHAPTER TWENTY-ONE
Rachel

I am completely enraptured in Adam's story, when suddenly I hear a knock at the front door, and immediately jump to my feet.

Sneaking over to the window, I covertly take a peek through the curtains.

"Shit! It's Ethan, and a couple of Jaxon's Beta Squad goons!" I whisper, ducking down.

"I thought you said you scared them all off?" Adam says, crouching behind the couch.

"I did!" I whisper forcefully.

"And I also recall you saying that only the Don Supreme himself would have the balls to show up here?!"

"Yeah, well," I snap, quietly closing the door to the office. "I guess that *technically* applies to Ethan too."

"What?!"

"In a way, it applics to him too. As I said, it's complicated!"

"Again," Adam snaps irritably. "Understatement!"

Another knock at the door.

"Fuck!" I say, running my hands through my hair anxiously.

"What do we do?"

"Can't we just ignore them?" He asks.

"Um, not really. I can't exactly tell them I *wasn't* home while under house arrest, Adam."

"Shit, good point," he says.

More knocking bangs against the door, this time louder than the first. He stands in front of the painting that hides the tunnel entrance, straining to get a better view out the window.

That's it! The tunnel!

Scrambling over to him, I pull the hidden lever switch on the picture frame.

"Get in."

"*What*?"

"Look, I can't ignore them because they still have a key. Which means there's nothing stopping them from just coming inside the house," I say as the picture door swings open.

"So we're leaving?"

"Not *we*, just you."

"Wait, what?!" Adam says, his eyes wide. "You want me to leave? Without you?"

"No! I just want you to *hide* until I can get them to leave!"

He glances into the dark hole in the wall.

"You mean…in the tunnel?"

"No, Adam in my magic fucking portal device!" I whisper sarcastically, as more knocking continues. "Yes, in the damn tunnel!"

"What do they want?"

"Well, last I checked I can't read minds so I can't be sure, but I can only assume it has something to do with me yeeting the maid's vacuum over the balcony!"

"What if it's not that?"

"Then I'll figure something else out," I say, waving him toward the tunnel aggressively. "But they don't know about you, or about the tunnel, so it's the safest place to hide you."

"No, I'm staying with you," Adam says firmly, shaking his head. "I don't trust them. Especially Ethan."

I roll my eyes.

"Look, I get he threatened you for beating his son to a pulp, but he's a good guy. Unlike Jaxon, Ethan's reasonable," I say forcefully. "But if he knows you're here, there's a good chance that he, or the men with him, will kill you."

"Yeah, that sounds really fucking *reasonable*, Rachel!" Adam hisses.

"Oh, you know what I meant!" I whisper back, as more knocking echoes through the house. "And I'm sorry, but I'm not willing to take chances with your life!"

"I'd like to see those fuckers try," Adam growls, reaching for his gun.

The doorbell rings twice.

"Oh for Christ's sake!" I snap, pushing Adam toward the tunnel. "I appreciate your bravery, but I promise, you can be brave another time. It's the Mafia, there's always plenty of opportunities!"

Finally, Adam relents and steps into the tunnel.

"But what do I...I mean, what am I supposed to do in here?"

"What?" I ask, exasperated. "I don't know, contemplate life? Or pretend you're a ghost for all I care. Just do it quietly!"

"No, Rachel," Adam snaps, now rolling his eyes at me. "I meant what do I need to do to turn on the fucking *lights*."

"Oh..."

Oops.

I'm momentarily embarrassed, However, the doorbell rings again and I'm snapped back to the present.

"There's a bar on the door that locks it in place," I rattle off quickly, hearing more pounding on the door. "Once I close it, throw the bar on, then hit the light switch. It takes a minute, but it will come on once the door is locked. I'll open it when the coast is clear!"

"And if something happens to you?!" Adam asks. "What then? I'm just stuck in the tunnel forever?"

"If something happens to me, just walk the path to the other side, switch *off* the lights, and enter 0752 on the keypad. The entrance should open."

"*Should*?!" Adam asks, a slight nervousness in his tone.

But as the doorbell starts ringing again, I forcibly shove him in the tunnel and close the door. I hear him mumble something about the code on the other side, and then what sounds like crashing.

"Ow! Fuck!" he yells. "You could've mentioned there's some goddamn stairs here, Rachel!"

Shit! I forgot to tell him about that.

But I also can't have him making any noise, or he will give the tunnel entrance away.

"Well, that's your fault! You walked up the same steps!" I say, hissing at the picture. "But just keep it down in there! You're a ghost, remember?"

Then without another word, I turn and bolt toward the study doors, flinging them open and stepping into the foyer. Apparently just in time too, as I hear the sound of a key being inserted into the lock of the front door.

"Just a second!" I shout in the foyer. "I'm coming!"

Fuck! Why do I feel like I'm forgetting something?!

I glance around frantically.

But knowing Adam is really my only secret, and he is currently locked in the tunnel, hopefully still alive after falling down the stairs, I bend over and start fluffing my hair vigorously.

Better to look like a lazy bitch, than a sneaky one.

Then I open the door.

"Jesus Christ!" I demand, faking a yawn. "Can't a girl sleep around here? Or are you people determined to drive me insane?"

"Good morning, Miss Valentine," Ethan says politely. "Or should I say, afternoon. May I come in?"

"Um, I'd rather you didn't," I snort, crossing my arms across my body. "But I assume that's not really a *question*, is it?"

Ethan smiles.

"That would be correct, Miss Valentine," he says quietly. "Considering the complaint filed by the cleaning ladies, and the chef that Mr. Pace hired *specifically* for you, he intended to come by himself, but I told him it was probably best if I came instead."

Double fuck.

"So, may I come inside?"

"Fine," I say, rolling my eyes. "But only if you cool it with the Miss Valentine shit. You know how much I hate that, Ethan."

Stepping out of the way, I open the door for him completely, allowing him to step inside with me, but he turns to the men with him.

"I'll only be a moment," he says with a smile, holding his hand up. "Just wait here for me please, gentlemen."

"But, Sir," the tall dark-haired one says, glancing up at me nervously. "Mr. Pace said that we were to never leave you—"

"I will tell Mr. Pace that you *did* accompany me, Alexei," Ethan says, his eyes now cold, and his voice stern. "But you *will* wait here, do you understand?"

The men look at me, and then at Ethan, before stepping back down onto the porch.

"Yes, Sir," the one called Alexei says with a nod. "We will wait here."

"Good lad," Ethan smiles.

He steps inside and I close the door behind him.

"So," I say as my heart immediately starts pounding. "What can I do for you?"

Silently, Ethan walks over to the busted tile in the middle of the floor and touches the pieces with his foot.

"You know, your father once told me that these tiles were all imported Italian marble," he says, picking up one of the pieces. "They're usually all cut from the same stone, and so they are incredibly hard to replace."

He looks up at me.

"…And incredibly hard to break."

Way to go me.

"Well, the vacuum was really heavy," I smile, with a bitchy little wink. "Also fuck my father and fuck his fancy tiles."

Ethan chuckles.

"Yeah, I can understand why you feel that way."

I can't explain why, but something about the way Ethan says this disarms me slightly.

I've been angry with Ethan, but I don't know if I actually have a valid *reason* to be angry with him. Perhaps it was the fact that Ethan was always the one calming me down after one of Jaxon's fuckups, or the one cleaning up his messes. Perhaps that's what made me think of an accomplice to Jaxon's behavior.

But deep down, I know that's not true.

What is true, however, is that Ethan was the one who kept in contact with me when I moved to Texas. He was the one I called when I desperately needed updates on my daughter.

He was also the one who volunteered to write the letter to Jaxon, telling him that I was never coming home.

Knowing a bit more of Ethan's past, explains more of how he sees the world. The fact that Ethan was once Mikanos Pace, the eldest son of Stephanos Pace. He was *the* heir and future Don

257

Supreme.

But he chose not to become the Don and heir to the Pace fortune, and instead chose a humble life of military service. However, when circumstances forced him to choose between his new life and his family, Ethan chose his family. And when his brother Dimitris was unable to conceive, Ethan volunteered as a donor to insure the Pace family line continued.

Through *his* son, Jaxon Pace.

Which meant that ultimately, Ethan apologizing and cleaning up on Jaxon's behalf, or giving me updates on my daughter, was nothing more than a father and grandfather doing what he could to protect and prosper the family he loved.

And perhaps the reason I could never understand, is because I didn't *have* a loving family. I had an asshole father who cared more about expensive Italian marble than about anything that was important to me.

"You know," Ethan says softly. "The staff weren't trying to irritate or pester you. They were here to make your life easier."

I swallow hard.

Could I tell Ethan about Adam? Could I trust him?

No. It's too much of a risk.

The last interaction Jaxon and Adam had, involved Adam kidnapping and interrogating Jaxon with a taser in an old, abandoned warehouse. And Jaxon, being the antagonistic asshole he is, somehow pushed Adam so far that Adam nearly killed him.

I still wonder what Jaxon said that upset Adam so bad?

"I know," I say, licking my bottom lip and glancing into the study. "I just wanted some time. *Alone.*"

Ethan stares at me for a minute, and then sighs with a nod. But then, to my horror, he walks toward the open study doors.

Oh shit. Oh shit. Oh shit.

I scramble quickly to follow after him, praying to God Adam is silent in the tunnel.

"You know," he says, walking into the room, surveying all of the collected famous art on the walls. "Jaxon isn't one for praise. Or apologies."

"I actually do know that," I say, sarcastically.

"...But he wouldn't be alive without you."

Ethan turns back to face me.

"You had a choice that night," he says, his heavy stare now

appraising me. "You could have chosen not to help Charlie and the team find Jaxon. But you did. And I'm curious as to *why?*"

I bite my bottom lip and cross my arms across my chest.

"Why?" I ask, taking a deep breath. "Because I know that Jaxon is the best hope of safety for Jessica. And even though you people think I'm a shitty mother—"

"I don't think that, Rachel," Ethan says firmly, cutting me off and momentarily making me lose track of my thoughts.

"Well, to the people who do think that," I say quietly. "I only ever want what's best for her. And I know that unfortunately, Jaxon is it."

"And do you actually believe that?" He asks.

The authority with which he asks nearly compels me to answer immediately, reminding me that this man was once indeed bred and trained to be a leader of men. He also has impeccable instincts and zero tolerance for bullshit.

…Or lies.

"Yes," I say, clearing my throat. "Jaxon can protect her in ways I can't. And with my brother on the loose, we all need protecting. Otherwise I wouldn't be here. As a prisoner."

Ethan stares at me, and then sighs.

He takes a step toward me, placing his hand in his pocket.

"I know this isn't ideal," he says quietly. "But Jaxon isn't…"

His voice trails off and he rubs his chin.

"He's not as stubborn as he used to be," he says before looking up at me. "The fact that you're here, and not in the bunker should be testament enough for that."

"You'll excuse me if I don't jump for joy," I say tilting my head to the side. "He still seems pretty fucking stubborn to me."

Ethan chuckles.

"Just give him time," he says softly. "You've saved his life more than once. As well as *mine*."

I say nothing, feeling my entire body tremble as I stare into Ethan's bright blue eyes.

"You've given him a gift he could never repay, Rachel. Several of them, in fact. He just needs time to see it."

I shift uncomfortably, a chill making me shiver as I lower my eyes to the floor.

"I've also *taken* from him," I whisper, trying to keep my voice quiet enough that Adam cannot hear it through the door. "And we know how unforgiving the Don Supreme can be."

I can't even look at Ethan as I say this. The guilt from the bullet I fired that hit Natalie in the stomach, killing their unborn child nearly suffocates me where I stand.

I want to tell Ethan it was all just an *accident*. A horrible mistake that happened too quickly.

I desperately want to explain that in the scuffle with Jaxon to take the gun back, I didn't even feel myself squeeze the trigger… and I didn't even know I hit her.

But I can't.

I simply stand here, staring at the dark oak hardwood floors of the study. Saying nothing.

Suddenly I feel Ethan's hand gently touch my shoulder.

"As I said," he says softly, his voice tender. "Just give him time."

Slowly, I look up at him, finding his face empathetic and kind.

"When he finally learned the truth about his parentage, I thought he might never forgive me," he says. "But, Jaxon, well, he surprised me."

He smiles with a nod.

"He might just surprise you too."

I wish I could believe that.

I know that Ethan means well. And I know that he just wants to give me hope that my relationship with Jaxon and Natalie will improve. But I don't see how it can.

"Tell me," Ethan says, his eyes drifting to the table in the study. "Do you usually drink coffee from *two* coffee cups?"

Fuck. That's what I was forgetting.

Immediately my stomach plummets through the floor as Ethan moves to the cups sitting on opposite sides of the table.

"I…I…" I say, my heart racing as I frantically try to think of some explanation. "I didn't like the first cup I made."

"Uh huh," He says, leaning in closer. "So why does only one have lipstick on it?"

He moves to the couch where Adam was sitting.

"And considering that Jaxon deliberately chose all female staff for you, to not make you uncomfortable," he says, sniffing loudly. "It seems strange that one of them would be wearing a male's cologne."

"Well," I say, feeling my cheeks heat. "You never know these days."

"Mmhmm," he says, turning back to face me.

He turns his inquisitive gaze to me, and I panic.

"Look, it's not what you think," I say quietly, my words choking in my throat. "I promise."

"And what do I think?" He asks, taking a step toward me.

Shit. He knows. Of course he knows.

"It's not Michael," I say quietly.

"Well, I'd kind of assumed as such," he says, crossing his arms. "Because as you just said, there'd be no reason for you to volunteer for Jaxon's protection if you just planned on inviting him back here with you."

Ethan and I lock eyes, silently staring at each other for what feels like an eternity.

"Where is he?" He finally asks, clearly referring to Adam.

"Hiding," I reply, trying to hide the way my breath is shaking.

My mind is racing.

Adam beat the ever-loving fuck out of Jaxon a week ago. If anyone has reason to hate Adam, it's Ethan.

Is he going to punish me? Will he take away my protection? Will he search this house top to bottom until he eventually finds Adam and then…

"Do you trust him?"

Ethan's question, barely above a whisper, surprises me.

"I…I do," I say softly. "That's why he's here. We had things to discuss. Things to work out."

"I can only imagine," Ethan says, his eyes still sternly scanning mine. "But quite a risk should anything *not* work out."

My eyes fall from his, his words reflecting my own deep-seated concerns about any kind of relationship with Adam.

"I guess that explains why you were so enthusiastic about clearing out the staff this morning."

I bite my lower lip.

Closing my eyes, I take a deep breath and ask the question I have to ask before it's too late.

"Is there any chance that you could just *not* say anything to Jaxon about this?"

Ethan stares at me, contemplating my request. And then without another word he turns and starts walking to the door.

"Ethan," I say, following after him, grabbing his arm gently.

"Please. I know I'm asking you for a massive favor here, but I need time, okay? Just to figure things out. Can you at least give me that?"

He sighs.

"I won't lie to Jaxon, Rachel." He says quietly. "I've done enough of that already."

Fuck.

I shut my eyes and feel my stomach twist, realizing that any momentary progress we've made, and the tiny fraction of peace I've had having Adam here is about to be taken away from me.

"But," he says softly. "I'm also *retired...*"

"What?"

"I don't work for Jaxon anymore," Ethan smirks at me. "So, I don't technically have to tell him anything."

"Oh..."

"However," he cautions. "As I said, I won't *lie* to him either. I don't know how you managed to finagle getting your secret guest here, but I suggest you *keep* him a secret. Because while I can pretend I didn't see any extra coffee cups, I can't say the same for any of the staff."

Oh my God.

Without thinking, I throw my arms around him, hugging him tightly.

"Thank you, Ethan," I whisper, feeling him gently squeeze me back. "Thank you."

"I'm sure I don't know what you're referring to," he says softly. "But just don't make me regret this. I have enough of those to last a lifetime."

I nod, releasing him.

"And if you're fine cooking for yourself, I'll arrange to have a grocery order dropped at the door. And I'll delay the cleaning people until next Friday. So, if your *friend* is still here, make sure you hide him well."

"That works," I say, still in shock.

He reaches for the doorknob but stops, turning back to face me.

"And if anything goes...wrong," he says quietly. "Promise me that you'll get yourself somewhere safe and call me. *First.*"

Oh wow.

The emotions that this simple statement evokes within my

chest nearly cracks me in half, and all I can do is nod.

He didn't have to do this. He could have just as easily killed me, or Adam, or thrown both of us on the street. But he didn't.

"Until next time, Miss Valentine," Ethan says with a polite smile, and without another word, he opens the front door and walks out.

"So what you're saying is," Adam says slowly. "Ethan knows...about us."

I nod.

"And you trust him not to say anything? To Jaxon?"

"I do," I say, tucking my hair behind my ear. "I can't explain why, but I do."

Adam stands with his arms across his body, rubbing his chin.

"Well, I guess we have to hope that trust isn't misplaced," he says softly.

"Seems like there's a lot of that going around lately," I say gently. "We've all got some skin in the game now."

He stares at me for a moment before sighing heavily, apparently accepting my assessment.

"But, it also means we're on our own for dinner," I say looking toward the kitchen. "And my culinary expertise is limited to scrambled eggs."

Adam snorts, the first smirk since his emergence from the tunnel skating across his face.

"Fortunately for you, I've got a bit more," he says, nodding toward the kitchen. "Let's go see what we've got."

And for the first time in hours, I finally relax a little. I open the refrigerator as he heads into the pantry.

"Do we have eggs and bacon?" he calls.

"Um, yes?" I ask, raising my eyebrow. "But I thought we weren't doing more scrambled eggs?"

"We aren't," he says, emerging with a block of cheese and a package of spaghetti. "I'm making you carbonara."

"What's that?"

"Food. Food that's delicious and easy," Adam says. "So you

263

can keep talking."

"Me?" I snort. "I mean technically you were the one on the story deck when we got interrupted."

"True," He shrugs, grabbing a pot from the cupboard and filling it with water. "But now I'm cooking. So, for the time being, my story is on hold, and you get to tell me what happened after Jaxon showed up at your apartment and beat your brother's ass."

"I mean, that was the gist of it," I shrug. "As much as I hated using my pregnancy as a way to get Jaxon's attention, I knew it would. I knew that he would drop whatever, or *whomever*, he was doing and drive immediately over to my house. I just didn't expect he'd possibly be saving my life in the process."

"What did he do with your brother?"

"Oh his goons carted Michael off somewhere," I say, pulling a strand of purple grapes from the bowl on the counter. "The minute I was loaded with a Mafia baby was the moment I became the safest woman in the city. No one could touch me."

Adam raises his eyebrows as he starts chopping a small slab of bacon into pieces.

"That's certainly one way of putting it," he says, his chopping becoming slightly aggressive. "Did you…confront him about the woman you saw him with?"

I nod.

"He confessed everything," I say quietly. "Her name was Polina, and she was the sister of Roman Antonov, the man he was trying to do business with. Apparently, she'd been really aggressive in her advances and Jaxon felt somewhat obligated to go along with it for the sake of his father's business proposal."

Adam looks up at me, his 'are you kidding me?' stare likely mimicking my own.

"Yeah…" I say.

"Prostituting your son for business," he says as he puts a pan on the stove. "Sounds pretty on brand for the Mafia."

"Jaxon said that she was really drunk, and being really aggressive, and they fooled around a bit, but she ended up passing out before…"

My voice trails off as I toss the rest of the grapes back in the bowl, my appetite suddenly nullified at the very memory of that conversation.

"And you believed him?" Adam asks quietly, dumping the bacon into the pan.

"No, not really," I shrug. "He had the reputation of being a man whore, and I knew that *everyone* couldn't be wrong. However, I could look past it, because technically I'd had Yuri in *my* bed just a few hours prior."

"Did you tell Jaxon about Yuri?"

"No," I say, lowering my eyes to the granite countertop.

"I assume because you were worried Jaxon would kill him."

"No," I say matter-of-factly. "That sounds more noble. But I simply didn't tell him because, well, I guess I just liked watching him grovel."

"Oh," Adam nods, without turning around. "I see."

"Yeah, I know, that sounds horrible," I roll my eyes. "But I was angry, okay? Everything Jess had said to me the night I found out I was pregnant was true. For months I'd been putting my entire life on hold for Jaxon, and I resented him a little for it. Regardless of whether it's right or wrong, I knew the only reason I slept with Yuri in the first place was because I saw Jaxon there that night with that Russian slut. It was retaliatory."

"I get it," Adam nods, dumping the pasta into the boiling water. "But I'm sure I don't have to tell you that it never ends well."

"No, you don't," I say, trying to hide my annoyance.

I shift uncomfortably on the stool.

"Well, go on," Adam encourages. "Continue."

"Anyways, he was shocked by the pregnancy," I say, tucking my hair behind my ear. "But then he also asked me what I wanted to do about it, which was…surprising."

"He might just surprise you too."

Ethan's words from earlier ring in my ears, ironically finding my own example of Jaxon's capacity for growth.

"Why was it surprising?"

"Because, that's not typical behavior for a Mafia Don."

"But Jaxon wasn't a Mafia Don yet, right?" Adam asks.

"True but even mafia-dons-to-be are obsessed with legacy. And heirs. So my assumption from the get-go was that I had no choice in the matter."

"But," Adam says, pressing his hands on the counter top and sighing heavily. "Jaxon gave you one."

I nod.

"It's a credit I will give him," I sigh. "He didn't force me, and he wanted me to know I wasn't forced."

Adam says nothing, his clear disdain for Jaxon overpowering his ability to say anything nice about him whatsoever.

Kinda cute actually.

"Well, anyways," I continue. "Once I told him that I was committed to having the baby, he was excited. Nervous, but still excited. He called his parents on the spot and told them that he had important news to tell them, and that it couldn't wait. And then he told them that he was bringing a guest to dinner…"

"You're…pregnant?" Jaxon's mother, Ismena, gasps.

"I am," I nod, biting my lip.

"Out!" Dimitris, Jaxon's father, suddenly thunders at the servant refilling his wine glass. "Now!"

"Would you like me to step out, Sir?" Ethan asks from his usual post in the corner. "For your privacy?"

"No, no," Dimitris says, shaking his head. "You can stay, Ethan. I think you're going to want to hear this too."

That's odd. Not sure why Ethan would be invited to stay?

"When did you…I mean how long have you known?" Ismena asks gently, folding her hands on the gigantic solid oak table in front of us.

"Well, I took the test yesterday evening."

"And you two waited this *long* to tell us?" Dimitris asks, looking sternly at Jaxon.

This long? It's only been twenty-four hours, dude.

"Well…I-" I start to say, but Jaxon interrupts me.

"Rachel tried to text me last night," Jaxon lies, placing his hand on top of mine as it begins to shake. "But I didn't see it."

"That's what your men are supposed to be for," His father scolds. "They are meant to keep your shit together. Keep you in the know. If they can't do that then maybe you need—"

"They do," Jaxon snaps back. "My men are reliable."

"Clearly not," Dimitris grumbles. "Especially if you have a

potential heir out there in the world, unprotected for a full twenty-four hours. That's—"

"Dimitris," Ismena suddenly interjects. Her tone is quiet, but firm as is the glare she gives her husband, that seems to say a dozen things with just one word.

He looks at her silently before nodding.

"What your father means to say," Ismena says, her eyes lingering on Dimitris before smiling warmly at Jaxon and I. "Congratulations, Sweetheart. We are so happy for you both."

"Thank you, Mom," Jaxon says affectionately, squeezing my hand gently.

"I'm sure you're both a little shocked and a little scared, but I promise parenthood isn't as bad as you—"

She coughs suddenly, covering her mouth with her cloth napkin. At first it starts out softly, but then quickly progresses into something much deeper…and more concerning.

Jaxon did mention that his mother had been ill recently.

"Mom?" Jaxon asks, pushing his chair back.

But Dimitris is already on his feet, moving to his wife and pouring her a glass of water.

"Αγαπημένη," Dimitris whispers tenderly, asking her a question in Greek as he gently rubs her back between her shoulder blades. However, Ismena smiles and shakes her head. Holding his concerned gaze, she whispers something back to her husband, in his native tongue. Dimitris sighs, kissing her forehead before scooting his chair closer to hers.

"Forgive me," he says, turning back to us, his tone noticeably softer. "But my wife has informed me that I am handling this like a bit of an ass. Obviously this is a bit of a shock, and we will have to adjust a few…things…on our end, but we can pivot."

"Things?" Jaxon asks, confused. "What things?"

"Things we can discuss at a later time," Dimitris says as he waves him off. "What's most important are the two of you. Now, I assume you have discussed your plans for the wedding?"

"*What?*" I say, my voice squeaking from my throat.

"The wedding?" He repeats, looking between me and Jaxon. "I assumed that my son has already explained to you that there is protocol for this kind of situation."

"Um, no," I scoff, looking up at Jaxon. "What wedding?"

"We, uh," Jaxon says, clearing his throat. "Hadn't quite gotten that far yet."

"Well, that's fine," Dimitris says with a smile. "We have people that can assist with whatever arrangements you need. You're also welcome to take the South wing and decorate the apartments however you see fit. Unless, of course you want to move—"

"Wait, wait, wait," I say, looking frantically between Jaxon and his parents. "We haven't decided if we *want* to get married yet."

"Oh my," Ismena gasps, closing her eyes.

"That's not really how this works, Rachel," Jaxon says. "We can talk about that later."

"Um, yes it *is*," I glare at him, gritting my teeth. "It works however *we* say it works, Jaxon."

"No, Sweetheart," Ismena says gently. "There's rules. Protocol. You have to get married. For everyone's sake."

"I'm sorry but no we…er…*I* don't." I say, shaking my head.

"Yes you do," Dimitris says coldly. "It's not up for negotiation."

"Excuse me?!"

"Rachel," Jaxon cautions. "Just stop talking. We can discuss this later."

"No, Jaxon," I snap at him. "I said I wanted to have the baby, but I never said I wanted to get married."

"It's not that simple," Jaxon hisses.

"And it's not up for discussion," Dimitris says firmly. "My son is a Pace. And he's the future Don Supreme."

"I don't care if he's the fucking King of England!" I practically shout as I push my chair back from the table and stand up. "I'm not being bullied or forced into marriage!"

"Sweetheart, no one is—"

Ismena starts to say but she can't even finish her sentence before she is coughing again.

As I stand here shaking in my boots, trying to catch my breath, Dimitris's attention is pulled from me and back to his wife. He motions for Ethan to come forward and the three of them have a short, whispered conversation.

"Do not worry about this, my love," he says pleadingly. "I will handle this. Please, just go rest. I will come find you later. Ethan, will you please help her back to our room?"

Ethan nods as Dimitris leans in to kiss his wife's hand.

It is then that I realize that the chair she has been sitting in the entire time has actually been a *wheelchair*, as Ethan slowly backs it up and out of the room. But as she is wheeled away, the cloth napkin she'd been holding falls to the floor.

...And it's covered in bright red blood.

Holy shit. Jaxon's mother is very sick.

The ornately decorated dining room falls as silent as the grave, spotted only by Dimitris's slow and deliberate footsteps as he walks over to the napkin.

 Picking it up, he stares at it for a moment before folding the blood-soaked fabric into his fist, gripping it tightly.

"I'm only going to say this once," Dimitris growls, glaring at Jaxon and I. "I have far more important things to care about than you and your childish bullshit."

"I'm not a ch—" I start to say.

"Then stop acting like one!" He thunders loudly, making me jump. "You know, I was going to spare your girlfriend this conversation, because I felt it was unsightly for a lady, but since she doesn't have any regard for decorum, why should I? Perhaps she needs to hear it."

He takes a step toward the two of us, and I instinctively retreat behind Jaxon, my heart pounding so loud I can hear it in my ears.

"I got a call from Roman Antonov's father today," Dimitris says, turning his attention to Jaxon. "He wanted to know what I thought about a marriage between you and his daughter Polina. Apparently, he thinks it was a good idea, considering she told him that *you* fucked her last night."

"*What?*" I whisper, all the air being sucked from my lungs.

"That is *not* what happened," Jaxon growls. "We did not sleep together. She came onto me, and I didn't want to offend Roman so I—"

"I don't fucking care what you did and didn't do!" Dimitris shouts, throwing his wine glass and sending it shattering on to the floor. "I care about this family, as you should too!"

"I do care about this fucking family!" Jaxon shouts back.

"Let me tell something, young man, if you think you're going to lead someday as the Don Supreme of this family—"

"I *am* going to lead this family," Jaxon snaps back forcefully, glaring at his father.

"Then I suggest you stop risking our reputation, our safety, and our business relationships just to wet your fucking cock!"

"That's not what fucking happened here!" Jaxon thunders.

"Yeah?! And what about her?" He shouts, waving at me. "Are you going to tell me you *didn't* get this girl pregnant?"

Jaxon grits his teeth but lowers his eyes, unable to respond.

"Wake up, Son! You're going to be a father now and have a child! And yet you're out here acting like one! Pull your head out of your ass and get your fucking priorities in order!"

Jaxon balls his fist and steps up to his father.

Oh my God, he's going to fight him?!

But just before it comes to blows, Ethan steps into the room.

"Sirs, Mrs. Pace is asking for you. I think you should come with me," He says, carefully appraising the situation he just walked into. "*Both* of you."

Without another word Dimitris turns and walks quickly from the room, with Jaxon hot on his heels.

I have no words. I simply slump into my chair, feeling the tears stream down my cheeks and regretting ever getting involved with Jaxon, and the entire Pace family.

CHAPTER TWENTY-TWO

ADAM

Rachel spins her fork around in her carbonara.

"Wow," is all I can say.

"Yeah," she whispers. "My shit-u-ation was pretty clear to me then."

"What happened after that *pleasant* conversation?"

"Well, the entire evening was derailed by Ismena's declining health. They called in a doctor, and we spent the night there."

"Did she die?"

"Not that night. But everyone was on high alert, and so none of us slept a wink," she says, taking another bite. "And that's where I overheard them talking about me."

"What?"

She snorts.

"Yeah. As I said, none of us could sleep," she says, gingerly playing with a piece of bacon with the end of her fork. "I'd heard there was a massive library at the Pace Manor, so I went for a walk and tried to find it. But, when I did, I heard them."

"Who is *them*?"

"Jaxon, Dimitris, Ethan," she sighs, grabbing her wine glass. "They were talking about Ismena and then me, and my family. None of it was very flattering."

"Jaxon too?"

"To his credit, he was doing his best to defend me," she says, spinning the wine inside the glass in her hand as she sits back against the chair. "But I'm sure you can imagine the things being said when your mother is known for being *the* stripper who pinned down a Mafia Don."

"Jesus," I say, turning my attention back to my food.

"It wasn't the first time I'd heard people talking shit," she sighs. "But this was harsher somehow. Like it just confirmed for me further, that I wasn't good enough for Jaxon. And considering the deal the Antonov's were trying to make, Jaxon knocking me up had thrown a big ass wrench in their business negotiations."

"But, it doesn't sound like Jaxon *wanted* to marry that girl."

She shakes her head.

"What Jaxon wanted didn't matter. And had he not knocked me up, I guarantee he probably would have married that bitch. You have to understand, Jaxon, at his core, has always been a family man. He was born and bred for his role as the Don Supreme and would always do whatever was asked of him. If his parents told him to marry that girl, he would've done it."

"But they didn't?"

"No," she says softly. "The heir in my womb was far more important."

"Was Roman Antonov upset? Like, was he offended?"

"Meh," she shrugs. "The Russians were weird. They just didn't get offended over shit like that. At least Roman didn't. And even though his father was technically in control, like Jaxon, Roman was starting to sit in the driver's seat more. Like Dimitris was doing with Jaxon."

"How cute," I snort.

"And I guess apparently, the sister was pushing for the match more than anyone else was, and I think Roman knew Jaxon wasn't that interested in it. So once I came into the picture, I provided a good enough excuse for him to say no. He couldn't allow his sister to marry a man with a bastard heir out in the world."

"So," I say, grabbing my wine to try and hide my face. "I take it you didn't agree to marry Jaxon, even after all that."

She shakes her head.

"No. I didn't," she whispers. "I did, however, negotiate with him to get Jessica out of jail."

"What?"

"Yeah," she smiles. "I was kinda proud of that. I told him I'd consider his marriage proposal, but only if he helped post Jessica's bail. In the end, he made a phone call and got the assault charges completely dropped."

"But what about the—"

"Drugs?" Rachel says, interrupting me. "I forgot about them. So they stayed stashed in my bag. And whether or not she knew, Jess didn't ask about it so I kind of forgot about it."

"But what about her charges? I thought you said the girl ended up in the hospital? I mean that had to have warranted a felony at least."

She shrugs.

"I don't know about all that. All I know is, he made a phone call and sent a car to pick her up. She was back at the apartment when I got home the next day."

I shake my head.

"Wow. It's like you people live in an alternate reality," I say, pouring myself another glass of wine. "So what, you said you'd think about it, and that was good enough for Jaxon's father?"

"No, not really."

"Oh, so he pushed back against his father?"

"No, he didn't do that either. He just sort of dropped the subject of marriage entirely. He said we could discuss it at a later time, but then a bunch more shit happened."

She takes another bite and looks up at me with a polite smile.

"This is really good by the way."

"I'm glad you like it."

"Where'd you learn to make this?"

"Well," I smirk. "The last few years I've had trouble sleeping at night. I would inevitably end up watching this late-night cooking infomercial show called *Cook-ing for Dummies,* with this ex-celebrity chef named Sebastian Cook."

"You know," Rachel says, pointing her fork at me. "I think I've heard of that show! That's the guy who teaches you how to make easy dishes with ten ingredients or less—"

"While also not-so-subtly plugging his line of cookware." I finish. "Yeah, I don't own any of that cookware, but I definitely taped a few episodes. Thought I should know how to make something besides just plain old mac and cheese."

"Just make it with bacon, pepper, and eggs," Rachel winks at me. "And then you can call it *carbonara*."

I stare at the plate of food.

"No shit…" I snort. "I never really thought of it like that."

She giggles into her wine glass.

"I mean, you have to admit, it's a lot of the same ingredients."

"Don't let an East Coast Italian hear you say that," I say, shaking my finger at her, as she hides her smirk with her hand. "Here I was thinking I was impressing you with my culinary expertise, and you go calling it fancy mac and cheese."

And for just a second, the serious nature of our conversation is interrupted, as the two of us share a laugh.

"For what it's worth," she says, still giggling softly as she gently toasts her wine glass against mine. "Whatever you call it, it was delicious."

"You know," I chuckle, taking a drink. "Sometimes you're a bit of a *brat*."

"At your service," she says, saluting me.

"Not now," I say, winking at her. "But maybe later."

A wickedly devious grin skates across her face before she tries to hide it.

Fuck she's hot.

I stare into her dark brown eyes, visions of me dumping all of the dishes off the table and ramming my cock deep inside of her race through my mind.

However, I don't want to *only* fuck her.

There is a part of me that still wants Rachel to let me make love to her. Perhaps a part of me that needs to know she'll *let* me make love to her, to know that we are serious.

"But," she interrupts me. "It's your turn."

"What?"

"For the story?" She says, dumping the rest of the bottle of wine into her glass. "You're up."

"I think we'd need another bottle for that," I say downing the rest of my glass.

"Good thing the cellar is well stocked," she says as she takes my plate. "So tell ya what? I'll do the dishes while you get more wine."

"You're going to do the dishes?"

"You sound surprised."

"Well, in my defense you did give me a big speech about not knowing how to boil water."

"Don't let the fancy house fool you, Mr. Westwood," she says as she walks over to the sink. "I've been on my own for a while. You can get away with not cooking, but you'll run out of dishes if you don't wash them."

"Fair enough" I chuckle.

But just before I turn to walk into the wine cellar, I catch a glimpse of her curvy ass in her leggings and suddenly nothing else matters.

I can make love to her later. Right now, I'm going to fuck her.

She turns the faucet on, but just as she runs the first dish under the water, I wrap my arms around her waist.

"Adam," she gasps. "What are you…what are you doing?"

"Don't turn around," I whisper darkly against her neck. "You just keep pretending you're a good girl, and wash the dishes."

"Excuse me?!" She starts to say, but before she can turn around I wrap my hand around her neck

"I said," I growl, squeezing her throat and biting her neck softly. "Wash. The. Fucking. Dishes."

I feel her shudder.

With one hand on her hips, I slowly slide the other down her breast, taking my time to squeeze it before continuing down her stomach. I slip my fingers inside the front hem of her pants, and she shivers, feeling me rub the thin fabric of her panties against her pussy.

"Ohhh, fuck," she gasps, nearly dropping the dish in her hand.

"Now, now, don't go getting distracted, Miss Valentine," I say softly, sucking on her earlobe as I press harder against her clothed pussy, sliding my finger back and forth across her slit. "Can you stay focused?"

"Ye…yes…" she moans as I hook my fingers in her leggings and start to pull them down.

"I don't see any scrubbing," I say as I stop, deliberately pulling her body against my throbbing erection.

I feel her tense.

"Hey now," She snaps irritably. "You don't get to—"

But I immediately grab her throat again and pressing her head back against my shoulder

"Yes, I fucking do, Princess," I growl wickedly, trailing my tongue up her throat. "Because as I said, you're a *brat*, Miss Valentine. And you should know from experience that I don't negotiate with brats. Do I?"

"No…" she breathes heavily.

"So, if you want me to continue, you're going to keep washing the dishes, and let me play with your body, however I please. Do you understand?"

She nods.

"That's a good girl," I say, kissing her cheek gently. "Now get back to work."

I can feel her pulse racing under my fingers, making my cock ache with knowing how turned on she is. With shaking hands, she picks up the dish and slowly starts rinsing it under the water.

I snake my hands down her body once again, gripping both her breasts this time, and squeezing her nipples until I hear her whimper.

"As I said," I say, grabbing her leggings again. "Don't worry about what I'm doing."

Slowly I pull them down, bending down to kiss her thighs, noticing the goosebumps forming on her shaking legs. I pull her panties down, slipping my hand between her clenched legs.

"Open," I command, pushing them apart and standing to my feet again.

"Shhiiiiit!" She moans, tiling her head to her left shoulder as I slip my finger inside of her.

"That's my girl," I whisper, kissing her beautiful, exposed skin on her neck. "You are so very wet. Is that because you secretly like it when I just take your body and use it like this?"

"Yes," she breathes.

"Then I suggest you don't stop. Or I'll stop too. And you'll get nothing."

She frantically starts rubbing soap all over the dish in her hands as quickly as possible before running the dish under the water. I finger her hard and fast, working my fingers in and out of her mercilessly until she's practically soaking my hand.

With one arm wrapped around her waist, holding her shaking

frame, I wrap the other around her body and start strumming her clit.

"Adam...." She whispers, clumsily setting the last clean dish on the counter beside the sink.

"Yes, Baby Girl?" I ask, freeing my cock from my jeans.

"Please...just...just..."

"Is this what you need?" I say, rubbing my cock against her.

"Yes!"

"Good," I say, biting her neck as I slam myself inside of her. "Because I need it too."

"Damn," Rachel says, sighing deeply as we settle back into the study. "That was different. I can't believe I let you talk to me like that."

I smirk to myself, pouring us each a glass of wine.

"You didn't seem to mind," I look at her over the top of my glass.

"Oh, I didn't," she grins, biting her bottom lip. "I just don't usually let most people talk to me like that."

"Well, I hope I'm not like most people."

I clear my throat, watching with satisfaction as the faintest of blushes settles across her cheeks as she smiles at me. Reaching forward she takes her glass from the coffee table and sits back on her couch.

"No," she whispers. "You're not."

I can't explain why, but something about the way she says this makes my heart beat faster.

Rachel flips her hair back, grabbing a pillow and settling in against the corner of the couch, stretching out her legs.

She's so beautiful, even when she isn't trying to be.

Especially when she isn't trying.

"So," she says. "We've concluded the dinner and dicking. Now I'm ready for serial killers."

"Dinner and dicking," I repeat, nearly snorting on my wine. "You sure as hell have a way with words, Miss Valentine."

"Yeah, yeah, yeah," she says waving me on. "Less

compliments, more confessions, please and thank you."

I laugh.

"Alright alright," I say, crossing my legs. "Well, it took us nearly two months of investigating and tracking before we had our perpetrators. They were a couple, on the lower end of high-society, who looked eerily similar to the profile I crafted for Roger." I say as Rachel kicks off her slippers.

"Martin Naveau, a forty-year-old architecture professor, and his art-gallery owning wife, Stella, had inserted themselves into one of the most prestigious and ultra private kink clubs in Manhattan."

"Almost *exactly* what you described," Rachel says.

"After our intelligence team hacked their way onto the Naveau's internet history, they found Stella's *art* for sale on the dark web. Art which consisted mostly of scarily accurate oil paint canvas recreations of the corpses we found in the woods in graphically lewd positions, selling a minimum of six figures a pop."

"Holy shit." Rachel gasps softly.

"And that was just a fraction of what her life-sized clay sculptures were going for," I continue. "We concluded that Martin and Stella must've been taking directly from the old adage about "life imitating art," but instead of paying a model to sit for long periods of posing time, decided to find models that didn't need to take breaks...or oxygen."

"Pesky inconvenience," Rachel winks at me.

"We learned from their friends that Martin and Stella were up to their ears in debt, and were considered the poorest couple of their trust-fund social circles. We could only assume this led them to harbor a vicious disdain for the increasingly high table of Manhattan's elite,"

"And come up with a way to strike back," she nods.

"Exactly. And after a few conversations with the connected facilitators, and the reasonable assurance of my informant's anonymity, I learned that the couple were referred to as *Kat&Mouse*, a femdom couple known for group scenes and for inviting their affluent playmates to their studio for sexy painting and photography sessions."

"And let me guess," Rachel says, taking a sip of her wine. "Those sessions involved the participants being imprisoned, defiled and abused in the worst of ways…and certainly never allowed to leave their canvas laden death factory."

"Correct," I confirm with a nod.

"But there must've been some form of evidence *at* Stella's gallery." Rachel says, her eyes wide. "I mean a droplet, a hair follicle a—"

She suddenly stops herself, pressing two fingers to her lips.

"Sorry, I don't know what came over me there."

But I'm grinning like a fool.

She was really getting into it.

"No, no," I say, waving her off with a smile. "It's cute that you're enjoying it. I usually don't tell these stories because they are too dark for most people."

"Well I like your stories," She blushes. "And I sure hope that *I'm* not like most people either."

"You're definitely not," I whisper, trying to keep my desire for Rachel in check. "But I like that."

"But I interrupted your story," she says bashfully.

I laugh.

"Well, you were right. We did think there was at least some evidence there. We were going to bet on it, and prepared for weeks, with separate teams following each of the couple at all times of the day. Myself, Scarlett, and another operative, familiar with BDSM, went undercover within the club, seeing if one of us could foster a relationship with the Naveau's."

"And did you?"

"Yes," I nod. "After orbiting their activity within the club for weeks, Stella finally approached Scarlett."

"As a submissive?"

I grin.

"No, as a *Domme*."

"Oooh," Rachel says, rubbing her chin.

"Because we knew that the majority of their victims were males, Scarlett was able to successfully convince Stella that *I* was her sub, and that I was available for play with outside Dommes upon request. She agreed to loan me to the Naveau's for an evening at Stella's studio for some erotic modeling."

"What I would give to see *those* photos." Rachel says playfully biting her lip

"There was never going to *be* any photos," I say, raising a

281

brow at her. "On the night of the meeting I was picked up by Martin in an unmarked van from my hotel and blindfolded. We had a silent ride back to the gallery, with my team tailing us the entire time."

I stop to take a drink of my wine.

"Everything was going according to plan…until the fucking bike boy."

"Bike boy?" Rachel asks.

"A bicycle delivery boy noticed our van as he was dropping off an order and tipped off the press. Within ten minutes, the media were swarming the location and all of a sudden, chaos erupted in the gallery," I say, tapping my finger on the outside of the glass. "Stella pulled a gun. As did I…"

"But you're still here," Rachel says quietly, her eyes glued to mine. "So I assume…"

I shake my head.

"She didn't walk away from that exchange," I say darkly. "But her fucking husband did."

"What?!" Rachel gasps.

"He abandoned his psychotic little muse without so much as a second thought, and snuck out the back into the sea of press like he was never there."

"So you lost him?" Rachel asks.

Well, here we go.

"Not for long," I say, clearing my throat. "It took another four months, but we tracked him down to Danbury, Connecticut. Which was only an hour from me."

"Well, at least that must've been convenient."

"No," I whisper. "It was *deliberate*."

"What?" Rachel says quietly.

"I made a lot of mistakes in that investigation," I shift on the couch, leaning forward on my knees. "The biggest was my assumption that Martin didn't care about his wife. He did. And I killed her."

Rachel's eyes go wide.

"Yes," I say, seeing the realization in her eyes. "I became his next target. And I was too fucking slow."

"Roger?" I ask, opening my ringing cellphone in the middle of the night. "Did we get him?"

I look at the clock.

3:27am

"Adam, Oh thank God!" Roger says frantically. "You've got to listen to me—are you at home?"

"Uhh, yeah I'm home," I snort, rubbing my eyes. "I already told you people ten times that it's my anniversary."

Instinctively I roll over and reach for Candace, but instead my hand finds only the softness of the new silk sheets I bought her as a gift for tonight.

"Adam listen to me," Roger says, his voice strained. "You were right, okay? About everything."

"Well, thanks Rog," I say sarcastically. "But you didn't have to call me at this hour to tell me—"

"Except about his target," Roger interrupts. "Adam, I know you're not going to believe me, but *you're* it."

I sit up in bed, suddenly wide awake.

"What did you just say?" I ask, my eyes scanning the dark room.

Where's my wife?

"I said you're the target, Adam," Roger repeats. "You and Candace need to leave and get out of town, and I mean ASAP!"

I try to flick the switch of the light on the nightstand, but it doesn't turn on.

Damn it. Cheap-ass bulb.

"Candace?" I whisper loudly, trying to keep my voice soft enough so as to not wake the kids.

"We found his hideout, and everything you said we'd find." Roger says quickly, as I grab my gun from the drawer next to me.

"Candace?" I whisper again, this time a bit louder, as I hold my hand over the receiver. "Oi, Cici! Where you at?"

I stumble to the door, tripping on my shoes that I left in the middle of the floor when Candace and I started stripping off after dinner.

That was definitely a fun evening.

Smashing my toe on the dresser, isn't though.

"Goddamnit!" I grunt.

"...But, Adam, he *knows* we've been tracking him for at least

283

a month," Roger continues.

"Yeah, well I tried to tell you that having Ghostrider and Maverick try and remotely hack his computer was a mistake," I say, pulling on my sweatpants. "He's too smart for that."

I try to flip the switch on the wall, but it too does not come on. I look outside, rain gently splattering the window.

"Fuck!" I sigh loudly.

"What? What is it?!" Roger asks nervously.

"Nothing, I think the storm must've knocked down a powerline or something, because I've got no power," I say. "Anyway, go on, why do you think I'm his target?"

"What do you mean your power is out?"

"Um, there's only one meaning for that," I say. "Storm, I guess."

But just as I do, I look up and see that the lights are on at my neighbor's house across the street.

"That's odd," I say quietly.

"Uh huh," Roger says awkwardly. "Is your wife...*around*?"

"Um, no actually?" I snort, grabbing my sweatshirt from the hook on the back of the door. "I assume she's in the bathroom or comforting the kid or something. Why? What's the matter?"

"Because...Shit," he sighs. "I guess, well...I guess there's just no easy way to say this."

"Then just say it?"

"Well, this guy's got newspaper clippings, and pictures of you everywhere," Roger continues. "...And also of *Candace*."

I freeze.

"*What* did you just say?" I ask, my voice barely above a whisper as I poke my head out into the dark hallway.

"I said," Roger says quietly. "He's got pictures of your wife on this wall."

"Candace?" I shout, this time loud enough to wake the kids as my son starts crying.

"Roger, I have to let you go," I growl into the phone.

"Adam, I don't know if that's a good idea I'm send—"

But before he can say anything I close the phone and shove it in my pocket. Something in my gut is screaming even louder than my son whose voice echoes through the darkened house. I flick the light switch in the hallway, but just like the others I've tried, nothing happens.

"Cici, the baby is crying," I shout, using my voice to detract from the squeaky floorboard in the hallway as I step closer to my son's room.

The fact that she hasn't responded at all, is very concerning. And when I step into my son's nursery I am immediately confronted with the reason.

"I'm flattered to hear you think I'm smart, Mr. Westwood," Martin Naveau says, as he stands behind my wife, pressing a black blade to her neck. "And apparently, I'm even smarter than you are right now."

My wife sits, shaking, tears streaking down her face in the nursery rocking chair.

"Apparently," I whisper quietly. "But you did bring a knife to a gunfight."

I whip my hand up, pointing it at him.

"And I have really good aim."

"Adam, no!" Candace sobs, throwing her hands up to stop me.

"Oh, I would listen to Cici here if I were you," Martin says. "Because as I was just explaining to your wife, this blade is obsidian. Custom made. I know from *experience*, that with very little pressure I could cut through the layers of her skin like it was butter. I trust you know it too, since you have seen some of my wife's work. Well, my *late* wife's work."

I pause, noticing the slight cut already dripping blood down her neck.

"Alright, alright!" I snap.

"Now kick your gun over."

I obey, lowering my gun to the floor and kicking it with my foot. He catches it with his foot.

"That's a good boy," he sneers, tauntingly.

My son wails in his crib.

"It's alright buddy," I try to comfort my son.

"It's fine," Martin says. "I think the little one knows that there's a big bad monster in his room."

"Now you're just flattering *yourself*," I say, my hands still raised as I frantically try and scan the room for anything I can use as a weapon.

"No dickhead," Martin hisses at me. "I was referring to *you*."

"Me?" I snort. "I think you have me confused. I fight for the good guys, remember?"

"No," he whispers darkly. "You killed my wife."

"You killed over a dozen people," I glare at him. "And you abandoned her—"

"You killed my fucking wife!" He roars in the dark room "So now you're going to watch as I kill yours!"

He grabs Candace's hair, exposing her neck as he holds the blade to it, her throat pulsing as she sobs silently.

I want to plead with him to stop.

No…that's exactly what I cannot do.

This man is a *psychopath*, and pleading with a psychopath is the equivalent of giving them an orgasm. It would be giving him exactly what he wants.

Unable to think of anything to say, I start laughing. I chuckle to myself, licking my bottom lip before bursting into a loud boisterous laugh.

"Stop that," Martin says, the smile instantly fading from his sallow face.

But I keep laughing.

"Stop it," he repeats, but I simply continue laughing. "I said stop it!"

"I'm sorry, I'm sorry," I say, pretending to wipe my eyes. "It's just so funny that you think that is a *threat* to me."

"What?"

"You think killing my wife would hurt me?" I snort. "I mean, if anything I should thank you for doing me a *favor.*"

"Wh…what?" he says.

"You think I want to be doing this work? Or even marry this whore? She was a stripper for god sakes! I was just stupid enough not to use a rubber, and we all know how that ends. We've been married for three years, and let me tell you, this bitch can nag. Seriously, she never shuts up."

Martin's face is completely blank, his stunned expression only highlighted by the glow of the moonlight.

He doesn't know how to respond…which is what I want.

"Adam, why didn't you take out the trash like I asked you, blah, blah, blah," I say in a high-pitched voice. "Why do you never change the baby, you always leave it for me to do…"

I laugh again.

"And the baby? Well, let's just say her pussy was only halfway

NICOLE FANNING

decent *before* the baby. Completely destroyed after."

"What?" Martin repeats.

I see that on the table, only a few steps away, is a big thick book of children's stories, and decide that's my best bet.

If I can distract him long enough to get Candace away...

"Please, just do it," I say, pressing my hands together as if I'm praying. "I'm beggin' you, man. Do it. I am dying to get back in the field again. The ladies *love* single fathers. I'd be pulling in pussy left, right and center! Hell, maybe we could even go do it all together."

Martin slowly starts to lower his knife, confusion still painted on the deep lines of his face.

Got him.

"Adam?!"

My partner Scarlett's voice suddenly echoes through the dark house, and before I can process it, I grab the book and fling it directly at Martin.

Instinctively he ducks, and I grab Candace, pulling her away.

But that's all the time I have before Martin lunges at me, digging the blade into my arm and rib cage.

I put my hands up to stop him, as he jabs at me continuously. I kick him hard into the bookcase.

"Adam!" Candace wails.

"Get Andrew and get out of here!" I shout as an enraged Martin comes flying at us.

She scoops the screaming infant as I do my best to fight him off, landing a couple of good punches, but feeling his dagger continuing to slice at me. He grabs me but loses his footing in the sheer amount of blood now pooling on the floor and the two of us go tumbling to the ground.

With all my might I struggle to keep his hand with the razor-sharp knife pinned, but I'm losing blood and consciousness. I feel him flip on top of me wriggling the wet blade away from me, but just before he is able to bring it down on my neck two gunshots ring out and his head explodes all over me.

A practically headless Martin slumps backwards into the wall, as Scarlett hits him with two more bullets.

Just like I taught her.

"Adam?! Oh my God, Adam!" I hear her say, as the room goes fuzzy.

I hear my wife sobbing, and my son wailing…and then everything goes black.

"Holy. Fucking. Shit."

Rachel's face is pale as she whispers under her breath. She shakes her head.

"I…I'm sorry," she says, practically gasping. "I don't know what else to say."

I chuckle.

"That's more than what most people manage when I tell them this story," I shrug. "Then again, I don't tell most people this story. Tends to be a bit…unsettling."

"I can see why," she says quietly, shifting on the couch. "But, you're sitting here, so…"

"I survived," I nod. "But just barely. I was in a coma for nearly two months. I had seventeen stab wounds, needed several transfusions, surgeries and hundreds of stitches."

"Jesus Christ," she says softly.

"Oh yeah, there was a priest too."

"What?"

"Well, barely anyone thought I was going to pull through, not even my doctors, so I guess they called in a priest for last rites or some shit," I chuckle sarcastically. "Which is funny to me, because I was raised Lutheran, so…"

"It's not funny to me," Rachel says, her eyes falling from mine. "That sounds horrific, Adam."

Taking a deep breath, I pick up my wine glass and inhale, savoring the earthy citrus scent that fills my nostrils.

"Yeah, it was horrific too," I say quietly into the glass. "And it wasn't even the worst part."

"What?"

I close my eyes, knowing that by simply starting this story, I've stepped off the dock into a sea of painful memories that are already threatening to pull me under.

"My wife," I say softly. "The experience was traumatic."

Rachel says nothing, as she looks down into the glass in her hand.

"Obviously because it's horrific enough to suffer a home invasion with a psychopath threatening to kill you and who very nearly kills your husband," I take a large gulp of wine. "But also because the things I said that night, to *distract* the psychopath, were pretty horrific too."

Rachel inhales deeply, rubbing her arms before pulling a blanket from off the back of the couch.

"Yeah, I assume that took time to heal too."

"Except," I say slowly. "It didn't. It was the beginning of the end for us. We started fighting all the time. We stopped sleeping together, and then we stopped sleeping in the same bed at all. We tried therapy. We tried doctors. Nothing worked. And that was when she started turning to the harder drugs."

I throw back the rest of my wine.

"Wow," Rachel says quietly. "Did she…overdose?"

I stare at her for a long moment.

"Something like that," I whisper, clicking my tongue inside my mouth.

"*Something*," She repeats quietly as she bites her bottom lip.

"Yup," I say. "Something indeed."

"Correct me if I'm wrong, but considering that you're not exactly subtle I'd say that's your way of telling me we've reached the end of what you feel like sharing this evening," she says, leaning forward on her knees. "Am I right?"

I say nothing, unable to respond.

She takes a deep breath and nods, clasping her hands together.

"Well, I guess that means I'm up," she says as she stands to her feet. "But considering it's on Jaxon Pace's dime, I say it's high time for more wine."

She grabs the empty bottle from the table and heads to the door of the study.

"You know, Agent Westwood," Rachel says softly, playing with the tag on the wine bottle. "I'm not always the fastest when it comes to catching on to things. But I'm not an idiot either."

"I never said you were."

"Good. I've learned that people will say what they want to say when they're good and ready," she continues. "So, I'm grateful for what you have told me, and I won't pressure you to continue."

She looks up at me, her brown eyes burrowing into my soul.

"But, I've also learned that it's never just *something*," she says softly. "It's either nothing…or it's *everything*."

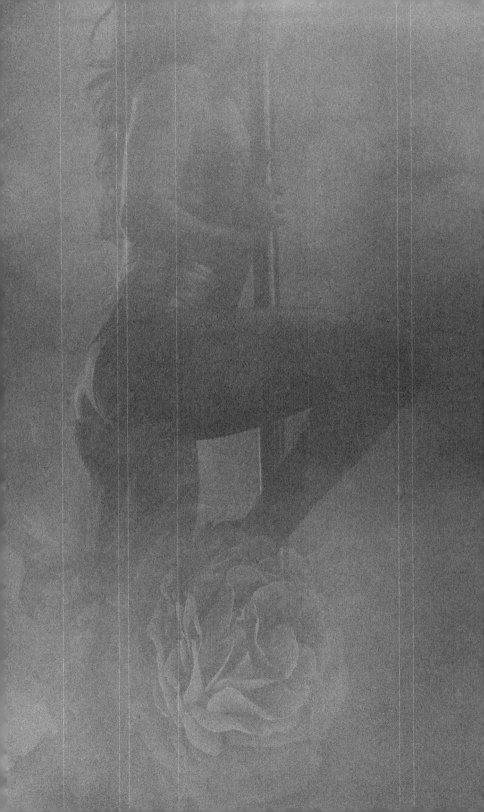

CHAPTER TWENTY-THREE

Rachel

After we told Jaxon's parents about the pregnancy, things kind of calmed down a bit. At least for a minute. Yuri kept calling, but I just ignored him.

Jess was able to keep her job at the club, but given her actions against another dancer, she was put on probation. Del allowed her to work the bar, wait tables, and do private dances, but she wasn't allowed to be on the mainstage.

And neither was I. But not because of Del.

Because of *Jaxon*.

Technically, he didn't want me anywhere near the club. Obviously for my protection and that of the heir within my womb, but also, I suspect for his *pride*.

To be fair it couldn't have been easy for him. I was pregnant with his child, but I also had a bit of notoriety at the club. I had regular customers, several of whom were men in the Pace Family Mafia. No matter how progressive or generally reasonable Jaxon was compared to previous dons-in-training the fact remained that my line of work made him uncomfortable. And it made his parents *very* uncomfortable.

And to make matters worse, I had refused his proposal. Well, not so much as *refused* as I told him I just had to put it off. While it was true that Jaxon was willing to marry me, watching my parent's misery as a result of a forced shotgun wedding made me hesitant to sign on the dotted line.

Jess told me I was crazy not to just agree to that on the spot.

It was true that marrying Jaxon would make my life a lot more comfortable. It meant that I wouldn't struggle anymore or want anything ever again. I wouldn't have to work, I wouldn't have to worry about money, which was incredibly tempting, given how many nights I went to bed hungry and exhausted.

But I also wouldn't have any freedom ever again.

The wives of Mafia Dons were treated like royalty. But even royalty has its restrictions. And similarly, to the monarchy, in our syndicate a Mafia Don's wife was expected to do three things: look pretty, stay silent, and produce heirs. Multiple heirs, to protect the family's legacy.

Well, I didn't give a fuck about *anyone's* legacy. And I had no intention of becoming just another disaffected debutante turned Mafia baby making machine.

…Because I know what would *happen* to those heirs.

Should I have a *son*, he would become the heir apparent. And like both Jaxon and his father, our son would be trained from a very young age in the violent and dangerous ways of our world. Training that was ultimately in preparation for his successful completion of *The Trials*, which were the excruciating, deadly tests that solidified Don Supremacy.

I don't know if I could handle that. So, I hoped for a *girl*.

But perhaps the biggest reason that I put a pause on Jaxon's proposal, was because I knew he was proposing out of duty, and not love. And while I loved him, and we had incredibly passionate sex and generally enjoyed each other's company…I was never really sure if Jaxon truly loved me.

His inherent sense of duty and protocol guaranteed he'd be there for our child, and support us in whatever we needed. And for now, that was enough. The way I saw it, if we were meant to fall in love and be together, we could sort that out after the baby was born. But I didn't just want him to just be willing.

I wanted Jaxon to *want* to marry me.

And not for his duty, or legacy, or even for his inflated pride… but because he loved me. And until I was sure of that, I left that part of my heart off the negotiation table.

His parents demanded a blood test, and before we even left the Manor the next day, their private doctor came out to conduct one, confirming my pregnancy. Jaxon's father also wanted a paternity test, but Jaxon vehemently refused, saying that he knew it was his, and that was enough for him.

Dimitris wasn't happy, but Jaxon's mother pulled rank and told him to drop it, so he did.

Strangely enough, Jaxon's parents' relationship gave me hope that maybe Jaxon and I could have that too. The kind of love that was forged from equality and respect, not just attraction and chemistry between the sheets.

They insisted we do everything we could to keep the baby a secret as long as we could, in order to keep the press out of the picture for as long as possible. After we found the best obstetrician in the state, my appointments would be conducted offsite.

Jaxon and I had to compromise on some things.

Even though we were both committed to secrecy, Jaxon was still worried that word would get out. He wanted to assign me a bodyguard for protection, but I declined. I didn't want to feel like someone was babysitting me, but also wanted to have a little piece of my own privacy for the little time I had left. I knew everything would change when the baby was born, and I needed time to grieve the life I was leaving behind. Thankfully he relented.

However, he did not relent on everything. He was adamant about me leaving my exotic dancing days behind me as it could bring shame to me, his family, and of course, our child. He knew the baby was his, but he also knew that gossip spread faster than the truth. And people love a good rumor.

But unlike previous arguments we'd had about this, this time I agreed. I hadn't told him about Yuri, and part of me still felt guilty about it. If Jaxon learned the truth, I knew two things for certain: First that he would certainly kill Yuri. And second, he would be furious with me. He had gone out on a limb with his father fighting the paternity test, and vouching for my character, if Jaxon learned that I had not been faithful…

I couldn't bear to think about it.

So after I made my case about needing the community I'd built with my girls at the club, as the only family I had, he agreed to let me work at the bar. And, it was kind of a blessing, because for the first two weeks my morning sickness had me randomly nauseous. And spinning around a pole wouldn't have been a great idea for me anyway.

A few nights a week, Jaxon would stop by at the end of my shift to take me home, and things felt *normal* for a while.

…And then it all came crashing down.

"I've got two of three here, I just need a second for the rest," Raegan, the pretty bartender with the pink short buzzcut hair says, setting two drinks down on my tray. "They're going to VIP."

"An *Appletini*? Really?" I snort, turning to appraise the group of men crammed into the section. "Who the fuck ordered this?"

"That would be the Birthday Kid," Jess laughs, appearing with her tray beside me. "Turned twenty-one tonight, and his friends brought him here. One of them said he's a *cherry*."

"Oh God, I love virgins!" Raegan gasps, leaning on the bar, resting her head momentarily on her fist. "Cherries are always so sweet and appreciative. Which one is he?"

"Uh, well, I'm gonna go out on a limb and say he's probably the one with three chin-pubes, a boner, and eyes bugging out of his skull," Jess snorts. "You could spot him a mile away."

Immediately, I find the young, brunette, pale-faced kid sitting in the first row, with his jaw hanging open as Crissy performs her pole routine. Around him, a group of much older boys holler and encourage him to put dollars in her panties.

"Aw, he's so adorable," Raegan giggles, setting two small water bottles on the bar for us. "Go give him some love for me, will ya, Rach?"

"Yeah, that's if the poor kid can even talk after watching Crissy perform," I say, nodding toward the awestruck kid. "Little guy is gonna get a dry mouth if it stays stuck open the entire time."

"Oh God, don't make me fucking laugh," Jess snorts. "That Jersey twat has nothing on you. You were, and will forever be the absolute best pole-greaser I know."

"Wow," I laugh, taking the water bottle. "That's a term I haven't heard before."

"You like it?" Jess smirks, scrunching up her nose.

"No, not really," I laugh.

"Too bad," Jess laughs too, swallowing the last of her water before tossing the bottle directly into the trash can across the bar from us.

"Well, thank you," I smile. "But those days are behind me."

"Yeah I know," Jess crosses her arms and raises her brow at me. "Because of some insecure ass-potato Mafia manchild."

"Who also just so happens to be the reason Maggie's charges against you were dropped," I say, raising my finger at her. "So perhaps you should go easy on my baby daddy."

"Finnnne," Jess shrugs. "But, I'll always encourage you to dance. You know this. I mean hell, you were the only girl I've ever been jealous of. You know, on stage, that is."

"Oh stoppppp," I roll my eyes, pushing her slightly.

"I'm serious!" Jess shrugs, playfully narrowing her eyes at me. "I only shacked up with you so I could learn all your secrets."

"Secrets?" Rae says, putting the last of the drinks on the tray. "Who's got secrets?"

"Me, apparently," I laugh, picking up the tray.

Making my way across the bar, the men at the regular tables whistle and catcall, apparently loving my hot pants and white button down with sleeves rolled up almost as much as they loved my stage outfits.

Part of me *does* miss it. Because even though I don't want to admit it to Jess, I do have some idea of how good I actually am. When I was first starting out, I remember working so hard at perfecting my skill and routines. It was my art, and it gave me such a rush of serotonin.

Crazy to think that I will likely never do that again. And a little sad too.

Crissy's set concludes just as I set the drinks down at the birthday kid's table.

"Whoa," he says as he turns back from the mainstage, his buddy slapping him on the shoulder. "That was so amazing! I've never seen—"

The minute his eyes find me, they grow to reflect the size of dinner plates.

"Holy Guacamole," he says, his jaw hanging open. "You're like, really, really pretty."

I chuckle.

Cherries. Gotta love 'em.

"Well, hiya, Sugar," I say, winking at him. "Someone told me that it was your birthday. Is that true?"

He nods, still staring at me a little drunk and deliriously.

"What's your name? What do you do?"

"Ash...Ashton," he smiles up at me, a big goofy grin on his face. "And I'm in the Mafia. I just started. God, that's kinda weird to say."

I giggle, deciding his I innocence warrants a little bit of grown-up flirting.

After all, it *is* the kid's birthday.

"Well, that's not that uncommon around here. We get lots of Mafia guys who like to come look at pretty things," I say, gently touching his cheek, before leaning in to whisper, deliberately giving him a view down my shirt. "But, just a little piece of advice, I wouldn't go around telling people that."

"Oops!" He laughs, drunkenly. "Good point. You won't tell anyone, right?"

"Don't worry, Sugar, my lips are sealed," I wink, placing my hand on his and giving it a good squeeze.

Staring down at my hand on his, he gulps so loudly I can hear it even above the music blaring in the club.

Hah! Mission accomplished.

"Happy Birthday, Darlin," I say, scooping up the empty glasses onto my tray. "But I gotta get back to work."

I wink at him one last time before turning and walking out of VIP, smiling to myself as I hear him plead behind me.

For a moment, I feel a little bad. I probably did go a little overboard, flirting with some young kid. My boyfriend and baby daddy would likely strangle him just for looking at me like that.

But it just felt so good watching him drool all over himself like that. Like it always did. It was a headrush, and a little boost to my confidence which had taken a lot of hits lately.

And it wasn't like it actually *meant* anything. For me, flirting was a sport. Getting the attention of men, and learning what they liked, was an art form I had perfected a long time ago to entertain myself. Like dancing, it made me feel powerful, and desirable.

And I didn't give the kid my name or anything, so there was really no way he could get in trouble for a little innocent fun.

Besides, what Jaxon doesn't know, can't hurt him, right?

After collecting a few more empty glasses from a few more of the high-top tables I return to the bar. That's where I find Del and Raegan talking to one of the guys from VIP.

Well, more like *arguing* with the guy.

"What do you mean she's not available?"

"I don't know what part of that needs explaining, Sir," Del says, a sarcastic smile in her voice. "I've already told you four times that she's not available for private dances."

"What, are you her fucking mother or something?" The guy snaps angrily. "It's the kid's first time, and we're paying good money to be here tonight. And he wants her."

"I don't care what he wants, she's not available."

As I approach, Raegan looks up at me and quickly shakes her head, motioning for me to avoid the conversation.

But it's too late, because the guy slams his hand down on the bar and turns around, looking directly at me.

"Ah! There she is!" He says excitedly.

"Sir!" Del yells, holding up her finger before quickly making her way around the bar.

"Hey gorgeous," the man says, walking over to me. "How are you doing, sweetheart?"

"Um, fine?"

"My little brother, you know the one who was practically wetting himself the minute he saw you? Yeah, he thinks you're the hottest girl in this place, and he wants you to give him a lap dance for his birthday."

"Excuse me, Sir!" Del says, appearing by my side, now visibly angry. "I've already told you that she's unavailable."

"Seems to me that she's available," he shrugs.

"Well, I'm—" I start to say.

"It's not up to her," Del snaps firmly. "Management has said otherwise. She cannot perform."

Wait...what?!

"What?" Jessica says, joining the conversation and voicing

my silent sentiments. "What do you mean management said she can't perform?"

"Jessica," Del growls, glaring at her. "This has nothing to do with you, so why don't you just get back to work. You're already on thin fucking ice as it is, young lady."

"Yeah I might be, but *she's* not," Jessica scoffs, pointing to me. "She's the best dancer in here, and I think if she wants to dance for the kid, she should be allowed to!"

Del glares at Jessica.

"You and I both know that's not how this works," she says through gritted teeth. "It came from...*management*."

However, the way she says the word tells me that management had nothing to do with this at all. The instruction to ban me from performing came from Jaxon Pace.

"This is fucking ludicrous!" The man laughs. "I mean, I thought this was a strip club for crying out loud?"

"It is, and you have your pick of any of the other dancers here," Del says with a frustrated but polite smile. "But I've been given explicit instructions, from *management*, that this young lady is not allowed to perform."

"Unfuckingbelieable," Jessica laughs, crossing her arms.

"I'll even make an exception and let you have this one if you like," Del says, motioning to Jessica.

The man shakes his head, but then looks Jessica up and down, considering her.

"Well, I suppose," he says, smiling at Jessica. "She's kinda hot too."

But something inside me snaps.

Apparently, me choosing not to perform out of respect for Jaxon wasn't enough. The asshole had gone over my head and reached out to my place of employment and told my house mom that I wasn't allowed to perform.

Fuck. That.

"You know what, no," I say, plastering a sweet smile on my face. "I'll be happy to dance for your brother."

"Really?! That would be great!" The man says, slapping a wade of hundred-dollar bills into my hand. "Whenever you're ready, obviously. He's going to be thrilled."

"Rachel," Del cautions as the man runs back to VIP. "You know who called and—"

"Yeah, I know, Del," I snap back. "I know Jaxon Pace thinks that he gets to decide what the fuck he gets to do with my life, but he doesn't."

"But what about the…" Del says, glancing at my stomach.

"I'm fine," I shrug. "I promise."

"I don't know, Rach," Del says, shaking her head. "I mean Jaxon called me directly. He made me promise to only have you at the bar. If he finds out—"

"He won't," Jess says enthusiastically, cutting her off and snatching the tray from my hands. "Come on, it's just one dance Del."

"And it's the kid's birthday," I say, throwing my hair in a ponytail. "It's not like I'm doing anything dangerous, he's a cherry for crying out loud!"

"This really isn't a good idea," Del shakes her head.

"Listen," Jess says, gently touching her arm. "You already know the situation. You know how miserable and sick she's been, and you know that her whole life is going to change once this baby comes. Just let the girl have a little fun tonight. Please?"

Del stares at her and then at me, the confliction evident on her face as she weighs the risk. However, this woman has always looked out for me, being the closest thing I've had to a mother since I started working at the club. Besides Jess, she's the only other person I've told about my situation, as well as my fears regarding losing a sense of my identity the moment the baby is born.

Perhaps that's eventually why she relents.

"Fine!" she sighs loudly, throwing her hands in the air. "One dance, Rach. And just this one time. Don't make me regret defying an order from Jaxon Pace."

"Don't worry, Del," I grin wickedly. "I do it all the fucking time."

"I'm serious!"

"As am I," I laugh, throwing my arms around her and hugging her. "But yes, I will only do it this one time, and if anything gets back to Jaxon, I'll make sure he knows that you tried to stop me."

"Yeah, yeah, yeah," She rolls her eyes, shaking her head. "Just hurry up, make it quick, eh?"

"We got this!" Jess says, turning to me. "What song do you want to dance to?"

But the moment our eyes lock she already knows.

"Got it," she grins, reaching into her pocket and pulling out her favorite red lipstick. "Go throw this on, and I'll go tell Donnie to play your song after Isla's set."

I swipe it out of her hand and rush backstage to put it on. I feel my heart pounding in my chest, at the thought of defying Jaxon Pace. But he had crossed a line. That wasn't respect, that was control.

And I refuse to give him that much control of my life.

After a quick refresh, I make my way back out onto the floor, crossing the velvet rope into VIP.

Nodding to Donnie, I unbutton the front of my white button up, and tap the birthday kid on the shoulder. He turns around just as *Cherry Pie* by Warrant starts playing on the speakers.

"Holy shi—" the kid exclaims as I straddle him, his brother and the men around him excitedly slapping each other.

Gently, he puts his hands on my waist as I roll my hips against his, shoving my tits in his face.

Whistles, cheers, and screams erupt around the room as I grind on him, running my hands through his hair. The boy shudders, smiling from ear to ear. Laughing to myself, I wrap my hands around his neck and throw my head back in a slow circle, my breasts heaving against my shirt.

That's when I see his face change.

The man beneath me, who was just having the time of his life, has gone completely pale, a look of absolute terror now painted unmistakably on his face.

That's odd.

"You okay there, Sugar?" I purr in his ear.

"Rachel!" Jessica whispers, suddenly materializing next to me. "Stop."

She is staring at something behind me, the same look of surprise and fear reflected in her eyes.

I turn to look, and suddenly I understand.

Standing just inside the entrance, is Jaxon Pace and his entire entourage, including my brother...and Jaxon's *father.*

Holy. Shit.

I slide off of Ashton, whipping around just as a furious Jaxon steps into the VIP area, snatching Ashton by the throat before throwing him onto the table beside us.

And if that wasn't horrific enough, I now notice that Roman Antonov is here too, with his entire security team, and his bitch-faced sister. The very same gorgeous sister who had wanted to marry Jaxon.

I am so fucked.

Jaxon steps in front of me, his body heaving with rage.

"Rachel," he whispers venomously. "What the fuck are you doing?"

But I can't answer. I don't have an answer, and I have forgotten all my words.

He places his hands on his hips, and chuckles to himself.

"Have you lost your mind?" He bites his lip, unable to look at me. "Go put some fucking clothes on."

I open my mouth to say something.

"Now!" He roars, making me jump.

I can feel the rage radiating from him, like waves rolling off his body.

"Hey, asshole!" Jess snaps, glaring at Jaxon, pulling me away from him. "You don't get to speak to her like that!"

"I will speak to her however the fuck I want," Jaxon growls.

"Jess—"

"Oh, I bet you fucking will," Jess snarls, getting in Jaxon's face.

Oh my God, I need her to stop.

I know Jess is just defending me, but she isn't making this situation any better.

One, because while we're talking, the rest of the Pace-Antonov entourage has stepped into VIP, sending the lingering civilian patrons scrambling out in every direction.

And Two, because she knows nothing about the proposed deal with the Antonov's, or the paternity test, and therefore doesn't understand *why* Jaxon is so furious right now.

But I do.

"That's another one of your unalienable rights, isn't it?" Jessica growls. "I get to speak to whomever I want however I want because I'm the great Jaxon Pace!"

Jaxon's bodyguards surround us, including my brother who glares at me, his lip twitching.

"Yes, that's exactly how that goes," Jaxon hisses at Jessica, narrowing his eyes at her. "Fortunately for you, it's *also* the same

303

reason you're standing here and not still sitting in a fucking jail cell, so I suggest you sit the fuck down and shut the fuck up like a good little girl."

Shit. Jess is definitely not going to take that well...

Before I can even stop Jessica from physically attacking Jaxon, one of Jaxon's men grabs her and stops her blow.

"Fuck you, Jaxon Pace!" She screams at him, trying to swing at Jaxon around the massive ginger man. "You pompous fucking asshole!"

"Jesus Christ," Roman Antonov chuckles to the men around him, rubbing his chin with amusement. "And I thought only Russian women were crazy bitches."

"Yeah, I am a crazy bitch! But you? You're a piece of shit, Jaxon! Do you know that?!" She says, still struggling. "Get off of me!"

"Jess! Stop it!"

"Ma'am, step away from Mr. Pace," the bodyguard says firmly.

"Of course! Wouldn't want anything to happen to our precious future Don Supreme!"

"Jess! Just stop!"

"No, Rachel!" Jess snaps loudly. "Because this dickhead doesn't understand you're the one sacrificing your job, your friends, your happiness, and your life for him!"

"Get her out of here!" Jaxon roars as the bodyguard forces Jessica backstage.

"*Rachel*?" Roman asks, turning to one of his men. "Wait a minute, is *this* the woman?"

"Hold the fuck up...*this* is the slut you chose over me?!" The bitchy blonde woman next to Roman scoffs, her jaw dropping. "The one who is *pregnant*?"

Oh fuck...

"Pregnant?!" Michael interjects loudly. "You're fucking pregnant?!"

Fuck. Fuck. Fuck.

Jaxon's face is absolutely terrifying. His jaw tenses and his eyes close, his fist clenching.

"You fucking bastard!" Michael roars, suddenly launching himself at Yuri.

But since Yuri just happened to be standing directly next

304

to Roman, Michael's body slams into the Russian mob boss, causing all of Roman's men to draw their weapons.

"What the fuck?!" Roman snaps.

The Pace Mafia men also draw their guns, and suddenly screaming erupts from around the entire club as everyone rushes for the exit, the staff also head for the door or opt to retreat back into the locker room.

"Whoa whoa whoa!" Dimitris thunders. "Hold your fire! Hold your fucking fire!"

"Hold your fire!" Roman shouts as very confused and very scary looking Russians watch Yuri and Michael punching and clawing at each other, smashing into tables.

"Charlie, get Rachel out of here!" Jaxon shouts.

"Michael! Enough!" Dimitris roars.

"You knocked up my sister!"

But at the exact same moment the words leave Michael's lips, Yuri manages to snatch his gun from his belt, shoving it hard against Michael's throat.

"No I fucking didn't!"

"I saw you leaving her fucking apartment!"

"She was already pregnant, you cunt!" Yuri fires back, grinning acidly before shoving Michael off of him. "But, you know, I guess I *did* enjoy shooting my load inside of the bitch and not having to worry about it."

Oh. My. God.

Michael's hand moves for his gun, but Ethan is faster, pulling his and aiming it at Michael.

"If you think about touching that gun, son," He growls. "I will shoot you myself."

With the club evacuated, and the music off, the entire club goes silent. Jaxon turns to look at me, his face blank.

Terrifyingly blank.

"What...what did you just say?" Dimitris says quietly, walking up to Yuri.

The quietness of his voice, mixed with the cold convoluted look of disbelief on Jaxon's face causes my entire body to shake. The men in the room lower their weapons as Dimitris Pace steps into the center of the men.

"Um, what?" Yuri gulps, the intimidating build and presence of the Chicago Don Supreme causing him to lose his nerve.

"What did you just say?" Dimitris repeats. "Word for word."

I want to die. I want to evaporate into thin air.

Because everyone, including Dimitris, *knows* exactly what Yuri just said.

"I...I...I," Yuri stammers nervously.

"You slept with Rachel?" Dimitris asks.

Yuri's eyes go wide, and he says nothing, glancing at me and then at the stoically statuesque Jaxon.

Jaxon doesn't turn around to face Yuri, he doesn't even blink, he just continues to glare at me.

Roman snaps a command in Russian, making Yuri jump, presumably demanding that Yuri answer Dimitris's question.

"Yes...but she was...already pregnant," Yuri says quietly.

"What the fuck?!" The bitchy blonde woman interjects.

"Polina, let it go," Roman snarls. However, she ignores him, storming toward us.

"You said that we couldn't get married because he got this bitch pregnant," Polina snaps, staring at me. "That's what you said, Roman!"

Roman growls something at her Russian, gesticulating and rolling his eyes, clearly frustrated.

"How can you even be sure it's your baby, Jaxon?"

"Exactly what I'd like to know," Dimitris says, glaring at me.

The wheels behind Jaxon's eyes turn so visibly that I can hear his thoughts out loud.

He knows this baby is his, but he also knows his father's deal has been ruined, and that the sister of the Russian boss is pissed, and that he's just been humiliated in front of everyone.

So while he knows this baby is his...he also *hates* me.

But if Jaxon denounces me here, if he removes my protection, one of these men, from one of these families, will be ordered to kill me. And they *will* kill me.

"It's my baby," Jaxon says quietly.

The men in the room begin to murmur, both in English and in Russian, before the room fell silent again. Too silent.

"Okayyy then..." Roman says, rolling his eyes sarcastically, clearing his throat. "Well, I guess, congratulations...I *think*?"

The entire room seems to be a silent conversation about me, everyone either hating or judging me. Dimitris walks toward the two of us, refusing to look at me.

"Jaxon," he whispers, his name almost a plea for his son to recant his statement. "Are you certain?"

"It's my baby," Jaxon repeats. "I'm the father of her baby."

"But…but how can you be *sure*?!" Polina scoffs.

"Enough, Polina," Roman warns.

"What?!" Polina snaps. "I mean, I'm only saying what we are all thinking."

"Polina! Shut the fuck up!" Roman snaps stepping toward us, rolling his eyes. "This is not our business."

"But…But…it's not *fairrrr*!" She whines, "This bitch fucked up everything! Jaxon and I were going to be married! Baba already agreed!"

"He only told you that to shut you up! Because you're an annoying, irritating, relentless fucking earworm!" He barks at her, doing a talking motion with his hand. "Yap, yap, yap, yap!"

"Fuck you, Roman! I'm angry and I want someone to pay for this!" She screams at him, glaring at me.

Jaxon has said nothing the entire time. His eyes have not moved from me, not for one second. As if he wants me to sit in this horrible, icky, awful feeling, and understand exactly how much damage I have done.

"I'm serious!" Polina howls. "Someone should pay for the whore's transgressions!"

Roman sighs, placing one hand on his hip and rubbing his eyes with the other, cursing under his breath.

"You want someone to pay, eh?" he says, nodding. "Alright, fine, Polina. Someone will pay for the fucking whore!"

Before anyone can even think to react, Roman yanks his gun from its holster, and fires one shot.

…Into *Yuri*.

Polina and I jump, the gunshot also finally shaking Jaxon from his trance. He whirls around, stepping in front of me as nearly every gun in the room is drawn once again. But the moment Yuri collapses back into the table, his body thudding to the floor, Polina immediately lets out a blood-curdling wail.

"Oh my God!" She screams, rushing to Yuri's side. "Roman! What the fuck have you done?!"

Polina cups Yuri's face, and sobbing over him in her native tongue as he chokes on the blood gurgling from his mouth.

Oh my God…

"You wanted someone to pay, and now someone has paid!" Roman snarls remorselessly. "I told you to stop being a fucking whore, and getting in the way of my business."

"Eeeeeeeeeek!" Polina screams at the top of her lungs, staring down at her shaking hands now covered in Yuri's blood. "Oh my God! No!"

"You think I didn't know about your little relationship? About you fucking this *mudak* every time you think my back is turned, eh?!" He says, snapping to his men with a Russian command. "I know, Pol. I know *everything,* and I see everything. I told you, I am fucking *God*."

"No, you're a monster!" She wails as Roman's men pick her up off the floor. "I will tell Baba!"

Roman says, laughing viciously. "Sweetheart, Baba knows you've been ridden more times than the town bicycle! If anyone is a *whore*, it's you, Sister."

"Yuri!" She wails as Roman's men drag her past me. "Oh, fucking God! Noooo! Yurrrri!"

Jesus Christ! She...she loved him.

Roman's men remove her, but as she passes by Jaxon and I, Polina's tear-stained face suddenly glares up at me, her eyes finding mine.

"You stupid bitch! This is all *your* fault!" She screeches, lunging at me, prevented by Roman's bodyguards.

Jaxon pushes me further behind him, putting himself between the two of us.

"You will pay for this! Do you hear me, you fucking whore?! I swear to God, you will pay for this!"

"Yap, yap, yap, yap," Roman barks at her teasingly, rolling his eyes. "Someone just put her in the fucking car. Use the trunk if she can't stay quiet."

Polina is dragged, screaming, crying and cursing at Roman and I, in both languages, all the way out of the club. Her brother then snaps his fingers, pointing to Yuri's corpse.

"Get him out of here, too. Before he starts to smell. I hate the way the dead ones smell."

"Mr. Antonov," Dimitris says, clearing his throat and staring as Yuri's body is picked up and carried out behind the men. "I apologize for all of this. But I assure you, that wasn't necessary. We don't want any trouble."

"Pfft! It's fine," Roman says, chuckling to himself, waving Dimitris off. "My grandfather used to say that '*you can't avoid that which is meant to happen.*' He lived life on the edge the way we do, so you know...meh,"

He shrugs.

"In that case, I never liked that grimy little fuck anyway. And you know, sometimes it's good to cull the herd."

"But, what about your sister? We did not mean to offend her—"

"She's spoiled, so life *itself* offends her," Roman shrugs, looking at the men behind him who join in a hearty chuckle. "My father only sent her on this trip with me because he got sick of her yapping in his ear all the damn time. Polina has always had a knack of sticking her nose where it doesn't belong. And she's always been a slut. Which is why, in good faith, I never would have truly supported the match."

He locks eyes with Jaxon.

"You deserve better than my slutty sister."

But Jaxon says nothing, instead he just nods, forcing a polite smile for Roman.

I don't know when I stopped breathing, but I can feel my body shaking. That really just happened. All of that came out. And a man just died.

...All because of me.

"Well then!" Roman claps his hands together loudly, looking around at the empty, silent club. "It seems we now have the entire place to ourselves. The whole club is VIP! However, it also seems we have killed the mood. I think we need a drink."

"Samuel," Dimitris says, calling forth one of his dedicated security detail. "Get Mr. Antonov the best bottle of vodka behind the bar. And then go find Del, tell her to get the bartenders back. Immediately."

"Yes, Sir," he nods.

Roman smiles to himself before turning back around, his eyes falling to Michael, still heaving, and covered in blood, with his hands behind his head, with Ethan's pistol pressed into his back.

"Perhaps, if we can remove the last of the *hotheads*, we can get some girls and vodka, and get back to our business, yes?"

"Of course," Dimitris smiles politely before turning to face Ethan and Jaxon, "Just give us just a minute...to handle our *business.*"

He means me.

"Alright, move it," Ethan snaps, pushing Michael forward toward the door. "You're off duty. Indefinitely."

I now find myself alone with a silent but furious Jaxon Pace.

"Jaxon…" I try to say, but I choke on my words.

Suddenly he grabs my arm, ushering me out of the room.

"Wait…what are you doing? Where are we going?" I ask.

But Jaxon nothing, instead pulling me down the hallway and straight out of the door to the alley.

I gasp, the cold Chicago air hitting my skin and realize that my shirt is still unbuttoned.

Oh shit. Jesus Christ.

Embarrassed, I start to rebutton it quickly as Jaxon turns away from me, rubbing his chin.

"Jaxon," I whisper. "I'm…I'm so sorry."

"You know, that's funny," Jaxon chuckles, turning away from me. He continues, his laughter getting louder and slightly more unhinged as he runs his hands through his hair. "You're sorry. Yeah, that's funny."

I can't imagine what he's thinking.

"I am," I say pleadingly. "I don't even know what to say right now."

"You don't know what to say? How about you explain why you're pregnant, and yet you're still out here, pulling this shit?! Huh?!" He laughs sarcastically. "Or how about we discuss me going out on a limb with my family, only to have you turn around and embarrass the fuck out of me? Right after we agreed to a compromise that *you* wanted! How about that?"

"It was nothing, Jaxon, I swear!"

"No, it absolutely *is* something!" he snaps, storming toward me, backing me up against the cold concrete of the alley wall. "My father saw that, Rachel! How the fuck am I supposed to explain this to him, eh? The man who just witnessed the mother of my child, and *his* grandchild, riding on *my* men like a bitch in heat?!"

His presence engulfs me, his massive frame towering over me, blocking all the light in the alley.

"On my fucking *men*!" He roars in my face, slamming his fist hard into the brick, sending dust sprinkling down the wall. "How do you think that makes me look?!"

Although I know Jaxon would never hit me, the sheer rage in his face, and the way the vein in his neck pulses makes me jump. In all our fights, I've never, ever, seen him so angry.

He glares at me before pulling away.

"Fuck!" He shouts, hunching over, his voice echoing off the stone walls. "God fucking dammit!"

"It was just a dance, Jaxon," I plead, walking toward him and grabbing his arm. "They needed someone to fill in and—"

He rips his arm away from me.

"Get your hands off me." He growls so lethally it sends a shiver down my spine.

"Please, believe me, it was nothing!"

"And Yuri?" He snaps. "What was Yuri, Rachel? Because it sounds like he just confessed that it was a hell of a lot more than a fucking dance! In front of everyone!"

Fuck.

"What did he say, again?" He spits, narrowing his eyes at me and rubbing his chin. "How did he drop that lovely little piece of information?"

He smacks his hand against his leg and snaps his finger.

"Oh, wait, now I remember, that's right!" He clicks his tongue. "That he enjoyed shooting his load inside of you, because you had already told him you were pregnant!"

He closes his eyes and shakes his head.

"...*inside* of you," he whispers to himself, before chuckling. "Unbelievable."

The look on his face is absolutely heartbreaking. I close my eyes, feeling the hot tears streaking down my cheeks.

"Look, Jaxon, I was just lonely!" I say, imploring him. "I didn't think you were coming back. You hadn't responded, or called, and everyone was saying that you ghost like this and just—".

"I was literally in the middle of the fucking *Trials*, Rachel!" He laughs, his voice echoing off the walls in the alley. "The Trials! I know you know what those are! I was risking my life every day, being tested and tortured in ways you can't even imagine. That night was my first day back in civilization and I didn't even want to be there. At all."

"I know that now, but I—"

311

"I thought you knew me better than that," he says, pressing his hand to his chest. "Everything I've ever done for you is to help *you*, make your life better. And every single step of the way, you've fought me."

My words strangle in my throat, my heart feeling like it is suffocating within my chest.

"And now," he says, snorting loudly and gesturing down the alley. "Not only do I find out that you couldn't wait, but also that you're sleeping with the fucking Russians?!"

"I was distraught Jaxon, didn't know what I was doing!"

"Bullshit!"

"That night," I say, trying to summon every ounce of my courage. "I showed up to the bar to tell you about the baby, and you were with Polina. I saw you with her!"

"I was never *with* Polina!" He shouts at me. "I was only entertaining that vapid bitch because she was Roman's sister. Yeah, we got drunk and fooled around, but that was that. And yeah, that was a mistake. But you know what I did? I *told* you about it Rachel. I fucking told you! Because I thought you deserved that! Meanwhile, I have to find out from your brother that you *fucked* Yuri?! The same night! A fact that you conveniently forgot to mention!"

"You're right, I should have told you, it was just a mistake, Jaxon," I beg. "It was a stupid mistake."

"Yeah, and so is *this*."

He glares at me in absolute disgust before turning away from me and walking away.

"No! Jaxon!" I cry, running after him. "Wait, please!"

"Wait? *Wait*?! Tell me, what should I wait for, Rachel?" He snaps, clicking his tongue. "For you to be something you're not? Or maybe for you to wake up and realize that I've only ever tried to support you and make your life better?"

"I know you have, I was an idiot," I wail.

He laughs, throwing his hands on his hips.

"You know," He says, biting his bottom lip. "Your little bitchy friend—the same one I pulled a hundred strings to keep out of prison? Yeah, her hinting that I somehow was selfishly and deliberately demanding you be miserable for my own gratification was just the icing on the fucking cake."

"Jaxon, Jess didn't speak for me!"

"No, but you *think* it," he says, wagging his finger at me. "And you see, therein lies the crux of our problem, Rachel."

He throws his hands in the air in frustration.

"I didn't want you to quit dancing because I have some twisted sadistic desire to see you miserable and unhappy. I'm not trying to stifle you or suffocate you."

"I know!"

"I wanted you to quit dancing because I have a family and a reputation to protect! A family that now includes *our* unborn child, who doesn't get a say in this. I was trying to protect their reputation, which I thought was what I was *supposed* to do as a father. I thought that's what we were both supposed to do!"

"It is, and you have," I say tearfully, my words strangling in my throat. "Look, I just made a mistake, Jaxon. That's all."

He stares at me, the pain, frustration, and disappointment so viscerally painted on his face. He licks his bottom lip, and chuckles to himself before shaking his head.

"You know, I thought you were different. God, I really did," he whispers to himself, rubbing his chin. "I know you had a hard time growing up in our world, and I respected that, but I thought you understood what it meant to be with me. What pressures I have, and will always have, riding on me. I thought that you, of all people, would understand what it's like to have your life decided for you."

I open my mouth to respond but nothing comes out. I don't know how to get my remorse across to him.

"What a fucking fool I am," he whispers painfully, he wipes his mouth.

"Jaxon, I—"

"You know what," he scoffs quietly, throwing up his hands. "No. I'm done."

"No! Jaxon! Please!" I plead as he starts to back away from me, shaking his head. "We can fix this! I know we can!"

"No, we can't," he says, his face cold, as if I am suddenly a stranger, someone he's never met before. "Because I can't be worrying about what trouble you're getting up to, or what shame you're bringing to my family. I have enough shit to worry about as it is."

"Please!" I wail. "Jaxon, I need you. *We* need you!"

He closes his eyes, as if the mention of our unborn child is

313

almost too painful to acknowledge.

"Look, I'll support you and the baby, because that's my job, but I'm done being a part of these little manipulative games you play. Find someone else to toy with."

"It's not a game," I sob, feeling my chest heave. "Jaxon, please. Believe me."

"That's just it," he shrugs, shaking his head. "I can't. I'm tired of fighting."

His words rip through me like a bullet.

"I can't be with you all the time, always. And it's clear that having a warm body in your bed is all you need. You might be willing to disrespect yourself, Rachel, but it's the last time you fucking disrespect me."

No, no, no. This cannot be happening right now!

He turns to walk away, and I reach for him, grabbing his arm, only to feel him pull away.

"I do respect you, Jaxon!" I shout, clawing at him. "Just give me another chance, please! I can do better, I promise!"

"No," he whispers. "You can't, Rachel."

He continues walking down the alley, but as I chase after him, my heel catches in a hole in the shoddy pavement and I twist my ankle.

"Ow! Shit!" I wince, collapsing to the ground.

But Jaxon doesn't stop. He's so angry and so fed up that he just keeps walking.

This is it. I'm going to lose him. Right now.

Despite the stabbing pain in my ankle, I get up and start limping after him.

"Will you please just wait?" I cry, practically yelping from the pain. "Just talk to me?"

"I'm done talking," he says. "And I'm done waiting."

"Jaxon," I beg, leaning against the stone wall in the alley, unable to continue chasing after him. "Please don't do this...I *love* you!"

"No. You. Fucking. Don't!" He suddenly roars, turning around and glaring at me, a fury in his eyes I've never seen before. "You know how I know? Because this is the only time you've ever said it. Right here, right now. And you know what? It's fine. Because I don't fucking love you either. Not anymore. This is over. You and me? We're *done*."

All of my words escape me and I watch, helplessly, as Jaxon Pace storms down the Alley, out of view.

…And out of my life.

I collapse into a ball, sliding down the wall to the dirty pavement, sobbing. In an instant, my world has shattered, and it's all my fault.

I was wrong. He was right. About everything.

Jaxon *had* loved me, and I hadn't been able to accept it. He *had* tried to protect me, and I had fought against him. And now here I sit, wallowing in my sins, unable to take any of them back. Jaxon and I were over. Really over.

I sit there, clutching my knees against my body, sobbing for what feels like forever, the only sound being the passing of the occasional car on the street, and my occasional sobs.

But then, I suddenly hear the sound of a car coming from down the other end of the alley.

"Yo, yo, look!" I hear a man say. "What do we have here?"

"Dude, it's the girl from earlier! She's crying!"

"Hey, honey, you alright?"

Huddled in my little ball of agony, I ignore them, hoping they will just leave me alone.

I really don't need this right now.

"Hey Kitten," he says gently. "Are you okay? Do you need help?"

Apparently not.

"I'm fine," I lie. "Please just leave me alone."

When I look up, I see that it's the man who paid for the lap dance for his kid brother.

"No you're not," another man's voice says, and I turn to see that standing behind him is the same kid brother who got choked and thrown across the room by Jaxon.

Well at least he's okay. Though he probably hates me.

"Look, I'm sorry," I say, wiping my mascara from my face. "For what he did to you. I had nothing to do with—"

"Shhhh," the kid says, leaning down next to me. "It's okay, alright? Few bumps and bruises, but nothing I couldn't handle. I didn't know you were the boss's girl."

"Not anymore," I say, choking back a sob.

"Oh shit," he says, shaking his head. "I'm so sorry. But seriously, it was so worth it. I loved it."

315

"I'm glad," trying to muster a smile. "But listen, I'm just having a bad night, alright? So, please just pretend you don't see me."

"No, please," he says sympathetically. "Let us help you."

"That's okay," I say, standing to my feet.

However the moment my ankle hits the pavement the searing pain returns.

"Ow!" I wince.

"Sweetheart, you're hurt," the kid says.

"I just twisted my ankle," I say dismissively. "It's nothing."

Glancing back at the door Jaxon and I walked out of, which doesn't have a handle to open it from the outside, I now realize I have to walk all the way down this alley just to make it back into the club.

But, *Jaxon* will be back inside the club.

Along with his men, and his father, and all of the Russians. All of whom now likely look at me as if I am common street trash.

Fuck, maybe I am.

"Look," the brother says, walking over to me. "You said you're not with Jaxon Pace anymore, right?"

I shake my head.

"Well then he won't care what you do. We have a car right here. Why don't you get in, and we can just take you home?"

Home. That sounds delightful. Anywhere but here.

The kid smiles at me and extends his hand.

"Okay," I finally say.

The Cherry Kid helps me to the car, with his older brother opening the back door.

"Josh, scoot over, make room for the lady," he says, and I slide into the middle of the back seat.

He slides in next to me, and closes the door behind him.

"Thank you," I say, wiping my eyes again. "If you make a left at the end of the alley, it's just right down the street."

The car starts moving, however, at the end of the alley, it does *not* turn left as I instructed.

"Um, hi," I say, reaching forward and tapping the driver on the shoulder. "Sorry, but I think you needed to turn left back there to take me home."

But the guy next to me takes my hand and sets it back in my lap before leaning in and whispering in my ear.

316

"We said we would take you home," his hot whiskey breath filling my nostrils. "But we never said it would be *your* home, now did we, Kitten?"

And suddenly my grief-stricken brain understands.

I have just made a horrible mistake.

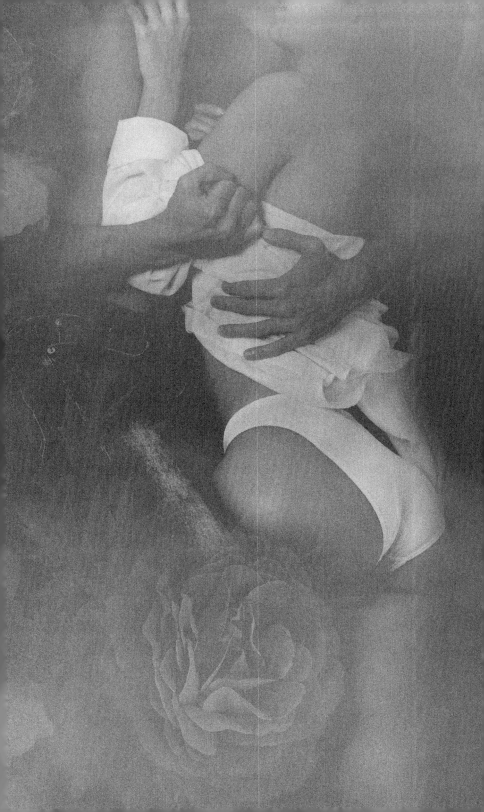

CHAPTER TWENTY-FOUR

ADAM

"So wait," I say, feeling my stomach twist. "You're saying that they…"

"They raped me," Rachel says, her eyes locking with mine.

I stare at her, simply unable to comprehend anything she just said to me.

"But," I say, my words choking in my chest. "This was the virgin kid, right? I thought you said he was nice?!"

She chuckles quietly to herself.

"Yeah, apparently being thrown onto a table for touching the boss's girl changes you," she says, clicking her tongue. "They were furious with me and decided to let their little brother have his way with me for revenge. And just for fun."

"No," I say, shaking my head.

"For three days." She continues, taking another sip of wine. "I was tied to a table and assaulted. In nearly every way you can imagine. But, I guess as an FBI agent, I can assume you can imagine a lot."

My heart is pounding in my chest.

"At first I tried to fight back," she says softly. "But that, well, that only made it worse."

She leans forward on her knees and spins the wine inside the wine glass in her hand.

"Jesus," I whisper, swallowing hard. "I can't even..." my voice trails off, but I realize that there's no way for me to even begin to comprehend what she's been through.

I shake my head.

"I can't imagine the strength it took to survive that."

She snorts quietly.

"You misunderstand, Adam. I wasn't trying to *survive*," she says, a sad smile on her face. "At that point, I had just stopped fighting. I was just waiting for the end to come."

Her words feel like acid in my veins.

I close my eyes, trying desperately not to picture the unimaginable horrors she must've endured over the course of those three days. Horrors that she's now casually discussing with me over a bottle of wine.

"I knew realistically it was only a matter of time before the novelty wore off, and then they would kill me. They'd have to," she whispers, every word palpable in the small study. "So I just gave up."

I can't move. I can barely think.

"There was something freeing in it though."

"Freeing?"

She sighs.

"Something, I don't know, powerful, I guess?" Rachel continues. "The moment you hit rock bottom—and I mean *actual* rock bottom, not just some over-inflated plateau of sadness, it's almost a comfort. Because you realize, at the very least, that you can't *fall* any further. You know right then that you can't lose anything else, because you've already lost everything and everyone you care about. And since you don't see a way up or out, there's an acceptance that happens. That this is, in fact, the end, and no one is coming to save you."

"So then," I ask cautiously. "What happened?"

"Someone *did* come to save me."

"Jaxon," I whisper, trying to hide my rage at the mere mention of his name.

She nods.

"Turns out, Jessica got in touch with him the next day after I didn't come home. He had people out looking for me."

"How generous of him," I growl under my breath.

"Apparently one of the guys liked to run his mouth, and he told someone who went in search of Jaxon Pace."

I down the rest of my wine.

"One minute I was lying tied to a table, and the next the door was smashed in and Jaxon and his Alpha Squad came storming into the room. He called paramedics and I was taken to the hospital where I spent a few days."

"Did the prick at least stay with you during your recovery?" I ask, my hand instinctively balling into a fist.

"Yes," she nods slowly. "We both apologized, and—"

"Wait, what do you mean you *both* apologized?" I snap, unable to contain my fury any longer.

"Well, yes, we both apologized," she says, confusion blanketing her face. "I wasn't innocent in the situation, Adam."

"Um, yes, Rachel," I snort. "You fucking were. You were absolutely innocent. You were abducted and raped."

"But I cheated on him."

"I don't care if you fucked every one of his men in front of the prick! That still doesn't mean that you deserved to be raped, Rachel!"

"I never said it did," she snaps back. "But Jaxon didn't rape me, Adam. And he obviously felt horrible about it."

"As he fucking should!"

"I'm just saying that I wouldn't have been in a position to get abducted and raped had I not been having that conversation about me cheating on him in that alley that night."

"Wrong! You wouldn't have been in that alley that night had it not *been* for Jaxon!" I'm shouting now. "He pulled you out there, the least he could have done was pull you back inside. No matter how mad he was at you, or how justified he was, or thought he was, he still never should have left you alone in a fucking alley in the middle of the city."

I shake my head.

"I mean, here he is, lecturing you about the morality of being the mother of his child, and yet he just left you, on a fucking street corner. What did he think was going to happen?"

"Well, in his defense—"

"Do not defend him right now, Rachel," I say through gritted teeth.

"I'm not!"

"You are. And I don't know what's more frustrating: the fact that he left you there, or the fact that you're justifying his failure by trying to share the blame."

She sighs deeply.

"Why is it so hard for you to admit he has faults?"

"Believe me I know he has faults. Adam!" she shouts at me. "I'm well aware of his faults. And I don't make excuses for him."

"Bullshit."

"Okay, I have in the past," she admits, rolling her eyes "But this was different. If I hadn't put him in the position, *I* put him in—"

"No," I say sharply. "Okay, yes, you cheated on him, and that was wrong. And perhaps, yes, you embarrassed him in front of his men and his business partners—which was also wrong. But *your* actions did not justify *his* actions. An eye for an eye makes the whole world blind, and just because Jaxon was hurt, doesn't mean he had to hurt you in return."

"But he didn't hurt me, Adam," She says. "Those men did. I know you like things to be black and white but this just isn't one of those things. It's complicated."

"It's really not though…" I growl.

"Jaxon and I have known each other a long time, there's a lot of layers to the shitshow that was our relationship."

"Fucking understatement," I growl.

"…And I'm sure it's really easy to sit on the outside and cast judgment on our messy little lives, when you don't know what it's like to actually be in a situation like that."

"No, I don't," I reply firmly. "But I know I wouldn't have done that to you. No matter how pissed I was."

"You don't know that," she says, her eyes breaking from mine. "You can't know that."

"I know I'd never have left you alone in a fucking alley, Rachel!" I snap, my blood boiling. "Not ever! I could be furious with you, but it wouldn't negate my concern for your safety."

She stares at me for a long moment before lowering her eyes

to the floor.

"You haven't lived it, Adam," she finally whispers, so quietly I can barely hear her. "So you can't make promises like that."

Wrong.

I chuckle sarcastically to myself, rubbing my chin.

"You know, after the home invasion, things broke down for Candace and I, and it wasn't long before she started cheating on me. She wasn't even careful with it."

Rachel looks up at me, a look of surprise on her face.

"As soon as I was sent off on assignment, she'd drop the kids off with her parents, and hit the bar. Eventually I caught on, and decided to investigate. And wouldn't you know, one night I caught her with her mouth around some asshole's cock, in a shitty bar outside of Poughkeepsie."

"Oh shit," Rachel whispers.

"Yeah, I beat his ass, and yeah, I was fucking furious with her, and yeah, part of me hated the very sight of her. But you know what I didn't do, Rachel?" I say, narrowing my eyes at her. "I didn't *leave* her at that shitty bar to fend for herself, all by herself, and no ride home. I put her drunk, unfaithful ass in the car, drove her home, and took myself to a hotel where I drank myself into a coma for a few days."

I pound my chest with my hand.

"Because that's what a fucking *man* does! A man does what's right! He does what's right even if he doesn't want to, even if he doesn't have to, even if they don't deserve it, and even if it's fucking hard!"

I bite my lip, still shaking my head and sighing deeply.

"...*Especially* when it's fucking hard," I whisper.

Leaning forward on my knees I run both my hands over my head, trying to reign in my frustration. If I had any remorse for how badly I had beaten Jaxon Pace during our little warehouse interrogation, a week ago it has now completely evaporated.

I should've hit him fucking harder.

Fuck that I should've killed him.

"Look, I know you don't want me to apologize to you because you think I'm pitying you," I sigh, still holding my head. "But the truth is, in some ways I *do* pity you, Rachel. Because that wouldn't have happened, had Jaxon been a better man to you."

I look up, finding her staring at me. The pained expression on her face, combined with the uncomfortable realization reflecting in her eyes, shatters my tattered heart inside my chest.

No woman ever deserves to be exploited like that, least of all Rachel, who's only crime was simply wanting an ounce of compassion from the man who claimed to care about her.

She deserved *better*.

From Jaxon, from her parents, and from literally every person in her life. And yet somehow, every single one of them systematically failed her. But perhaps what cuts the deepest, is that I now understand Rachel really didn't *know* that she deserved better.

…Because she had never known *better*.

And knowing what I know about her life, and everything she's been through, I find it truly remarkable that she's survived this long.

Her lip trembles and she looks away. Standing to her feet she sets down the wine glass on the table.

Shit. What have I done?

"Rachel, I didn't mean to…" I mumble, sighing deeply. "Well, what I mean is…I wasn't trying to—"

"It's fine," she says quickly, turning back to me with a smile on her face. "You know, I think I'm just tired. It's late."

"No, I'm—" I start to say, but it's too late.

Without another word, she picks up the wine bottle, leaving her glass behind on the table and walks out of the room.

Great job, Adam. You uncompassionate fuck.

I can hear Rachel's footsteps on the stairs and lean forward on my knees, cradling my head in my hands and kicking myself for letting my detest of Jaxon Pace overrule my empathy.

And while it's true that *I* never would've left her in a Chicago alley simply because I was angry, maybe she's right. Maybe because I hadn't grown up in their world, or lived the experiences they had, I couldn't truly appreciate where she was coming from.

Maybe I just let my emotions cloud the issue.

Jaxon Pace may have abandoned her, but it *is* slightly unfair to blame him for her rape. No matter how I personally felt about the fucker, I can't imagine he'd let such an offense slide without some sort of repercussion for those responsible. He might be the asshole who hurt her, but he'd also shown some respect for the mother of his child. Occasionally anyway.

Here she was, opening up to me about an incredibly horrific experience, which as I understand is not easy for her to do…and I flew off the handle.

I have to go fix this. Immediately.

Jumping to my feet I hurry up the stairs after her. Part of me kind of assumed she would've already locked me out of the room, but I find the door ajar. Gently, I knock three times.

"I don't know why you're knocking," she says, turning on the fireplace. "Seems a bit redundant to do on an open door."

"Well, I didn't want to invade your space," I say gently. "May I come in?"

"Um, yeah, obviously?" She snorts, shaking her head. "Kind of a stupid question."

My question might seem innocuous, but there's a deeper reason behind my asking. Rachel has just divulged a heartbreaking story detailing her consent being revoked, and all I want to do is remind her that with me, she still has it.

I step into the room.

"Rachel, forgive me, but I didn't like the way that conversation ended." I say quietly. "I want to fix that."

"There's nothing to fix. It's fine," she says, sitting down on the bed. "It's been a long day, and I'm just tired. I think I need sleep."

I want her to talk to me about how she's actually feeling, but I also don't want to press. Not now. Not after that.

"Do you, uh," I say, clearing my throat. "Want to be alone?"

She fidgets with something on the comforter.

"I…I don't know," she says, looking away, biting her lip. "Maybe? I…I don't…"

No. She doesn't.

Carefully I make my way across the room to her, slowly and intentionally. Sitting down in the chair across from the bed.

"Look, I know the story you just recounted was traumatic," I say gently. "And I—"

She rolls her eyes.

"Oh for fucks sake, Adam," she snaps, suddenly throwing her hands in the air. "How many times do we have to go over this? I don't want your fucking pity!"

"It's not pity, Rachel. It's empathy."

"Well, I don't want that either!" She shouts, her voice cracking as she jumps to her feet, storming past me toward the bathroom. "I'm not upset!"

"Okay, that's fine. I'm just saying that if you were, I'm here. And it's completely normal."

"Well you know what? Maybe I'm not normal, okay? And maybe I like it!" She snaps, stomping back over to me. "And for the record, I'm not some specimen for you to dissect, okay? All of this happened a very long time ago. It's in the past, it doesn't bother me anymore. I'm over it!"

However, the tears in her eyes and the quiver in her lip tell me the exact opposite, and within seconds I am on my feet beside her.

"Something can be in the past and you can be over it," I whisper softly. "And it still can hurt."

"You know what," she snaps, tears streaming down her cheeks. "I don't need your stupid pity, or your empathy, or… anything! I don't want any of your psycho-babble-bullshit. You get that? I'm…I'm fine! I'm…over it!"

She runs her hand through her hair, her voice cracking. And without thinking I close the distance and pull her to me. The moment her skin hits me, she immediately falls apart in my arms, sobbing against my chest.

"I'm not weak," she mumbles against my chest. "I'm not."

"I know, Rachel," I whisper in her ear.

She says nothing, simply sobbing into my shoulder.

I wish more than anything that I could take her pain away. But I can't. There's nothing I can do to undo what has been done to her. And I don't know how to fix this.

But I do know I can hold her and let her know that she is safe.

"I'm here," I say softly, kissing the top of her head. "Okay? I'm right here. And I've got you."

This is the first time that she has truly let her walls down with me, and I doubt sincerely she intended it. When her sobs finally begin to quiet, and her breathing slows, I gently rub her back and press my lips to the top of her head.

"Get into bed," I say quietly. "You do need to sleep."

"No, don't…don't go," she whispers against my chest, gripping me tightly. "Please."

I smile to myself.

"I'm not going anywhere," I say softly. "Get into bed, and let me hold you."

"Do you want me to take my clothes—"

"No," I say, cutting her off, my tone gentle but firm. "Tonight is not the night for that."

"Oh," she says, confusion echoing in her eyes.

But even this makes sense to me now. Nearly all of her interactions with men have been either traumatic or transactional.

Hell, I don't know if she's even ever had someone who just wanted to be with her, and spend time with her, without expecting something in return.

"Rachel, I'm not going to have sex with you tonight," I say, brushing the hair from her face. "But I will stay with you, and hold you all night, because that's what I want to do with you. But only if you *want* me to."

The light returns to her eyes, and she nods gently.

"Okay," I whisper, nodding toward the bed. "Go on then."

She finally peels herself from me, and grabs her pajamas as I walk over to my bag removing my other pair of sweatpants. The two of us strip down in silence before climbing into bed.

Her true fragility is clear to me when, unlike her usual hostile response to vulnerability, she simply folds into my arms without a word.

Hours later, I wake in the darkness, my body jolting, and my heart instantly racing. It's almost as if some loud noise has startled me, and now I'm just a few seconds behind.

Instinctively, my eyes scan the dark room, adjusting slowly to the pale moonlight casting haunting shadows around the room. But find nothing.

It was nothing. Just a nightmare.

I close my eyes, my heart still pounding in my chest as I groggily start my grounding techniques. My first partner, Scarlett, taught me some tricks to calm my anxiety when my PTSD randomly rears its terrifying head in the form of a night terror.

What's my name?

Adam.

How old am I?

Thirty-Seven.

Where am I?

The Valentine Mansion. With *her*.

Rachel Valentine, the sleeping brunette, laying in the crux of my shoulder. Her breaths are deep, slow, and relaxed, much different than how they were an hour ago when she was shaking and twitching.

I stare down at her as she shifts, placing her hand on my bare chest. Her hair smells of the vanilla-passion fruit shampoo I used this morning in the shower, having left mine at the hotel. Her long dark curls lay messily around her face. Gently, I reach down and stroke it back behind her ear, kissing the top of her head. I can't be sure, but I swear I see her smile.

God, she's so fucking beautiful.

Slowly, my heart rate starts to settle just by looking at her.

Her.

The singular word for the woman has completely uprooted, disrupted, and challenged every single foundation of who I am.

…And everything I'm *not*.

I thought I knew who I was before her.

I've been a few things to a few different people throughout my life. I wasn't popular, but I also wasn't disliked. I easily blended into the crowd, nothing more than a background color. Which honestly just made my work with the FBI even easier, as they liked agents who were invisible in plain sight. And because of that job, I was able to travel a bit and have experiences I doubt I would've had otherwise.

I used to say my job gave me a life. Because as a young man, I was so excited to flash my big bad FBI badge, and too foolish to see that an incredible life was right in front of me the whole time. I had a wife I loved, and two beautiful boys, but I had missed so much being so preoccupied with the notoriety of my job.

Until that job cost me everything.

And then it was too late. It was a lesson I had learned the very hardest of ways, and now I simply had to live with.

But even after I had grieved for my family, and even after I was ready to try and put myself out there, I found the world even colder and dating even more exhausting than the first time around.

It was always the same hamster-wheel. The same questions, same flirty conversations, same disappointments, same arguments, and the same eventual break-up.

So, I just stopped trying.

I spent enough time alone that I was happy with myself. I was a decent looking guy, so when I really craved a woman's company, I had no problem finding one for a night or a weekend, or a professional for the occasional punishment or domination I desired when the mood struck.

But even from the beginning, Rachel was different.

There was an edge to her. Something sharp and dangerous. And yet, still unpredictable and exciting.

She was never the same old rinse-repeat cycle I was used to because it was clear she wasn't trying to be the same version of anything. Every single day to her was an adventure, and she longed for the thrill of anything that made her heart beat faster, anything that made her feel free.

And yet, it's clear to me that she's not just a free spirit, drifting aimlessly through life by fate or chance. No, that accidental existence would be far beneath her, and far too simple. And Rachel Valentine could *never* be that simple.

There's loyalty to her that is incredibly unique. For a girl labeled as unreliable, untrustworthy, and uncaring, she sure cared a lot. Which just told me that a very real, and very fragile heart still thundered away inside of her. On multiple occasions she had risked her life for people who might not have done the same for her, or who had openly betrayed her...like Jaxon Pace.

But at the same time, while Rachel might want to feel free, she also wants to belong. Deep down, she wants to be kept, without being imprisoned. And loved without being suffocated. Not by just anyone, but by someone who is willing to stand in her storm, because they truly love her.

Rachel's contradictions make sense to me. They are the residual aftershocks of the complete love she's never felt, and the *better* she's never had.

Has she ever known love? True, honest, love? I don't know.

I don't know if anyone has ever loved her correctly.

...But I want to be the one who finally *does*.

Because what I realize, here in the dark, is that I *do* truly love her. Completely. Truly. And honestly.

Even if I'm not ready to tell her, and even if she's definitely not ready to hear it. No matter how insane that is, or how terrifying it may be, and even despite all of my own glaring faults and inadequacies,

I'm not a perfect man. I've made plenty of mistakes. And I have plenty of my own regrets and demons who stalk my nightmares. But maybe all my trauma and all the lessons I've learned, have prepared me for this moment right here. With *her*.

Perhaps all my broken pieces are exactly the sacrifice she requires to fill in the cracks so she can feel wild enough to fly her crazy flag, yet safe enough to fall apart.

That's why here in the dark, with Rachel wrapped up in my arm, I make her this simple silent vow:

I will be patient for her.

I will be understanding for her.

I will be compassionate for her.

I will be forgiving for her.

I will be better for her.

And maybe, just maybe, I'd be better for it.

CHAPTER TWENTY-FIVE

Rachel

I wake the next morning before Adam.
Curled against his strong chest I feel his slow and steady breaths beneath my hand. Careful not to wake him, I shift gently so that I can look up at him.

He's so pretty.

I still can't believe that he's here, with me. And more shocked that he's stayed, despite all my gruesome stories.

After we crawled into bed, he stayed true to his word; he simply held me. All night. Never letting go for even a minute. At some point I guess I asked him why he came there with me, and what he truly wanted out of this, and what he hoped to achieve.

"I just want you, Rachel."

That was his answer.

Direct, concise, and a little cheesy.

But, honestly, I guess cheesy is pretty standard for Adam.

We talked for hours until eventually I fell asleep, right here on his chest. And here I had remained until the morning, laying cuddled up with this beautiful man. Which is a feat in itself.

I've never been one for cuddling. Maybe it's because I've spent so much time on my own, but I've really never understood the point of needing or even wanting someone's hands all over my body if sex isn't involved. Excessive touch, without climax, always made me feel smothered and suffocated. Even with Jaxon, who rarely lingered long after the deed was done.

If anyone had asked me six months ago for non-sexual intimacy, I'd have charged them double.

But…I don't mind *Adam's* touch. I never have.

Back when he was just a client, I spent several nights with him after our transactional business had concluded. And last night he just held me close, stroking my back with his fingertips. There was something so natural about my place in his arms, and it felt so comforting, and safe.

Jesus Christ, now I'm the one being cheesy. Fuck this shit.

The weirdest part for me though, is having to reconcile myself to the fact that our *relationship* hasn't imploded the way I thought it would. At least not yet anyway.

But perhaps that's because Adam is not as vanilla as I thought he was…or as innocent. There's still lots I don't know, but he's definitely lived a harder, darker life than I assumed a run-of-the-mill FBI Agent would.

Adam wasn't the devil Jaxon was, but he also wasn't a saint.

…And I like that about him.

I try to shift again, but this time Adam wakes.

"Good morning," he says, rubbing his eyes.

"It will be after coffee," I yawn, feeling his arm wrap around me, pulling me closer. "I'm far more pleasant after coffee."

"Well, I guess you could just ask the cook to bring some up," he stretches, winking at me. "Oh wait, never mind. I guess that means making coffee is on you, Miss Valentine."

"And I'd say, considering I did that for you, so that no one discovered you here, and killed you, I'd say coffee is on *you*, Agent Westwood."

"Hmm, I suppose you have a point," he chuckles, with a yawn, stretching his muscular arms above his head.

God he's sexy.

"Although," I say, resting my chin on his chest, and running my hand slowly down his chiseled bare chest. "There are other ways we could wake up."

But just as my hand reaches his belly button, he gently stops me with his own.

"Rachel," he whispers, clearing his throat. "Why don't we wait on that for a minute, huh?"

"What?" I ask, confused. "Why?"

I can't help it, but a part of me reacts to his refusal as if I've been struck, having never been turned down for sex before.

"Because last night was intense, yeah?" he says, sighing deeply. "And I...well, I don't want to feel like I'm taking advantage of you."

Oh. Yeah, as I said: cheesy as fuck.

"That's the stupidest thing I've ever heard, Adam," I snort, unable to stop myself.

"I'm serious."

"As am I," I scoff. "As I said, I'm fine. It was a heavy memory, but I've processed it and I'm past it. And now I want to fuck."

Hooking my leg around him, I pull myself on top of him, feeling his erection pressing against the thin panties I wore to bed.

"Rachel," he tries to protest, but I ignore him, grinding myself against him.

His face strains, and I hear him breathe in deeply, his body shuddering under my touch. But just when I think he's going to give in and let me, he flips me over on my back, pinning me beneath him.

"Oh you want to be on top, huh?" I grin, biting my lip. "Okay then."

"No," he says firmly. "I want us to *wait*. Just for a little bit."

"Why should we wait?" I say seductively, ignoring him, and continuing to grind myself against him from underneath.

He sighs, and then hangs his head.

"Come on Adam, you know you want to fuck me," I groan, winking at him and feeling his hard erection pressing into me.

"I do," he says, "But I don't *just* want to fuck you, Rachel. I want to know that there's more than just sex between us."

"Well there might be lots more Adam, but you're kind of killing the mood right now," I say, rolling my eyes. "I'm not trying to process all of my emotions here, just have some quick, casual, morning sex and—"

Suddenly he grabs my chin, leans in and kisses me hard,

knocking all the wind from my lungs.

"And I want to know," Adam says, he growls. "That I can make love to my *girlfriend*."

I immediately stop moving. And breathing.

"Believe me, I love fucking you, Rachel. And, I…" he says, clearing his throat. "I also care about you. Deeply."

"As do I, but—" I start to say but he kisses me again, silencing me once more.

"Look, you asked me last night what I wanted? Well, I want a relationship where I know I can have both. And I want it with you."

"We will have that," I say defensively, threading my hands up into his hair and kissing him softly. "I'm sure we will."

"Well until I know that I can have that, and until I know that you'll let me make love to you and not just fuck you like a wild animal all the time—"

"Mmm, now you're talking," I giggle, biting my lip and moving to kiss him.

But again he stops me, pressing his forehead to mine instead.

"Until I know we can have both, I think I'm going to hold off on fucking you."

"What? Why?" I whine.

"Because that's when I'll know you're serious about this, with me."

"Of course I'm serious," I snort, trying to grab his cock. "I'm just also serious about getting this d—"

However, he blocks me once more.

"Rachel, sex with you means something to me. And I know we're good at it. But you allowing me to make love to you is different, it's how I'll truly know it means something to you too," he says, leaning in and kissing me again, making my brain go fuzzy. "So I'm not saying no to sex altogether, I'm just saying that making love to you is how I'll know we're on the same page."

"I can't believe I'm getting cock-blocked by something as silly as this," I pout, irritably.

"Well," Adam says with a smug little grin. "As *someone* eloquently said last night, it's never just something. It's either nothing, or it's everything."

Did this motherfucker just use my own words against me?!

And before I can even think of anything to say in response, Adam climbs off of me, and slides off the bed.

"Why don't you just lay here, and think about how pissed you are at me," he chuckles arrogantly as he walks toward the door. "Don't worry, Princess, I'll go make the coffee."

He opens it and steps into the hallway, just as I launch my pillow directly at his head.

To his credit, Adam made up for not fucking me by bringing me breakfast in bed, where I remained pouting.

However, after a cup of coffee and a few bites of his delicious sausage and mushroom strata, I felt slightly more forgiving, even if I was no less horny.

But two can play at this game.

And if he was going to try and resist fucking me, I was going to make resisting as hard as I possibly could.

This meant joining him in the shower, and accidentally rubbing against him. And then deliberately taking my time to wash every single inch of my body very, very slowly. Or walking around the bedroom afterwards, in just my panties, trying to "decide" what to wear, then intentionally choosing something form-fitting and low-cut, to showcase all of my delicious curves.

Adam may have suspected what I was doing, but he was powerless to stop me. He was also now forced to *adjust* the bulge in his pants nearly a dozen times before he eventually decided to excuse himself, and just go make more coffee.

Rachel:1 Adam: 0

Satisfied with my revenge and armed with a fresh cup, I flip on the gas fireplace in the living room as we settle back into the couches. Instead of diving right back into the heavy shit, we spent some time talking about some of the easy stuff.

Adam had been pretty good at baseball. Really good, actually, and had even been offered a sports scholarship to a couple of pretty prestigious schools. In another life, he likely would've gone pro, had he not joined the Bureau and dedicated his life to fighting criminals.

Since I hadn't had a semi-normal childhood, I didn't have the long list of hobbies he had. But I did have some musical artists I liked, a few authors, and a handful of old movies I enjoyed.

He asked me if I could live anywhere in the world, where would I go, and I told him that after spending the better part of my life holed up in dingy apartments in overcrowded cities, I'd love to live on a horse ranch somewhere in the mountains, far away from everyone else.

It was a nice reprieve, but eventually we circled back to the conversation about what had happened to me.

Adam of course reiterated that I didn't have to tell him anything I didn't want to share. But part of me wanted to. Because deep down, I meant what I said in the car the other night I wanted him to know me. Completely.

And while I might not like the story, I knew that I needed to get it off my chest.

So I told him everything. About how after the incident Jaxon moved me into The Manor to live with him. He really didn't give me a choice, but I also didn't object. But this wasn't what *anyone* wanted.

Jaxon wanted to get married. I just wanted to breathe.

And his parents wanted me gone.

They could barely look at me. Perhaps it was because I had wrecked their plans for a *worthy* match for their son, or simply because my messy existence, and the chaos I brought with me, shamed their family.

At least that's how it felt to me.

Jaxon denied it of course, but I could feel their disgust with every sideways glance, whispered conversation in the library, or the occasional passive comment muttered under their breath when I'd brave a family dinner.

He could deny it all he wanted, but I knew the truth. Every whisper within the walls of Pace Manor echoed what I already knew: I wasn't what Ismena and Dimitris wanted for their son. And I wasn't what *anyone* wanted for the future Don Supreme.

And honestly, I couldn't blame them.

After all, I was a stripper and occasional escort who had gotten pregnant with Jaxon's bastard child and then refused to marry the most eligible bachelor in the city. But if that wasn't enough drama to rival a primetime reality show, I had also just been kidnapped and raped, and by now our entire syndicate knew all the gory details of what had happened to me.

…And they knew because of Jaxon.

Jaxon's *response* to my assault is the very reason his name is whispered in secret like he's the Boogeyman, and why the entire city of Chicago fears him to this day.

He went *thermonuclear*.

And being the volatile personality he was, it was incredibly visceral. No one, including Ethan, could talk him down, and he unleashed a slew of retribution killings so vicious that left the entire underworld of Chicago terrified to leave their homes.

Nathan Myers, was the first casualty. He was the informant who approached one of Jaxon Pace's Alpha Squad regarding my whereabouts. He was a low-level smuggler who worked for Dakari Nam. He was also a friend of Aaron, the oldest of the brothers who had raped me. On the second day of my kidnapping, Aaron met Nathan at a bar for drinks. At some point, Aaron asked him if he wanted to "see something amusing," and invited him back to the house that they were holding me at.

When Nathan arrived and saw that *I* was that *something*, he was appalled, and despite Aaron's offer, Nathan refused to touch me. However, he was younger, smaller, and far less vicious than any of my captors, and was understandably terrified, afraid they might kill him if he tried to stop them from having their "fun" with me.

In his way, he did what he could to distract them, plugging them with so much alcohol that they fell asleep and could no longer rape or torture me. But knowing he didn't have the keys to the padlock around my neck, and knowing there was no way he could get them off of the drunk Aaron without waking him, he promised to leave and get me help.

And he did. Nathan snuck out and went straight to the Pace Mafia, who at that point were already searching for me. Ultimately, Nathan Myers was the reason Jaxon, and his men were able to find and rescue me at all.

However, Jaxon did *not* see it that way. At all.

Jaxon saw Nathan as a *coward*, whose inability to intervene the moment he saw me chained and abused, resulted in my extended torture. And he punished him for it. He gouged out Nathan's eyes, and sliced off his ears, before setting the mutilated man loose in the sex district. Poor Nathan stumbled feebly around before ultimately stepping off a curb in front of a city bus, ending his misery.

Some part of me felt a little bad about what happened to Nathan, because he hadn't been the only one that the brothers had invited back to assault me. None of the rest of the spectators, or occasional participants did anything to help. But Nathan did. He was the only one. And so for him alone, I felt the slightest pang of remorse.

But not for any of the rest of them, all of whom were tracked down by Jaxon and his Alpha Squad, and who all met very similar fates.

I know, because in some cases Jaxon asked me to confirm whether or not I recognized a suspected assailant. But if I'm honest, I just said "yes" to them all. In those three days, I had been beaten, starved, and so badly dehydrated, that so much of that experience was just a hellish blur, and I didn't care if they were guilty or innocent. I wanted all of them to suffer.

As did Jaxon. Who didn't stop with just the participants.

He would kill anyone for even *mentioning* my name.

When he heard that Sebastian Macron, one of Antonio Luca's top enforcers, had made a joke at my expense, Jaxon showed up at the man's home and mercilessly beat Sebastian to death with an ashtray…in front of his terrified wife and kids.

But Jaxon saved the worst for the men who had raped me.

Aaron, Josh and Ashton Sutton were taken to the Pace Family's *Dolor Domas*, a torture house masquerading as a farmhouse outside the city.

Jaxon then informed them that for their crimes against me, and therefore *his* family, he was invoking the most barbaric and cruel of our Mafia syndicate's punishments against the Sutton family: The *Sanguis Purgatio*, which was known in our syndicate as a "blood cleansing." It meant that Jaxon intended to wipe out their entire family line all at once…and for *good*.

While the three brothers had been tortured for days, he and his men had tracked down and rounded up every single living member of their bloodline, and after removing all six of my rapist's eyelids, the men were forced to watch as Jaxon executed every single one of them.

In a small act of mercy, perhaps as an expectant father, or

more likely at Ethan's urging, Jaxon chose to spare the only two children within the Sutton family, who were cousins of the brothers. As innocents, they were collected, and placed with reputable upper class families, under new names and aliases.

But that was only the beginning.

After watching in agony the assassination and dissolution of their family line, tourniquets were then placed around each of the brother's limbs. Systematically, and without anesthetic, their hands, feet, eyes and tongue were removed and tossed to the pigs. Lastly their genitals were also removed, and thrown into a meat grinder, after which Jaxon forced the men to consume their own flesh, forcing every bit down their throats with a cattle prod. What was left of the brother's mangled bodies were then tossed into the pig pen...to be eaten *alive*.

Did I feel bad for them? Fuck no.

No, on the contrary, I *watched*. I watched all of it.

Their torture couldn't undo what had been done to me, but somehow, hearing them scream in horror and agony for hours on end, healed the tiniest little fraction of my soul. Or what was left of it anyway.

Jaxon made sure that the syndicate understood that anyone caught even saying my name would have their throats ripped out. And for a while, it worked.

However, in our world, whispers could never truly be silenced, and so in his blood-thirsty quest for vengeance, he had inadvertently *broadcasted* what happened to me to the entire underworld. Behind closed doors everyone was talking about my rape.

...And about our baby.

Within days of me moving to Pace Manor, my face was plastered on dozens of salacious tabloid articles about how Jaxon was "slumming it on skid row," courtesy of that raggedy cunt, Celeste Donahue. This meant that despite his family's efforts to quiet all of the noise around me, there were sleazy paparazzi posted outside the manor at all hours of the day. Meaning that for the first few months I couldn't leave, even if I wanted to.

But even then, I had no reason to leave. I had no one to see.

The girls at the club had been the only family I had.

But because Del had openly defied Jaxon's orders, he fired her and effectively banished her from the city. Because of this, most of the girls there refused to speak to me. Some out of fear, others out of anger. Which meant that that night at the club had been the last time I would ever set foot in the place.

Jess of course visited a few times, if only to give me updates on life outside the walls, but her visits were usually infrequent and short.

I was in hell, and Pace Manor was nothing more than a fancy prison cell within that hell, where everyone hated me. But, ever my knight-in-slightly-dented armor, Jaxon valiantly defended me, and what was left of my honor. He tried to be supportive and sympathetic.

At least I think he did. But I started to see him less and less.

Eventually he calmed down enough to stop cutting people up, but even then he was still busy learning how to be the damn Don. He also had to deal with an onslaught of paparazzi, gossip, as well as fallout from the other Dons in the syndicate, many of whom had lost men in Jaxon's revenge rampage.

I wish I could have appreciated his efforts for what they were, on behalf of us and our baby. But all I saw was his late nights getting later, and me trapped and going stir crazy in a house I clearly wasn't welcome in.

I was suffocating, and I blamed him for it.

And just when all the noise around me was starting to quiet down, Ismena died, and the impossibly cold Pace Manor somehow got even *colder.*

Jaxon was devastated. But Dimitris was inconsolable.

He started drinking a lot and became increasingly violent and angry. He'd fly off the handle and look for any excuse to execute anyone for anything.

I felt like I was trying to navigate my way through a landmine field, and the stress started to affect my health. After one of my appointments with the OBGYN, the doctor told me that my blood pressure was nearing dangerous levels, and that if we didn't do something to alleviate some of my anxiety it could be dangerous for the baby.

That's when I had enough. While I could accept the mess I had created, I wasn't about to let anyone endanger the little life growing inside my womb.

The night I decided to confront Jaxon…

I sit in the chair facing the door, bouncing my foot on my knee and glancing up at the clock waiting for the lights to finally turn off outside the window.

4:34am

Wow, this is a new record. Even for you, Jaxon Pace.

I'd been listening to the conversation Jaxon was having with Roman Antonov through the open window ever since the two of them stumbled back to the manor three hours ago and posted up on the patio with more booze.

I heard all about Roman's ongoing war with the Irish back in New York, and how the two mafia clans have been squabbling over territory and shipping rights for the last fifty years. I also learned that the reason that Roman and his father, Nikolai, had ultimately sought the Pace's out, was not to *join* our syndicate, but rather to *prevent* the Irish from doing so.

For the last fifteen years, the Irish had been vying for a spot within the Chicago underworld. But, they were unpredictable and carried a heavy blow to anyone they disagreed with. To the Pace's their volatility made them a liability they couldn't sanction, and so they had ultimately declined their request.

But Jaxon, the burgeoning businessman, had taken it a step further. He had traded the support of the Pace Family in the Antonov's affairs, to leverage Roman's contacts in the steel industry. On top of growing his shipping empire, he had become a bit of a real estate entrepreneur as of late. Specifically, he was interested in transporting the high-quality, but low-cost steel that came from Lipetsk. With it, Jaxon was going to build a luxury hotel, a massive skyscraper, right here in the heart of Chicago that would be the pinnacle of opulence and decadence.

The door in front of me suddenly bangs open, making me jump. Jaxon stumbles inside, drunkenly singing to himself. His clothes are disheveled, and the man smells like he took a swim in a pool of vodka.

"Oh!" He hiccups, practically falling onto the bed. "You're still awake?"

Well he *attempts* to, anyway.

"I couldn't sleep," I say icily, watching him sit up and pathetically struggle to take off his shoes. "I've been messaging you all day, but I didn't know you were going to be drinking with the ridiculous Russian all night."

"Well, neither did I," Jaxon snorts, chuckling to himself. "But he's entertaining as hell."

"That's lovely, but I have something important to talk to you about."

He sighs, rolling his eyes. "Now? I'm…I'm a little drunk."

"Yeah, you know, I figured that much out for myself, actually," I bite back, annoyed.

"Ugh," he groans. "Can we just not do this right now, Rachel? As I said, this isn't really a good time for me."

"No, as a matter of fact, you *didn't* actually say that," I snap back at him. "Because you never say anything to me. About where you are, or what you're doing, or when you'll be home. And it's never a good fucking time for you, Jaxon. Because you're always with this person or that person, and you're not here with me, and our fucking child!"

"Well, excuse the hell out of me," he snorts sarcastically. "For the record, I'm just out here trying to build a life for us and our child!"

"Oh really?" I growl, crossing my arms across my body. "Because the only thing I see you building is a fucking hangover! And don't play that game with me, Jaxon Pace. Let's be real, the only person you're doing it for is *yourself*."

He sighs loudly, shaking his head.

I take a deep breath, trying to swallow the absolute frustration I have for this entire situation.

"Look," I say, throwing my hands up defensively. "As fun as this is, I really don't want to fight."

"Could've fooled me," he snips back.

"But I need you to listen to me, and I can't get a fucking word in with you, because you're never here!"

"Alright Rach," He snorts, throwing his hands up in the air. "Jesus fucking Christ. You want to talk? Let's talk. What is it that you need to say that can't wait until the goddamn morning?"

"I can't be *here* anymore, Jaxon," I plead, standing to my feet. "I can't do it anymore. Trapped inside this house, day after day. I need air. I need sunlight."

"Then go step outside?" He scoffs, shrugging.

"No, it's a metaphor, you fucking moron," I growl sarcastically. "I don't want to be here anymore. I hate it here."

"Oh, I'm sorry, is the gigantic sprawling Pace Manor not good enough for you, your highness?" He glares at me, clearly offended. "You're saying you'd rather go back to your shitty, roach-filled apartment with Jess?"

"If it meant I'd have company occasionally besides your angry drunk father," I hiss back at him. "Then yes, I think I would!"

"Do not," he growls, "ever say a word about my father."

"Or what, Jaxon?" I shout at him, crossing my arms across my body. "Go on, tell me what will happen if I do, huh? Will you haul me off to the cells? No, of course not, because what would people think about the future Don Supreme treating the mother of his firstborn *heir* like that? Or perhaps if I speak ill of your father I might spontaneously burst into flames? No, although that would be a hell of a fucking feat if I do say so myself."

My blood boiling as I take a step toward him, shouting in his face as loudly as I possibly can.

"So, forgive me, but I'll say whatever the fuck I want about your alcoholic, lunatic father, starting with the fact that he's lost his mind, and gone completely off rails!"

"You don't think I *know* that?!" Jaxon shouts back, his face now red, the vein in his neck pulsing.

"If you do, than what the fuck are you doing about it?!" I shout back at him. "I'll tell you: absolutely fucking nothing!"

"I told you, I'm building us a life, Rachel!"

"And I'm building you a fucking *legacy*, Jaxon!" I shout at him, pointing to my stomach. "A baby. Your heir."

My words seem to stop him in his tracks. His eyes drift down to my hand across my belly.

I cave, suddenly sitting down on the edge of the bed.

"My doctor told me today that my stress and blood pressure were through the roof," I sob. "That being here, in this house with you, and your father could be detrimental to our child! And the truth is, you don't care!"

Jaxon is still for a moment before sitting down on the edge of the bed opposite me. He sighs, running his hand through his hair.

The silence in the room is palpable, every deep breath he

draws seeming to echo my own frustration.

"I do care," he says softly. "Of course I care about you and our baby, Rachel. I…I can't believe you think that."

The gentleness in his voice stirs something within me, because in some small way, I *do* have pity for him. I know Jaxon's tired, and I know how hard he's working. For all his faults, he's done far more for the sake of his duty than any Don would've done before him.

"I have no idea what I'm doing," he says quietly. "Or what I'm meant to be doing. I'm just trying to build something new, for us, and for our family. But I also know that this baby isn't what you wanted, and I know that you're doing this for me."

"Well, not *just* for you," I say, biting my lip, my hand delicately cradling my stomach. "I want to meet her too."

He looks up expectantly.

"*Her*?" He whispers.

Oh shit! I didn't mean to let that slip.

I hadn't figured out the right way to tell him, but suddenly he's on his feet, walking around the bed, and my heart starts pounding in my chest.

What is he going to think about it not being a boy?

"You mean," he says, standing in front of me. "We're having a *girl*?"

"Yes," I whisper, feeling like I am momentarily unable to breathe. "I found out today. The doctor says it's a girl."

He stares at me, his bright blue eyes burrowing into mine. And then without another word, he drops to his knee, gently pressing his hand to my stomach.

"A girl," he says softly. "Who will be the most loved little girl in the entire world."

Oh my God. He's actually…happy.

He doesn't know it, suddenly it feels as if for just a moment, the entire world has been lifted off my shoulders. Closing his eyes, he kisses my stomach, muttering something in Greek against the thin fabric of my shirt.

"I promise, little one," he whispers. "That I will always keep you safe. And that as long as I live, you will never, ever, know the terrors of this world. For you are, and will forever be *mine*."

CHAPTER TWENTY-SIX

ADAM

"So Jaxon wasn't upset." I say, clearing my throat. "You know, about her being a girl."

Rachel shakes her head.

"No, on the contrary," she smiles softly. "He was thrilled."

I shift uncomfortably in my seat. The thought of Jaxon Pace even touching Rachel, let alone having a baby with her, makes my insides twist.

Why? Because I know, from experience, how intimate the act of having a baby with someone could be. Hearing the heartbeat. Feeling the baby kick. Picking a name. Setting up a nursery. All of these were huge milestones that I enjoyed with my wife when she was pregnant with both of my sons.

Even if your relationship with your partner was rocky or difficult, the act of creating a life is beautiful and powerful. And even if you can *only* be unified in loving that child, it still moves you and changes you in ways you aren't prepared for.

But it also *binds* you to that person. Forever.

Now here I sit, reminded that even if, by some miracle, Rachel and I find a way to make this work, the woman I love will forever have a connection to some insufferable asshole that has hurt her in unforgivable ways.

And that if I truly love her, I will have to forgive him too.

A thought that disgusts me to my core.

How do I even go about trying to do that?

I hate Jaxon. For all the ways she loved him, and for all the ways he failed her. But my hatred doesn't change the fact that he's the father of her child.

I don't know the details of why Rachel left Jaxon. Nor do I know how things went down with him getting full custody of their daughter. Every time I've asked, she dodges the question, or straight up changes the subject. Which tells me that she's not *ready* to tell me. But so far, I've heard at least dozens of valid reasons as to why she would've been justified in that decision.

I'm fine waiting for her to tell me when she is ready, because I know she's trying to show me her world.

So no matter how nervous I may be, or unsure of her feelings, this remains the biggest confirmation that she wants this enough to *try*. And if she can try, I can try too. For us. For *her*.

I will be better for her.

"So, Jaxon was thrilled," I say, smiling politely. "But what about his father?"

Rachel's momentary smile drops.

"In his way," she says quietly, shifting. "Jaxon did step in and try to sober him up, so at some point he congratulated us. But also managed to slip in that typically boys ran in the family, and would likely follow."

"What an ass," I snort.

"Honestly, I didn't care what Dimitris thought," she shrugs. "This was a weird instance where the Mafia's patriarchal policies actually benefited and protected my daughter. She would get a normal life, or as much of a normal life as one can expect as a Mafia princess. But she wouldn't be groomed and trained for The Trials. Which was one of my biggest fears."

"What, uh," I say, taking a sip of my coffee. "What are The Trials? You mentioned that Jaxon had been radio silent because he was off doing that, but never actually explained what they are?"

"The Trials are a rite of passage," Rachel says, sighing and leaning her arm back on the back of the couch. "Back when the Mafia first started, The Trials were a series of tests to determine the validity and capacity for a leader to take up the mantle of Don Supreme. There's a lot more procedure to it, but basically each Mafia clan would select a champion to represent them, and the four champions would compete."

"You mean power isn't automatically transferred?"

"It didn't use to be," she continues. "It used to be that every time a Don Supreme would die, every clan would go through this process, fighting and vying for supremacy. But that ultimately proved to be very convoluted and, well, *messy*."

She means deadly.

"So, instead, the elders decided that for the sake of peace, the Supremacy should stay with a family as long as possible."

"Jesus," I chuckle, shaking my head. "It's so crazy to me that you guys have all this…procedure."

Rachel snorts.

"Chaos only works if it's *organized* chaos baby," she shrugs.

"Apparently," I say, clicking my tongue. "Anyways, I'm sorry for interrupting. Please, continue."

"Well, they agreed that the line of succession should default *first* to the firstborn eligible male heir of the Don Supreme. He would not have to compete for the Supremacy, only complete it. It also ended up being good for the men, you know? To see their new leader, the man they've sworn to protect with their very lives, complete the tests that confirm his competency to lead. And so, as long as he was over the age of eighteen, and successfully completed The Trials, he was the new Don Supreme, and life could continue on without much mess, chaos or disruption."

"And you mentioned that a male heir would've been groomed and trained for these tests?"

She nods.

"From the moment he could walk," she says, crossing her arms across her body. "Just like Jaxon was."

I do my best to keep my face stoic and unbothered.

But everything Rachel is telling me is mind-blowing. The idea that this complicated underworld exists is shocking enough, but the fact that it's so intricate and complex, is absolutely mind-blowing.

"What happens in the event that a Don Supreme didn't have

351

a son?" I ask.

"Then he would select a champion from among his ranks. But all the other Dons, from all of the major clans, would be allowed to put forth a champion as well, and the balance of power could shift." Rachel says. "If they passed all the tests."

"And when you say tests…?"

"There's four of them. They cover different elements of leadership," she says, pulling her legs up on the couch. "The Gauntlet is a test of your physical strength and endurance. The Tower is a test of a champion's intelligence and cleverness. And the Tribulation is simply just torture, to desensitize you to pain and test your resolve under pressure. And the Judgment is the final test, which is an individual test of your emotional stability… and *integrity*."

Miraculously, I manage to stop myself from snorting, or making some offhand comment about "honor among thieves."

"So, yeah," Rachel sighs, taking another sip of her coffee. "That's why male heirs are necessary. And why I was thrilled that *my* baby would never be subjected to that cruelty, danger and pain."

"I want to say this will be my last question," I say, rubbing my eyes. "I don't know if it will be, considering that was a lot of information, and everything you tell me about the Mafia seems more confusing than the last, but what happens should more than one champion pass all of the Trials?"

"Well, first of all, it's usually skewed in favor of the current ruling family, because naturally they've dedicated all their time and resources to preparing that champion. And as I said, these tests are deadly, one tiny misstep and you could die, so that's what happens to a lot of the underprepared champions. So, it's very rare that there is more than one that survives. However, the champions compete individually, and are scored by the heads of the Mafia clans," Rachel shrugs. "But you can imagine that a mob boss is only interested in propping up their own guy, so the numbers usually are too close to call. So, in that case, there would be a fight…to the death."

"Wow." This is all I can say.

"I told you that it was complicated," Rachel chuckles. "And I imagine it's hard for you to comprehend that we heathens have any laws. Or *honor*."

"I know *you* have honor," I say, before my lips can stop me. *Shit. That was...sappy.*

But Rachel smiles softly, lowering her eyes to the floor.

"Well," I say, clearing my throat awkwardly. "What ended up happening to you? You know, with not feeling happy or safe at the manor, or around Jaxon's father?"

"He bought me a house."

"What?"

She nods.

"Technically, it was a townhouse, and technically it was a temporary situation until the baby was born. At which time I agreed to move back to Pace Manor with his heir," She smiles. "But it gave him time to sort out what was going on with his grieving father. And it gave me my own space. It had four bedrooms so I even got to set up a nursery, and since it was much closer, Jessica came to visit all the time. He also gave me a driver, who would take us wherever we needed to go. And there was a protection detail, obviously."

"How generous of him," I say, clicking my tongue.

"Yeah, *generous* is the word I'd use," Rachel says, pursing her lips and crossing her arms. "Considering all the stories Jess told me throughout my pregnancy. Things she'd heard, rumors about Jaxon fucking this bitch, and that bitch. So yeah, I guess I'd say he was pretty fucking generous indeed."

"Wait, he cheated on you, while you were *pregnant?*"

Rachel laughs.

"You sound surprised."

"Well, I mean, he just risked his neck for you," I say, shaking my head. "And you just told me how excited he was to be having a baby with you?"

"He was also a man, Agent Westwood," Rachel shrugs. "A rich, and fairly attractive man, who had been raised to think he was entitled to the world and everything in it. Add in a little alcohol or the occasional party drugs, and that's a recipe for a decent amount of *generosity.*"

The bitterness in her voice is clear, a lingering scar left from an open wound.

"It was like every fucking time we got to a good place, or I thought we were at a good place, or I at least thought we were on our *way* to a good place, there was another...*pothole.*"

She closes her eyes, a sarcastic smile painted agonizingly on her face.

"Here was this incredible man who could defend my honor, build skyscrapers, pass The Trials, and buy me townhouses, but apparently fidelity is a concept Jaxon hadn't mastered yet," she sighs, her face suddenly falling into sadness. "Or I don't know, maybe he just didn't love me. At least not in the same way he apparently loves Natalie. Or maybe he just couldn't love me like that."

Part of me feels relieved to hear her talk about her extremely rich and extremely powerful ex-boyfriend like this. While another part of me feels sorry for the pain she must've felt, and still feels. And still, *another* part of me feels guilty as hell.

…Because I gave this misery to someone.

"Sometimes love has nothing to do with it," I say softly. "I know that no one wants to hear this, because it isn't very empowering, but sometimes sex is just sex. It's therapy."

"Correct me if I'm wrong," Rachel says, raising a brow at me. "But I feel like that's a cryptic sentence, especially from a guy who told me he cheated on his wife, but then never actually got around to telling me about it."

"I know," I say quietly.

"And wasn't it you who gave me some high-handed speech this morning about real relationships need to be more than just sex?"

"No, I said that I need mine to be," I say with a smirk, always impressed by her ability to never miss the opportunity to get a subtle bratty jab in. "And believe me I only know that because I learned that lesson the hard way."

"What lesson?" She asks.

"A lesson in *balance…*"

After our showdown with Martin Naveau, the weeks and months of my recovery were long and painful, and not just for me physically.

Candace and I may have survived a serial killer, and Scarlett may have put him in the ground, but Martin's ghost still haunted our hallways. And our lives.

Unable to clean the massive blood stain off the floor of my son's nursery from where Scarlett blew Martin's head off and where I had nearly bled out, we decided to put our house up for sale. We moved. We went to therapy, both as a couple and also individually. At some point we were both prescribed antidepressants and relaxants. Practically everything.

But nothing worked.

In fact, all it seemed to do was drive us further apart.

Having been dragged out of her bed by a psychopath, Candace couldn't sleep at night, and especially if I was there. This led to the two of us sleeping separately, and our sex life crumbled to pieces.

At first I looked at getting back to work as a blessing, a distraction from the misery that was my home life and relationship. But with no way to reconcile my long hours, on the road, with her anxiety about my safety, the two of us drifted further apart.

Our trauma was like an infected sore that refused to heal. Every time something difficult happened, it would rip open and ooze its bacterial pus over all the rest of our healing. Over time the two of us just became numb to the pain.

We became numb to each other.

After my workplace-ordered therapy sessions concluded, I told myself I didn't need to return. But I should've. Because as my marriage deteriorated, so did I. And the next time I found myself tracking a serial killer, I found myself with a clear line of shot.

…But I couldn't take it.

It's not that I wasn't allowed, it was that the paralyzing fear about whether this killer would track me down too, should I *miss*, had me unable to pull the trigger. The killer got away, and went on to kill another three people before she was eventually caught.

No one on my team blamed me for this, but I blamed *myself*. I blamed myself for being unable to protect Candace. I blamed myself for my failed marriage. I started to question if maybe I was permanently damaged, sharing genes with a father like mine who could do the horrific things he'd done. I started to question if I was ever going to be able to feel good again.

Little by little I was shutting down.

…Until Scarlett saved me once again.

"Let me see your gun," Scarlett says, holding out her hand.

"Um, okay?" I say, handing it to her.

If anyone else asked for my gun, I would've told them to fuck right off. But Scarlett is my partner, and she is the one person I trust more than anyone else in this world.

Especially since I caught my wife sucking that guy's dick two months ago.

"I don't understand, Scar," I say, slapping my hands on my jeans as we walk along a long warehouse hallway in the industrial district. "Why are we here? At this warehouse? I mean, we already caught the killer?"

She pulls a key from her pocket to unlock the door at the end of a long hallway.

"This isn't about the killer," Scar says, pushing the door open. She flicks a switch, causing the lights to buzz on above us. "This is about you. And your therapy."

"My *what*?"

When the room flickers to light, my jaw immediately drops. Inside of this dusty warehouse, in the middle of nowhere, is a meticulously crafted sanctuary of leather, whips, chains, and more sex furniture than I can count on first glance.

The bones of the warehouse might be old, but *this* room has been renovated. A gigantic four-post bed sits in the background. The walls are covered in hooks, cuffs and restraints, while the bulk of the space is filled with hand-carved mahogany chairs, benches and tables. Each piece is more ornate and detailed than the last, leather and steel coming together in every deplorable assembly you can imagine.

This isn't a warehouse…This is a *dungeon*.

"Why are we *here*? What the hell is—"

But before I can finish my sentence, a sharp cracking sound echoes through the air, and pain on the back of my legs sends me collapsing to the floor.

"What the fuck?!" I shout, turning to look at her. "Ow!"

"I just told you why we are here!" Scar snaps at me loudly, her voice echoing off the walls. "So stop asking pointless questions and get on your knees."

"Excuse me?!" I gasp, the searing hot pain coursing through my body like a bolt of lightning. "This isn't funny, Scar! That really fucking hurts!"

"Good!" Scarlett whispers remorselessly. "Now, *kneel.*"

Fuck that!

Scarlett has obviously lost her mind.

But just as I try to stand, I hear the whooshing sound of the crop whipping through the air, feeling it strike me again across the back of my thighs.

"Aw! What the fuck!" I shout, the stinging pain nearly blinding me. "Scar, why are you doing this?!"

"It's therapy," she says, cracking me again, sending me tumbling to the ground. "And you're in dire need of it."

I've barely had time to breathe before her crop connects with my back, knocking the wind from my lungs.

"I know all about your past, Adam," Scar smirks, at me, whacking the back of my legs. "I was there, remember? I was standing right beside you when you told Roger about why you were the right...*fit* for the Naveau job."

"Scar, I—" Again I try to stand, but this time she whacks me twice, each time harder than the last across the backs of my thighs, keeping me on my knees.

"See I've been unsure what to do about you. You've been slipping a lot lately. I considered whether I should report this to HR, but then I remembered what you told me," she laughs, circling me, this time cracking me hard across my ass. "About your occasional...*preferences.* And about how, when you were feeling really low, those preferences helped you heal. Took me a minute to realize what you might actually need, might be something I am actually qualified to provide."

What the hell?!

"See, I've been building this space for the last five years," she chuckles. "Little passion project of mine to let off a little steam with the right *playmates.*"

"Now, just wait a—"

Before I can stand, or try to grab the crop from her she whacks me again.

"Ow! Fuck!"

"Exactly," she says, leaning down and grabbing my face. "That's exactly what you need. A good fuck. But not on your terms, little pet. On *mine*."

"Scarlett," I gasp, still trying to breathe, my body reeling from the pain. "I don't want to fuck."

She smiles, and continues to circle me, cracking her crop every time I try to get off my knees, keeping me there.

"As I said, Adam," she says, the sound of her boots connecting with the cold hard floor and echoing off the walls. "This isn't about what you *want*. Hell, it isn't even what I want. It's about what you *need*. It's therapy."

What the fuck is going on?!

"Scarlett, just tell me what you want?" I ask, trying to move away from her, only to meet the end of her crop once again.

"I want you to get your shit together, Adam! I want you to act like the fucking man I know you to be!" She snaps at me angrily. "You're a goddamn federal agent for crying out loud. You're a man who is one of the best and bravest men I know! A man who is smart, strong, fearless, a good husband, and a great fucking father!"

She walks around in front of me, once again grabbing my face.

"This *isn't* you Adam! You're not this pathetic, terrified, sniveling pussy-ass bitch who's afraid to pull the trigger when he needs to!" She shouts at me, shoving me back down on the floor. "Three people are dead, Adam! All because you can't work through your shit!"

She's right. Fuck I hate that she's right.

Her crop collides with the back of my thighs again, making me groan and collapse down on the floor once again.

"You're my partner," Scarlet snaps at me. "I need to trust you to have my back."

"You can!" I say, defensively. "You can trust me, Scarlett! You know this!"

"No I fucking can't trust you! And do you want to know why? Because you don't even trust yourself, Adam!" She shouts at me, snapping me with the crop again.

"Arrrgh!"

"You're a failure!" She snaps, whipping me again. "You're

weak! You're dropping the ball! You're disappointing the people you care about most! And you know what? Your incompetence and failure is fucking dangerous! And I'm done tolerating it!"

With every sentence, the hard crop connects with my ass and thighs, sending the painful debilitating shock waves through my body.

And when she finally stops, I don't even try to get up.

Her crop, and her words, have shattered the last remaining fragments of my pride, and I simply don't have the mental strength to object anymore. Or even to stand.

Brought literally to my knees, I sit here, shaking, my body wracked with the stinging pain.

And that's when the tears start flowing. Tears I had bottled up and hidden away in the darkest parts of my soul.

"You're right," I break, sobbing on the floor, as Scarlett simply circles me menacingly. "I've failed them. I've failed them all. As a partner. As a husband. As a father. As a friend."

I don't have the energy to fight emotions that arise in me, pouring out here on the floor. I simply let it happen, right there in front of Scarlett.

Suddenly she stops, right in front of me.

…But I can't even *look* at her.

Because despite being her partner for the last four years, I don't feel like I have any right to look at her right now. All my pride, all my arrogance, has disintegrated.

Scarlett is right. I *have* failed everyone I care about.

Hearing movement, I instantly flinch, expecting the crop again, but this time instead she reaches forward and gently pulls my chin up to look at her.

As I finally open my eyes, I see her face smiling warmly down at me.

"That's right, Pet. You have fucked up. Big time," she says gently. "But this is where I can help you."

"H…how?" I whisper.

"I can help you leave all that weakness here," she says softly. "All of it. All your insecurities. All your fears. All your failures. This can be your therapy. I can help you face it, overcome it, and then you can leave it here, in this room."

Softly she strokes my cheek with her thumb.

"And maybe once you've purged yourself of all this guilt and bullshit you keep carrying around, you'll remember the badass motherfucker you were born to be." She purrs, leaning in. "And start fucking acting like him again."

I don't even feel her lips press against mine. I can't feel anything. I can't even think. At this moment in time I am empty of all thoughts and feelings. I am nothing.

But somehow, that's *exactly* what I need to be.

"Your partner…was a *Domme?*" Rachel asks softly. "That's who you cheated on your wife with?"

I nod, sighing deeply.

"Look, I know that this isn't going to make sense," I say quietly. "But before you judge me, I need you to know that this wasn't love. It really was just therapy. It felt like so much of my life was completely out of my control for so long. I had so much guilt about not being able to protect my wife, or satisfy her. I hadn't been able to perform my job. At this point in my life, I was frozen with guilt and fear."

Rachel says nothing, her eyes glued to mine.

"I *loved* my wife," I say, my voice nearly cracking. "I had committed to her, and to our life, and I was determined to keep that promise, even if that meant I had to overlook the drinking, the drugs, even the cheating."

She nods.

"I did *not* love Scarlett. And she didn't love me," I shrug. "It was simply *stress* relief. There was no romance or feelings between us, it was simply sex and therapy. She helped me work through the guilt and baggage I was carrying, because ultimately it benefited her."

"What?" Rachel asks gently. "What do you mean?"

"When I felt low, or when things felt heavy, I could allow myself to retreat to subspace," I say, swallowing hard. "I could relinquish control, and allow her to think *for* me. It was the first time anyone had taken my burdens and worries from me and given me room to just…breathe. And when it was over, I had the benefit of a release, a clear head and the serotonin."

"Why?" she asks.

I rub my chin with my hand, trying to think of a way to explain this strange dynamic.

"I think it was that aside from the relief I felt relinquishing control, it also satisfied my sadomasochism, which is something I enjoyed in my younger years. And so while she broke down my insecurities, she also helped me build a sense of pride from being able to survive whatever ridiculous tortures she inflicted during our sessions."

I watch as Rachel considers my words and then nods.

"Okay I guess that makes sense," she says softly.

"Back then, I wasn't the kind of guy who was going to sit in therapy and talk about my fears, worries or inadequacies," I sigh, rubbing my hands together. "Where I came from, that's not how it was done. Men unfortunately didn't discuss their struggles. They just dealt with them, in miserable silence. But this dynamic with Scarlett, still allowed me to do that. I didn't have to talk about my issues. I could simply just be. And even though it might not make sense, I found peace and clarity in that subspace."

Running my hand over my head I take a deep breath.

"As I said," I say softly, "I know this might not make sense, but in some weird way, it actually helped me."

"How?" Rachel asks.

"It cleared my head. Allowed me to be more present," I nod. "I was a better husband for it. I didn't spend every single interaction with Candace replaying every mistake I'd made, because I had already dealt with that in the dungeon. Which in turn made me more thoughtful, more loving, more present and kinder."

I bite my lower lip.

"We started making progress in repairing our marriage, and we even started being intimate again," I say quietly. "That's when she got pregnant with my second son."

"And," Rachel says quietly, shifting on the couch. "How did all this work with Scarlett?"

"Scarlett and I were strictly business," I say sitting back against the couch. "After that first impromptu session, we followed the proper protocol and discussed our boundaries, limits and safewords, that sort of thing."

"She had safewords too?" Rachel asks. "So, you were more of a *switch* with her. Kind of like you were with *me* sometimes?"

"No," I say, shaking my head. "With Scarlett I was solely a submissive. However, occasionally she would *demand* I take control. But even then it was still her calling the shots."

"I see," Rachel says, biting her lip. "So you had it for when she was topping from the bottom."

I nod slowly.

"But as I said, this was just a moment in my life. It was necessary at the time, but I could never go back to that role in a full time capacity again," I say, locking eyes with Rachel. "As you know, from some of *our* very first sessions, I enjoy some aspects of domination, but I'd say I'm more of a switch. In a 95-5 split. Meaning that occasionally I enjoy it and even benefit from being dominated, but now that I've found other ways of coping and dealing with things, I prefer to be the one in control."

"Yes, I know you do," Rachel blushes, a small smile tugging at the corners of her lips. 'And for the record, you're good at being in control. And being, ya know, *dominant*."

For the first time since we started this conversation, I feel like I can breathe, her reaction giving me the smallest fraction of hope that telling her this hasn't been a giant mistake.

"I'm curious to know how it worked," she asks, sitting back against the cushions. "Like did it interfere with your job or your partnership? Was it awkward?"

I shake my head again.

"No, actually, it wasn't. Some of the first parameters Scarlett and I set were that this was, and would always be strictly professional domination. Therefore, we operated in this 'what happens in the dungeon stays in the dungeon' capacity. We could speak freely while we were *in* the warehouse, but it shut off the moment we walked out that door."

"Wow," Rachel whispers, tucking her hair behind her ear.

"I think it only worked this way because of who we were as individuals. We had been paired together because of our similarities and were both able to compartmentalize this as just a facet of our association. To us, it was just another job. We never discussed it in text, or during work hours, not even in private. Never even in an offhand comment or joke," I say, licking my bottom lip. "And it worked somehow, because those boundaries kept it feeling like it *was* just therapy. And not an affair."

"How long did it last?"

362

"About half a year, maybe slightly more," I sigh. "But, when I started doing better, Candace and I started doing better, and that's when Scarlett and I severed our dynamic completely."

"With no hard feelings?"

"As far as I know," I say, sitting back in the chair. "No."

"How can you be sure?"

"Well, I guess I can't be totally sure," I shrug. "But I wasn't her only submissive, and one of her other playmates ended up becoming her fiancé. But by that time Scarlett and I had already ended our dynamic, and were strictly work partners at that point."

"So you did stop seeing her," Rachel says, biting her lip.

My chest hurts, knowing how hard this must be for her to hear, and how unflattering I must look to her.

"Yes," I nod. "Scarlett taught me to control my feelings and impulses better. And how to better compartmentalize the harder things for dissection later, which became my *ledger*."

"What's the ledger?"

"The ledger is what I was explaining to you on the car ride here," I say gently. "I took the balance I learned in BDSM, and applied it to my work. For every life I take, I will save a life in return. To keep the guilt at bay and balance the scales."

Rachel nods, pulling her legs up and under her as she sits back on the couch.

I study her face, my heart racing.

What is she thinking right now?

"Look, Rachel," I say, clearing my throat. "I realize that this makes me look selfish and probably...shitty. And I imagine, when compared to your baggage with Jaxon, probably really, *really*, shitty."

"I mean, technically your wife cheated on you first so..." she says. "So it's not like what you did was even that bad."

She shrugs, looking off toward the window.

And then suddenly it makes sense.

Perhaps the reason she put up with Jaxon's bullshit for so long, the reason she stayed, wasn't just for the sake of their daughter. It was because on some level, Rachel felt that because she had cheated on him first, that she *deserved* it.

Fuck.

I hate Jaxon Pace. I truly cannot stand the pompous prick. But unfortunately, in this regard, we are more similar than I'd like

363

to admit. Jaxon and I *both* made promises to women we loved. Incredible, selfless women who were also risking their lives to bring our children into the world.

And then we *both* went and broke those promises, for extremely selfish reasons.

But if I am going to love Rachel, better than Jaxon ever did, I have to *be* better than he was…and better than *I* was too.

Without a word, I get up and cross over to Rachel's couch, sitting down beside her and taking her hands in mine.

"I need to say something to you, and I need to be clear," I say, taking a deep breath. "Whatever *my* reasons were for cheating on Candace are irrelevant. It was still wrong. I'm not telling you this story to brag about some stupid conquest, I'm sharing this so that I can be accountable and honest about mistakes I've made. Just because I benefited, or learned something in the process, does not in any way negate the fact that I cheated on my wife. I hate that I did it, and believe me when I say, I've paid for it. Dearly."

Rachel says nothing, but the way her soft brown eyes burrow into mine, nearly guts me.

"My wife didn't deserve my betrayal," I say softly, feeling my heart throbbing in my chest. "And neither did *you*, Rachel."

Her chest heaves, and her lips quivers.

"But I…I fucked up," she whispers.

"You made mistakes, sure. But so did he. So did I. That's humanity. Sometimes we hurt the people we love. We are flawed, foolish and fucked up little creatures. If we're lucky, we learn a few lessons on the journey. I learned that when you love someone, and I mean *truly* love them, you don't trade in *daggers*. You don't want to hurt them simply because you're hurting."

She looks back up at me, and a single tear streaks down her cheek.

"Rachel, I can't promise you that I'll never hurt you. I wish I could. But what I can promise you, is that I will never, ever, hurt you like *this*. I'm not that man anymore."

The heartbreaking look on her face nearly shatters me.

"I wouldn't blame you if you didn't believe me," I say quietly. "Hell, I barely believe it myself. But, I—"

Rachel suddenly leans forward and kisses me. Her kiss is soft and gentle. She pulls away, pressing her forehead to mine.

"I *do* believe you, Adam," she whispers against my lips. "Of the very few things I believe in this world, I believe in *you*."

Her words obliterate me.

I had made peace with my brokenness. I had accepted it as my way of life. But as Rachel says this, somewhere deep inside my chest, I feel one forgotten broken piece of my heart slide back into place.

I suppose it's fitting in a way.

Perhaps the peace I truly need can only come from the girl whose very existence is chaos.

And maybe the only heart capable of gluing mine back together, is the one that was just as broken, making from the ashes a beautiful mosaic from all our misery.

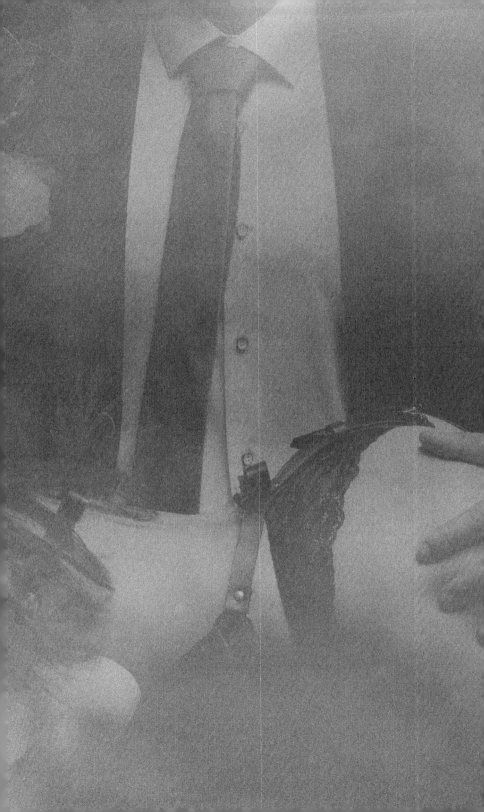

CHAPTER TWENTY-SEVEN

RACHEL

I kiss him, unable to stop myself.

His hand slides up my cheek, pushing his tongue into my mouth, as he lays me down on the couch cushions, kissing down my neck. He climbs on top of me, slipping his leg between mine and deliberately rubbing his knee against my clothed pussy.

I groan, grinding myself against him, while slipping my hands the inside of his shirt and deliberately scratching down his back, digging my nails into his skin

"Arrgh!" He winces, throwing his head back in shock.

I giggle. However, my response evidently pisses him off as he immediately snatches my throat, squeezing tightly.

"Fuck woman," he growls. "You make me so goddamn…"

His voice fades out as he kisses my neck, biting and sucking against my skin.

"What?" I breathe. "What do I make you feel, Adam?"

He grins, crushing his lips to mine before pulling back.

"Crazy," he whispers.

His response is breathless and raw, and it makes me giggle.

"Oh, you find that funny, do you?" He asks, raising a brow at me. "You enjoy driving me insane?"

"Little bit," I smirk, biting my bottom lip.

"I'd be careful if I were you," he growls against my skin, slipping his hand between my thighs and squeezing my pussy between his fingers.

"Or what?" I grin smugly. "I think you forget that you told me this morning you're going to remain a celibate until I agree to make love. So really, what can you do to me?"

But to my surprise he chuckles softly, licking his lips.

"Oh Miss Valentine, I haven't forgotten," he growls, looking up at me, fire burning in his eyes. "That was a *kindness*."

He bites my bottom lip, sucking hard and wrapping his hand in my hair. Suddenly he pulls it tight, making me gasp and forcing my head back, exposing my neck.

"Do *not* mistake my kindness for weakness, *princess*," he growls, tracing his lips along my jawline and down my collarbone, the stubble from his chin tickling me. "For a man who willingly confronts *his* darkest desires, is definitely not afraid to play with *yours*."

Holy. Fuck.

Every other thought in my brain evaporates in an instant.

"Get up," he commands.

Before I can obey or even regain my composure, he stands, still gripping my hair at the base, pulling me up with him. With his other hand he yanks my leggings and panties down before pulling me across his lap, pinning my arms beneath me.

"Do you remember your safe word?"

"What?" I breathe, feeling my heart pounding.

"Your safe word."

"Well, yes, it's *Mozart,*" I gasp, as he releases my hair and instead wraps that arm around my waist. "But, Adam, what are you—"

"Good." He says, and suddenly his hand comes down hard on my ass.

"Eek!" I yelp.

"You think you're smart, eh? A little smartass?" He says, positioning himself so that one of his knees forces my legs open, the other pinning me in place. "Let me show you what smartass bratty little girls get."

368

He smacks me hard again across my right ass cheek, before slapping the other one.

"Ow!" I gasp. "Shit!"

Again, he slaps me hard, twice on each side.

"While I might occasionally find utility in a little submission," he says, smacking my bare ass again. "It also means that I understand the role of a submissive *intimately*."

"Fuck!" I shout, as he delivers yet another stinging blow to the other cheek. "That really hurts!"

"That's the point," he says, rubbing my sore bottom with one hand. "I told you I wanted to make love to you, and instead of acting like a big girl, and talking about your feelings, you've decided that you're going to avoid it, and act like a brat, throwing a tantrum. Because you're that desperate to get fucked."

"No! I'm not! I—"

But I can't finish this sentence as his hand suddenly cups my pussy, making me gasp.

"No?" He whispers, rubbing my bare clit with his hand, as I shudder, my body nearly seizing in his hand. "You mean you're *not* desperate to have this hole filled?"

"I…I…" But my brain turns to mush as he strokes my sex, teasing my entrance with his thumb.

Suddenly I *am* desperate for it. For all it.

"Oh God…" I groan.

"That's what I thought," he says.

He pulls out and cracks his hand against my ass, hard.

"Fuck!" I shout, trying to get away from him, but finding it impossible as he holds me fast.

He rubs my bottom gently, minimizing the sting before again stroking the outside of my pussy, teasing me.

"God, you're so fucking wet. And you have such a beautiful ass," he says, running his hand over my backside and making me tense. "Shame to see it so red."

But instead of striking me, I hear him lick his fingers and then shove them deep inside me. I jump, the sheer sensitivity combined with the vulnerability of my position as he moves his fingers around inside of me aggressively.

"Oh my God, Adam!" I shout, my legs shaking.

"Now," he growls. "Please know, I am going to keep my promise. You're not going to get this dick until you agree to let me make love to you."

"Please, no!" I plead, Adam still working his fingers in and out of me. "I need it! I am desperate for it! And I—"

"But," he interrupts my pleas, pulling out and rubbing my clit quickly. "I might let you cum, but only if you admit what a little brat you are."

"Oh Godddd…"

Again he pulls his fingers out of me, running two on either side of my clit and making me tremble. However, just as I am getting used to the incredible sensations, he stops, immediately spanking me again on each cheek.

"Fuck! Ow!" I groan. "Stop! Okay, okay! I'm a brat!"

He squeezes my increasingly sore ass in his hand, running his hand over my smooth throbbing skin before slapping my pussy, making me jump.

"And are you going to behave?" He says, slapping it again. "Stop being such a desperate little slut and just be patient?"

"Yes! Yes!" I yelp frantically.

He shoves his two middle fingers back inside of me, using his thumb to rub my clit at the same time.

"Eeeeeek!" I shout, feeling his long fingers flicking my G-Spot deep inside me, and sending waves of pleasure all throughout my body.

"What are you, Miss Valentine?" He says, pulling all the way and then pressing all the way back in. "Tell me. Nice and loud."

"I'm a desperate little slut!" I moan.

"Louder!" he says, working me harder.

"I'm a desperate little slut!" I shout, my words echoing off the walls of the old house as I feel him pushing in and out of me. "I'm *your* desperate little slut!"

He freezes, as if what I said wasn't what he was expecting.

My ass is throbbing, my pussy is dripping, and my heart is pounding, unsure of what comes next. I feel him shift, and brace myself for another crack on my ass. But instead, he leans in, pressing his lips to the back of my neck.

"Say that again?"

"I am *yours*, Adam" I breathe. "All yours."

"Yes you are," he growls against my skin, kissing me softly and shoving his fingers back inside, strumming them around inside of me. "You, are my bratty little *Princess*."

"Fuck yes!" I shout, feeling my climax nearing.

"Tell me what you want," he says, suddenly pulling out of me again just before I cross over the edge. "And be sure to ask nicely."

"Please let me cum," I whine. "Please! I...I...I need it!"

"Good girl," he whispers, shoving his fingers back inside of me. "Go on then, cum for me, Princess."

And without hesitation, I obey.

"Wow," I smile, breathing deeply. "That was amazing."

I am sprawled across Adam's chest, the two of us laying across on the couch.

He kisses my forehead, his hand up the back of my shirt, softly trailing his hand up and down my skin.

"Perhaps I should be a brat more often," I giggle.

Adam says nothing, chuckling beneath me, gently swatting my now re-clothed bottom.

"Ouch!" I laugh. "That's actually still sore, you know."

"Oh, I know. That's the point." He growls wickedly, gently pulling my chin up to look at him, kissing me softly. "Gives you a little reminder of how naughty you are."

For a second I am lost in his eyes, and it takes me a moment to realize that I'm just staring up at him.

Stop it, Rachel. Quit grinning like a fool.

Turning, I lay my head back against his chest, trying to dial back the feelings blooming in my chest.

Feelings are dangerous. They always have been. Which is why, after all of the pain I went through with Jaxon, I am so hesitant to let myself feel them.

In my heart I know Adam *is* a great guy, and a good man, but there's still so many questions. There's still so much I don't know about him.

And there's even more that Adam doesn't know about *me*.

Telling him about the rape was hard, and even though he was incredibly sweet, in the back of my mind I still know it wasn't the *scariest* thing I have to tell him.

There's still at least two skeletons in my closet that I'm not ready to unveil. Not yet anyway.

"Hey you okay?" He asks gently, running his fingers through my hair, momentarily disarming me. "Don't tell me I spanked *too* much of that bratty attitude out of you."

I snort, rolling my eyes.

But the softness of this moment is making me feel oddly vulnerable. Too vulnerable in fact.

Distance. I need a bit of distance.

"Mr. Westwood, my attitude is grafted into my marrow," I say, sitting up and leaning back against the opposite end of the couch, facing him. "Hate to break it to you, but you could spank my ass until it is as red as a tomato, and I'd still tell you to go fuck yourself."

"Good," He laughs, throwing one arm back behind his head and grabbing my foot with the other. "I prefer the challenge."

Fucking asshole. Why does he have to be so...perfect?!

There's something about his relaxed posture, and the smug but sincere smile on his face that threatens to undo any remaining resistance I have. My brain and heart feel as though they are at war with each other.

"So," he says, crossing his arms across his chest. "Where did we leave off? I think it's your turn, if you're feeling up to it?"

Opening a can of worms and leaving sappy girl hours? Yes.

"Well, pretty sure I was telling you about being pregnant, and hearing rumors about all of Jaxon's extracurriculars," I say, with a false smile. "Although, before we get to the horrific tale that was my birth experience, I have a *worse* story for you."

"Oh yeah?" he chuckles. "And what's that?"

"My mother."

I had no desire to meet Valerie Valentine.

She was dead to me from the day she walked out on us.

That was until Michael showed up, claiming to know where she was living. I tried to put it out of my mind. But I couldn't.

Michael obviously had his own agenda, which he tried

repeatedly to push on to me. He seized every opportunity to tell me about Jaxon's infidelities in an effort to convince me that I couldn't rely on or trust him to take care of me, and that I should be concerned about my own inheritance.

I told him I didn't care about our stupid inheritance, as I had lived this long without it anyway.

But in the end, I changed my mind, and took the address.

I would see her. Not for his agenda, but for my *own*.

Perhaps it was my raging third trimester hormones, but I had questions, and unfortunately, I knew that she was the only person who could answer them.

Coincidentally, I changed my mind just in time, as I found Valerie Valentine at *Peaceful Passage*, an assisted care hospice facility in Milwaukee, dying of stage four lung cancer.

To be honest, I was unsure if she would even recognize me. But from the moment I stepped into her room that morning, and she looked up from her crossword puzzle, she knew.

"Well, fuck," she shrugs, throwing the newspaper down. "I guess I should have assumed this day would come."

"I'm sorry?"

"Honey, don't play dumb. You're like looking in a mirror," she says, crossing her arms. "If that mirror was also a portal back in time about thirty years. You've even got the bun in the oven.""

"You know who I am?" I say, setting my coat down on the chair.

"Good. Then I guess that spares us an awkward conversation."

She laughs.

"Considering you look like you're about to pop," she says pointing to my stomach. "And you're *not* wearing a wedding ring, I assume there's going to be some awkward conversation anyway."

This fucking bitch…I hate her already.

"I can't wear my ring," I lie, unwilling to allow my bitchy mother to have any of the upper hand. "My fingers are too swollen from the pregnancy."

She stares at me for a moment before shrugging, picking her newspaper back up.

"So whose kid is it?" She asks, without looking at me. "Hopefully not some unemployed dirtbag who—"

"It's Jaxon *Pace's* child actually," I smile, watching as her eyes go wide and she nearly drops her pen. "So, no, not an

373

unemployed dirtbag. Or alcoholic Mafia Don, like Daddy."

"Well then," she says, staring at me awkwardly for a minute. "Good for you I suppose. I assume you know the sex?"

"It's a *boy*," I lie.

Fuck her.

I know Valerie Valentine is just searching for any way to pick apart my happiness, and I refuse to give her anything.

"When's the due date?"

"I'm thirty-eight weeks," I say, rubbing my stomach. "So, any day now."

"Full term? Hmm," she replies looking back down at her crossword. "I'm surprised the Pace's allowed you to leave the city when you're that far along."

"Well, a lot has changed in thirty years," I say, sticking my nose up at her. "I go where I want, when I want."

Technically this was also a lie. Technically it was two.

While I had an assigned driver, and bodyguard, I definitely did not get to go where I wanted when I wanted. All of my movements were closely monitored.

Additionally, I *had* been instructed not to leave the city by my doctor today, but Jaxon hadn't been there to hear it. The father of my child was too busy, off touring his building site for the hotel, with the repeatedly-drunk Russian man, and had apparently forgotten about our last doctor's appointment.

However, since my driver and bodyguard were not *allowed* in that room, no one heard the doctor tell me this interesting little tidbit besides me. And since I had been stewing on seeing Valerie for weeks, and denying Michael's repeated offers to take me himself, I decided to piss everyone off at once and go see the bitch myself. On my own terms.

But even though I'm doing my damnedest to not let Valerie get inside my head with all her pointed questions, designed specifically to make me feel shitty, I do feel a little bad about lying about the baby being a boy.

Mostly because I am thrilled about my baby being a girl, and I have absolutely no shame in it. Even if she would.

But Valerie doesn't have a *right* to information. Nor does she have a right to my honesty. She only needs to know what I feel like telling her. Which is that I'm happy, healthy, and have everything her selfish, childish, narcissistic ass never got.

I want her to be jealous of me. I want her to hurt.

And she looks like she is.

Her small, weak, sick frame sits rotting in her wheelchair, the tube in her nose attached to an oxygen bottle. She looks old.

Part of me hates her with every fiber in my being. She left me and my brother with that monster of a man, in an effort to save her own skin. And if what Michael told me was true, unlike her original deal with my father where she got nothing, she had been getting alimony every month for the last two decades.

Which meant that Valerie was still being rewarded.

...For *abandoning* us.

I wonder if any part of her even feels bad for it?

"I think the answer you're looking for," she says, without looking up at me. "Is *Yes*."

"Excuse me?" I ask, taken aback.

"The answer you keep asking yourself, and probably drove all the way here to find," she continues, scribbling furiously. "But are now too cowardly to actually ask."

Umm...what?

"And what question is that?" I ask.

"About whether or not I knew what might happen to you and your brother if I left," she says, sighing and setting the folded newspaper down in her lap. "After I left you alone with your father. And the answer is *yes*."

It takes me a minute to put together what she just said, but when I do, my blood instantly boils.

"So," I say quietly, my lip twitching. "You're saying you knew that dad would abuse us?"

"Oh please," she snorts, waving me off. "*Abuse*!? That's what you call getting smacked around a bit once in a while? Hah! Honey in my generation it was just called *childhood*! You kids always want to make mountains out of molehills. You all want to claim to be a victim of some horrible tragic childhood."

"It was a hell of a lot more than just getting smacked around," I hiss at her venomously. "And it was a hell of a lot more than once in a while!"

"And yet," she says, shrugging. "You survived, didn't you?"

Oh no she did not...

"How dare you," I growl my fist clenching.

"Excuse me?" she scoffs, pressing her sallow spotted hand

on her chest. "How dare I? How dare *I*?! You're goddamn right I fucking dared! I dared to live a life where I wasn't the one taking the brunt of his rage, protecting the two of you!"

"So instead you decided to just pass on that mantle of abuse and rage to us?!" I hiss at her. "Your fucking *children*? You're actually bold enough to sit here and say you feel no remorse?!"

"Hey, honey, I suffered too!"

"And I suffered *because* of you!" I shout at her.

She jumps, shocked by my rage, starting to cough.

"I didn't get a choice in being born! And I certainly didn't get a choice in being born to you, and the unfortunate genetics that had me *looking* more like *you* every day! So yeah, you did give that mantle to me, and I took the brunt of it for far longer than you. I didn't get a fucking choice in that either!" I seethe, glaring at her. "But you sure got a choice in *abandoning* me, and leaving me trapped in a dark world I didn't understand with a fucking monster!"

"You know," she says, coughing louder. "I think this conversation is done."

"It's really not," I growl. "I'm far done with you."

"Well, last I checked, you've got no leverage. Which means that you can't make me do anything I don't want to do," She laughs, still coughing. "So, I think it's time to go."

"I don't give a shit what you think," I snort.

"Nurse? Nurse!" She calls, ignoring me. "Can someone please remove this woman? And I need a tank change! Now!"

"She's not out there," I say coldly. "I made sure that no one would be around for this conversation."

"Nurse!" She calls, this time more quietly as she furiously fusses with the knob on her tank.

I smile, walking over to the door and opening it wide, glancing out into the empty hallway.

"Nurse!" Valerie gasps, this time quietly, banging on the table in front of her.

But no one is coming.

That was something I *hadn't* lied about.

Valerie flails around for a moment, choking, coughing, and banging on the table, all while I hold the door open with a smile, waiting for what I know is inevitably coming next.

Finally, she looks up at me, and points to the full oxygen tank in the corner of the room.

"Alright, fine! I'll talk but I need help! Please!" She mumbles, her face turning red.

Gotcha, Bitch.

I close the door, and lock it with the key I swiped off the nurses station down the hall when she was distracted. Walking across the room, I grab the full canister of the life-saving oxygen and walk back over toward her.

Placing my hand on her old tank, I suddenly freeze.

"Please!" She gags, clawing at her neck as she struggles to breathe. "I'm...I'm going to die."

"I know, and you know what Valerie?" I whisper, leaning in close. "That's called *leverage*."

"Did you have a pleasant visit, Miss Valentine?" Max, the driver asks as we make the turn and pull onto the onramp for the highway.

"What?" I ask, suddenly pulled from my trance.

"With your aunt?"

Oh, that's right, that's what I told him.

"It was...interesting, I suppose," I shrug, buckling myself in. "And yet somehow unsurprising."

He smiles.

"Well, I'll get you home safely, ma'am," he says politely. "I've got to be honest, I'm not sure how the boss would feel about us being all the way up in Milwaukee. I hope he's not upset with me for this."

"Well, considering he's probably ten vodka-tonics into his afternoon with the alcoholic Antonov, I imagine he isn't feeling much of anything," I say bitterly. "So I think you're safe."

Max makes no comment in return, but in the rearview mirror, I catch his eyes. And the hint of a smirk.

For some reason, I find Max is the easiest to be around, out of all of Jaxon's men. While I don't doubt that he would valiantly protect me if there was trouble, as instructed, he's young, and relatively quiet.

I roll my shoulders on the back of the car seat, struggling to get comfortable and replaying the events of the last hour, which *had* been quite interesting indeed.

That's when I feel the *pop*.

It's awkward, like the feeling of a rubber band being snapped, mixed with the feeling of a joint popping, but deep inside…in my core. But before I have time to even acknowledge what that was, I suddenly realize that I am leaking. *Everywhere.*

Holy. Fucking. Shit.

"Uh…Max?" I ask, my voice shaking. "How close are we to the nearest hospital?"

"I'm not quite sure, ma'am," Max says, confused. "I think it's a few miles away."

"You need to take me there. Immediately. And have someone find Jaxon Pace," I breathe, my heart starting to pound. "Because I'm going to have this baby. *Today.*"

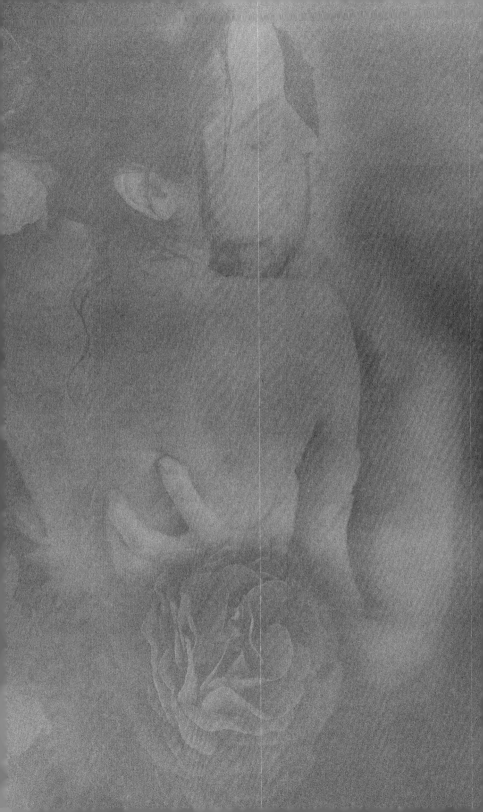

CHAPTER TWENTY-EIGHT

ADAM

"Holy shit!" I gasp. "You went into labor?!"

"Well, yeah," Rachel chuckles softly. "That's kind of the end goal for pregnant ladies."

"No," I say, rolling my eyes. "I mean, that day, in—"

"Milwaukee. Yeah, I know. Believe me I wasn't too keen on that either," She sighs, throwing her hands in the air. "Of all the places, of all the days, it had to be when I was hours away from Chicago. And Jaxon."

"What did he do?" I ask.

"Well, I had been correct that he was off somewhere, fucking plastered with Roman Antonov," she says, clicking her tongue. "Jaxon is anything but predictable."

"Did he make it in time for the birth?" I ask.

"Nope," she shakes her head. "No one did, actually. People informed Dimitris fairly quickly, but the problem was Jaxon and Roman. Apparently these two idiots decided to shake their security teams and do some drunken inner-city bar crawl. So for a couple of hours, no one could find them. Until, of course, they ended up getting arrested for drunk and disorderly conduct after smashing a shop window like a couple of drunken teenagers."

"I thought you said Jaxon's team was always with him?" I ask, slightly confused. "Like they were never supposed to leave him?"

"Oh they weren't, and believe me Dimitris was furious," Rachel says, nodding. "But he was literally furious with everyone that day. He was pissed at Max for taking me so far outside of the city. At Jaxon for acting stupid. At Jaxon's Alpha Squad. At Roman Antonov. At all the cops who arrested Jaxon and Roman. I honestly think the man lost track of everyone he was pissed at. And had I not been in labor with the firstborn heir of the Pace family, I honestly think Dimitris would've let Jaxon and Roman just sit and sober up in jail. But lucky for them, he didn't and bailed them both out."

"So what happened?"

"Well it took a few hours for them to find them, and then it took a couple of hours and a dozen phone calls to get them released. And then ended up fighting against traffic, since apparently it was too windy that day to take the chopper."

Of course they had a fucking chopper. Why wouldn't they?

"How long did it take them to get to you?"

"I'm not really sure," she shrugs. "I know I was in labor for nearly three hours with just Max by my side. I guess there were complications, and I ended up needing to have an emergency C-Section."

She looks down at her sleeve, biting her lower lip.

"All I know is that it took them a really long time to get there," she says quietly. "But to be honest, after my water broke, the whole day became a bit of a blur."

"They usually are," I smile gently. "Especially the first time."

"Were yours at least easy?" She asks, looking back up at me.

"Well, it was for me, but I wasn't the one pushing a baby out of me," I snort softly, rubbing my chin. "So I'm probably a bit unqualified to answer that."

Rachel smiles, the setting sun casting a warm glow on her pretty face.

"It was an experience though," I say, smiling to myself. "The most incredible experience I've ever had."

"Were you there for the birth?"

382

"Both times," I nod. "First time I got lucky. I had missed a lot of the day-to-day stuff, being off on assignment a lot of the time, but fortunately she went into labor on a Saturday morning, when I was home. And for her second pregnancy, I refused to miss anything."

"Could you *do* that?" She asks.

"Not really," I say, shrugging. "But considering I had survived a deranged serial killer who tried to murder me and my family, let's just say the department was more than generous in granting me a special leave of absence."

"Ahhh," she nods.

"I got to experience a lot of the things I didn't get to do the first time around. I mean, every doctor's appointment and every Lamaze class you best believe I was there with her. I was there for all of it."

Rachel blushes, her eyes falling from mine.

Oops.

It occurs to me that perhaps I shouldn't be bragging about being a present partner after she just confessed to not having one for her own daughter's birth.

"Anyways," I say, clearing my throat. "Yeah, it was amazing. I mean, gross as fuck, but yeah, still amazing."

Thankfully, this makes her laugh.

"Sorry," I chuckle along with her. "That was probably rude."

"Just a little," she says, still giggling.

"It was just so *messy*," I say, waving my hands around.

Rachel says nothing, but raises her brow at me.

"Oh, shit!" I say, trying to backtrack my callous remark. "I'm not saying that any of that is your fault, as the lady or anything."

"Well, that's a relief…"

"I just mean that," I say nervously. "There was just a lot of blood and different kinds of…fluids. If I'm totally honest, I have a weak stomach sometimes, and I got a little nauseous and dizzy the first time around. And, I uh, well…I nearly fainted."

"Wait, wait," she laughs harder. "You're telling me that the hardened FBI Agent, who spends his days dealing with gory crime scenes all day, fainted watching his son coming into the world?!"

"Hey now, I said I *nearly* fainted," I say defensively. "And when I go to a crime scene, I know what to expect. I had no idea what to expect here! And, it seemed like there was always some more shocking thing happening minute to minute!"

"I bet changing diapers was a rude awakening for you," she laughs, wiping her eyes. "And your weak ass stomach."

"Oh God," I say, closing my eyes. "Don't even get me started on those. I swear, some of those things were damn near radioactive! I mean, I can't even look at guacamole anymore!"

Rachel loses it, her giggle becoming contagious enough that eventually I can't help but join in.

"Pretty sure I will forever hate the smell of digested crushed peas until the end of time," I laugh.

"Okay," she says, finally getting control of herself, wiping her tears of entertainment away. "I needed that."

"So, I'm sorry," I say, after the two of us have composed ourselves. "I didn't mean to interrupt your story. You said you had a C-Section, and then your daughter was born?"

"Yes, Sir," she smiles. "And she was perfect. Absolutely perfect and absolutely beautiful."

"And what happened once Jaxon eventually made it to the hospital?"

But the moment I ask this question, I instantly regret it. The smile fades from her face. And she shifts uncomfortably on the couch.

"Nothing good," she says quietly.

The room falls silent.

"I'm sorry, would you excuse me for a moment?" Rachel says, standing to her feet.

"Of course," I say, but I've barely finished before she's already out of the room, and headed upstairs.

Five minutes go by, and although I keep anxiously waiting to hear her footsteps creaking on the stairs, I tell myself it's nothing.

But when those five minutes turn into ten minutes, my profiler brain instinctively kicks into gear.

I remember the way she got quiet, and the way she bit her lip.

Surely my question about Jaxon showing up was reasonable, but perhaps there is something more serious that I missed?

Immediately I stand and head upstairs, listening for any movement, but finding the second floor quiet.

"Rach?" I call, knocking on the bedroom door, which sits slightly ajar. "Are you okay?"

There is no reply, and for a moment I wonder if maybe she went into another room somewhere on this floor.

But then I hear what sounds like the sound of water running.

I peak my head inside the bedroom, finding it empty but seeing the light on in the ensuite bathroom. Stepping into the room, I find every article of clothing Rachel was wearing strewn haphazardly, leaving a trail toward the closed bathroom door.

What the hell?

"Rachel?" I ask, knocking on the door. "Is everything okay?"

"You can come in," she calls from inside.

I open the door, and to my shock and surprise I find Rachel, sitting in the large clawfoot tub…taking a bath.

"What is it?" She asks, innocently.

"Um," I say, looking at her confused. "Forgive me but that was a really long *moment*. I was starting to get a little worried about you."

"Oh, no, I'm fine," she shrugs. "I just felt cold and decided that a bath would probably warm my bones."

"Oh, okay," I say, smirking to myself. "Well, I won't disturb you. I'll let you enjoy your bath then."

"Wait, so," she says as I turn to leave, sounding confused. "That's it?"

"That's what?" I ask.

"You're just, okay with me just coming up here and deciding to take a bath?" She asks, quizzically. "I mean, without telling you?"

"Well, I'll admit your delivery was a little strange," I shrug. "But no, I'm not upset with you if that's what you're asking."

She stares at me, as if I'm the one suddenly acting bizarrely.

"Why not?" she asks.

I chuckle to myself, walking back into the bathroom and closing the door behind me.

"Rachel," I say gently, leaning on the marble countertop "Do you want me to be upset?"

"No, I don't," she says quickly. "I just sort of assumed you would be."

This time I say nothing, instead just raising a brow at her.

"It's just…the conversation was heavy, and I felt like I needed a minute to myself. Just to process things, and then I," she says, biting her lip. "Well, I came up here, saw the tub, and thought a bath sounded relaxing…"

"Alright," I say calmly. "All of that makes sense, I suppose. The only thing that still doesn't make sense to me, however, is why you thought I'd be *upset* with you because you suddenly needed a break from our conversation?"

Her eyes find mine, and I smile politely.

"Because you're *allowed* that, you know," I say. "This isn't an interrogation. It's a conversation. So if the topic is too much, or if the conversation becomes too heavy, or if you're just not interested in having it anymore, that's okay. You can step away and say no. You don't need my permission."

She sighs, the worried lines in her forehead dissipating a little.

"No, it's not that," she says, shaking her head. "It's just…"

She stares at me for a long moment, before lowering her eyes to the water.

"I just didn't want to *lie* to you," she says softly. "We said no lies, and for my part, I've done a really good job of keeping to that. Because for the first time in my life, I want that honesty with someone, and you deserve that from me, Adam. But, back there, I don't know, I just felt myself fighting the urge to lie to you. So I decided to come up here and take a bath. Just to clear my head."

Oh wow.

Of all the answers Rachel could have given to me, this was the one I least expected.

"Well, I appreciate your honesty," I say, leaning forward on my knees, stroking my chin. "Do you want to talk about what made you want to lie to me?"

She nods, taking a deep breath.

"It was the birth," she says, pulling her knees up to her chest and wrapping her arms around them. "I don't know why, but you were talking about how amazing your experience was, and I realized that mine…Well, let's just say it was far from amazing."

"I see," I nod quietly. "I'm sorry. I sincerely didn't mean to make you feel self-conscious at all."

"No, I know that. I guess I just had this moment where I realized how *normal* your birth experience was, and how abnormal mine was and I felt really insecure," she says, rubbing her arms. "So much so that I considered pretending that everything about the experience was fine just so that you don't look at me like I'm some freak."

Her words shock me to my core.

It occurs to me, that of all the horrific stories Rachel has told me thus far, somehow *this* is what makes her uncomfortable. And not just uncomfortable, but uncomfortable enough to actually consider lying to me.

The physical act of bringing a child into the world is dangerous and terrifying enough, but knowing what I know about Rachel something tells me that this was more than that. It's clear to me that whatever trauma she endured; the experience stuck with her more than anything else she's survived.

…And yet, she still chose *not* to lie to me.

Rachel isn't one for overt displays of affection or affirmation, and I've learned with her that sometimes I have to read between the lines a bit. And what this tells me, is that she *chose* me, over her fear.

This moves me deeply, but as I try to think of something to say, nothing comes to me. So, I do the only thing I can think of.

Immediately I pull my shirt over my head, and then undo my belt, and step out of my jeans and socks.

"Wait…what are you doing?" She asks me, a look of shock on her face.

I walk around behind her and step over the edge of the large tub.

"Jesus Christ, Woman!" I gasp the moment the extremely hot water hits my skin. "How has your skin not melted off your fucking bones?!"

She giggles.

"I don't know, I guess I'm just used to being in hot water."

"Very funny," I breathe softly as I settle in behind her.

After adjusting to the hellish water temperature, I wrap my arms around her and pull her back against my chest.

She says nothing, but brushes her hair to the side, leaning her head back against my shoulder.

"Thank you," I whisper back, kissing her shoulder. "For choosing not to lie to me."

"Adam, I…I," she pauses softly. "I don't have a lot of good things about me. Or even good stories to tell you. But whatever good I do have, I want to give it to you. I want you to have all of it."

"There are plenty of good things about you, darlin" I say

gently, running my hand up and down her arm, kissing her ear. "You've just spent so much time focusing on the negatives. We just have to make an effort to work on that."

She places her hand on mine, turning her head back so that she can look at me.

"I want to," she whispers softly. "But I don't know if I can change that narrative. Or the way I see things. Or people."

I kiss her cheek, taking a minute to get my thoughts in order and just enjoying the feel of her body against mine.

"Look, I know I don't come from your world, so I may not always understand parts of it," I say quietly. "But I understand *darkness*. And I know what it's like to live with it. Or as a prisoner in the shadows of your own mind."

"What do you mean?" she asks softly.

"Sometimes, when we experience trauma it imprints on us. It can taint the way we see the world, or even people. It's like the rose-colored glasses have come off and now we're forced to walk into every situation with invisible scars, where we're subconsciously gauging everyone we meet for how much of a threat they could be to our peace."

"Yes," Rachel whispers, wrapping her hand around mine, as I gently kiss her bare shoulder.

"I know you think you're broken or tainted," I say softly. "And since I can't convince you otherwise, for the time being I just want you to know that you're not alone in that feeling. *All* of us feel broken in some way or another. And there is no set timeline on healing. You can take it at your own pace."

I feel her trembling, and squeeze her tighter.

"If there was a way that I could take these painful memories from you, or undo the things that have been done to you, I would. In a fucking heartbeat," I whisper against her ear. "But since I can't take away the bad memories, what I want to do is give you *new* memories. Ones that cancel out the nightmares, and bring you joy and peace. And if I do that, even for one brief moment, then my time on this earth will not have been wasted."

Rachel says nothing, but I watch as her breathing deepens, her lean shoulders rising and falling with the increasing rhythm of her heart. She wipes her eyes before taking my hand and bringing it to her lips.

"I promise, Adam," she whispers softly. "You already *do*."

CHAPTER TWENTY-NINE

RACHEL

"Congratulations, Miss Valentine," the nurse says. "Thank you," I say, gently rocking my newborn daughter in my arms. "I think she may have fallen asleep though. She's not sucking anymore though."

"Ope! Look at that," the nurse chuckles sweetly. "That's pretty common with newborns. They just doze right off. Would you like me to put her in the bassinet here? So that you can rest a little?"

"That's okay," I say, adjusting the gown to cover my breast. "I don't think I'm done holding her yet."

"Understandably," The nurse smiles, "Well, skin-to-skin time is the best thing you can do for her right now, so if you're okay, I certainly encourage it."

"I'm very okay," I say, without looking up. "In fact, I don't know if I will ever be able to let her go."

"My wife said the same thing," Ethan's voice says gently from the other side of the curtain, making me jump.

"Oh hello, Ethan," I say, double-checking that my gown is closed completely. "I didn't know that you were here yet."

"My apologies, Miss Valentine." He says politely. "May I come in? I come bearing gifts."

"Yes, of course."

He steps around the corner, carrying a vase with bright pink roses in it and a tiny stuffed teddy bear in a little lace dress, likely purchased from the gift shop below.

"Those are beautiful," I say, as he sets the flowers down on the table next to me.

"I thought so. I also went ahead and brought your hospital bags from The Manor. Figured you might want those," he says, producing my diaper bag and small suitcase I'd had prepared for weeks. "The car seat is already set up in the car as well."

"Oh my God," I gasp. "Thank you so much for thinking of all those things. It all happened so quickly that I didn't have time to send messages to anyone. And Jaxon wasn't answering his phone so…"

My voice trails off, and I bite my lip.

"Speaking of," I say quietly. "I assume if *you're* finally here then he can't be too far behind?"

"Both of the Pace men will be up shortly," he says, his eyes finding mine. "They just needed to…exchange a few words."

"What?"

"They were engaged in a heated discussion," Ethan says, an uncharacteristic tinge of frustration in his voice. "And apparently a two-hour car ride wasn't enough time to finish said discussion."

"Oh…"

They were arguing?

"But as a father myself, I know how exhausted you must be," he says with a warm smile. "And I didn't think it appropriate to have them come up here and disturb your peace, so I gently *suggested* that perhaps they work it out downstairs before coming up."

Oh wow.

Not that I disagree. For one thing, everything is calm and tranquil on this side of the maternity floor. And I'm also a bit annoyed with Jaxon for prioritizing business over the birth of his child and for not answering my phone calls when I went into labor.

392

I'm about to ask Ethan where Jaxon was and what he was doing, but then I notice him staring at the beautiful little pink bundle in my arms. The smile on his face melts my heart, making me forget about everything else in the world.

"Would you like to say hello?" I say, offering her to Ethan.

"Oh no, I don't want to intrude," Ethan says, clearing his throat again. "This is your time to bond and be together."

But something about the way he is still smiling at the baby tells me this is more of a formality, and less of the truth.

"Tell ya what," I say, sitting up in my bed. "I'll trade a few moments of bonding for a wet washcloth and my toiletries bag from the front pocket of that bag suitcase. That way, you can't feel guilty because you're technically doing me a favor and giving me a chance to freshen up before the tornado that is the Pace men arrive."

"Fair enough," Ethan chuckles.

He unzips the suitcase, pulling a washcloth and the small black pouch from inside. Stepping into the ensuite bathroom in the room, he wets and rings the cloth before handing it to me and setting the bag on the tray next to me.

I lean over, and Ethan gently takes the baby from my arms.

"Well, hello there," he says, smiling down at her. "Why aren't you just beautiful."

He rocks her gently, speaking to the sleeping little girl softly while I quickly wash my face, brush my hair, and reapply my deodorant. He's just handed her back to me and readjusted my pillows when I distinctly hear Jaxon's curt voice echoing down the hall.

"Rachel Valentine?" I hear him ask impatiently.

"Room 237, Mr. Pace," the poor nurse says nervously. "She's in bed two."

"*Bed two*?!" He snaps. "You mean, the mother of my child is *sharing* a room?! Why isn't she in a private room?"

"W…well, technically right now she is. There's no one else in that room, Sir," the nurse stammers. "I promise she's the only one in there."

"And it will remain that way!" Jaxon growls angrily. "If any of you want to keep your fucking jobs that is."

Jesus Christ. He's such a snob sometimes.

"Tornado warning," Ethan mutters sarcastically under his

breath, stepping back into the corner.

And within seconds Jaxon Pace blows through the door, rushing into the room.

"Oh my God, Rachel," he says, excitedly, looking distinctly relieved. "I'm so sorry I'm late. How are you? Are you feeling alright? Was it difficult? Are you in pain? Do you need anything?"

He looks over at the empty bassinet, a look of panic flitting across his face.

"Wait," he says nervously. "She's not here? Where is she? Why is she not here? Did they take her? Is something wrong?"

"Jaxon," Ethan says softly. "You've just asked the girl ten questions in less than ten seconds. Just take a breath, and *look*."

Jaxon swallows and turns back to me, his eyes finally falling to the bundle wrapped in my arms.

"Oh my God," he breathes, the expression on his face immediately shifting from anxiety to joy. "Is...is that *her*?"

"No, this one is just a loner," I snort quietly, watching as it takes him a second to completely register my joke.

"Can I...hold her?" He asks gently.

"Of course you can," I say, offering him to her. "She's your daughter after all. Just be careful with her head."

He reaches down and tenderly takes her into his arms.

"I can't believe it," he says softly. "You're actually here."

"I'll go stall Dimitris, and give you two a moment," Ethan says quietly, heading for the door. "Congratulations."

I mouth my thanks to Ethan before he steps out into the hallway.

"Hello, little one," Jaxon whispers, staring down at our daughter as if she is an angel descended directly from heaven.

While I might still be irritated with him, temporarily I forget my frustrations, melted by the reverence and gentleness this man is projecting.

"You," he says softly. "Have no idea how loved you are, and how wrapped around your tiny little finger I already am. I promise, you will never want for anything in this world."

He looks up at me, the biggest smile on his face.

"Thank you," he says sincerely. "For this. For her. She's absolutely perfect, Rachel."

"She is pretty perfect," I say, feeling my cheeks heat.

"Now we just have to think of a name," he says, rocking her

back and forth.

Oh shit...

"Um, well," I say, swallowing hard. "Technically, I kind of already gave her one."

He looks up at me, confused.

"You weren't here, and they asked me what her name was, and I guess I just kind of said the first name that came to me," I say nervously.

"What did you pick?"

"Jessica," I squeak out quietly.

Jaxon says nothing, staring at me.

"I'm sorry, I'm sure we can change it if you want," I blurt out defensively. "But Jessica is the only person who has actually been like family to me, and I thought maybe because your name is Jaxon and they both start with a J that it kind of went together and—"

"Rachel," he chuckles. "Relax. It's alright."

"So," I say anxiously. "You're not mad?"

"Why would I be mad?" he says, smiling down at Jessica. "You just gave me a daughter. A healthy, beautiful daughter."

"That I did," I whisper.

"You're her *mother*, call her whatever you want, I don't care. I only care that she's here."

Holy. Shit.

"She still needs a middle name, though," I say, smiling up at him. "You mom told me she liked the name Eliza or Elizabeth, so I was thinking, maybe we could go with one of those?"

He smiles at me, and nods before looking back down at the sleeping baby in his arms. He leans down and kisses her forehead, closing his eyes.

"Jessica Elizabeth Pace," he says, smiling and pulling back to look at her. "Something tells me that the whole world is going to know your name someday."

Dimitris wasn't as keen on our choice of names as we were, suggesting instead that we go with something more traditional of the Pace family. But Jaxon promptly overruled him.

After what Ethan told me about how the two of them had fought the entire ride to the hospital, I was just grateful that Dimitris eventually let it go, and it didn't escalate into round two on the maternity floor.

However, even though he and Jaxon didn't agree on the name of our daughter, they *did* seem to agree on torturing the poor hospital staff out of their minds.

They were unbearable, constantly scrutinizing every single thing the nurses did and questioning everything the doctor told us. They also insisted that Jessica and I be moved to one of the private client birthing suites within the first hour of their arrival, effectively removing the room from the circulation of scheduled deliveries with no remorse. And if that wasn't irritating enough, the nurses and doctors found themselves having to not only deal with the prickish Pace men, but also having to work around the dozen or so strapping bodyguards they had posted up outside the suite.

Needless to say, I was grateful when the day was coming to a close, and Dimitris suddenly decided to head back to Chicago, leaving Jaxon and I to get some sleep in the room *alone*.

He was just finishing his goodbyes right as the night shift Doctor came in to introduce himself.

"Well, Miss Valentine," Dr. Milburn says. "Everything looks good, your bloodwork looks normal, and the nurse said that they've been able to keep your pain under control?"

"Yes, they have, thank you," I nod.

"Good, well I will send the nurse in to get you tucked in so that you can go ahead and get some sleep then," he says, turning to Jaxon. "If you have a moment, Mr. Pace, could I talk to you for a second?"

"Which one?" Dimitris snorts. "There's two of us here, ya know."

"The father," Dr. Milburn says, masking whatever frustration he might have with the slightly inebriated Dimitris Pace, who had been sneaking sips from his platinum flask for the last hour.

"That's me," Jaxon says, slightly annoyed. "But my father was just about to leave anyway."

The three men step into the hallway as Gemma, the only nurse who didn't burst into tears today from Jaxon and his father barking orders, slips into the room. She adjusts my pillows and helps get me comfortable, before grabbing my water cup.

"I'm going to go get you some more ice water, love," she says. "We have to keep you hydrated."

"Don't be surprised if I'm asleep by the time you get back," I yawn, settling back against the pillows.

But apparently, Gemma forgets to close the door and suddenly all the noises from the hallway are loudly filtering into my room. *Ugh. Seriously?*

While I could just wait for Gemma to return, I decide not to wait that long and just get up and close it myself. After carefully making my way out of the bed and walking to the door, I am just about to close it when I can suddenly overhear the conversation happening outside.

"Wait, wait, wait," Jaxon snaps, irritably. "What do you mean that I'm *confirmed* as the father. Of course I'm the fucking father you moron, I'm on her damn birth certificate."

"No, Sir, I only meant that we just obtained the results of the rapid paternity test we conducted, and I was just informing you that you were confirmed as the father," Dr. Milburn says, his voice slightly anxious.

What?!

"What paternity test?!" Jaxon barks loudly, echoing my thoughts. "I never ordered a fucking paternity test you asshole!"

"*You* didn't," Dimitris says, clearing his throat. "But I did."

I watch through the crack in the door as Jaxon turns to face Dimitris.

Ethan, who stands between the two men sighs and hangs his head.

"Excuse me?" Jaxon hisses, lethally. "You did *what?*"

"Thank you, Dr. Milburn," Ethan says warningly. "Now would probably be a good time to check on your *other* patients."

The Doctor nods, quickly excusing himself and scurrying off down the hallway.

"So let me get this straight," Jaxon growls, stepping closer to Dimitris. "You're telling me, that you went ahead and ordered a paternity test for my daughter, after I explicitly told you I didn't need one?!"

"Jaxon," Ethan cautions. "I understand you're upset but I highly recommend you keep your voice down."

"Listen, Son," Dimitris says, the alcohol slightly slurring his words as he shrugs defensively. "I know you love Rachel and all, but let's be real. We all know the girl's reputation. You needed to be sure that you weren't yoking your cart to your neighbor's horse, you know what I mean?"

Jaxon *snaps*.

Grabbing his father by the shirt, he backs him up and slams against the wall, knocking over a picture, sending it shattering to the floor. Down the hall, a nurse yelps, ducking behind the nurse's station.

Both of their Alpha Squads try to intervene, attempting to pull the two men apart, but Jaxon is refusing to let go of his father's shirt.

"Jaxon!" Ethan whispers forcefully, trying to keep his voice low. "There are women and children on this floor. This is not the place for this kind of behavior!"

"What the fuck makes you think you have the right, to interfere with my family?!"

Jaxon releases his father, shoving him away from him.

"I am the Don Supreme," Dimitris says, out of breath. "And in case you forget, this is my family too!"

"You had no fucking right!" Jaxon snaps at him. "Get the fuck out of my sight, you drunken asshole!"

"Excuse me?!" Dimitris breathes, shocked. "You don't get to talk to me that way, young man."

"I think I just did," Jaxon fires back. "I'm sick of your poison. You and me? We're done!"

Jaxon turns and starts walking back toward the room.

"Get back here!" Dimitris snaps angrily, taking a step toward Jaxon, causing Jaxon to turn around.

But Ethan suddenly steps between them, addressing Dimitris.

"Go home, Αδελφός," He says, darkly. "You've got a long drive back to Chicago. Tonight is not the night."

Dimitris glares at him, breathing heavily. Finally he turns and storms off down the hallway.

Once he disappears, Ethan turns to Jaxon for a moment, who stands furiously in the middle of the hallway glaring after his father.

"I can't believe he would do that," Jaxon growls.

"I know you're upset," he says firmly. "But you have a brand

398

new daughter, and a woman who just brought her into the world. *They* need you right now. Go be with them."

With my heart pounding in my chest, I walk back to my bed and climb in, closing my eyes and turning my head away from the door.

I'm not sure how much time has passed when I finally hear it creak open and Jaxon steps into the room, but I do know that I pretend to be asleep when he kisses my forehead. And as he lays restlessly down on the couch beside me, I can feel the tears streaking down my cheeks, staining the pillow.

"Holy shit," Adam says as the two of us lay in bed together. "So Jaxon's father ordered a paternity test because he didn't trust you?"

I nod.

"Did you tell Jaxon that you overheard it?"

"Eventually," I sigh. "Obviously I had no interest in going back to The Manor with him, and our baby, as we previously agreed, and I had to tell him why."

"I imagine he did not take it well," Adam snorts.

"He took it better than I thought he would," I shrug. "But that's because he was seriously considering leaving the family at that point."

"What?"

"He was really upset, so much so that he stayed with me, at the condo, and didn't speak to his father for weeks," I look down at my hands on the comforter. "Honestly, that was the happiest we'd ever been, actually. At least it was for me. We were just a normal little family, spending time with our newborn daughter. He was dedicating himself completely into his hotel business and said repeatedly that he was leaving that life behind."

Adam turns in the bed, rolling onto his side and staring at me. I smile at him politely, before lowering my eyes from his.

"It was the only time I thought that maybe, just maybe, we *could* work, you know?" I say quietly. "If he left all that shit behind him."

"But?"

"You never get to just *leave* the Mafia," I bite my lip. "One way or another, they never really let you go."

"So Dimitris forced him to come back?"

"In a way, I suppose."

"What do you mean?" Adam asks. "How did Dimitris get Jaxon to come back and take over?"

"Well," I sigh. "He *died*."

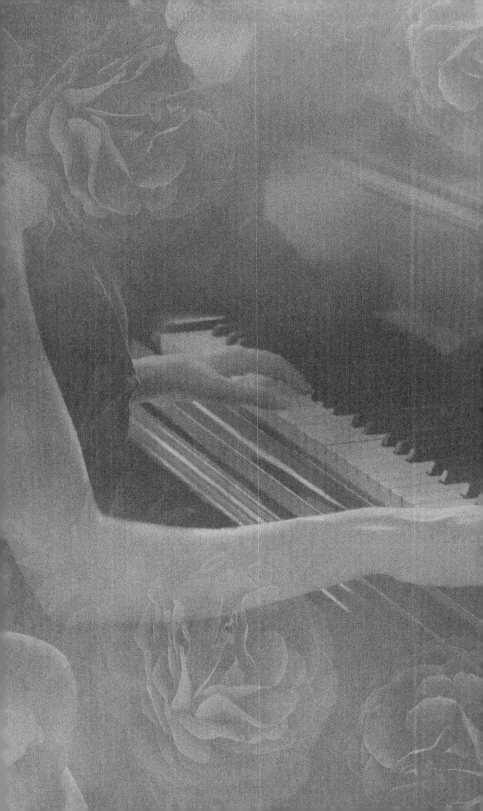

CHAPTER THIRTY

ADAM

The next two days at the Valentine Estate pass relatively uneventfully.

I get the entire backstory on how Jaxon took over the Mafia, with all of the recently discovered information.

I get the full story behind Ethan White, the right-hand man of both Dimitris and eventually Jaxon Pace, and how he was actually a Pace *himself*. Ethan's name at birth had been Mikanos Pace, and he was the eldest son and heir to Don Supreme Stefanos Pace…before he decided to quit the Mafia and join the military.

Stefanos was furious. He gave his son a portion of his inheritance, as well as the new identity of "Ethan White," before telling him that "Ethan" was no longer part of their family, and to never return. He then proclaimed his younger son, Dimitris, would succeed as the new Don Supreme.

There was no way for Stefanos to know, but the action he took that day would forever change the Pace Mafia…and the Pace family itself.

I learned how after a few years in service to his country,

Ethan had learned of a plot to destroy his family, and despite their estrangement, chose to seek out and reconcile with his brother. They fought together, and Dimitris sustained heavy injuries, but they ultimately won. And with his younger brother now the Don Supreme, Ethan chose to rejoin the mafia, rededicating his life to the protection of his family.

The syndicate thrived under Dimtris's leadership.

However, due to the severity of his injuries, Dimitris was unable to give Ismena a child. Which meant there would be no heir. So after exhausting every avenue, the couple did the only thing they could think of…And they went to Ethan.

Ethan already had several children of his own, and was technically of the same bloodline, so for Ismena and Dimitris, he was the ideal option candidate to be a sperm donor. And so through in-vitro fertilization, the Pace legacy continued, and Jaxon Pace was born.

Jaxon was loved and cherished, but he was only ever meant to know Dimitris and Ismena as his parents. Ethan was around, but was more of a watchful protector. He spent his time mentoring Jaxon, and teaching him to be the man he is today, never revealing his true relation to him.

However, when Jaxon fought with his father, and decided to leave the Mafia, that's when everything fell apart.

And it fell apart quickly.

While Dimitris was able to reconcile with Jaxon, he was *not* able to convince him to abandon his burgeoning hotel empire, and recommit himself to becoming the next Don Supreme. This unfortunately put the Pace Family at risk of losing the power they had held exclusively for decades. Unwilling to just abdicate, Dimitris quickly scrambled to select another champion from within his ranks, to compete against the other families' champions in The Trials.

And in a completely unexpected move, Dimitris chose a candidate no one expected: Michael Valentine.

After his father's death, a traumatized adolescent Michael Valentine spent several years in and out of therapy programs. When these ultimately proved unsuccessful in helping him cope with the horrors he endured, Dimitris and Ismena, stepped in and took the young man under their wing.

At sixteen Michael was the youngest recruit in the family's

history. Perhaps the Pace's thought that the grueling training would provide the discipline and structure the boy lacked.

And aside from the occasional violent outburst, they were correct. For the most part, Michael thrived within the structure of Mafia life, at least for a few years. His fearlessness in the face of danger made him stand out from the others, and he progressed quickly through the ranks. And despite Jaxon's reluctance, Michael was even hand-picked for the heir's protection detail.

Perhaps Dimitris thought that Michael's skills as well as his ruthlessness would come in handy when competing for the Supremacy. And at first, it looked like he had made a good choice, with Michael completing the first three tests as flawlessly as Jaxon had. But then it came to the fourth test, *The Judgment*.

According to Rachel, The Judgment was a test designed to test a champion's emotional integrity and sense of morality. A quandary, selected by those closest to the champion, would be presented. The champion would then have to decide between mercy or punishment, with punishment often equating to death.

Michael *failed* this test.

Not because he delivered the wrong judgment, but rather that he took little to no time to hear testimony, review facts, consult the elders, or even deliberate in his decision of death.

This was a massive disappointment for Dimitris. And one he did not handle well.

While Michael was exiled from the Pace Mafia, Dimitris went back to Pace Manor, and planned to do the unthinkable: assassinate his only son, Jaxon Pace.

Why? Because according to a distraught and likely drunken Dimitris, who was far from the fair and noble Don Supreme he used to be, the loss of power was a shame he could not bear, and it was "better to have a dead son, than a disobedient one."

As a back-up plan to Michael dying or failing in The Trials, and Jaxon's adamant refusal to take over as Don Supreme, Dimitris wanted to clear himself of any embarrassment or shame at his son's refusal to continue the Pace Family legacy. He had even gone as far as to draft documents preparing for the liquidation of Jaxon's assets upon Jaxon's *untimely* death. And so, when Dimitris returned to the Manor that night, he planned to murder his son.

But Ethan stopped him.

Miraculously, Ethan had discovered Dimitris's vile plan while his brother was supervising The Trials, and confronted him, right there on the lawn of Pace Manor. He told his brother that he wouldn't let him kill Jaxon. But when Dimitris wouldn't relent, Ethan had to make an impossible choice between his brother, and Jaxon. And he chose Jaxon.

That night, Ethan changed the course of history, for everyone involved.

Although in time the truth would ultimately reveal itself, in the beginning, Ethan stayed on as Jaxon's right hand, choosing to keep his true identity and relationship to Jaxon a secret.

Jaxon, after briefly grieving his father, ended up taking up the very mantle he had refused, becoming the new Don Supreme.

According to Rachel, Jaxon had accepted this role in an effort to better support his men and family, by protecting them from a bloody civil war. However, it meant that *her* role in Jaxon's life, as well as their daughter's, had now become a more crucial one.

I also learn that following the death of both of his parents, Jaxon did require Rachel to move to Pace Manor, both for her safety, as well as for the safety of their daughter. However, their hopes of living a peaceful, and quiet family life at his ancestral home were constantly undermined. Either by Michael, causing chaos and unnecessary bloodshed around the city as a way to cause friction between Jaxon and city officials, who relied on Jaxon to keep the *unspoken* peace within the underworld.

…Or from rumors of the overworked and exhausted new Don Supreme, using drugs and recreational sex to keep up with the stresses of his new fast-paced responsibilities.

They fought constantly.

Rachel kept her condo in the city, simply as a space for her to retreat to when she couldn't bear to be around Jaxon. She moved her friend Jessica into the condo, both to give Jessica and her kids a better home environment, but also for the company. And although she found herself trapped on the sick carousel ride of heartbreak and apology-gifts on a weekly basis, she still held out hope that Jaxon would eventually grow out of this phase, and stop acting like a narcissistic twat.

But, this is something I *understand.*

I knew better than most what it was like to love someone who hurt me.

And so over the next two days, Rachel divulges aspects of her past that would seem gruesome and illogical to a normal person, I also slowly dissect my own whiplash reality with Candace.

Oddly enough, our parallels are terrifyingly similar.

I tell Rachel about how after ending my *therapy* affair with Scarlett, things were surprisingly good for a time between my wife and I.

But then my work started demanding more and more of my time, and the lonely hours at home with young kids proved to be more than she could bear.

I tell Rachel about thinking I deserved Candace's infidelity, one for the trauma she endured, but also for the affair she never knew about.

I justified *everything*.

I justified tracking Candace's phone to various bars and hotel rooms, to retrieve my wandering wife. I justified finding various pills hidden in bottles of expired medication around the house. I even justified getting the phone calls from the hospital after she overdosed in a grocery store bathroom.

And yes, occasionally, I would consider leaving. Getting the divorce, taking custody of the kids. But, just like Rachel's belief that Jaxon was only going through a phase, I too believed my wife would eventually sort out her shit.

Everything would be fine. I just had to be *patient*.

Coincidentally, however, patience is something I'm also learning with Rachel.

After the experiences I had with my wife, I assumed putting together the pieces of Rachel's puzzle, even with our earlier bumps in the road, would be a walk in the park.

But I was wrong.

Rachel's personality is far more complicated, and emotionally volatile than any woman I've ever been with, and certainly more unpredictable.

But perhaps it is exactly this personality that attracts me to her. And perhaps it is exactly my previous experience that has granted me the patience to navigate the choppy waters of her soul, and allow me to slip into her harbor.

…Even if I'm still actively trying my damnedest not to cave and slip into her physical "harbor." Which is proving harder than I thought.

But I know my reasons for abstaining.

Rachel is not complicated, volatile and unpredictable by accident, but rather default. Having been denied any kind of relational stability, either from her family or from Jaxon, Rachel's default quantifier had defaulted to *sex*.

She had only ever experienced the feeling of security, compassion and attention within the parameters of a strictly sexual relationship. Because of this, sex had become the only way she identified her worth. And so, even with people she truly cared about, like Jaxon Pace, sex was a transaction. One in which she provided a service, and received the momentary, but painfully temporary feeling of affection, desire and love.

But this was a hollow kind of love.

In fact, it wasn't love at all. It was emotional prostitution.

And I didn't want to be her client, I wanted to be her *soulmate*.

So no matter how long it takes or how patient I have to be, I am resigned to be better for her, and determined to show Rachel that sex alone did not equate to intimacy, and that intimacy was only a *part* of love.

However, on the third day of my dick-sabbatical, it appears Rachel has reached her threshold when she corners me in the kitchen as we start to make dinner.

"So, I have a question," she asks.

"Shoot."

"There isn't like, *another* reason that you don't want to…"

Her voice trails off as she carries a bag of potatoes over to a cutting board on the counter.

"Another reason?"

"Well, I'm not trying to complain," she says, shrugging. "And I will admit I have enjoyed you sleeping next to me, because you're hotter than a furnace."

I chuckle to myself, opening the fridge and pulling out some chicken breasts I started marinating the night before.

"But like every morning I notice that you're…*excited*," she says, gently clearing her throat. "And I just wondered why, if you're already there in bed with me, you didn't want to fuck."

Reaching around me I pull a pan from the cupboard above the stove.

"Does not fucking bother you that much?"

"No!" She says quickly, stiffening. "I don't even care."

"I mean, it kinda *seems* like you care," I say, trying to hide my smirk.

Admittedly watching her try and pretend that my three-day cock-hiatus *hasn't* been driving her crazy is bringing me the slightest bit of amusement.

Given the massive erection I woke up with this morning, with a handful of her perky tits and her thick ass sleepily rubbing against the head of my cock, it's been damn near painful to resist yanking her thin panties down and just shoving my cock deep inside her.

Especially since she's started wearing such tight clothing around the house, and deliberately sleeping in *just* panties and a tank top.

"I just don't understand it," she shrugs defensively. "Are you refusing to fuck me because you're just not attracted to me anymore or something?"

Her face is beet red as she glares at me before aggressively yanking a potato from the bag and hacking it open with a giant knife from the block.

I cock my head to the side, narrowing my eyes at her. I don't even need to say anything, because even *Rachel* knows how ridiculous that statement is.

She knows damn well how badly I want her. Always.

Just like she knows that I'm not actually *refusing* to fuck her, I'm simply refusing to *only* fuck her.

Perhaps that's why I find this pouty mini-tantrum of hers so amusing, especially when the whole point of this exercise isn't to deny her intimacy, but to work on a different part of it: *feelings*. And after all our recent conversations, she knows this.

So Rachel's not actually asking me this question because she wants an answer. No, she wants a *fight*. She's hoping to bait me into an argument in which I give in to her desires.

But I won't.

She's acting like a brat. And we don't negotiate with brats.

"I'm pretty sure," I say calmly. "That I've already explained my stance on this. More than once."

"Right," she scoffs, rolling her eyes. "And I get that you don't want sex to feel *transactional*, or whatever you said. But I feel like we should still be able to fuck."

"And we will," I say, turning back around to face her. "But I

409

told you, that I just need to know that in *addition* to fucking your brains out, I can also make love to you."

She rolls her eyes again, crossing her arms.

"See," I say, pointing the spatula in my hand at her. "That right there is why I'm holding off on fucking you."

"Why? Because I think making love is ridiculous?!"

"You don't actually think it's ridiculous, Rachel."

"Yes I do!" She says defensively. "It just sounds so…soft. And I'm not a girl who is interested in soft sex."

"See, I might've believed you, if you didn't just admit that it *sounds* soft," I grin. "Which tells me that you've never actually tried it."

"I…I…that's not what," she mumbles. "I mean…I've sort—"

"Remember," I caution with a grin. "We agreed: *no lies.*"

"Ugh! Fine! So I've never tried it, okay?" She grunts, adorably annoyed. "Big fucking deal! I don't want to! It sounds stupid, and I'm not interested in trying it!"

"That's fine, sweetheart," I shrug. "But I'm not interested in *just* fucking. I want to know that we're building something real and to me, that's the indicator."

"Why?!"

"Because it's different."

"How different?" She demands, her hands on her hips.

This girl…

I take a deep breath and walk around the island so that I'm standing in front of her.

"Because, Rachel," I say softly. "It's where the pageantry and bullshit stops, and the walls come down. It's where I don't just throw you on the bed, choke you, pull your hair or spank your ass, but—"

"…Now all of *that* sounds good to me," she interrupts with a snarky little smirk.

"Oh really?" I say, crossing my arms across my body, and narrowing my eyes at her. "Weren't you just telling me a few nights ago that you wanted to feel *real*?"

Her smile fades, and her eyes get wide.

"Well…yeah," she says, shifting uncomfortably.

"That's exactly what making love is all about. It's not just fucking and orgasms, it's a raw, and deeply emotional experience. It's me getting lost in all of you. Adoring you, savoring you, appreciating every single inch of you. It's where you take down every barrier, every wall, exposing every vulnerability, and you do it *because* you trust me to love all your broken pieces," I say, my eyes holding hers. "It's more than just loving you physically, Rachel. It's about running my finger down the spine of your soul, seeing who you truly are, and reminding you that I love every page of your story."

Rachel stares at me, her chest heaving.

"Pout about it if you want, throw your tantrum if you need to," I smirk, gently running my thumb along her cheek. "But that's what I want to have with *you*."

A few seconds pass between us in silence before Rachel seemingly snaps out of it, clears her throat, and quickly looks away from me, running her hand through her long brown hair.

"You know, you say a lot of sappy things, but that might be the sappiest thing you've ever said, Adam," she snorts loudly.

But I'm not buying it.

Because even from where I'm standing, I can see her cheeks turning the brightest shade of crimson.

Gotcha, Princess.

"Suit yourself," I say, shrugging and turning back around, if only to hide the massive smile on my face.

I take the opportunity to grab a tray and some wax paper, setting it next to her for the potatoes, before starting the oven. We sit in the silent kitchen for a few minutes before I hear her slowly start quartering her potatoes, far less aggressively.

"So," she finally says, breaking the silence. "Does that mean we are…?"

"Are we what?" I ask, turning back around.

"I don't know," she shrugs, tucking her hair behind her ear. "Exclusive?"

I chuckle to myself.

"Rachel, you're a Mafia princess, under house arrest in her childhood home, and I'm a suspended FBI agent who willingly jumped into that house arrest with you. I don't know how much more *exclusive* we could be."

"Okay, first of all, I'm not a princess!" she snaps, annoyed. "I've already told you that, repeatedly. And second, I meant, are we exclusive once we get *out* of here?"

Using a fork, I slowly transfer the chicken into a glass baking pan.

"You mean *if* we get out of here,"

"You know what, Adam? Never mind!" She suddenly snaps, slamming the potato in her hand on the cutting board and storming out of the kitchen.

It rolls off the edge and onto the kitchen floor as I stand here, stunned.

Well, shit. That was short lived. Good job, Romeo.

Unfortunately it takes Rachel storming off for me to realize that I just overlooked her uncomfortable mannerisms, and the sheepish tone in her voice, completely missing the reason for that entire line of questioning.

I throw the chicken in the fridge and walk over to the sink, quickly washing my hands and kicking myself for fucking that up so royally.

She'd had a reaction to what I said about making love.

I was just starting to get through to her.

Quickly I head down the hallway to find her. Since I didn't hear her go out the front door, or the obnoxiously creaky stairs on the main staircase she couldn't have gone far. Sure enough I find her in the study, sitting on the piano bench just staring at the keys. But she doesn't look up at me as I walk into the room.

"Rachel, I'm sorry," I say quietly.

"It's fine."

"No," I say, gently walking around in front of her and kneeling down. "It's not fine. And I'm sorry."

I reach for her hand but she quickly pulls it away.

"Look, I realize what I said might be construed as me being dismissive, or wanting to be with other people and—"

"I don't care if you are," she snaps. "You're a grown man, Adam. You can do what you want."

Reaching for her hand, she tries to avoid me again, but this time I catch it in my hands and hold it firmly.

"*This* is what I want."

"Is it though?" She asks, sarcastically.

"Yes, it is," I say, waiting for her eyes to find mine. "If it wasn't, I wouldn't be here right now."

"Yeah, well, you might be if I'm just a target to you. Or one of your assignments. Or maybe you're just using me for information to get insight on Michael and—"

I immediately cup her face in my hand, pressing my lips to hers, kissing her deeply. At first she tries to pull away, but when I kiss her again, eventually I feel her relax.

I pull away, pressing my forehead to hers.

"Rachel, you are not a target, and you are not an assignment," I whisper against her lips. "You are the woman I want to be with. So much so that I would risk everything just to be here with you, okay?"

She swallows hard, but does not move.

"What I said was insensitive, and I'm sorry. I fucked up."

"I never said you fucked up."

"No, but I did," I say, shaking my head. "See, I told you the other day not to be afraid to ask me things, and then I also made that big speech in there about wanting you to be vulnerable with me and experiencing true intimacy. But then when you tried to communicate what was on your mind, I dropped the ball."

Her eyes fall from mine for a moment but then she looks back up at me.

"I'm sorry," I repeat, emphasizing my sincerity. "I hate that the first chance I get to work through some of this baggage with you, I…Well, I let you down. I really want to get it right for you, because I want to be a better man. Both for myself, *and* for you."

"You are," she says quietly, biting her lip.

"I'm trying," I say, stroking her cheek with my thumb. "But I'm a little out of practice so I'm going to screw up and say dumb shit sometimes."

A smile tugs at the corners of her lips.

"But please, never doubt why I am here with you. I'm here because I believe that underneath all the mistakes we've made, we have something *real*."

I swallow hard, my heart pounding in my chest at the weight of my own words.

"And I don't want to screw *that* up. Because that's what's most important to me, and it's been a long time since I felt that. With anyone."

She stares at me for a moment before putting her hand on mine, pressing against her cheek.

"Neither do I," she whispers so softly I can barely hear her. "I'm just really not good at the vulnerability thing, Adam."

"No shit, Sherlock," I wink.

This makes her giggle, and I finally exhale.

"I've told you what I've gone through, but I still have this fear that maybe because of the way we started—"

"Rachel, don't give a fuck about how we started." I say firmly. "I want you, all of you, exactly as you are to feel comfortable talking about whatever is on your mind."

"I'm just afraid of what we talked about in the tub," she says softly. "Like I know you say it's okay, and that you want to know the truth about my life, but it doesn't stop me from feeling like a shit show when I tell you these messy stories. And then I start to spiral and worry that something I've told you, or that I will tell you will taint your view of me."

She stares at me, her big brown eyes locked on mine.

I smile, looking down at her small hand in mine before bringing it to my lips and kissing it softly.

"Rachel, please hear me," I whisper. "Who you were, and what you did before me doesn't bother me in the slightest. I want to hear your messy stories because they are part of you, and part of how you got to where you are. But I've never once looked down on you. In fact, I admire you."

"You...*admire* me?" she whispers.

"Are you kidding? Baby girl, every challenge, every struggle you've ever had thrown at you, you've survived. And not just survived but have come out stronger and more resilient. How could I not admire you?" I say warmly. "I promise there is nothing you could tell me that could make me think less of you because there's nothing in your past that you need to be ashamed of."

Tears well in her eyes and she bites her lip, looking down at our hands intertwined.

"I *want* to tell you everything. It's just...terrifying."

"I know," I say softly, pulling her off the bench and into my lap. She straddles me, placing her legs on either side of me. "So don't rush it. Remember we're going to take this at our own pace, okay? We'll get there."

"Thank you," she whispers. "For being patient with me."

"Of course," I say, gently wiping her tears away with my thumb. "I might not always get it right, but I promise to do my best, Princess."

She rolls her eyes, and shakes her head, but this time she doesn't pull away.

"Why do you insist on calling me *that*?" she chuckles.

"Because you keep insisting that you're not a princess," I wink, smiling against her lips. "And I've decided I disagree."

I thread my hand into her soft curls and kiss her deeply, pushing my tongue into her mouth. Slowly I work my way down, kissing my favorite beauty mark on her neck.

"And also" I growl, sucking gently on her earlobe, making her moan. "Because I know that it drives you fucking crazy when I say it."

The way she moans, makes my cock swell inside my pants.

God I bet she's so fucking wet right now.

"Jerk," she whispers, gripping my shoulders hard. "But you know, you should be careful playing with fire, Adam. Especially since your pussy-deprived cock is so hard it's practically *inside* me already."

Oh shit...

She grinds her sex against my throbbing erection, and all the air is sucked out of my lungs.

I want her, and she knows it.

She kisses me, and presses her forehead to mine.

"I know you want to make love to me," she says, working her hips up and down, making me shiver. "But what if we find a middle ground between the two?"

"Such as?"

"Such as," she whispers, pressing her tongue to my neck. "What if I acknowledge that you want more than just a physical relationship with me, and you acknowledge that I'm just not quite ready to make love. What if I don't say no, and instead I just say not right *now*?"

I smile.

Touché, Miss Valentine.

"Well, then I'd probably have to find a middle ground between what I want to do to you, and what you want me to do to you."

"Such as?"

"Spread you open across this piano and lick your pussy until your screaming wakes your dead-ass neighbors."

I watch with utter satisfaction as her jaw drops.

"That sounds good," she whispers, her cheeks flushing with color once again. "I could consent to that."

"As you wish, Princess," I growl, grinning wickedly.

Hours later, I wake in the darkness, the moonlight filtering in the thin gray shades of the tall bulletproof glass windows. I roll over sleepily, reaching across the bed for Rachel.

But my hand touches only fabric.

She's not here.

This is where I would normally panic, but then in the distance I can faintly hear the soft sounds of music playing somewhere in the house. Pulling myself from the warmth of the soft down comforter, I stumble groggily toward the door, glancing at my watch.

3:15am

Christ, Mafia princesses keep weird hours.

The record must've changed, because suddenly I recognize the unmistakable slow and sorrowful tones of Beethoven's *Moonlight Sonata*, echoing throughout the old house.

In nothing but my sweatpants, I make my way down the creaky dark oak steps and across the cold marble foyer to be met by quite a sight.

It wasn't a *recording* I heard from the upstairs bedroom, it was Rachel, playing the baby grand piano in the study.

With only the fireplace glowing softly in the corner, and the moonlight filtering through the paned glass of the study window, she looks hauntingly beautiful. Without a stitch of makeup, and sitting in just her thin tank top and panties, she completely takes my breath away. Her long dark brown hair is brushed to one side, and her arms flex as she immaculately delivers each note, completely lost in the heartbreaking piece of music.

She's good. Really good, actually.

I remember her telling me she played as a kid.

Granted at the time, I thought she was Annie from North Carolina, a girl who took classical piano lessons and who dreamed of being a concert pianist when she grew up.

Hey, I guess part of what she told me was true.

But watching her now, I realize just *how* good she really is. Her bare feet instinctively press the pedals down, as her hands

NICOLE FANNING

brush the keys with feeling and intelligence, lingering for each
emotional musical breath before moving on.

What could she have been, had anyone invested in her?

The thought pricks my heart, despite knowing she would
likely scold me for pitying her, yet again. However, it's not just
pity I feel for Rachel.

I *love* her.

As the song transitions from its famous slow and mournful
progress to the fast-paced crescendo celebrated by so many
pianists, Rachel is so lost in the Sonata that she doesn't even look
up. Her eyes close as her fingers immaculately tap each and every
note with precision. And given that no sheet music sits before
her, it's clear that she is playing this entire piece from memory.

I realize I am witnessing a rare moment.

So much of her personality is loud, messy and disorganized.
Like a meteor speeding for earth at terminal velocity, Rachel
possesses little to no self-control. And she *embraces* it.

But even with the boisterous bedlam that is Rachel Valentine,
there is little unnecessary malice in her actions, but rather a
unique authenticity. She might be crude, dangerous, or even
vicious when provoked, but unlike her psychopathic brother
she's not an inherently mean or vicious person by nature.

Her unpolished and callous exterior is simply a survival
mechanism contrived through her trauma to pull her through the
horrific events of her past.

Rachel may be chaotic, but at least she is *genuinely* chaotic.

What's more, she knows exactly who she is. And she has no
intention of changing. Not for me or for anyone else.

However, I have no desire to change her.

Because I don't love her for who she could be, I love her for
exactly who she *is*.

Every scar, every wound, every crack in her armor, is just
another piece to the mysterious puzzle of a woman who sits before
me. The tragedies she has endured, the sacrifices she has made,
and the hard lessons she has learned, have added incomparable
depth to her existence. There is a captivating strength to her
survival, and a profound fragility to her mayhem.

And as I stand here, watching her broken heart bleeding onto
the piano keys, there is no denying the beautiful catastrophe that
is Rachel Valentine, has enraptured me completely.

417

I might not be able to change what has been done to her, but I can change what happens to her from this point forward. I can keep her safe, give her the acceptance she craves, and love her to the best of my ability.

Which is exactly what I intend to do.

The song finishes.

"Are you going to linger in the shadows all night?"

"Depends,"

"On?"

"Does this spooky serenade intend on *lasting* all night?"

She smirks, sitting back against the bench.

"No, I think I'm done."

"Please," I say, holding up my hands and stepping into the room. "Don't stop for me. It was perfect."

"Oh I promise it wasn't," Rachel scoffs to herself. "It was actually wrong. Substantially."

"How?"

"I skipped the entire second movement."

"What?"

"Well, technically a lot of people do. Mostly because this sonata itself is a bit of an enigma."

"How do you mean?" I say as I walk in and sit down on the couch across from her.

"Most sonatas typically follow a very common three-part format. The first starts off fast, the second movement slows down, and the third movement is usually short and fast."

"No grand finale?"

"Not before Beethoven," she smiles. "Mr. B was a rebel in his time. Once he started writing sonatas, he actually preferred to have *four* movements instead of three. And his fourth movements were typically longer and more dramatic. But even then, he didn't adhere to that *all* the time. It was like he hated being boxed into any set format. He would occasionally like to change things up a bit, and Moonlight Sonata was one of his more riskier pieces. He skipped the standard fast first movement, and started instead with this slow and captivating melody. Then there was this minor breath in the piece, where he had this bright and uplifting brief second movement, and ended with a jaw-dropping finale."

I smile to myself.

She's so excited to be telling me this.

"However, what most people hear in Moonlight Sonata is two parts-the slow and the fast. When in reality, it's actually supposed to be three parts. But, a lot of the time pianists will skip the second movement and just continue to the finale. That's what I did just now."

She laughs to herself. But the moment her eyes lock with mine she blushes and looks away.

"I'm sorry," she whispers, biting her lower lip. "God, I think I got a bit carried away with musical theory."

"I liked it."

She shakes her head, clearly embarrassed that she got lost talking about something she loved.

"Rachel," I say, calmly. "I enjoyed it. And I enjoy that you enjoy it. How is it that you know so much about this?"

"My tutor," she says quietly. "We could only play the piano when my father wasn't home, or he would bitch about the noise. But we took advantage of every opportunity where he was out of the house. He taught me mostly the classics. Bach, Mozart, Wagner, Chopin, Tchaikovsky. But Beethoven was his favorite."

She tucks her hair behind her ear.

"Which meant he was my favorite too."

"You cared for this man," I whisper, watching her nod.

"He cared for me. I just wish I could've..."

Her voice trails off, and she flinches.

She still feels guilty for his death.

Even now as I sit here reminded that this very man bled out in the other room, I wish I could remind her that she wasn't responsible for his death. But I know she already knows this, and I also know that knowing something, doesn't take away the sting of a painful memory.

So, I decide to change the topic.

"You know, I wasn't sure I was going to tell you this, but before you got taken captive by Jaxon, I actually had planned to take you to the opera."

"What?"

Her jaw drops, and she looks at me, her face transfixed in confusion and astonishment.

"Yeah," I chuckle to myself. "The day before you went missing you said you were going to come by the hotel, remember? You had mentioned you liked classical music, and I had never been to the opera myself, so I went and bought two tickets to see La Boheme opening night. I was going to ask you out for a date… you know surprise you."

"What?" She repeats. "You bought us tickets? To the opera?"

I nod.

"But when you didn't show up that day, I went down to your brother's club, even though obviously I didn't *know* he was your brother then, but I went there to try and find you."

"What happened?" she asks.

"Well," I chuckle, biting my lip. "I ended up getting the shit kicked out of me just for mentioning your name."

Rachel stares at me, her chest heaving.

"That's why you were in the warehouse that night," she whispers. "When they came to rescue Ethan."

"I guess so. All I know is I woke up on the other side of the city, alive, and untethered. Which seemed like a miracle, given Michael's whispered reputation around town." I say, clearing my throat. "And the reception I got when I went back to the club—."

"Wait, you went *back*?" She gasps. "Why?"

"Because," I shrug. "I had your ticket. And I guess I thought that if you were alive, maybe the offer would…tempt you out of hiding."

"You really wanted to take me to the opera," she whispers, her eyes glued on me.

"I did," I whisper gently. "Badly."

"You wanted to take me to the opera so badly that you would risk getting your ass kicked a second time, or even getting shot, all to take me on a…*date*?"

Her eyes are locked on mine, paralyzing me in place.

"In retrospect, I suppose that probably wasn't the best idea," I say, swallowing hard. "Since it probably got back to your brother, and may have given him the idea to actually go and blow up the opera so I do feel a bit bad that–"

"That's why you were there that night," she whispers, interrupting me. "You were there, still hoping I would show up."

That's when I see her lip quiver, and dark brown her eyes well with tears.

"Yes," I say quietly, lowering my eyes from hers.

The silence that fills the room is electric.

"Do you…" she whispers. "Do you *love* me, Adam?"

Her question stuns me, and my stomach instantly drops.

Although I've admitted it to myself, I haven't dared say it to Rachel, simply out of fear that she would bolt.

How long am I going to keep this to myself?

It's true, so much of us has been wrapped up in lies, both innocuous and intentional. And through it all, both of us have clung to the tattered remains of our relationship like a life raft weathering the storm of our tumultuous truths.

But all of my painful transparency will mean absolutely nothing if I deny the most important truth of them all.

"Yes," I whisper, my eyes finding hers. "I do love you, Rachel. And I've loved you for a long time."

She stares at me for what feels like an eternity, completely still, and completely silent.

And then, without a word she stands to her feet and crosses the room, straddling me and kissing me deeply. At first I am so stunned by her reaction that I can barely move, but slowly my hands wrap around her body and pull her flush with me, my kiss matching her fervor.

She pulls away slightly, pressing her forehead to mine.

"I love you too, Adam," she whispers, her voice cracking.

Holy. Shit.

"And," she says, taking a deep breath. "I want you to make love to me. Right. Fucking. Now."

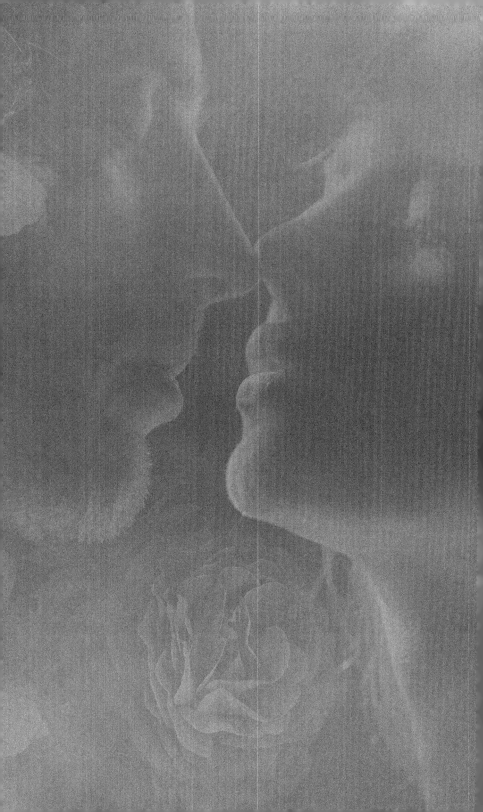

CHAPTER THIRTY-ONE

Rachel

"What did you say?"

Adam sits beneath me, in only his gray sweat-pants, his words echoing in the silent house.

Moment of truth, Rach.

My entire body starts trembling, but not because I regret what I just said to him.

No. I'm trembling because I *don't* regret saying it. I know what I said, and I know the truth behind it.

I *love* Adam.

And for perhaps the very first time in my life, I *mean* it.

"I said," I repeat, my voice trembling. "That I love you, Adam Westwood. And I want you to make love to me."

The moment the words leave my lips, his soft hands cup my face, kissing me passionately before threading up into my hair.

"As you wish, Princess."

Without another word, he lifts me by my thighs, wraps his arms around me, and carries me out of the study. I would normally object, but tonight I don't, instead relishing the warmth of his bare chest against the thin fabric of my tank top.

He carries me up the staircase and into our bedroom, laying me down on the sheets.

"Lift your arms," he commands, his voice hoarse and raw.

I obey and he sits down beside me, pulling my top over my head. The gas fireplace glows warmly in the corner as my heart pounds, as he gently runs his hand over my naked breasts.

He looks at me with a raging fire in his eyes, his muscular arms flex as he takes his time caressing my skin, teasing my nipples with his thumbs. Squeezing me, he leans in and begins sucking on each of them as he runs his hands down the length of my body.

"You are so beautiful, Rachel," he whispers.

The reverence in his voice, and the soft gentle way he says this makes my entire body tingle.

"I want to see *all* of you," he says, slipping his hand between my legs, rubbing his fingers against my panties. "So we need to do something about these."

"Oh my God," I moan, as he deliberately teases me through the fabric.

"Whose little pussy is this," he says, burying his face in my neck while continuing to rub my sensitive clit.

"It's…yours," I gasp, the sensitivity making me squirm.

"And who am I?"

"My…*boyfriend*," I whisper, the very word making my whole body tighten.

"That's right," he says as my eyes find his. "And I want you to know that I choose *you*, Rachel Valentine, and *only* you."

He hooks his fingers inside my panties and slowly slides them down my body.

"And that a body this beautiful," he breathes, spreading my legs and kissing the inside of my thigh just above my knee. "Is going to require me to take my sweet time, appreciating every inch of you."

He pulls off his sweatpants, revealing his massive, throbbing erection before climbing on to the bed. He slides between my legs, presses the back of my thighs up against my stomach and burying his face in my pussy. Delicately he slips his tongue just inside the lips.

"I love your body, but I especially love this pussy," he whispers against my sensitive clit. "The softness, the smell, and the taste."

"Oh God, yes!" I moan, arching my back and pressing my pussy harder against his face.

I feel him run his finger down my slit before pressing just the tip inside of me, before shoving all the way in.

"Adam," I groan, leaning back against the pillow, feeling my legs start to shake.

Yes, I feel vulnerable and slightly exposed, but instead of normally running from such feelings, somehow this time it's positively electric. As if my entire body *wants* to feel every single kiss or touch. I've waited so long for this, and it feels so good.

"God I love it when you get messy for me," he growls. "How your body just can't help itself."

Oh fuck!

He lets go of my legs, and pulls the covers down around us, encapsulating us in the sheets before pressing his body against mine. And for the first time in days, I feel his hard erection, pressing eagerly against my pussy.

I want him. It's inappropriate how much I want him. I feel desperate to have his cock inside me.

Holy. Fucking. Hell. Why do I find this so hot?!

"Tell me," he says, kissing my earlobe, slowly grinding his cock on the outside of my pussy. "What are you to me, Rachel?"

"I...I'm..." I whimper as he teases me, knowing exactly what he wants me to say, but my brain suddenly struggling to remember how to speak.

"Go on," he grins wickedly, as he grips his erection in his hands, deliberately rubbing it gently against my clit. "I want to hear how much you believe it. I want to hear you own it."

"I'm your..." I whisper, my heart pounding loudly in my ears. *"Princess."*

"Very good," he says, kissing me.

He positions his cock right at my entrance.

Oh God!

"And the last, probably most important question," he asks, pushing deeper inside of me. *"Why* are you my Princess?"

"Because," I breathe, unable to stop myself any longer. "Because you love me."

He smiles, in a way that is somehow contrary to the filthy tone in his voice and the way he's been deliciously teasing me.

Then I feel him push his cock inside me, thrusting in slowly, pressing all the way in.

"Oh…My…God…" I gasp, wrapping my hands around the back of his head, as he pulls out and back in again.

I run my hands down his back, hearing his rapid breathing, feeling him swell inside of me.

"Have you missed this cock, Princess?"

"Holy fuck," I breathe, feeling every inch of him thrusting in and out of me. "Yes!"

He buries his face in my neck again, and I arch my back, feeling his breath on my skin as I squeeze my legs around him, pulling him deeper inside me. Kissing down my skin he wraps his tongue around my erect nipples and sucks hard, making me gasp.

Time slows and every touch, every kiss, every breath feels different. I don't just *want* Adam, I want him to permeate every single molecule of my body and imprint himself forever.

"Look at me," he says gently.

My eyes find his, feeling the rhythm of his thrusts increase.

"I love you, Rachel" he breathes, shuddering slightly. "I love all of you. For exactly who you are."

"And I…" I whisper, feeling my body clench around him. "I love you too."

The world around us fades away as the two of us climax together. Our breathing slows as we savor every second of orgasmic bliss.

That's when I see the smile on Adam's face, and it's as if something clicks into place for me.

"I love all of you. For exactly who you are."

These aren't empty words. They have meaning and worth.

Just like *me*.

Which is something Adam has always made me feel. The way he talks to me, and treats me, makes me feel worthy and *seen*. For exactly who I am, because he has never asked me to be something I'm not.

For most of my life, I have needed my walls and my protection. Vulnerability has only ever brought me misery and pain…until Adam.

Adam makes me feel *safe* enough to be vulnerable.

This man truly loves me. And he loves me completely, in

ways my broken heart didn't even realize it needed to be loved.

Maybe I didn't deserve the pain. Maybe I didn't deserve to be broken by people I trusted. And yet somehow I always managed to survive. Because that's who I am. I'm a survivor.

However, as I lay here, tangled up in his arms, feeling discarded parts of me come back to life, I realize that for the first time in my life, I don't feel like I'm *just* surviving anymore.

For the first time in my life, I'm actually living, and I've never felt more alive than I feel, right now, with him.

So maybe, all my suffering had not been in vain.

Because if it took all the pain, and betrayals, and heartbreak, to bring me to this moment, right here, with him…then all of it was worth it.

Adam and I made love until the sun came up.

That's when I cried.

I don't know how it started, or even *why* it started, but somewhere between obliterating my walls and soaking in our ecstasy, the gravity of the moment hit me, and a landmine of suppressed emotions bubbled to the surface, and I just burst into tears. And I mean *a lot* of tears.

"I'm fine," I say, wiping my eyes, laughing. "I…I don't even know why this is happening. I don't know what's wrong with me."

"Nothing is wrong with you," Adam says, immediately pulling me into his arms. "I promise."

"Something clearly is," I say, burying my face in his chest, my entire body shaking. "I've never cried after sex before. And it's not like you hurt me, or I'm sad, I feel good. I'm happy."

"That's good," Adam says, rubbing my arm. "Happy and good is how I want you to feel."

"But then why am I crying like a lunatic if I'm happy, Adam?" I weep, a whirlwind of complicated emotions flooding my brain. "Did you break my brain? Or did you shake something loose?"

"No, Baby Girl," he chuckles softly into my hair. "I promise this is normal."

"This is not normal, Adam!" I shout into his chest.

"Rachel," he says, holding me tightly. "You have just done something completely new and slightly terrifying. You surrendered to the moment and allowed yourself to be naked emotionally. That's bound to trigger an emotional response, and sometimes that response is a few tears. So just take a few breaths, and find your center."

"This is embarrassing," I say, taking a deep breath. "I love sex. I've had a fair amount of it. I've never ended up a bumbling mess afterwards."

"Well, as I said, making love isn't just sex," he says, turning on his side to face me, stroking my hair behind my ear. "It's sex of the *soul*. And it can only truly happen when you have a real connection with someone."

I take another deep shaky breath, and then another, slowly feeling my elevated heart rate start to settle.

"For what it's worth," he says quietly. "That meant the world to me. And I enjoyed every second of it."

Oh wow...

"Even this?" I ask, sarcastically chuckling.

He smiles, and then leans in and kisses me.

"Especially this," he says against my swollen lips.

"Why?"

He looks down for a moment, his brow furrowing.

"Because I know vulnerability isn't easy for you," he says gently. "Anytime you let your guard down with me, whether it's talking to me about music, or even just falling apart in my arms, is a moment you're trusting me to protect your heart. And there's no greater compliment."

I stare at him, wondering if he's even real. And then, unable to stop myself, I lean in and kiss him softly.

"I suppose vulnerability isn't all bad," I say, settling back against the pillows. "And I guess love-making-sex wasn't as boring as I thought it would be."

He chuckles, kissing the top of my forehead, his fingers gently stroking the length of my arm.

"Sweetheart, nothing with you could ever be boring," he says sarcastically. "You're like adding kerosene to a forest fire."

"I'll take that as a compliment," I smile.

"You should," he smiles in return.

But then, it fades almost as quickly as it appeared, and he looks down at the small bit of distance between us.

Oh no...that can't be good.

"What is it?" I somehow manage to squeak out, my anxiety spiking once again.

"Rachel," he says, swallowing hard. "There's something I haven't told you."

"Worst. Sentence. Ever." I say, chuckling nervously.

"...And I feel like I owe you an apology."

"No, on second thought," I whisper, as all the air is sucked out of my lungs. "*That* is the worst sentence ever."

He smiles, but only in the polite way people do when they are trying to mask another emotion.

"I promised you that I would be honest with you, and I've kept that promise," he says slowly. "I want you to know who I am, where I've come from, and all the skeletons in my closet. Because I want no secrets with you."

"Nor I with you," I nod.

"But there's *one* skeleton we have yet to discuss," he says, closing his eyes. "One I've put off talking about, because, well...I was scared."

"Of?"

"Scared of scaring *you*," he whispers. "But I did plan to tell you, because I wanted you to know all the information before you..."

"Before I what?" I ask.

He sighs heavily, tapping his hand on the mattress and once again closing his eyes as if he's resigning himself to do something he really doesn't want to do.

I reach forward and gently place my hand on top of his, slowly stopping his nervous tapping.

"Adam," I say softly. "Hey, it's me, okay? Just talk to me, and whatever it is, we will...well, we will figure it out."

Whoa...now who sounds cheesy?

He looks up at me, his other hand gently touching my cheek.

"Do you know when I first knew I loved you?" He asks.

I shake my head.

"I knew I loved you, the night you interrupted my interrogation of Jaxon Pace," he scoffs quietly. "When I saw you standing there for the first time, after fearing the worst for months, I felt like I could finally breathe again. Like I could actually feel my dead heart practically come back to life."

Oh shit...

"And then when you left with him," he says, licking his lip and raising his brow. "Oh I was furious. And jealous. And heartbroken. Now, I'm not a therapist or some emotional expert or anything, but I'm smart enough to know that you can't feel heartbreak if you didn't first feel love. So that's when I knew it was real."

"But," I say softly. "We both still wanted each other. Even despite the lies, and the bullshit we had to sort through."

"True. But it was quite a pile of bullshit, and quite a hill to climb, and despite my irrational hope that we *could* make it, I wasn't sure that we *would*," he says. "And so being here in this house with you? And hearing you say that you love me? Well, fuck, that was just the best of everything."

I can't deny the smile tugging at the corners of my mouth.

...Even if I'm terrified of what he's about to tell me.

"But anyway," he breathes. "My point is, that in a perfect world, I would have told you this story, *before* you fell in love with me. I planned to do it that way. I just didn't think we'd..."

His voice trails off, but I know exactly what he means.

"No one could plan for this, Adam," I say softly. "Kerosene on a forest fire, remember?"

He snorts, and nods.

"I wanted to tell you this *first*, but I was too afraid," he says, sighing deeply. "Hell, I still fucking am."

"Well," I smirk, winking at him. "How about you stop being a pussy and just tell me what this final skeleton is, so that we can talk about it and move on?"

"Because that final skeleton," he whispers. "Belongs to my wife."

"What do you mean?" I ask, confused. "You told me that your wife died?"

"What I told you was true," Adam nods. "But I didn't tell you that *I* was the one who *killed* her."

CHAPTER THIRTY-TWO

ADAM

The look on Rachel's face is indescribable. It's almost as if she's experiencing too many emotions at the same time, and her face is just frozen.

"Your wife died…because you killed her," she repeats slowly. "And that's your final skeleton?"

Closing my eyes, I nod, taking a deep breath.

"It's the only thing I've been truly terrified to tell you about me, and my past," I whisper. "And, again, I don't want to ruin the mood, but I also don't want to wait any longer to tell you. Because you need to know."

Rachel says nothing, continuing just to stare at me.

"As I said," I say softly. "Ideally, I thought I would have more time to tell you, before we…well, before love was involved. But that's not how this worked out."

She sighs, looking down at our hands intertwined.

"I just have one question," she says quietly. "And I trust that you will be honest."

I nod once, my heart now pounding in my chest.

"Did you not tell me, on *purpose?*"

"No," I say firmly. "Again, the intention was always to tell you everything, but as you now know, there's a lot to this story, and we just haven't gotten to it yet."

She nods, seemingly chewing on her lip.

"But," I say, taking a deep breath. "I want to tell you now. I need to tell you. So that there aren't any feelings of secrecy or dishonesty. And before this goes any further."

"I mean, it's gone pretty far already," she says, raising a brow.

I can't reply. I can't even move.

Everything I've told her *has* been the truth, including my reasons for holding off. Yes, I was afraid, but I also needed her to know the whole story. What happened with my wife and I both was a long time coming, but also a shocking and horrifically unfortunate surprise. And the only possible shred of hope I have of Rachel understanding, is for her to learn all of it, in exactly the order I've told her.

However, I also know that if I lose her now, after everything we've been through together, it will crush me. Completely.

But I have to tell her.

It's now or never.

"I know," I finally choke out. "And I acknowledge that there's no easy way to tell you this, but there's also no other way for us to move forward another day in our relationship without it. And so, if you will allow me, I'd like to tell you now."

Rachel stares at me for a long moment before nodding her consent.

Hell, at least that's a start.

I take a deep breath.

"So, I've told you about how my work, and the casualties of that work, put a strain on our relationship. And I told you about how after the trauma, my wife started abusing various substances to cope with her anxiety, depression and loneliness. I also told you about how that led to my affair with Scarlett."

"You said that you paid dearly for it," Rachel whispers, her eyes flitting to the giant gas fireplace. "Did she find out?"

"No," I say, shaking my head. "But even still, the universe is rarely so lazy or unbalanced as to not deliver a bit of karma."

"What do you mean?"

"Guilt," I say, swallowing hard. "Turns out, no matter how

justified you think you might be in an action, and how convinced you are that no one will get hurt, they do. Especially when it comes to secrets. And dishonesty."

I sit up, positioning my back against the headboard as Rachel decides to flip around on the bed so that she's facing me.

"You see, because every action has a reaction. And they always have consequences."

"But you said that you didn't love Scarlett," Rachel says gently. "That the time you spent with her wasn't romantic, it was strictly therapy. And even I can understand that...sentiment. Sometimes sex is just sex."

"That's true," I nod. "But regardless if that time is simply a physical act or therapy, it's still *time*. At the end of the day, it was just more time spent away from Candace."

"But...you said that time away helped?"

"It helped *me*," I say. "But not Candace, who was already struggling with the amount of time I had to spend away for my work. And here I go, adding on additional time away, at a point in her life when perhaps she needed me the most."

"Ohh..." Rachel nods.

"Obviously it's not an exact science, but statistically, men cheat on their partners for the physical act of sex, or for the thrill of pursuit and conquest. Women, on the other hand, are more likely to cheat on their partners out of need or imbalance. They tend to only seek attention outside the home when they aren't getting it, or getting it in the way they need it, at home."

"Well," Rachel tucks a strand of her hair behind her ear, her eyes falling from mine. "I can certainly attest to that."

I nod gently.

"There's only so much anyone can take. And loneliness is brutal," I shrug. "In Candace's case, my absence, in a difficult point in her life made her lonely, which caused her to fuck other men. Men who were oftentimes the ones in possession and pushing her the substances she craved to cope with her day to day."

I swallow hard, the heaviness in my chest nearly suffocating me.

"So in a way, I guess you could say I indirectly had a hand in pushing her further into the arms of other men."

"No, Adam, you didn't," Rachel says, narrowing her eyes at

435

me. "I mean, I get what you're trying to say, and I know you are a man who takes responsibility for his actions. But when it comes to the breakdown of a relationship, it takes two for that. And believe me, I understand the headspace of a cheater, perhaps better than most. I'm not trying to step on any toes here, or disrespect your late spouse, but I made my choices. And so did your wife."

Even despite the uncomfortable subject material, I can't help but find Rachel's defensiveness at my own self-deprecation slightly adorable.

"I'm not disagreeing with you," I say gently. "I'm just saying I also made my own choices. And like I said, every action has a reaction. And every choice has a consequence. Right or wrong, black or white, our choices define us, and every selfish indulgence will eventually require its pound of flesh. Mine just came in the form of guilt."

"Guilt?"

I nod slowly, closing my eyes.

"Guilt is a mindfuck," I whisper, rubbing my chin. "I was already carrying baggage guilt over the home invasion long before I started having an affair. And even though, yes, my relationship with Scarlett carried no romantic or emotional attachment, that logic didn't exempt me from guilt. No matter how I tried to rationally reason away my sex-therapy sessions in Scarlett's dungeon, at the end of the day, it was wrong. Candace never would have approved, and I knew that, which is why I kept it a secret."

Rachel says nothing, looking down at her fingernails.

"However, where it really comes full circle," I scoff quietly. "Is that *because* of my own shame, I overlooked Candace's. Despite her drug use and blatant infidelity, I stayed with her. To me, it seemed like it was the universe's way of punishing me."

My throat closes around my words, knowing full well the impending pain and horror that I am about to unleash the moment I break the lock on my skeleton closet.

"But it *wasn't*," I whisper, closing my eyes. "You see, the scales always have to be balanced. And karma is very real. But in the end, the universe's actual punishment was so much worse than I ever could have imagined..."

"I think you're overreacting," Scarlett says, rolling her eyes and taking a bite of her hotdog. "I mean, so the new kid does a little hacking for fun on the side. What's the big deal? The guy works in *intelligence*, Adam. That's his job."

It's just after 11am, and the two of us sit in an old utility van outside of the New York Stock Exchange. We're currently fourteen hours into our stakeout of a suspected serial stockbroker murderer and have been discreetly following him to various parts of the city all morning. We were supposed to be relieved an hour ago by two other members of our team.

But they are *late*.

"Scar, the big deal is that the little shit is digging into the *personal* personnel files of people at the Bureau," I say, popping the last of my sausage into my mouth. "I mean, some of that shit is private for a reason. It's illegal for anyone to even look at it without permission. Best believe when I caught him doing it, I gave the fucker a piece of my mind."

"Which I'm sure went well," she says sarcastically, taking a swig of her orange soda. "Think of it this way, if he can get into it, then in theory anyone can. And if his job is to find leaks and holes in our *target's* security, why shouldn't he look for them in ours?"

Well...she has a point there.

"Seems to me the kid is just perfecting his craft," Scarlett continues. "And if anything, that's a work ethic *you* of all people should understand. Maybe cut the kid some slack."

"But that's just it," I say, shaking my finger. "He *is* just a kid. I don't even know his real name, because Roger only calls him by his callsign, which is only just encouraging that nonsense. So we're being asked to trust him, and accept him, but we know next to nothing about who he really is. I mean, can the little tyke even *drink* yet?"

"Who cares? It's not like you'd take him out for drinks anyway, Adam," She laughs, smacking her forehead in frustration. "Look, at the end of the day, he apparently went to a very good

437

school, and graduated early at the top of his class. From what I understand he was a bit of a prodigy. Which is probably why Central Intelligence picked him up."

"Right, but he wasn't there very long before he asked for a transfer? So, my question is why? What did he do wrong? Who did he fuck over?"

"Maybe he didn't do anything wrong though, Adam. Maybe he just wanted to see a little more *action*," she says, throwing her hands up in the air. "That job couldn't have been very exhilarating, and the kid probably just didn't want to sit behind a desk all day for the rest of his life."

"I don't know," I grunt, taking a drink of my sweet tea. "Those techy types make me suspicious."

"Well *I* like him," she shrugs. "Other than the fact that he stares at my tits a lot, he's really sweet. And regardless, Roger liked him, and he's part of our team now. So maybe instead of throwing this weird little hissy fit of yours, you should give him a chance. You know, you don't have to be distrusting of everyone, all the time, Adam."

"When you lived in a house with a serial killer for more than a decade," I say, shaking my head. "You're naturally distrusting of everyone, all the time."

Scarlett sighs, shaking her head.

I glance at my watch.

"So where the fuck is this little child prodigy?" I say, rubbing my eyes.

But no sooner do I say this however than the door to the van opens quickly, and in hops Ghostrider, and his partner Maverick, who is also a transfer from Central.

"Don't worry guys," he says jovially, making a finger gun. "I know who did it. It was Professor Plum, in the Library, with the candlestick."

"What?" Scarlett asks.

The fact that neither of us seemed to get his little joke, immediately makes him lose the smile on his face.

"Well, I just thought that…you know, since your name was Scarlett," he stumbles nervously. "You know, *Miss Scarlett*? From that old movie *Clue*?"

"Oh my fucking God," I sigh, rubbing my eyes and shaking my head at Scarlett. "Please tell me he did not just say that…"

'What?" He asks, confused.

"Kid," Scarlett snaps firmly. "We've both been on this stakeout for more than half a day, tracking his little worm all over the city. He's slipperier than a motherfucker, never staying anywhere for very long. So I suggest you get your head in the game before we miss him getting into his car, or calling a cab, because then all of this will have been for nothing."

"No it won't."

"Excuse me?" Scarlett whispers terrifyingly. "What did you just say to me?"

"I just said no, it won't," Ghostrider replies.

I glare at him in the rearview mirror.

"If you don't hit him," I growl looking at her. "I will."

"No, no!" He says, waving his hands defensively. "This morning after you guys tracked him to that nice little brunch place down on fifth? That place is delish by the way, they have really good avocado toast, but I prefer the eggs benedict myself, but with the applewood bacon instead of the cana—"

"Get to the point," Scarlett snaps.

"Sorry," he chuckles nervously. "Anyway, I had Mav here corner the waiter who took the perps credit card, and I slipped this sexy little tracking sticker on the back. So as long as the guy takes his wallet, we will be able to track him wherever!"

Both Scarlett and I sit here in silence, absolutely stunned.

If I'm honest, that *is* a bit impressive. But, I'm still suspicious of the little wankstain, and not about to give him any praise.

However, Scarlett does.

"Wow," she says, raising her brows with a nod. "That's pretty cool, Kid, I gotta say."

"Thanks!"

"Well, Adam," she says, turning to me. "What do you say we let these little rockstars take over, and you and I take their car and go home? They seem to have things under control, and I am in need of a long ass nap."

But being the protocol junkie that I am, I'm opening my mouth to say something about how they probably just violated a bunch of rules of engagement as well as suspects right to due process, when I feel my phone vibrating in my pocket.

As I pull it out, I realize that it's the number for my boy's school, and suddenly I have an uncomfortable feeling.

"Give me the keys to the Sed," I say, holding out my hand. The guy in the back, Ghostrider's nearly-silent partner, Maverick immediately puts the keys in my palm.

I grab my bag off the floor, and hop out, simultaneously answering the call.

"This is Adam Westwood," I say politely, walking towards the unmarked beige sedan.

"Oh! Hello there Mr. Westwood!" A very chirpy and bubbly woman says on the other end of the phone. "This is Principal Stevens, how are you today?"

"Fine," I grumble, yanking the driver's side door open and watching as Scarlett follows after me, motioning for me to pop the trunk.

"That's great!" Principle Stevens says into the phone as I start the engine. "Well, I was just calling to see how Andrew and Malcolm were doing."

Scarlett climbs in beside me, and I put the phone on speaker phone.

"Um," I scoff, rolling my eyes to Scar and pointing at the phone. "I assume they're fine. But I'd also assume you'd know better than me, as they attend *your* school."

"Well, that's just it Mr. Westwood, and why I'm calling you," The Principal says politely. "The boys missed school Monday and Tuesday, and we haven't been able to reach your wife, so I figured I would reach out to you."

"What?" I freeze, my stomach immediately twisting.

"Yes, Sir," The Principal continues. "I was personally overseeing the pickup lane on Friday, and I do remember talking with Candace for a minute, but neither of the boy's teachers have seen them since then, so we were just a little concerned."

"I'm sure everything is fine," I say, more to myself than to the woman on the phone. "Let me call my wife."

Without waiting for the Principal to respond, I end the call. Immediately dialing Candace.

But she doesn't answer.

"Come on, answer," I sigh, frustrated.

"Is she…?" Scarlett asks gently, not needing to infer further.

"Who the fuck knows," I groan, as the second call rings out once again with no answer. "It's not the first time she's gotten fucked up on a weekday, but the last time she at least arranged for a neighbor to take the kids to school."

Realizing how ridiculous that statement is only makes me angrier, as I try to dial Candace's parent's house, knowing that if she was planning on getting high, or going out, that's the first place she would have taken the kids.

"Shit, I just remembered Tom and Ronnie are in Aspen until Friday," I say, ending that call before dialing Candace again.

Pulling up the tracking app I secretly installed on Candace's device, I show that her phone is still at the house.

Well, that's good at least.

However, the fact that she is home, and she isn't answering, is a bit concerning for me. When I spoke to her late Monday night, she sounded a little drunk, but she wasn't slurring her words or anything.

Did she get high? Did she overdose? Did she get drunk and hurt herself and is unable to do anything with two young kids?

"Come on Cici, answer the fucking phone," I growl.

"I'm sure everything is fine," Scarlett says, trying to calm me down.

"Everything's not fine!" I snap at her. "You know, I put up with a lot of shit, and if she wants to fuck up her own life, I've already learned I can't stop her. But you don't go keeping the kids out of school because you're too fucked up to take them."

"Are we sure she's at home?"

"According to the app, her phone is at least."

"Do you want me to call the police?" she asks, not responding to my anger the way she usually does. "Have someone go over there to check on her and the kids?"

"No, if she is fucked up, that's the last thing I need is a police report and all that mess."

When I try her two more times and she doesn't answer I slam the phone down on the counsel. Scarlett rolls her window down and grabs the portable police light from the glove box.

"Just drive," Scarlett says, reaching out the window and putting it on top of the car. "If you hurry we can be there in forty minutes."

"I still have to take you back to your—"

"Adam, your kids are more important so just drive the fucking car," she snaps, buckling her seatbelt. "Just don't kill us on the way there."

And without another word I press the pedal to the floor and merge us onto the freeway.

In total, the drive took us thirty-eight minutes and some change. I spent the entire time still trying to call Candace while also reminding myself that if something truly bad had happened, like a fire, I would have known about it much sooner. And thankfully, when I pull down my street, nothing seems out of the ordinary.

The quiet little suburb looks as normal as it usually does around lunchtime. Mr. Jenkins the retired Vietnam veteran on the corner is out edging his lawn like he always does on Wednesdays, and Suzanne Waters, the stay-at-home mom is supervising her toddler twins playing in the sprinkler.

And when I pull up in my driveway, it looks exactly like the way I left it four days ago when they sent Scar and I out on this latest assignment.

I turn to her, trying to figure out what to say.

"Look, Scar, I—"

"I'm fine waiting here," she says softly. "I know. Just go."

I nod, before yanking the door open and bounding up the steps. Trying the door, I find it unlocked.

That seems suspicious, given her inherent fear of home invasion ever since the incident.

Wonder if she had company?

"Candace?" I say, walking in the door. "Hey, Candace!"

Realizing that I don't know what has gone on in my house, or who is inside of it, I take the precaution of making sure that my gun is accessible.

"Cici! Honey, are you here?" I shout.

The living room curtains are drawn and the TV is on. A pizza box sits on the couch cushions and a half-eaten slice is wrapped in a napkin atop the coffee table. The receipt is from yesterday, and the pizza is pepperoni, mushroom, and black olive, which is Candace's favorite. On the end table farthest from me is a plate of old dinosaur chicken nuggets and ketchup.

They've been here recently.

"Candace!" I shout again, clearing the kitchen and dining room quickly before making my way to the bedroom.

There's a weird smell lingering in the hallway, but it's hard to place. It almost smells like burnt plastic, or gasoline, or maybe it's bleach? However, there isn't a surface in this house that looks like it's been cleaned.

Well, at least since *I* picked up the house as best I could, right before leaving last week.

That's odd...

Pushing open our bedroom door, I find that the television is on in there as well, but no one is around. The bed is unmade, and the room is cluttered with piles of laundry, bills, and discarded water bottles, along with the faint but distinct scent of cigarettes. The room is a mess, far worse than my usually clean wife would've typically allowed.

If she was sober that is.

"Andy? Malcolm?" I call, swiftly moving on to the boy's room. "You guys here? Daddy's home!"

But there's no reply. Their room is empty, and their beds are unmade, and upon closer inspection I see both of their Toy Story matching backpacks discarded under some toys in the corner. Knowing that it was unlikely both of my children, who were so excited about their new backpacks, would have left them at home, it's clear to me that my kids are *not* at school.

"Candace! Andy! Malcolm!" I shout, again, checking the bathroom. "Is anyone here?!"

"Adam?"

I'm just about to head over to the garage to see if she's in there, when I suddenly hear my wife faintly call my name from our bedroom. Immediately I turn and race backwards, pushing open the door and walking around the bed.

That's where I found my wife.

She's lying on her side, on the floor, next to a pile of vomit.

"Candace!" I gasp, rushing down to her. "Are you okay? Jesus fucking Christ, what the hell happened?"

"Hi, Adam, your home," She groggily smiles up at me, adjusting her tank top and brushing her disheveled hair aside. "That's nice. I knew you'd come home soon."

"Yeah, I'm here, Baby," I say, gently pulling her upright. "Did

443

you fall? Are you hurt? Are you sick? Did you…"

However, it's at this exact moment when I notice the orange pill bottle underneath her. A bottle with two cigarettes inside that appear to be stained…or *wet*. It takes my FBI Agent brain less than five seconds to identify *why* those cigarettes are in that bottle, and why they look that way.

…They have been dipped in PCP.

The latest wave of drug busts happening in several states along the east coast involves dealers selling what they call *fry*, which are cigarettes dipped in PCP, formaldehyde, and other various chemicals. My suspicions are confirmed when I grab the bottle and pop it open, the smell of ammonia fills my nostrils, nearly making me dizzy.

I cough, slamming the lid back down and shaking it angrily in Candace's face.

"What the fuck is this?!" I shout at her, watching as she flinches away from me. "Is this fucking *PCP*?!"

I yank her up on her feet, seating her on the bed.

"You have to be kidding me right now!" I thunder, staring down at the bottle in my hand. "Please tell me this is a joke. Oh God, please tell me this is a joke, and you're not honestly doing this shit right in our home, where we live with our goddamn kids?!"

"I…I…" she mumbles, still clearly inebriated.

"Do you realize I could lose my job over this Candace? Having this shit in my fucking house?!" I shout at her. "Or that we could lose our kids?! Have you ever thought about *that*?"

"N…no…" she whispers.

"Where did you get it?"

"I don't know," she says sheepishly.

"You don't know," I snort, sarcastically, rubbing my chin, my rage building. "You really expect me to believe that?"

"Yeah, I don't know how that got there. That's not mi—"

"Oh, I see, it's not *yours* huh?!" I snap. "So if I make you go in that bathroom, and take a drug test right now, it's not going to show that you're doing PCP in my fucking house?!"

"Adam, honey," she chuckles nervously, her eyes still rolling around in her head. "I'm good, I promise."

"You want me to believe you're *sober*?!" I laugh viciously. "You're honestly trying to say that to me, right now? While I'm holding your fucking drugs in my goddamn hand?!"

"Well…I *was* sober," she says slowly, her eyes drooping.

"Yeah? So where are my fucking kids, Candace?" I snap. "Where's Andy and Malcolm, huh?"

"The boys? They are…they are at school."

"You sure about that, Cici?"

"Yes, of course, Adam," she says, waving me off. "It's a fucking school day."

"You know, babe," I say, clicking my tongue. "On that you're correct. Okay then, *Supermom*, how about you answer this riddle for me? Tell me why Principal Stevens called me today, on a school day, to ask me why my kids are *not* in school?"

"What?"

"Yuppp!" I snap sarcastically. "And you know what else she told me? She said that no one at the school had seen the boys since you picked them up on *Friday*. So, do you want to try that bullshit answer again, champ? Or do you want to tell me where the hell my kids are?"

My patience for this game is over, and a very real fear has set in, not knowing where my boys are.

"They are in school, Adam," she says indignantly. "I took them this morning."

"Candace…"

"Okay look, I kept them home Monday, because I forgot my alarm," she says defensively. "And Tuesday, I just wasn't feeling well enough to drive, and the neighbors weren't home–"

Fuck this bullshit.

"Where are my damn boys?!" I thunder, making her jump.

My heart races as a thousand thoughts, none of them pleasant, start flashing rapidly in my head about where in the world my two young sons could be.

"I'm telling you, Adam!" She yells at me. "They are in school. I took them myself."

"You took them *where*, Candace?! You're so fucked up, how the hell did you drive anywhere?!"

"Well, I was sober enough to drive *then*," she says, rolling her eyes. "I'm not perfect but I think I know when I'm safe to drive."

"Clearly not!" I snap. "So they aren't here, and they aren't at school, and I know they aren't at your parents house because they are in Aspen. So where they fuck are they Candace?!"

"I...I..." she says, rubbing her head.

"Adam?" I hear Scarlett knock loudly on the front door and hear it swing open. "Is everything okay? I could hear the shouting from the car?"

Shit. I don't want her to see this fucking mess.

"Oh my God, is someone here?!" My wife whispers frantically, her eyes wide as she feebly attempts to stand up. "Is it the cops?! Do we need to run?!"

"It's just Scarlett, she came with me," I hiss. "And no, we're not going anywhere until you tell me where the boys are."

"Adam?" Scarlett calls again. "Are you good?"

"I'm in here," I shout. "I've found Candace, but she's..."

I pause, closing my eyes and gritting my teeth together, embarrassed for what I'm about to say.

"She's here, and she's high out of her fucking mind," I say bitterly. "But Andy and Malcolm aren't here, and she's saying she doesn't know where they are."

"Oh shit!" Scarlett gasps.

"That's not what I said!" Candace snaps at me, hitting me on the arm. "Look, I've already told you a dozen times that they are at *school*! I drove the kids to school and then, yeah, maybe I came back here and got a little fucked up, okay? So the fuck what? What's the big deal?"

It takes everything in my power not to react.

I'm so sick of having these cyclical conversations with my dishonest, unfaithful, addict of a wife. I just want to put my head through the wall.

...Or at least my fist.

However, despite my rage, I know that Candace won't tell me if she thinks I'm going to be upset.

I have to calm down and try and get her to tell me the truth.

Because as of right now, my kids are missing and she is the only person who knows where the hell they are.

"The *big deal*, Honey," I whisper venomously, putting my hands on the bed, pinning her between them. "Is that you *didn't* take them to school."

"But I did–

"No you didn't," I say quietly, my tone dark. "I know you didn't, because the school called me today. And the Principal told me that Andy and Malcolm were *not* there. And unlike you, I know that the school doesn't have a reason to lie to me."

"Wait," she says, twitching anxiously. "The school called *you*? And they said the boys aren't there?"

I feel my diplomacy evaporate.

Fuck this shit.

My kids aren't here. I have no idea where they are. And so I have no way of knowing if they are in danger, and it's killing me inside.

"Where the fuck are my boys Candace?!" I shout, grabbing her by the shoulders. "Tell me where my fucking kids are or I swear to God I will call the cops and having your ass arrested for drug use, possession, and child fucking endangerment!"

"I dropped them off! At school I don't know!" She shouts, shoving me away from her. "I remember putting them in the car and driving them to school! I know I did! If they aren't there then…"

"I'm warning you, Candace," I growl, grabbing my phone from my pocket. "I'm done play–".

"Adam? Hey Adam!" Scarlett suddenly calls from the other room. "You might want to come see this."

"Give me a minute," I shout down the hallway before turning back to my wife on the bed.

"Cici" I spit. "Where are my kids? Where is the last place you know you remember *seeing* them?"

"In. The. Car." Candace snips at me. "I keep saying that and you're not listening. "I know that I put them in the car to take them to school!"

"Fine," I snap, pulling out my phone. "Have it your way. I'm done with this shit. Enjoy fucking prison."

"No!" Candace wails, feverishly trying to swat the phone from my hands.

"Adam!" Scarlett calls again, this time more urgently. "Get in here!"

"I said I need a fucking second, Scar!" I shout back, unable to keep my rage out of my tone, as I hold my phone away from Candace, who still attempts to grab it.

"Fuck that, get in here!" Scarlett snaps, and I hear banging around in the kitchen.

Goddamnit! What the fuck could she possibly need?!

But the moment I turn to walk into the hallway, my wife

immediately makes a dash for the window, clumsily trying to pop out the screen and climb out.

"What the fuck do you think you're doing?!" I shout at her, whipping out my handcuffs. "You're not going anywhere until we get to the bottom of this!"

"Adam, no, please!" She tries to protest, attempting to stand, but then nearly falling off the bed. "I don't want to go to jail!"

Quickly and professionally, I slap my first set of handcuffs on my wife's wrists before using my second set to secure her to the bedpost at the end of the bed.

"What are you doing?!" She screams, thrashing around violently, trying to kick me. "Adam?! Adam!"

In this moment, I don't even know what to think. This woman looks nothing like the woman I love. Not even anything like the woman I married. She looks unhealthy and unhinged. She's gone crazy, kicking and thrashing around, and screaming like a wild animal the moment I put the cuffs on her.

Jesus Christ.

"Adam! Get the fuck in here now!" Scarlett shouts at the top of her lungs. "Something is wrong!"

Scarlett's tone causes my attention to shift, and I bolt to the kitchen, where I find my visibly distressed partner pressing her head against the kitchen door that leads into the garage.

"Come here! Listen to this," she says, pointing to the door. "Does it sound like her car is running?!"

"What? Scar, what the hell are you talking about?" I ask, rolling my eyes. "Look, I'm not trying to be a dick but I'm dealing with a situation with my wife and I don't know where my fucking kids are and I—

"Adam, it sounds like her goddamn car is *running*!" Scarlett snaps, pounding on the door. "Doesn't it smell fucking weird in here to you? I noticed it as soon as I walked in. It smells like—"

"...*Exhaust*," I breathe, the scent now filling my nostrils.

Suddenly an extremely sickening thought hits me like a freight train, and my instantly stomach twists.

"I remember putting them in the car…"

My wife's repeated, confusing statements come flooding back to me as my stomach plummets straight through the floor.

Oh my God…No.

"I can't get it open because she has this fucking thing!"

Scarlett grunts, using her hand to flick the heavy bolt lock at the top of the door, an addition Candace insisted upon when we moved in. "Is there a key around here somewhere? Or do you have bolt cutters?!"

It can't be. It just can't. Please God. No.

"I...I..." I mumble, my brain starting to spin.

"Oh God you don't think that..." Scarlett's voice fades off.

No. That's just not...possible. There's no way.

But now, looking frantically around the filthy house I know that even if the key is likely around here somewhere, we are never going to find it quickly.

I turn and immediately run out the front door, racing around to the garage with Scarlett behind me.

Together the two of us lift the heavy garage door by hand, as the smell of exhaust and carbon monoxide from Candace's still-running SUV pours out in the driveway before the two of us can even push the door all the way up.

God please...let me be wrong.

Covering my mouth, I rush over to the car, but the moment I do, I am met with my living *nightmare*.

Because right there, buckled into the backseat, my two beautiful boys...are both *dead*.

"So that's the whole truth?" Roger sighs, as he stands in my living room, running his hand over his head.

I hear him ask the question, but I can't respond.

Andrew Scott Westwood is dead.

"Yes, Sir," Scarlett replies for me.

"Have you called or told anyone else?"

Again, I can't respond.

Malcolm Everett Westwood is dead.

"No, Sir," Scarlett replies for me once again.

"Alright," he sighs. "By all accounts, you know what should be done here, but I...well, I guess part of me can understand."

He looks around for a moment before cursing under his breath and running his hand over his head.

I know he's talking about whether or not he should call the police, and make me turn myself in. But I don't care. About a single goddamn thing.

My boys are dead.

"Since you called me, instead of the police, we are going to discuss this one time, and one time only. Then you two are going to do exactly what I say," Roger says quietly. "And if either of you ever try to rat each other out, or rat *me* out, for what we are about to do, I swear I will deny everything, and you both will spend the rest of your lives rotting in the worst prison in the United States. Do you understand?"

"Yes Sir," Scarlett nods.

My boys are dead.

"We need to work quickly. Get the scene set and then we need to get our stories straight, establish your alibis and make the appropriate phone calls to local police," he sighs. "When they show up, I'll arrive with Scarlett. You'll say that you called me when you happened on the scene, and you'll let me do the talking. I'll handle the rest on my end, so we can make sure things go the way we want them to."

My boys are dead.

He walks over to me, and places his hand on my shoulder.

"I wish there was anything I could say to make this better for you," he says quietly. "But I can't. I know that you, and Candace, suffered a lot for this department, so the least I can do is make it suffer a bit less for you. Will you allow me to do that?"

My eyes find his.

"Will you allow me to help you, son?" Roger asks.

"Son."

I had a son.

Infact, I had two.

Two beautiful sons. That are now dead.

…And so am I. There is nothing left of me anymore.

"Yes, Sir," I say quietly, uttering my first words since I cradled both of my dead sons in my arms.

And right before I shot my drug addicted wife in the head.

"I need you to realize and accept you're not going to like anything I'm about to say to you," he says firmly. "We need to set the scene and make this look like this was some form of a retribution killing, at least on the surface. It's *your* job to keep your emotions under control until the eye of the storm has passed. Now I need to know, before we start damage control, do you think you can do that?"

Can I do that?

My sons are dead.

My wife is dead.

My brother is dead.

My parents are dead.

Can I shut off my emotions and feel nothing at all?

Of course I can. After all, I have nothing. And no one left.

"Yes, Sir," I reply, feeling the last of my emotions leave my body, certain that I will never feel anything, ever again.

I sit on the bed at Valentine Manor, unable to move. I can feel the tears on my cheeks, and wonder when was the last time I actually cried about this.

"Your boss helped you cover it up," Rachel says quietly.

"Yes, he did," I whisper. "Best case, I tell myself that he wanted to keep me out of jail because he harbored some sliver of emotion for me."

I wipe my eyes.

"But," I sigh. "Some part of me always wondered if he only did it because he didn't want to lose me, or get any of the bad press on the team he was running. After all, they looked really sloppy at this point. And if he lost me, he knew he'd also be losing Scarlett too, she made that abundantly clear when she called him right after I...shot my wife."

Rachel lowers her eyes to her hands in her lap.

"So that's what happened," I say quietly. "It was classified as a triple homicide, and blamed on some non-existent drug kingpin that my wife was involved with outside of my knowledge. We held a funeral, and regardless of whether or not I liked it, life moved on."

"Do you...*regret* killing Candace?" Rachel asks.

I stare at her, swallowing hard.

"Truthfully? I don't know. Some days, no, I don't. But I've

learned since I lost my boys that death is a mercy. Living on the other hand is much harder than dying. And I think in some ways, when I walked into that room and fired that bullet, I put Candace out of her misery…and put myself in it," I say darkly. "So, yes, if I could go back I would make a different choice at that moment. I'd choose to send my wife to suffer in jail, living with the consequences of her actions…The same way I've had to live with them."

Silence settles over the room, as Rachel wipes her eyes, and crosses her arms across her body.

"The only real regret I have is that I didn't do what was best for me and my boys, and leave," I say, closing my eyes. "I should've done that before it was too late. But I just…loved her. So fucking much. I loved her past the point where it was healthy to love another human being."

I look down at my hands in my lap, flashbacks of pulling my son's lifeless bodies from the backseat of Candace's car playing in my mind.

"Sometimes I hate myself for not seeing this coming," I whisper. "But then again, how can you imagine the mother of your children doing something like this? You can't. You simply just can't."

"No," Rachel says gently. "You can't."

"I should've left," I whisper. Shaking my head. "Things weren't getting better, they were getting worse. I was being delusional, thinking we could work through it. But I should've fucking left. If I had, who knows what would've happened to Candace. But I know that at least my boys would still be alive. I'd make sure of it. And that's the shit that wakes me up in the middle of the night, like a knife straight through my heart."

My eyes wander to her face, staring at me with some pitiful mixture of empathy and sorrow, while the firelight flickers in the background.

"But that's it," I whisper. "That's the very last skeleton in the very last of my closets. I can now safely say that you know every single dirty disgusting and disturbing detail about my life."

Rachel nods slowly.

Part of me would give anything to be able to read her mind right now. But the rest of me is terrified to do so, and see the way she must see me now. Perhaps as nothing more than a wife-killer, and father who wasn't there for his kids when they needed him.

My stomach twists, and finding it near impossible to handle the suspense of what she's going to decide to do, after hearing all of this, I decide to make it easier on her.

"Look," I say quietly. "If you don't feel comfortable sleeping in the same bed as me, I'm happy to sleep in another room. Or if you want me to go, then I—"

"Adam," Rachel says, inhaling sharply. "I actually already *knew* this story."

"What?"

She nods.

"When you took Jaxon back to the warehouse to be interrogated, his men, and Natalie, came to me asking for my help in finding you," she says slowly. "I guess it all ended up being some bet between Jaxon and Charlie, about whether I would help find him, but yeah. Anyway, when all this was going down, they told me about how you had killed your wife."

Holy. Shit.

"But, at the time, I just assumed they were saying that to sway my decision, or maybe that they were just saying to make me not trust you."

I can't reply. I can barely breathe. My mind is spinning.

She already knew.

"But…I did trust you," she says, looking at me. "Even before I knew the reason *why*, I knew who you were as a man. And I trusted that you weren't someone just going around abusing women, or being violent for no reason."

"But…then why didn't you tell me?" I ask quietly. "Back at the motel, you *asked* me about her?"

"Because, like you said to me, I knew it needed to come from you," she says, her eyes finding mine. "And I knew it needed to come on your terms when you were ready to tell me."

All I can do is stare at her.

"So no," she says, sitting up on the bed and moving closer to me, cupping my face with her hands. "I don't need you to go anywhere or be anywhere but right here with *me*."

She kisses me again, and this time I pull her into my arms, and lay her down across the mattress.

This moment isn't sexual, but rather sweet and tender. The very thing I've been the most afraid of telling Rachel, is something she's already accepted about me. And despite being thoroughly convinced that I'd never find love or happiness ever again, because I couldn't possibly deserve them, somehow, I find them both. Right here in her arms.

"I love you," I whisper against her lips. "And yes, I know, I've probably said that a lot in the last few hours, but I don't give a flying fuck."

"I love you too," she whispers back.

"Maybe we should get some sleep?"

"Yeah…" she says slowly, but all of a sudden, her eyes fall from mine, and she bites her bottom lip.

"What?" I ask, gently lifting her chin to face me. "What's wrong?"

"It's nothing," she says, shaking her head.

But I'm not buying it.

"I'd say we're well past that now, wouldn't you?" I ask, raising my brow, and gently rubbing my thumb along her cheek. "Talk to me."

"Well, I know it's late and all. Err, *early*, I suppose," she says, taking a deep breath. "But I guess I was just wondering that since you shared *your* last skeleton, if perhaps I should share mine too?"

"You mean, that you have something you're afraid of telling me too?" I ask.

She closes her eyes, nodding once and pressing her lips together.

"Fair warning, it's a bit longer than your story was."

"It's okay, babe," I say, leaning in and kissing her slowly. "I've got nothing but time, so I'm ready when you are."

CHAPTER THIRTY-THREE

Rachel

The first few months after Jessica was born were incredibly difficult for us as a couple.

After Ismena died, Dimitris fell into a depression, and had regressed far from the benevolent Don Supreme he had once been. His suspicious death had left the syndicate in a place of confusion and turmoil, and had left Jaxon in charge of sorting it all out.

But not everyone was keen to just accept Jaxon as the Don. He might've been the heir apparent, but he was the youngest Don Supreme in the syndicate's history. And after having the prospect of a champion competition dangled in front of them, some of the other dons set out to test him, deliberately causing chaos, and brashly thinking that Jaxon wouldn't risk responding harshly so soon after taking power.

But they were *wrong*.

Similarly, to his response to my assault, Jaxon's response was swift, and vicious. He used these bad actors to send a message to the rest of the syndicate that mercy was not his first impulse, and if you crossed him…you would die. Screaming.

And they did.

When he could, he'd try to spend time with our daughter, but between building his successful hotel business, as well as trying to manage the Mafia's business, Jaxon's hours spent at home became less and less frequent.

And while I no longer had to deal with the uncomfortable forced proximity to his parents, I still hated the cold and increasingly lonely hallways of Pace Manor that had never felt like home to me. So I chose to spend most of my time at my condo with Jess and the kids.

I somehow managed to get Jaxon's blessing to work the bar at this up-and-coming BDSM club called the Apparatus Room.

Well, actually, it *wasn't* somehow.

I caught him cheating on me with some red-headed high-society trust-fund slut from uptown. And wouldn't you, *somehow*, that bitch ended up falling down a flight of stairs and breaking her ankle.

After getting my revenge, I leveraged their affair to get what I truly wanted out of Jaxon, which for me, was being able to go back to work. He reluctantly agreed, as long as I only worked behind the bar, with absolutely no exceptions to this rule.

It was as fair of a compromise as I would get from Jaxon.

I wish I could say that catching him cheating was the end of our relationship, but it wasn't. Of course it fucking wasn't.

No matter how much I hated it, or even *him* at times, my love for Jaxon kept me tethered to him. Our relationship became nothing more than a cruel and repetitive cycle of devilish Deja vu.

He'd cheat, and then I'd cheat to make him jealous. Then we'd break up, make up, and wake up to do it all over again.

Sometimes, depending on the offense, there might be lavish gifts involved in his apologies too. Such as in the case of the trust-fund cunt, he bought me a brand-new car as part of his apology. Not that I needed one, as Jaxon had permanently assigned me a bodyguard to make sure that I was safe…or perhaps to babysit me at work.

While I wanted to be strong enough *not* to take him back, on some level, I told myself that it wasn't necessarily *him* making these poor decisions, but rather the copious amounts of booze and stimulants he was taking to try and keep up with his ever-increasing workload.

But even still, one thing was clear. My limit for his bullshit *was* waning.

Which is why, at one of my postpartum appointments with my doctor, I made a massive decision without telling him:

I had my fucking tubes tied.

I knew he'd be furious if he found out, but I also knew Jaxon would never consider a vasectomy. And at some point soon, his Don brain would start kicking into high gear, and he'd start wanting to try again...for a *son*.

But I wasn't going to be just another baby-making machine for the Mafia.

Only Jess knew about my decision, and she helped me to and from my appointment, running interference so that my glorified "bodysitter" Max didn't ask too many questions while I was recovering from the sedation.

I figured that at some point, Jaxon would either discover the truth, or at the very least, decide to quit waiting around for my acceptance of his proposal. At which point he would probably marry someone more inclined to ignore his indiscretions and willing to give him a gaggle of kids.

Maybe then, my daughter and I would be free. And if he did knock up some more pliable broad, maybe he would not only let us leave town but maybe even help us disappear so that we could have some semblance of a normal life, instead of one permanently yoked to the Mafia.

One way or another, I was determined to eventually regain some of my independence back, someday, in some way.

But that day was far off.

For now, however, I was stuck in Jaxon's orbit, emotionally and physically, forced to live my life according to *his* desires, and his schedule.

A schedule that is getting increasingly difficult to accommodate. Or anticipate.

For example, on the day of our daughter's six-month checkup, we'd planned to attend the appointment together, and then Jaxon offered to take me to an early dinner before he had to attend one of his investor functions.

However, on the morning of her appointment, an hour before he was supposed to come and get me, he called to tell me that something was wrong in some contract his lawyers had proposed, and he wouldn't be able to make it. He asked me to reschedule it, but I declined.

I told him, albeit a bit *icily*, that the doctor was booked four months in advance, and despite Jaxon's insistence that they would assuredly move stuff around for *him,* reminded him that I was fully capable of attending her doctors appointments on my own, as I had already been doing it for most of my pregnancy anyway. Then I hung up.

He called a few times, apologizing and insisting he would come by after the function ended, but I just ignored him.

It ended up being a bit of a blessing, as by 4pm, I already had a throbbing headache, and was grateful that I could just have Max take me home.

However, just as I go to put my key in the lock, I hear what sounds like a scream come from inside the apartment.

"Max!" I shout down the hall, where my bodyguard sits in his designated chair. "Come quick!"

"Miss Valentine, wait!" Max shouts, bolting toward me. "Let me go first!"

But I don't listen, and instead, yank open the door.

"Shh, baby, why are you being so difficult?" A man's voice sounds from the living room.

"I said get the fuck off me, you creep!!" I hear Mandy shout, as something goes tumbling to the floor in the middle of the living room.

"Mandy?!" I shout, storming into the living room, with Max hot on my heels, pushing himself in front of me.

But that's when I see *Eamon West* standing there, holding Mandy around the waist, pinning her on his lap. He releases her the moment he makes eye contact with Max and I.

"Hello there, Rachel," he says, adjusting his shirt.

"What the fuck are you doing in my goddamn condo?" I hiss, pulling Mandy to me and putting myself in front of her. 'How did you even get in here?"

"Jess let me in," he says, shooting a glance at Mandy. "She just had to run down to the store real quick."

"She left you alone with her *minor* daughter, in my apartment?"

I say, crossing my arms across my body. "I highly doubt that."

"Your place huh? Guess it pays to get knocked up by Jaxon Pace," he points to my stroller. "Is that the little wonder?"

He takes a step toward us, but Max immediately steps between us, his towering frame practically engulfing Eamon's.

"That being said," Eamon says, sneering up at Max. "Suppose it is nicer than that cockroach infested place you guys used to have. You know, back when it was just my *patronage* paying most of your rent. Seems you've upgraded, honey."

"Oh, I was always above the likes of you," I spit. "And now, since it is my place, I don't even *have* to tolerate you being around. So you can either let your trash ass out yourself, or I can have Max here give you an express ticket to the first floor...out the fucking window."

"Don't worry," he says, throwing up his hands. "I'm happy to see myself out. Do give Jess my best."

Oh believe me, I will be having a fucking word with Jess.

Eamon chuckles, and heads for the door, opening and closing it loudly behind him, deliberately waking up my sleeping daughter. Once he's gone, Max turns to me.

"I'll be just down the hall, Miss Valentine," he says politely. "And I'll be sure he makes it out of the building."

"Thanks," I nod.

After Max leaves I immediately turn to Mandy.

"Are you okay?" I ask.

"Yeah, I'm fine," she says, wiping her eyes. "I don't know what the heck happened, but I was just watching TV with him and my mom before she said she suddenly had to go to the store. And the minute she left, he just pounced on me. But you walked in right after, so that's good."

"He's a pig," I say, stroking her hair. "I'm sorry you had to deal with that. Are you hungry? Do you want me to make you something to eat?"

She shakes her head.

"No thanks. But do you want me to take her?" Mandy says, pointing to the stroller. "Ivy is still down for a nap, I could put Jessica down too if you want."

"Sure, but only if you're feeling up to it," I say, tucking her pretty blonde hair behind her ear.

She nods, a smile skirting across her face as she takes the

crying baby from the stroller. However, the moment Mandy pulls her into her arms, Jessica stops crying.

"You know," I say, smiling at her. "You're pretty good with babies. I think she likes you better than me. You'll make a really good mom someday. I mean, if you want to be a mom that is."

"Aunt Rachel!" She teases, rolling her eyes.

"Hey you never know!" I shrug.

Walking into the kitchen I pull one of the premade bottles of breastmilk I'd pumped from the fridge and hand it to her.

"Well, I want to go to medical school before I start thinking of babies," she says, kissing the now smiling baby Jessica on the cheek. "So I don't know. I guess we'll see one day."

"That's a good plan, kid," I say, watching my daughter giggle as Mandy blows raspberries on her belly. "I have no doubt you'll figure it out."

She gives it to the baby and carries her down the hallway to the nursery, where Mandy's sister Ivy sleeps. It takes less than twenty minutes for Jessica to go down for her nap, and for the teen to retreat into her bedroom.

However, it takes nearly a full hour and a half for Jessica to return from the store. When she does, she nearly has a heart attack when she sees me sitting on the couch, in the dark.

"Jesus Christ, Rachel!" Jess exclaims, pressing her hand to her chest and collapsing back against the door frame. "You scared the shit out of me."

"Oh? Why's that?"

"Well, I just wasn't expecting to see anyone," she says, coming inside and closing the door. "I apologize, I thought you were supposed to be at dinner with Jaxon tonight?"

"It was canceled," I say, narrowing my eyes at her. "But I guess I'm confused, because even if I wasn't here until later, wouldn't you *still* be expecting to see someone here on this couch? Exactly where you left them?"

"What?" Jess asks quietly. "Who?"

"Oh, I don't know, how about fucking *Eamon*?" I hiss.

"I...I..." Jess mumbles.

"See, I thought that was odd too, you know, coming home and finding that slimeball in *my* living room, considering that you told me repeatedly that you were done with him. Especially after he did absolutely nothing to help you when you got arrested.

462

Except, ya know, proposition me for sex."

"Well, yeah…but—"

"…And then I also find it a bit weird, considering I explicitly told you about how you and the kids were more than welcome to move in with me, but only if you agreed to stop taking private clients at home. Which is still my home. You know, the same place where Jaxon Pace's *daughter* lives."

"I know, I know," Jess says defensively.

"But perhaps the weirdest thing, and the part I'm struggling to wrap my head around here the most," I say, gesturing with my hands. "Has got to be the fact that you left your daughter alone with Eamon West, for over an hour. Knowing exactly what kind of man he is, and also knowing I wasn't *supposed* to be home for a few hours."

Jess goes pale.

"So please," I say, crossing my arms tightly across my body. "Which of these things would you like to clarify for me first?"

"Rachel, I—"

"He had his hands all over your preteen daughter, Jessica!" I snap at her, jumping up and storming toward her. "Good thing she fought him off, and I arrived when I did because he's a fucking pig!"

"What?!" Jess gasps. "Oh my God!"

"Yeah! I walked in on him forcing her to sit on his fucking lap while she tried to fight him off, and I got to be honest, Jess," I say, my rage boiling. "It's not a good look, considering you left for so very long. It almost looks as if you knew that was going to happen and were giving your permission!"

"Of course I didn't know!" Jessica shouts back at me. "What kind of mother do you think I am? You think I would knowingly endanger my daughter?!"

"I don't know! That's what I'm trying to find out!"

"Fuck off, Rachel!" She hisses at me. "I love my kids, I'm not perfect, but I would never do anything to hurt them and it's disgusting that you would even think that!"

"Where did you go?!"

"I had to go pick up a prescription for Ivy!" Jess says, yanking a small prescription bag out of her purse. "And I got stuck on a bus that took too long! You know, not all of us have fancy new cars that we can just take all over the city whenever we feel like it just because our baby daddy is loaded!"

Her words feel like a slap in the face. I open my mouth to say something, but nothing comes out.

Had I been wrong? Did I assume too much?

"I'm sorry," I say quietly. "You're right, you didn't deserve that."

She glares at me for a second before sighing and shaking her head.

"It's fine," she says. "I know you're only looking out for Mandy, as you've always done. I just...I can't believe Eamon would do something like that."

"Jess, *why* are you seeing him again?" I ask, as gently as I can muster. "I mean you know all he does is use you."

"I know..."

"And he did nothing to help you when you were in jail, when technically he was most of the reason you ended up there in the first place."

"Well, no," she says, shrugging. "I ended up there because I have a temper, and I kicked that bitches ass."

I snort, shaking my head, trying not to laugh.

But Jess chuckles, and then I have to join in.

"Seriously, though?"

"I just..." Jess sighs, throwing her hands up. "I was lonely. Eamon is familiar. Surely you can understand that."

"Yeah," I nod. "I do. But you need to be careful with him. And I'm serious, he really can't come here. I don't trust him around the baby."

"I know. I...I think knowing that he touched Mandy is the final straw for me. I won't see him anymore. I promise."

And, per most of our arguments, the two of us silently hug each other, right there in the kitchen.

"Now," she says, breaking away and grabbing one of her bags. "I heard there's a masquerade gala happening at the Apparatus Room, that you just *neglected* to tell me about?"

"Well, yeah, because I wasn't planning on—"

But before I finish my sentence, Jess pulls two identical scandalous sailor costumes out of her bag.

"Um, no," I snort. "Absolutely not."

"Um, absolutely yes!" Jess counters. "You know damn well the twins used to get so much attention whenever we went to these events. Everyone loves twins! We can pull this off!"

"No, Jess," I laugh. "I just had a baby, I'm not sure I feel comfortable in something so…revealing."

"Your body is perfect, Rachel," Jess argues. "I swear all it did was give you bigger tits, which is kind of infuriating."

I laugh.

"But seriously, I promise this will make you feel sexy and powerful again. You need to get back out into the world in a fun way."

"Fun might be debatable in this context."

"It's the night of the USSO, so all those sexy sailors are going to be wandering around town, looking for fun that's a little bit more taboo…And you know how I love a sailor!"

"I know you just love *men*," I laugh. "Their profession doesn't matter to you."

"Come on, Rachel!" She whines pleadingly. "I heard the owner, Glow, was telling people she's going to go big with it! Apparently she wants the masquerade to become their biggest event of the year, and this is the first one, so you know it's going to be bumping!"

To be fair, I *had* heard all of this, actually. Glow Bourdeaux was my manager and had been planning for this party at her club for the last month. I had even pitched in and helped her with a few decoration ideas.

…I just hadn't told Jess about it for exactly this reason.

"Jess…"

"Look, it will just be a regular night out," Jess says excitedly. "Nothing too crazy. It's been so long since we had a night out that didn't end in a disaster."

Well, that's true I guess.

"It always gets crazy," I say, rolling my eyes. "Besides, Jaxon would never allow me to—"

"He would if you *invite* him," Jess winks.

"Tell you what," I say, crossing my arms. "He's supposedly coming over later tonight. If you can convince him, then I will go."

"Deal!"

If I thought that I was a good negotiator, I quickly learned I have nothing on Jess. Jaxon had been hesitant, but after Jess made her case about how it wasn't fair that I was wasting away inside this apartment, and that it would be good for people to see us together, he eventually relented.

Jess was beyond excited, convinced that our plan to go as twins would be the highlight of the party.

But it was exactly *this* fact that was making me nervous.

I wasn't ashamed of my post-baby body, in fact, I was enjoying my newfound curves more every day. And my slightly bigger breasts. But after spending over a year in relatively conservative clothes, the idea of putting on some scandalous little sailor costume, that left little to the imagination, seemed daunting.

Surprisingly, it was actually *Jaxon* who gave me the confidence to wear it. Because after Jess got done presenting her case as to why we should attend the masquerade gala, and we all went to bed, he insisted I try on the outfit for him.

…And he very much enjoyed it.

So, I decided what the hell.

The morning of the gala, I am awakened by Jess furiously knocking on my bedroom door.

"Oh my God," I groan, rolling over. "You can come in if you stop banging!"

"Sorry," Jess says, slipping into the room. "But I had to know what you thought of this!"

It is then that I realize that Jess has dyed her signature, long blonde hair brown.

"Holy shit! Jess!" I gasp, covering my mouth. "You…you dyed your hair?!"

"Isn't it great?" She squeals.

"It's gorgeous, but…you dyed your hair for a party? Why?"

"Well, it's not technically for the party per se," she shrugs, playing with her now brunette locks in the mirror. "I'd been considering a change for awhile, and this just gave me a great excuse to do so!"

I realize that my jaw is just hanging open as I climb out of bed and go stand next to her in the mirror.

"I had a wig, obviously, just in case. But I really wanted to see your stylist, because she always does such a great job," Jess says. "But she's obviously booked until the end of the year, so I wasn't sure it was going to happen, but then she called me to say she had a cancelation this morning and said I could have it if I could make it there in less than an hour. And I did!"

All I can do is just stare at Jess as she rattles off her story faster than the speed of sound. Having always known her, for over a decade as a blonde, it is a bit shocking to see the same girl standing here as a brunette.

"It looks amazing, babe," I say, running my hands through it. "As always."

"Thanks!" She says, practically dancing where she stands. "I love it! I've got to go show Mandy! Mandy! Hey Mandy!"

And just as quickly as she burst into the room, she runs out.

Good lord. She's sure excited about this party.

Shaking my head, I head to the bathroom to shower. I guess that there was *some* part of me that was excited to go out tonight. It had been a really long time, and if I was being honest I was going to enjoy being out with Jaxon.

Doors opened for him everywhere. No one refused him anything. Being with him was a power move in itself. There would likely be paparazzi and reporters there.

And even though, yes, there were rumors floating around about Jaxon having hooked up with other women, he never allowed himself to be seen publicly with any of them, and wouldn't have been caught dead getting photographed.

But he *would* with me, as I wasn't just some random booty call, I was his girlfriend and the mother of his child.

After everything this city has put me through, there selfishly is a part of me that will love rolling up to the club, on *his* arm, looking like a total bombshell, making tongues wag. Perhaps then the conversations around me will stop.

Since the plan was for me to come back with Jaxon at the end of the night, Max drove me and the baby over to Pace Manor where her nanny was going to watch her. Mandy would stay back at my condo and babysit baby Ivy, and since Jaxon was going to be with me, Max would stay behind outside and watch over the condo, just in case Eamon had the idea to try and be a creep while she was home alone.

The rest of the day was pretty normal, with Jess and I just hanging around with the girls, and puttering around the condo. The party at the Apparatus Room didn't actually start until 11pm,

467

but knowing Jaxon we wouldn't be arriving until at least 11:45 as he always liked to be the last to show up, and have a grand entrance.

When Jess and I finally have our hair and makeup done, and put on our matching costumes, we stand in front of my full-length bedroom mirror and stare at our matching reflections.

"God," I mutter. "We really do look like twins."

"Told you," Jess says, striking a pose or two. "Aside from your little beauty marks, we're nearly identical. Especially with these."

It's at this point she hands me one of two white cat-eye masquerade masks, in a shimmering black fabric.

"Oh gosh," I say, looking at them. "These are stunning, Jess. Where did you get these?"

"Grams made them," Jess smiles. "I mean, I picked the fabric and pattern, but she's a whiz with the needle."

Looking down at the gorgeous mask, as well as how hot I look in this costume, I'm suddenly overcome with emotion.

"Jess, I just want to say thanks for this," I whisper quietly.

"Oh no worries! I think Grams actually had fun sewing something. It's been so long and—"

"I mean for all of this," I say, turning to face her. "For the costumes, and for insisting we go out and do something. It's just been so long since I've felt good about myself."

My words choke in my throat. Jess turns to me and wraps me in a giant hug.

"Of course, Babe. What are friends for?" Jess winks, pulling back. "Don't cry, or you'll ruin *our* makeup."

My phone chimes, and there's a text from Jaxon.

11:22pm
Jaxon: Ready when you are.

"Well, Jess," I say, grabbing my purse. "Our chariot awaits."

We say goodbye to Mandy and head downstairs and find Jaxon waiting outside the car, in a full tuxedo.

"What no costume?" I ask playfully, stepping onto the sidewalk.

"So, Mr. Pace," Jess says as we step out onto the street. "What do you think of our look?"

Jaxon's face alone was worth wearing this outfit. The man looks at me as if he wants to devour me on the spot.

"I think I can't wait to take it off later," he says, his eyes finding mine after he rakes the entire length of my body with his gaze. "We might have to leave early."

My cheeks instantly heat, and I shoot him a wink.

Damn him for always being good with words.

"Not a chance," Jess says, rolling her eyes. "We're shutting the place down tonight!"

Ethan opens the passenger door and Jess climbs in as Jaxon extends his hand to me, pulling me close and kissing me softly.

"...Or maybe we could just find a dark corner." He whispers.

Holy shit...

"Maybe we will," I say, biting my lip.

He kisses me again, but then Jess starts knocking on the glass of the passenger window, and pointing to her fake watch.

"You know, your friend isn't the most patient of people," he says, rolling his blue eyes.

"That's pretty funny coming from you, Jaxon," I chuckle. "But no, patience is not one of Jess's qualities."

Opening the door I climb inside the backseat and he climbs in with me. The drive is quiet, but Jaxon can't seem to keep his hands off me in the car, whispering filthy things in my ear the entire time. And it feels so fucking good.

Yes, I know he can sometimes wander, but when he's with me, he's *with* me. And having him drooling all over himself has my serotonin spiking like crazy. This is the most beautiful and powerful I've felt in months.

And as he cups my face and kisses me, I think for just a second that maybe, just maybe, I *could* marry him.

Our car pulls up in the drop-off lane and we can all see the paparazzi outside, flashing their cameras.

"Well, I assume that means it's time to put our masks on," Jess says, pulling hers out of her purse.

But as I go to pull mine out, Jaxon stops me.

"Don't," he says quietly. "Let them see you."

"Oh," Jess says, confused. "So we're not wearing them?"

"You can if you want," Jaxon says politely.

"Well, it kind of breaks the look," Jess scoffs, sounding a bit annoyed. "And my grandmother made them for our *twin* costumes."

"Don't worry, Rachel can still wear it with you inside," Jaxon says, rolling his eyes. "I just think this is a good photo opportunity for the two of us."

Oh wow. "The two of us?"

If I thought I was melting before, it is nothing compared to him saying this to me.

Jaxon wants to be seen *with* me.

Our car pulls up in front, just as I grab his face and kiss him. The paparazzi start taking our photos. He gets out and opens the door for me, pulling me out with him. As he's used to this, he pauses and pulls me close to him, allowing the cameras to get the shots they want.

Thankfully, before I nearly go blind from all the flashing lights, he takes my hand and pulls me forward into the club. Once inside he helps me put on my mask and the three of us make our way through the crowd, stopping to casually mingle.

"Please tell me you're at least going to have *a* drink tonight?" Jess says.

"I don't know if that's a good idea," I say, apologetically. "I mean I'm still breastfeeding and—"

"Babe, you're not *feeding* tonight," Jess says, rolling her eyes. "Besides, one or two drinks won't kill you. Besides, you have loads of it in the fridge, and you're using formula."

"Well…"

"Jaxon," Jess says, tapping him on the arm and then whispering something in his ear.

He smirks up at me.

"I think one or two is fine," he says, winking at me. "Just take it easy, they probably will hit harder tonight since you haven't really drank alcohol in over a year."

"There," Jess says, putting her hand on her hip. "Your keeper has approved it. So what do you want?"

"Um, how about just a glass of red wine?"

"Lame but okay," Jess says. "I'll be right back."

The minute Jess leaves Jaxon pulls me close and whispers in my ear how incredibly hot I look. He's nibbling on my ear when I hear a voice, I absolutely despise coming from behind us.

"Jaxon!" Eamon exclaims, slamming his hand down on his shoulder hard. "Long time no see brother."

Any smile that Jaxon had only moments before now instantly dissipates.

"I didn't know you guys were coming," he says, moving to hug me.

However, I move away, retreating back against Jaxon, who immediately puts his hand up to stop him.

"And I didn't know they'd let you *in*," Jaxon says coldly. "But either way, I'd suggest you keep your distance from my girlfriend this evening."

"What?" He laughs indignantly. "I thought we were cool?"

"After yesterday? With the kid? No. No we are not."

"Well, that's disappointing," he shrugs. "But whatever. You two lovebirds enjoy your night huh? I'm sure I'll see you around."

And just as quickly as he appeared, he seems to disappear back into the crowd. The moment he's gone, Jaxon whispers something to his bodyguard who immediately nods and then walks off.

"Don't worry," he says, rubbing my shoulder. "Josiah is going to have him booted."

"Good," I say, taking a deep breath. "He makes my fucking skin crawl."

"That's Eamon," Jaxon says, rolling his eyes.

"That's one way to describe it," I mutter under my breath.

He leans in and kisses me, pushing his tongue into my mouth, while sliding his hand up my thigh and kissing his way up to my ear.

"So, it's up to you," he whispers. "But I heard the coolest thing about this place are the silhouette rooms. And I may have gone ahead and reserved one for the night."

This makes my jaw drop.

The silhouette rooms at the Apparatus Room are indeed one of the coolest parts of the club. Reserved for VIP only, they are essentially private playrooms that line the perimeter of the club. But what makes them exciting isn't just the fact that they come stocked to the brim with professionally cleaned toys and various sex furniture, it's the fact that each one has a glass window that faces *into* the club. A window that with just a flick of a switch can go from a fully blacked-out privacy window to an illuminated display, casting shadow silhouettes of the room's occupants.

...And their activities.

All around us, I notice that a handful of the rooms are already activated, showing various shadow couples participating in all manner of debauchery.

"As I said, it's completely up to you. There's no pressure."

"That," I say, leaning in and kissing his neck. "Sounds like one hell of a memory. I think we could definitely give these people one hell of a good show."

"I think so too," he growls, cupping my face.

"Oh God," Jessica's voice sounds beside us. "If you two are just going to make out the whole time I'm going to have to get plastered. I forgot how unsatisfying being a third wheel can be."

She hands me a glass of red wine before turning to Jaxon.

"The bartender said that you had your own bottle service already arranged," she shrugs. "And I only had two hands."

Jaxon snorts.

"Yeah, I always have a bottle of my own liquor dropped off beforehand because I don't trust the top shelf liquor at any club, it's always garbage." Jaxon says, arrogantly. "But I thought you were skilled at carrying multiple drinks. Aren't you a waitress?"

"I'm an off-duty waitress," Jess smiles at him sarcastically. "So you're on your own, Mr. Billionaire."

Jaxon chuckles, before signaling to one of his men to get him a drink. The man returns minutes later with a scotch on the rocks for Jaxon.

"Cheers!" Jess says, extending her arm in a toast.

We join her and then take a drink.

"Oof," I say, cringing a little from the bite. "Either that isn't great wine, or I've been sober for far too long."

"Probably both," Jaxon smirks, rubbing my arm.

"Hello Jess."

We turn and suddenly my heart nearly stops. Because standing beside us is Mags...the same girl that Jessica *stabbed* in neck with her stiletto all those months ago.

The scar on her neck has obviously healed and is barely visible, but going off the nasty glare that Mags is shooting at Jessica, it's clear that the scar on her heart has not.

"Maggie," Jess says, looking the beautiful girl up and down icily. "Didn't expect to see you here tonight. Don't tell me you're actually *dancing* tonight?"

"Oh gosh honey, I don't dance anymore," Maggie laughs,

rolling her eyes. "I'm actually here for Glow, on behalf of Lyt Vodka, maybe you've heard of us?"

"Nope, it doesn't ring any bells," Jess shakes her head, shooting her a bitchy smile.

"Oh it's a small batch distillery that my *fiancé* and I started seven months ago," she grins, flashing the engagement ring on her left hand. "And what can I say, things are going quite well. We've been so blessed."

"How nice," Jess says, her smile fading.

"It is. It really, really is. Of course it might not have been possible without the very sizable *donation* I received from Mr. Pace here," Mags says, shooting a more genuine smile at Jaxon, who adjusts his tie. "As an out of court settlement for not pressing charges for a certain *assault* a year ago?"

"Doesn't ring any bells either," Jess says, clicking her tongue.

"Oh well, some things just slip your mind I guess," Mags shrugs. "It's crazy to think how different my life is now. I suppose everything can just change on a dime!"

Jess is now straight up glaring at Mags, and at the very sizable rock that now decorates her finger.

"Well, anyways," Mags says, smiling at us. "I've got to go mingle, but it was so nice catching up. Good to see you, Rachel, and you too Jaxon. Congratulations on the new baby, by the way. Ben and I are so happy for *you two*."

Well, at least she doesn't hate me.

"Thank you," Jaxon says politely, rubbing my arm. "We are pretty happy as well."

And without another word, she turns and walks off into the club.

"If I didn't actually like these shoes, I might stab her ass again," Jess mumbles, rolling her eyes. "Snobby bitch."

"Jess," I admonish, rolling my eyes.

Soon after Mags leaves, we are approached by a gentleman wearing a very intricate leather outfit who informs our party that Glow Bourdeaux has offered Jaxon her private booth, as her apology for there not being a designated VIP area yet.

Impressed at her foresight, or perhaps observation at his detest for being approached by the general public, Jaxon accepts and passes along his gratitude before the three of us climb into the private owner's booth, decorated with a high top granite table, and seats made of black cashmere.

"Well, I suppose now that we're all alone, I should share with you my little surprise," Jess says, leaning into the table as I take another sip of wine. "I managed to find *these*."

From her pocket, she produces two little pink pills with smiley faces stamped on them.

"Jess!" I gasp, putting my hand on top of hers to hide it. "Is that…Is that *molly*?!"

"Maybe," Jess grins.

"Well, I'm not doing that," I say, shaking my head. "The alcohol is enough."

"Good thing I didn't bring the other one for *you*," she says, fluttering her eyes up at Jaxon. "I brought one for your man, who was so kind to let you come out to play tonight."

I look up at Jaxon, who looks just as surprised as I am, telling me he definitely wasn't aware of Jessica's little plan.

…But also seems somewhat tempted by it.

"I don't think that's a good idea," he says, swallowing hard, adjusting his tie. "I'm trying to stay away from that shit."

"And doing a horrible job of it, from what I hear," Jess says.

"Jess!" I snap.

"What, Rach?" She smiles at me sweetly. "I'm just saying, if he can party all over the city, why shouldn't he party with you too? Especially since a little birdy told me that the main silhouette room is reserved for Mr. Pace."

Jaxon stares at Jess, and then down at the pill in her hand, and then finally back up at me.

"Oh come on," she says, sliding to him across the table. "You two are already all over each other, why not pop that little diddy and have one hell of a night?"

As shocked as I am, and slightly uncomfortable, in a weird way, I kind of see Jess's logic. Jaxon did have a reputation for partying hard, and on some level the fact that he didn't do that stuff with me, and kept it from me, made me feel like I wasn't cool enough to share that experience with him. Like I was some boring old sweater.

I don't want to be a sweater. I want to be enough for Jaxon.

Maybe if I let him do it, he won't hide it from me anymore.

"Alright," I say, winking at him, and sliding my hand up his thigh. "You can do it. Just for tonight."

474

He stares at me for a moment before raising a brow at me, a smirk skating across his face.

"You sure?"

"Yeah," I say, biting my lower lip. "We do have a show to put on after all, remember?"

His mischievous little smirks fades into a wicked smile, and he swipes the little pink pill off the table and swallows it.

"Alright then," he grins. "Tonight's gonna be fun."

And it was…for a minute.

Because about thirty minutes later, just as the Molly was kicking in for Jaxon, and the two of us were busy grinding on the dance floor, I suddenly started to feel dizzy and nauseous. My skin started to feel hot, and my head started to throb.

Thinking it might be the loud music of the club, I told Jaxon that I was going to use the restroom, and if he was still feeling up to it I'd meet him back in the silhouette room.

I pulled Jess off of whatever random boytoy she was making out with and told her I needed her help.

Instead of going into the crowded bathroom, I pulled her back into the dancer's locker room, knowing that with the only dancers working tonight were out dancing, we'd have a bit more privacy. However, the moment we get back into the room I suddenly feel my legs give out from under me, and barely catch myself before falling onto the bench.

"Jess…" I groan, feeling increasingly terrified that even my words are starting to sound slurred. "Something…is…*wrong.*"

"No, babe," Jess says, reapplying her lipstick in the mirror. "This is totally normal."

"W…what?" I breathe heavily, the room starting to spin.

She presses her lips together several times, and straightens her tits in her shirt before finally turning back around and walking over to me.

"Here, why don't you lie down for a minute," she says, helping me lie down on the bench that runs down the center of the lockers.

For some reason, my thoughts are still clear, but my words

and body feel as if they are stuck in a vat of molasses.

"Something…is wrong…" I mumble. "Get…Jax…Jaxon."

"No, I think you're fine," she says. "Though I gotta say, I really didn't think it would work so fast."

"Wh…what?"

"Ah hell," she laughs, waving her hand. "Eamon said it was doubtful you'd remember much, if any, of this in the morning. Especially if I gave you the whole tablet. So, I suppose there's no harm in telling you, is there?"

Wait, what did she just say?! Eamon?!

"Tab…let?" I breathe, each syllable feeling harder than the last.

"Don't worry, it's just a little Rohypnol," Jess smiles at me. "You know roofies?"

What?!

"Oh, don't look at me like that," she sighs, rolling her eyes.

She suddenly bends down beside me, her face only inches from mine.

"Rachel, sweetie, I realize what I'm going to say might sound harsh, and probably going to be very upsetting for you to hear, especially given how long we've been friends, but I think you deserve the truth," Jess says, reaching out and stroking my hair. "I'm so appreciative of everything you've done for me, especially in the last few months. But I've got to be honest, babe. I'm tired. I'm tired of being jealous of you."

What the fuck?!

I want to respond, but I'm too shocked to even put syllables together.

"And I know I should just be happy for you, but it's not that simple. It's been so hard watching you two together for the last year or so, I mean you have no idea. Here you have this gorgeous, powerful man, buying you condos and cars, and asking to marry you," she says, gesturing around. "And you don't even want it! Meanwhile, I'm forced to survive off of scraps or charity."

Is she fucking serious right now?!

All I can do I stare up at Jessica, unable to reply, my body now refusing to speak at all.

"And I want you to know that I *tried* to find another way. I thought that if Jaxon moved on to someone else, and dumped you that perhaps my jealousy would go away, so I helped a few lost little lambs find their way into his club, or office, or bed. But then every single time, he'd always come back to you!"

I cannot believe this.

"And then I thought about just telling you about all this, because we share almost everything else," she says, with a shrug. "But I don't believe for a second that that applies to Jaxon. After all, you've always been very possessive of him."

Because he's my fucking boyfriend and father of my child!

"But let's be real for a second, I mean we can do that, right?" She continues, as if the two of us are having an active conversation and one of us isn't drugged and paralyzed. "You can't really want to be with him, because you don't even *want* to marry him. Otherwise, you wouldn't have gone and had your tubes tied. You can't even give him children. But you see, Rachel...*I* can. And I honestly think that's what I'm supposed to do here."

Oh my fucking God...

"And again, I want you to know that I tried to do this a different way. I tried just convincing one of the girls he hooked up with to just somehow get me their used condom or save some of his... well, you get the idea," she laughs to herself. "But apparently, he only trusts *you*. Like, he's so careful with not shooting his load off and he's even really strict about how he disposes of that stuff."

She laughs out loud to herself, waving her hand.

"Whatever, I'm rambling now, and wasting valuable time. Basically, the gist of this story is that I just want to get pregnant with Jaxon's baby," Jessica shrugs. "Because then I'd never have to worry about anything, ever again."

This fucking bitch is serious?!

"...But it's not like Jaxon would ever do it with me," she snorts. "I mean, he did have to pay all that money for Mags, and I just don't think that I'm really Jaxon's type I guess, because he's never even tried to hit it you know?"

Because you're supposed to be my friend!

"So when this little party presented itself, I had this brilliant idea for us to go as twins. That's why I went through with all of this. Because my plan was, that if I could get Jaxon a little fucked up, and get him to think I was *you*, then maybe he'd let his guard down and actually come inside me. Because even though he'd be pissed when he learned the truth, I'd still be carrying his baby."

I want to stab you in your fucking face, Jessica!

477

"So when I say this isn't personal, babe," Jessica says, smiling down at me. "I swear it really isn't. Well, mostly. And who knows, maybe you won't even remember this when you wake up. Eamon told me when he sold it to me that sometimes it causes memory loss. But, I guess we'll have to see."

She stands to her feet.

Even though I want to jump her and bash her head into the concrete floor, unfortunately all I can do is just lay here, helplessly, and watch.

"You should be safe in here," Jess says, bending down and kissing my forehead. "See, I'm not a total monster."

Yes you fucking are!

And without another word, Jessica turns and walks swiftly out of the locker room as I start to feel the tears streaking down my cheeks.

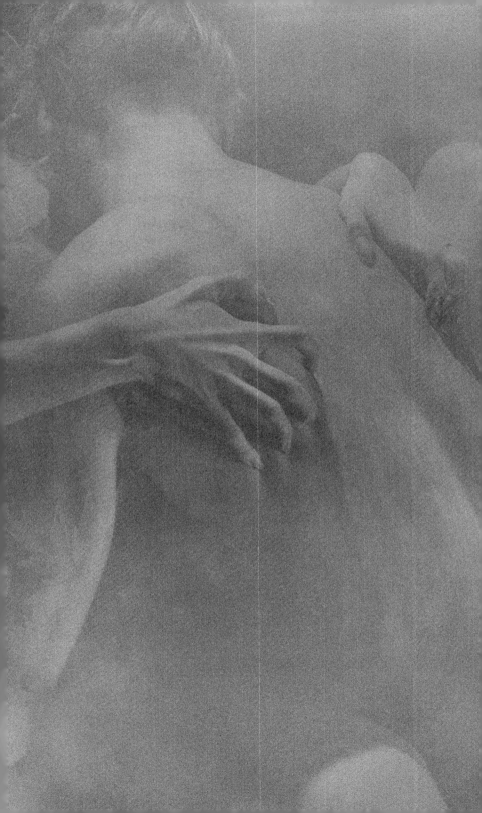

CHAPTER THIRTY-FOUR

ADAM

"Holy shit," I breathe. "That's definitely not where I thought that story was going."

"Believe me," Rachel says, darkly. "Neither did I."

"Were you okay?" I ask. "I mean, *aside* from the horrific betrayal from your best friend, of course. Like did you have any complications from the Rohypnol, or fall off the bench and hurt yourself?"

Strange as it is, especially after recounting a story as terrible as this, a smile begins to form on Rachel's face.

"What? Why are you smiling?"

"Because it's kinda cute," she says quietly.

"What's cute?'

"You are."

Her words stun me, and all I can do is blink at her.

"And why am I cute?"

She pauses, looking down at the comforter as she tucks a strand of her dark brown hair behind her ear.

"I haven't told many people that story," Rachel says. "But it's cute that you're the only person who's immediate concern was for *me*, and not about whatever drama ensued afterwards."

Oh...

"Rachel, I care about *you*," I say quietly. "And I'm sorry for any hurt the actions of other people caused you, but I don't give a fuck about any of them. I mean, outside of the fact that they hurt *you*. Baby Girl, at the end of the day, you are my priority. Just you. They mean nothing to me. You mean everything."

Without another word she leans forward and kisses me, pressing her body into mine and climbing on top of me.

"Well this is nice," I smile against her lips.

"I'm warning you, Adam," she says softly. "I'm not sure I know how to reconcile the way you love me."

I hear her sharp intake of breath, and feel her body tremble against mine.

"And I wish that I could guarantee that I would always react with the tact or even the softness you deserve," she says, her breath hitching. "But I know I can't. At least not always. I'm... damaged. And I see the world that way sometimes too. And I guess I just want to tell you, so that you know, no matter what I might say sometimes, that the way you love me is everything to me too."

I snake my hands up her back, pulling her closer to me.

"We're all damaged, Rachel. In one way or another. We're all just trying to use our broken pieces to fill someone else's cracks," I say softly. "But I want your damage, and any piece of you that I can get. And if any part of me, can help any part of you, you can have it. Because I'm all yours anyway, Baby."

I can tell my words have resonated, as her cheeks turn a bright shade of crimson, and she sheepishly tries to roll off of me and retreat back to her spot on the bed.

Oh no you don't, Princess.

"No, no, no," I say, grabbing her and pulling her close. "You can keep telling your story, but now that I've had you close to me, I want more of that. So get back here."

"You actually want to hear the rest of this story?"

"Only if you're ready to tell me," I say, stroking her cheek.

"Well, this is where it gets good," she chuckles darkly.

"Good is definitely a strange word choice," I say, clearing my throat. "But go on then."

"Well obviously I was just laying there, unable to move, and barely able to talk. Had I been just left there, completely alone with no help, who knows how long I would've been there before someone found me."

"What do you mean completely alone?" I ask. "You mean, someone else was in the locker room?"

She smiles, chuckles to herself.

"Turns out Mags was in the locker room. She heard it all."

"Oh wow," I say, raising my brows.

"She went to go find Jaxon, and tell him what Jessica had said to me, but at that point he was already back in the silhouette room, waiting for me."

"And I assume when *she* showed up, looking exactly like you…" my voice trails off.

"Yep. And of course, security for those rooms is already tight as well but when a billionaire is on deck it's impassable. Charlie was standing guard outside their room, but they were down the hall and the corner. Mags couldn't even get past the bouncer to tell Jaxon, and Charlie didn't have a line of sight to the security podium, so he couldn't see what was happening," Rachel continues. "But then Mags found Ethan."

"She knew Ethan?"

"He just so happened to be the one who had come to see her in the hospital on Jaxon's behalf," Rachel smiles. "For the settlement Jaxon offered her to not press charges against Jess."

"I see," I nod. "And I imagine Ethan was the most qualified person in that building to help you."

…Even if I personally don't like the fucker.

Rachel nods.

"As I said, Jaxon's team had medical preparations on hand for almost any kind of *crisis*. Luckily for me that included Flumazenil, which doesn't *always* work but can work in a pinch for a Don Supreme overdosing himself on benzos."

"…And coincidentally Rohypnol is a benzo," I say.

"Once I came too, I told Ethan what Jessica did, and where they were, and why no one could find them. Ethan insisted he was going to handle it, but I…well, I had another idea."

"Uh oh," I chuckle. "I'm gonna go out on a limb and say that I imagine your idea was less…diplomatic."

"While Ethan was arguing with the bouncers guarding the entrance to the rooms, I swiped one of their flashlights, slipped through, and walked off down the hall until I found Charlie," Rachel says darkly. "The minute he saw me without a mask, after thinking he saw me go into that room with Jaxon *with* a mask… he panicked and busted down the door."

"I bet Jaxon loved that," I say, trying to hide my smirk.

"Yeah I caught her on top of him riding him, both of them high out of their fucking minds," Rachel continues. "He took one look at me, standing there, and then shoved her off of him so hard she whacked her head on the glass silhouette window."

"Damn."

"And while she was down on the ground, I beat the living fuck out of that bitch with the flashlight," Rachel says, her eyes flitting to the fireplace. "And I didn't stop. Jaxon had to pull me off of her."

"Wait, what?" I ask, shocked. "Why would he do that?"

"Well, the silhouette window was still on," Rachel chuckles.

"So everyone in the club witnessed you…and her…?"

She nods.

"Yuuup. So yeah, he was just trying to do damage control," she shrugs. "In his defense—"

"I really hate it when you say that," I growl.

"I know, but in *this* instance," Rachel says firmly. "He really *didn't* know he was fucking her. He realized it far too late, and then here I come busting in, busting her up. A lot to process for someone who was just having the time of his life, thinking he was just fucking his girlfriend."

"…Who is now beating her doppelganger to death," I sigh. "Yeah, I still hate Jaxon, but on some level, I understand."

"Do you?" she laughs, raising her brow.

"No, not really," I say, quickly.

"Didn't think so," she laughs.

"I swear," I say, shaking my head. "It's really never a dull moment with you people."

"We're not a boring bunch, that's for sure," Rachel nods. "Well, anyway, the drug Ethan gave me to counteract the Rohypnol, sometimes requires more than one dose. Meaning that even after taking it, I guess you can still pass back out. And that's what happened. One minute I'm beating Jess's ass, and the next I just kind of collapsed. I woke back up at The Manor."

"Jesus Christ," I sigh, shaking my head. "What happened with the shitty doppelganger?"

"Jessica?" Rachel smiles, batting her lashes at me. "They called an ambulance, she had a shit ton of broken bones, a concussion, and a busted jaw. I mean, I let this bitch have it."

She shifts, the smile fading from her face.

"Never thought I'd ever have to fight with Jessica though," she says quietly. "For over a decade, she'd been my best friend in the world. No scratch that, my *only* friend in the world."

I take a deep breath, trying to think of something to say.

"Still hurts, honestly," she whispers, wiping her eyes.

"Betrayal always does," I say softly. "Because the worst ones come from the people we love, the people we are certain would never betray us, so it always hits like a car crash."

"Yeah, I was blindsided," she says, shaking her head. "Looking back, I can see all the little signs leading up to it. I thought her trying to get me to dump him was her trying to be a good friend. Or when she'd tell me about some rumor she'd heard about him fucking another woman, I thought it was just her looking out for me. I never thought she was actively plotting for the demise of my relationship."

"Jealousy does weird things to people," I say, stroking her arm. "It seems like she was a good friend to you, but only as long as you stayed behind her. Perhaps the minute you stepped into the spotlight, or good things started happening for you, she realized you didn't need her anymore."

"Maybe," she whispers. "I just, I don't know. You know, I'd been cheated on, and that obviously hurt. But it didn't compare to this. This broke me. And it's a big part of why I struggle to trust people anymore."

I see the moment her bottom lip trembles, and she immediately raises her hands to her face.

"It's such a mindfuck," she says, her voice choking. "I hate that she did this. I hate that she made me do what I did. She made me...ugly."

"You were not ugly, Rachel," I say, pulling her against my body, feeling her sobs against my chest.

"I was though, Adam," she sobs. "That night, I was *ugly*! But not just for what I did to her that night. For so long, I've just

485

held this…this anger. This hatred. Of anything good. Anything happy! Because when I was the happiest, when I *finally* let my guard down and allowed myself to think that maybe there could be some happy little fairy tale with Jaxon, and our daughter…the person I trusted more than anyone else in the world came along and just ripped that away from me! I would've never done that to her! I only ever wanted her happiness, why the fuck couldn't she just want mine?!"

I don't have an answer. Hell, I don't even have anything to say. All I can do for Rachel is hold her, so that's what I do. Pressing her tightly against me, letting her cry. Gently I kiss the top of her head, just reminding her that she's here, with me, and that her heart is safe.

After a few minutes I feel her breathing steady, and she pushes back from me, wiping her eyes.

"Anyway," she says, clearing her throat. "I woke up at Pace Manor. Jaxon called his private doctor, and he came and flushed the drugs from my system."

"What did he have to say?"

"Everything," she says, closing her eyes. "He just apologized, over and over, for everything. And like Mags had told Ethan everything she heard, so Ethan had obviously relayed that message to Jaxon."

"So he knew about the drugs, and how Jessica had planned this, and about the other women?"

She nods.

"Well, not to be an asshole," I say gently. "Even if Jessica *had* thrown those women in his path, he still went down it. He made the choice to sleep with him."

"He did," she agrees. "Jaxon acknowledged that. It didn't undo anything he'd done, it just provided context. And of course he had learned the truth about my procedure, from what Mags had told Ethan while they were working to save me."

"How did he take that?"

"Better than he would've had all the rest of this not gone down at the same time," she snorts. "He was shocked and surprised, but I think he also kind of understood. But because we obviously had bigger things to discuss, it got buried."

"I see," I say quietly. "So he wasn't upset, he was apologetic?"

"Beyond," she says, a sad smile on her face. "He apologized

486

repeatedly, for hours, over what happened that night, with Jessica. And eventually I told him that I forgave him."

"Did you?"

She shakes her head.

"No. I couldn't, and I *knew* I couldn't," she says quietly. "It didn't matter."

"What do you mean?"

She looks up at me, her dark brown eyes paralyzing me in place, as she takes a deep, heavy breath.

"I knew that was the end," she sighs. "I knew that no matter the why or how, the fact remained Jaxon had fucked my best friend. And there was no coming back from that."

"So you broke up with him?" I ask. "For good?"

She chuckles to herself, sitting up on the bed, and leaning back against the headboard.

"You can't just break-up with Jaxon Pace," she says, continuing before I can object. "Especially when we have a daughter together. No. That was never going to happen. He would never allow it. But I needed to get off of this carousel, and I knew the only way I was going to be able to do it."

"Which was?"

Rachel pauses for a moment, staring at me before closing her eyes.

"The worst thing I've ever had to do," she whispers, her lip trembling. "*My* skeleton. The only thing I've ever done that I have never been able to forgive myself for."

I stare at her, holding my breath, unable to move at all.

"I knew that I had to leave Jaxon," she says slowly. "But I knew that he would never let me leave with our daughter. And I knew if I tried to run, they would find me. And that would be the best case, because if *Jaxon's* men didn't find me, then other men would find me."

"What do you mean?"

"The other clans," she says darkly. "They would find us, kill me, and take her. Use her for bait, or worse."

"So I...." she breathes, her voice hitching. "I left her."

Holy shit.

"I knew that Jaxon was the best chance she had at safety, and a life that wasn't on the run," she sobs. "But that life couldn't be with me. So I had to do the hardest thing I've ever had to do,

487

which was say goodbye to my daughter."

Rachel suddenly bursts into tears, pulling her knees up to her chest.

"I've regretted that decision, every single day for the last seven years," she cries.

I try to reach for her, but she pulls away from me.

"Don't," she sobs, shaking her head. "I know what you must be thinking of me! And how much you must despise me right now!"

"Rachel," I whisper, reaching for her again.

She pushes my hand away once more but this time I grab her and pull her back to me.

"Rachel," I say as she continues to try and get away. "Rachel! Stop."

I wrap her in my arms, my face buried in her neck.

"Rachel, why on earth would I despise you?" I say gently against her hair that falls loosely down her shoulders.

"Because you *lost* your children, Adam!" she nearly shouts, her voice strangled by her emotions. "They were stolen from you. And here I am, abandoning mine! Leaving her the same way my bitch of a mother left me! I'm a monster!"

And just like that, one more tiny piece of Rachel Valentine falls into place.

In the same crippling way that my story about my wife had kept me paralyzed by the idea that she could run and not want anything to do with me, Rachel's biggest fear is me learning the truth about why she doesn't have custody of her daughter.

She sacrificed her rights in order to run from what was causing her pain. And Jaxon Pace, intentionally or otherwise, had caused her a lot of pain.

Using all of my strength, I turn a crying mafia princess around to face me, immediately cupping her face in my hands.

"Rachel, you are *not* a monster," I say firmly. "You held out for as long as you could, you brought a beautiful baby into the world, and you tried to make it work despite every single hurt he caused you. That doesn't make you a monster, that makes you a survivor."

"I left her, Adam," Rachel whispers, tears streaming down her face. "How could I do that?"

"Because you had to," I say calmly. "Sometimes it's just that simple. It's messy, and yeah the world is going to interpret it however they want, but you know you loved that little girl, and you also know that she'd be safe with Jaxon."

She sniffles, breathing heavily, her dark brown eyes falling from mine.

"And even though I don't like the guy," I say, swallowing hard. "I'd be willing to bet he would burn the world to the ground before he let anyone hurt that little girl. And you knew that too."

Her eyes find me, and she nods.

"We are taught to believe that love is meant to be perfect and flawless. Well, it isn't. Sometimes love is messy and doesn't look anything like we think it will. But that doesn't make it any less powerful or any less real," I say, stroking away one of her tears with my thumb. "So when you ask me how I see you? Well, I see a woman who has more grit, strength, and courage than anyone I've ever known. I see a mother who sacrificed her own happiness, and a life with her daughter, so that her daughter's life would be easier. You're a warrior, Rachel. I have nothing but respect for you."

Rachel smiles, a soft blush settling on her cheeks.

"Adam, I love you," she whispers softly. "But…you haven't heard the whole story yet."

"So?" I say, kissing her hand.

"Well, I'm just saying that you might want to reserve judgment on blindly giving me a blank check for forgiveness, love and respect, and all those other nice things you said about me just now." She whispers, closing her eyes.

"No," I grin.

"At least until you know the full extent of my sins."

"It won't make a difference, Rachel," I say gently. "It won't change how I feel about you."

"How can you say that? You don't know that," she says softly, her eyes falling from mine. "You can't possibly know that because you don't know everything I've done."

"Rachel," I say, locking eyes with her. "I've already made up my mind. There is no story you could tell me or no skeleton in your closet that is going to scare me away. I'm here to stay. But please, by all means go ahead, and tell me how the story ends…"

CHAPTER THIRTY-FIVE

Rachel

"**W**akey wakey."

I snap my fingers over my former best friend Jessica's face as she lays strapped to a hospital bed.

Slowly but surely her eyes groggily flutter open.

"Wow, You did it! That's impressive."

Her eyes squint under the bright fluorescent lights, highlighting her face, covered in blue and purple bruises I gave her while beating her with the flashlight.

"I overheard the nurse say that you'd be pretty out of it and were unlikely to wake up. But, hey, I guess turning off your morphine drip did the trick, eh?"

Jessica's eyes slowly find mine.

"Guess the story going around the floor is that you got into a pretty bad bar fight and broke your jaw," I snicker, watching Jessica flinching. "Oh, don't worry about trying to talk though, it had to be wired shut. But that's okay, you don't need to talk for this conversation anyway."

Her breath becomes ragged and she reaches toward her button to call the nurse. But, given that both her torso and hand are covered in plaster casts, she can barely move.

"Aw, Jess, what's wrong?" I tease. "Oh, you want to call someone, sweetie? Well, unfortunately they've already done their rounds, and they are very busy tonight."

I push the call button closer to her, but just out of reach.

"Tell ya what, I'll leave that there, and if you can reach it and manage to press it, I'll let you. Sound good?"

Her eyes flail about wildly, her immediate panic at being alone in a room with me becomes apparent.

Good. I want her panicked. I want her fucking terrified.

After all, you only get to *kill* your best friend once.

I pull out a bag from my pocket and walk over to her bed.

"Make room, *Twinsie*," I say, aggressively pushing her legs aside, making her groan. "Now, I can't stay long. Cuz you see, I'm leaving town. And also, since you've been tied up here. No one has likely been to see your kids in hours, but don't worry, we'll get to that in a bit."

"Mmmmpf!" Jessica moans.

"Kinda ironic, isn't it?" I sneer. "You here, unable to move, to talk, and me standing here holding all the power."

Jessica's breathing increases, and she continues to try and reach the button.

"But I just had to come congratulate you," I say sarcastically. "I mean you really put a lot of time and effort into your little plan. And you really got me this time."

I stare at her, watching her nostrils flaring. The monitor over her head starts flashing, indicating her heart rate is climbing. But since I've already silenced the alarm that usually goes off, no one will be coming to check.

"Jessica, Jessica, Jessica," I say, placing my hand on her leg. "You were my best friend. My girl. You knew me better than everyone, you knew everything about me. My past, my trust issues, and especially my struggles in my relationship with Jaxon."

Her eyes are wild and frantic.

"Can I ask a few questions? Like…what did you think was going to happen? Or how long were you pretending to be happy for me while plotting to steal the father of my child? When did you start telling yourself that if *I* didn't want to have his baby and marry him, that perhaps he should give *you* that opportunity? Cause I got to be honest, that's pretty bold."

"Mmpf! Mmmpf!"

"I'm sorry, honey, I can't understand you," I say with a grin.

She wails, unable to open her mouth and scream. I also notice the first beads of sweat starting to appear on her brow.

"I bet without that morphine to distract you from all those broken bones, concussions and lacerations, you probably feel like absolute shit right now. You've gone so long without a hit."

I lean in and whisper.

"I bet you can feel evvvvvverything."

She wails quietly, futilely thrashing her head back against the bed.

"Oh don't worry, there's no one that can hear you, the night shift nurse is occupied elsewhere. And your floor nurse, well, she's knocked out in the laundry room. Because obviously, I needed to borrow some scrubs."

"Mmmmpf!"

"I'm not going to stay much longer, I just wanted to drop by and see you one last time…just to cover my tracks."

Her eyes go wide again.

"Mmmpf! Mmmpf!" She grunts.

I pull the bag up on the bed with me, and unzip it.

"See, even though I interrupted your little tryst before Jaxon could finish, I can't have you getting well and causing problems for me, or Jaxon, or my daughter. So I'm going to handle business with you, and then I'm leaving town. For good."

I start pulling the items out of the bag. A vial, a syringe and some latex gloves. And Jessica's little pink pen case where she'd stashed her meth a year ago.

The moment she sees it I hear her breathing stop.

"I do have to hand it to you, you did succeed in dealing me and Jaxon a death blow. I mean, wow. You went *big*. But you know, I don't know if I would have ever found the strength to leave him on my own. So thank you, because you were just the nail in the coffin."

I notice her eyes are lingering on that pink pen case that I've deliberately left within eyesight.

"But as grateful as I am for your help in leaving him, I hope you understand that I just can't leave you hanging around."

"Mmpfh!"

Gingerly I pull on the latex gloves, a syringe and the vial. But, the first thing I do is grab her casted arm, and take the needle from the pen case.

"Now this might hurt a little."

I jam the needle down hard in between her fingers. I do it a few more times, just to be sure I've drawn blood.

…And maybe because I also am enjoying the sound of her muffled screaming.

Eventually the syringe is empty so I set it back in the open case on her food tray.

"You'll have to excuse the crude method, but I didn't exactly have a lot of time to come up with this plan," I say with a wicked grin. "But when they brought you in here you already had a whole slew of drugs in your system."

I grab her chart off the end of her bed.

"Ah yes, cocaine, GHB, opioids, heroin and methamphetamines," I laugh sarcastically. "Look at you, you little overachiever!"

She strains hard trying desperately to reach the button, but given the massive chest cast from the three broken ribs I gave her, she can't sit up.

"Sadly, after doing a quick internet search, the little amount in your pen case here unfortunately isn't enough to *kill* you."

I take the vial out and pull the cap off the syringe, pulling the liquid into the needle.

"But see this right here? This is Thallium. Max stole it from Jaxon's scientist guy, Akram?…Aram? Ahab? Or whatever the fuck his name is. I overheard him saying that it's super deadly in concentrated doses, and coincidentally it's also a bi-product of the meth cooking process. So naturally when meth is found in the bloodstream, or the patient has a history with drug abuse, they assume that's the culprit. You know, it was actually almost used to kill Jaxon?"

I laugh to myself, brushing my hair over my shoulder dramatically.

Jessica continues moaning and crying, staring down at her bloodied hand, and still trying to reach for that call button.

"Oh, I forgot you don't know, do you? Well, it was this whole thing. I guess Jaxon's father was trying to find a way to off him and make it look like an accident, because Jaxon was trying to leave the Mafia, oh my god. Dramatic much"

I smile down at her, narrowing my eyes at her. I pop my gum in my mouth and giggle.

"Blah blah blah, point is it was easy enough to get my hands on, and far easier than trying to cook up some meth and bring it here. I don't have the patience for that shit. But all you need to know is that when *this* enters your bloodstream, one by one your organs will start shutting down painfully. You'll die miserably and since like I said it's oddly hard to differentiate from meth, your friendly doctors will have no idea what's actually causing your rapid deterioration and will be unable to stop it."

I pick up the bag and lay the remainder of its contents on the bed. Her pipe, the drugs, everything.

"Mmmpf!" Jessica continues to grunt and cry, realizing she's completely helpless to her own fate.

"I'm also going to leave all this shit here. With your rap sheet, everyone will have to assume your addiction was just so bad you just had to make a mess of yourself trying to have a fix."

I pick up the needle and push it directly into her IV line as she begins to thrash violently against the bed.

"I was slow to your antics. Far too slow. But it all makes sense now."

"Mmmpf! Mmpf!" She grunts, looking up at me pleadingly, tears streaking down her cheeks.

I place my thumb on the plunger, but pause, looking down at her.

"I trusted you," I whisper, trying to hide my pain with my disgust. "I told you everything. I would have done anything for you. Hell, I even named my fucking daughter after you, Jess. I thought you were my best fri—"

I close my eyes and shake my head, unable to even finish the sentence.

"No, I won't call you a *friend* because you don't even know the meaning of the word."

She shakes and whimpers, still trying to reach for her call button, understanding now that's her only hope. She strains against her body cast, fighting the pain, which I know must be excruciating since I shut off her morphine.

But that button won't save her…I'd unplugged that too.

Even in this moment, when confronted with all the ways she's a shitty friend. All she cares about is herself. But I guess that's my fault. Since she's always been this way.

That's what I get for trusting people.

Jaxon and Jess, the only two people I trusted in the world, have both fucked me over.

…And ironically now they've fucked each other too.

While I know Jaxon was drugged out of his mind and truly believed he was fucking me when he was caught with Jess, it doesn't matter. This isn't the first time I've caught him with another woman, and certainly won't be the last. He can't help it. He's just a man-whore, and Jess is just a backstabbing little cunt who's never been above playing dirty to get ahead.

But I now have no doubts that had she succeeded in getting pregnant, she would've fully tried to oust my daughter.

Which *can't* happen.

Jessica gives up on trying to reach the call button, and looks up at me. The moment her eyes meet mine I feel nothing but hatred.

I lock eyes with her as I plunge the plunger down, forcing the concentrated Thallium into her IV.

Her eyes go wide, and she starts immediately crying, knowing that she's about to die.

"You fucked my boyfriend, Jess. And while I've come to terms with the fact that you're a lying, scheming, conniving bitch, you who had no remorse for fucking me over," I say calmly. "You were indirectly trying to fuck my *daughter* over, and put her life at risk. And that I will not allow."

Jessica begins frantically shaking her head.

"No. You knew what you were doing. You figured if I didn't want to accept Jaxon's obligatory proposal, that you'd just load yourself up with his bastard, and bring another support check into the world. I mean, what's another baby to you right? Just another bargaining chip for you to manipulate. And worth it, as *this* baby's daddy would be a billionaire and coincidentally the most powerful man in the city. You know, it takes a devoted kind of twisted to use your own kids as pawns for your sick little games. Oh, and speaking of your kids, don't worry. Once we're finished here, I'm going to go pick them up…and take them for a little drive."

"Mmmpf! Mmmmpf!"

"Speaking of, I should probably change," I smirk. "Especially since you're not long for this world."

I shut the door and walk over to Jessica's bag. I'm assuming one of the girls at the club must've grabbed it from her locker and shoved all her shit into it before the ambulance drove off.

I yank off the scrub top I stole from the nurse I knocked out in the hospital laundry room, and instead pull a black tank from the bag. Inside I also find a pair of jeans, her phone, wallet and keys. But I smile when I see the only item I was really hoping for was in the bag: Her signature robin's egg blue rhinestone *Jessica* sweater.

"Good thing I don't need this to get your kids to come with me, since they trust me," I grin. "But hey, everyone loves souvenirs, right?"

"Mmmpft! Mmmpft! Mmmpft!" She grunts hysterically.

"Oh God, don't act like you're suddenly parent of the year. Let's be real, you don't give a fuck about those kids outside of the payments their fathers guaranteed you."

She continues grunting and thrashing. Occasionally wincing from pain.

"You know what gets me heated too? The fact that you made me feel guilty for what I walked into with Eamon, where I caught him about to put his filthy pedophile hands on your daughter? Yeah, you knew. You knew what he was and what he wanted, and God forbid I hadn't come home then and stopped him, because I think you would have let him do it. If he paid you enough for it. Or, I guess if he gave you the right drugs, huh?"

She glares at me.

"You know, most parents want better for their kids than they had. Not you. No no. You think the world screwed you over. But that's your fucking child! She didn't ask to be born, and your only job was to protect her from people who would do her harm, no matter the cost!"

The significance of my words, knowing exactly what I just sacrificed to protect my infant daughter has my hands shaking.

Keep it together, Rach. Finish this.

"You're a shit mother! You knew all the signs and you deliberately left that sleazeball alone with her!" I snap at her.

497

I shake my head, rifling through the bag for anything else of value.

Silent tears now start streaming down Jessica's cheeks.

I grab her perfume and spray it all over myself before putting a medical mask over my face.

I grab Jessica's chart, and copy the last set of vital readings, alternating a couple slightly. According to the time on the sheet, it looks as if the nurse's rotation for Jess is every forty-five minutes. I notice the next rotation starts in five minutes, so I write the time down as four minutes from now, knowing it takes exactly five minutes to get to the front of the hospital.

With any luck, I'll be out of here and long gone before anyone actually checks on her and by then she'll be long gone. I gave her a dose of two ml of Thallium, which is more than two hundred times the lethal limit.

"Truth is, those kids will be better off without you," I lean in close. "I will guarantee it. And maybe, if they are lucky, the memories they have of their shit mom who only ever looked at them like they were breathing dollar bills, will get lost in time. They deserve someone who cares about them."

I walk to the door, turning off the lights, watching as her eyes start rolling back into her head.

"You don't deserve to be remembered," I say quietly. "I'll see you in hell, bitch."

It was surprisingly easy to get the kids in the car.

I brought Mandy a cheeseburger and fries, and made up a bottle for the baby. We ate, and then I told Mandy that her mother was in the hospital, and that they would be going to stay with their Grandma for a while.

…I just didn't say how long.

Mandy was thrilled to hear she was going to her grandmas, as I expected she would be. She packed a bag for herself while I packed a bag for baby Ivy and we were on our way.

I didn't call Doreen ahead of time, mostly because I didn't know what to say. It wasn't that I regretted what I did to Jessica, but rather I just needed a minute to process it. So when Mandy fell asleep in the passenger seat, and the baby nodded off in her carrier, I appreciated the silence.

At least I knew that these kids would be in a much safer, and substantially healthier living situation being cared for by their grandmother. There was no doubt in my mind that they would be better off with Doreen, than they'd ever been with their mother.

Even Jessica knew it too, which is why she dumped them off every chance she got. She just also knew that if she signed over custody, their child support would stop funding her drug habit.

Their own mother had been a roadblock in their happiness, and had been using them for profit. And God knows what else she might've used them for.

However, tonight, I had put an end to their exploitation. I just had to kill my best friend to do it. Well, former best friend.

But the scariest part about it?

I felt *nothing*.

That is until we pulled up outside of Doreen's townhouse, and I realize that this might be the last time I see these girls too. I take a moment to get my emotions under control before gently waking Mandy and telling her to go ring the doorbell while I gathered up the bags and baby carrier.

"Oh my goodness!" Doreen exclaims, standing in the doorway in her nightgown. "What an unexpected surprise!"

And just as I expected, she welcomed her grandchildren inside without so much as a second thought.

"Jess got into some trouble," I say, swallowing hard.

"What kind of trouble is it this time?"

"The kind that involves the police, drugs and the hospital."

Doreen sighs, shaking her head.

"Mandy Dandy, take your sister upstairs to the guest bedroom, and get settled in. It's late, and you should be sleeping."

"Yes, Grams," she yawns, picking up her sleeping sister and heading up the staircase. "Goodnight Rachel."

"Night kid," I say, swallowing back the last remaining glimmer of humanity I possess.

No. I can't afford that right now. Stay focused.

"Doreen, I feel like I need to be honest with you," I say quietly. "There's a good chance Jess might not make it out of this one. Rumor has it she overdosed."

"Dear God," she says, shaking her head. "I thought she was clean. She was doing so well."

"She wasn't," I say, closing my eyes. "She'd been lying to you. And to me. About a lot of stuff. It's bad. I feel like I don't even know her anymore."

Well, at least some of that is true. But I have to really sell this.

Doreen sighs, appraises me with the kind of compassionate concern only a grandmother could have.

"I know this is a lot, Mrs. Daniels," I smile. "And I know it's probably the last thing you're prepared to take on right now. But I think the girls need to stay with you. They aren't *safe* with her anymore."

"What?"

I stare at her for a long moment before handing her Jessica's blackmail box.

"Don't open it now," I whisper. "Or you won't get any sleep tonight. Just know that any confirmation about any suspicions you might've had, or the kind of mother she's been, or what she's been doing in front of these kids is in that box," I say, swallowing hard. "Everything you'd be protecting them from, by taking them in, is there. And I think it might surprise you."

"Oh my word," she whimpers, looking at the box in her hands. "Is it that bad?"

I nod.

"I know this is a lot to ask—"

"No, no," she says, shaking her head. "They are always welcome here."

I reach back into my back and pull out an envelope full of all of the cash I was able to find stashed around my condo.

"It's not much, but hopefully it will offset some of the costs," I say handing it to her. "There's also papers in there regarding her child support payments and schedules, along with contact information for the fathers of both girls."

"I thought—"

"I know that she told you the fathers were not sending support but that's not true," I say, handing her the envelopes. "They have been the entire time. And I'm also fairly certain that they would love to see their kids as often as you'd allow them to. I'm sure they'd find working with you a lot easier."

500

Doreen shakes her head.

"I don't know what's going to happen with Jess, or if she's going to pull through," I lie. "But I'm sure that if you reach out to her contact at family court, they can help you sort everything out. Or, I don't know, put you in touch with some resources or something."

The look on this poor woman's face as she stands here, having her entire world rocked by what I'm telling her, nearly breaks my heart.

No. I have no heart. I have to remember that.

"I know this has to be a massive shock, but you were the only person I knew I could trust to look out for those kids."

She stares at me, before nodding slowly, clearly still trying to process everything I've just dumped in her lap. She closes her eyes for a second and then smiles up at me weakly.

"Well, I…I should be going," I say awkwardly. "I'm headed out of town to see family. I don't know when I'll be back."

I stare at her for a long moment, trying unsuccessfully to come up with anything else to say. But there is nothing else to say. This is the situation, plain and simple.

Time to go.

"Goodnight, Mrs. Daniels."

I turn around and quickly open the door, wanting immediately to be as far away from this place as possible.

But just as I reach the car and yank the driver's side door open, I hear her call my name from the top step of her porch.

"Thank you, Rachel," she calls in the early morning light. "For having a heart."

I smile at her, but know the truth as she closes the door.

No. I have no heart. There is no heart left in me anymore.

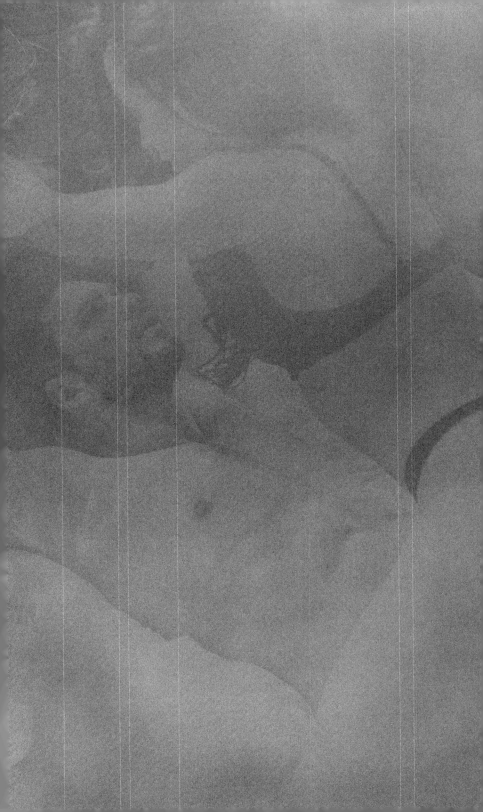

CHAPTER THIRTY-SIX

ADAM

"So yeah," Rachel sighs as the two of us take a shower together. "That was the day my heart shriveled up and died."

I rinse my head under the water before moving out of the way so she can get under.

"I can't imagine how hard that must've been for you," I say, passing her the shampoo bottle. "But that's not true, you know."

"What isn't true?" she asks, running her hands through her hair. The way the water trickles down her delicious curves has me momentarily distracted.

Fuck she's sexy.

"The part about you not having a heart," I say. "You do."

She laughs quietly, rinsing the shampoo out of her hair.

"I think there are loads of people who would disagree with you on that, Adam."

"If they truly believe that," I say, switching places with her. "Then they haven't been paying attention."

"Well, if there *is* anything left," she says, lathering up her hair again. "Then it's frozen solid."

"No, it's not Rach," I say, shaking my head.

"Oh, I promise it is," she chuckles. "But it's okay. I'm not ashamed of it, it's how I survived. You have to be a cold-hearted bitch to get by in this world."

"You are not a cold-hearted bitch," I say firmly. "So just stop talking about yourself like this. I don't need you to put on an act for me."

"Excuse me?" She says, scoffing loudly.

"You heard me just fine." I say, giving her a stern look. "I said to stop with the I'm-a cold-hearted-bitch routine. Maybe that shit worked on the little fuckboys you used to play around with, but I assure you, that's not me. I'm not buying that shit for a minute, because I know better."

"I don't know what you're—"

"Yes you do, Rachel. I know full well that you understand what I'm saying. And you know as well as I do that you're not a cold-hearted bitch."

"Yes, I am!"

"No you're fucking not," I snap, stepping out of the shower and grabbing a towel. "You know, I can listen to you tell me messy story after messy story, and not bat an eye. And I can sit with you on your bad days, hold you on your worst days, simply stand beside you and help you face your insecurities and fears if you need me to. But what I won't do, Rachel, what I *refuse* to do, is sit here and let you degrade yourself by saying you don't have a *heart*. Because nothing could be further from the fucking truth."

Even though I mildly feel like I'm scolding her, I still grab a towel for her too as I hear her shut off the water.

"Adam, I killed my best friend," she says as she steps out.

"Is that supposed to convince me? Rachel, I've killed people too, including my own *wife*," I scoff quietly "Your point is?"

"Yeah, but you told me that you regretted doing what you did," she wipes off her body with her towel. "And the difference here is that I don't regret it."

I chuckle to myself, wrapping my towel around my waist.

"I said I had guilt."

"Same thing," Rachel says, rolling her eyes.

"Except it's not, though," I say, grabbing my hairbrush. "Regret is what you feel when you did something, but upon looking back, realize it was the wrong choice. Guilt is what you feel when you deliberately do something that's wrong, or that goes against what society says is right. Such as killing a person in the line of duty. Was I justified? Yes. Does it still weigh on my conscience? Yes."

She says nothing, wrapping the towel around herself.

"The only regret I have is not getting my boys out of the situation before it escalated," I say quietly. "The rest is all guilt. Because it was a conscious choice. But regardless, that guilt tells me I still have a soul. A heart beating within my chest."

"What's your point?"

"I *know* you have regrets too, Rachel. You told me so yourself, remember? But having done things you wish you could take back doesn't make me think you're some monster who runs around hurting people. It makes me think you're *human*, because you can't make it through life without a few bumps and bruises and battle scars. Your ability to regret is directly connected to your ability to love. And it should be, because how can you ever hope to truly love someone if you don't have the humility to admit your own mistakes?"

She bites her bottom lip, staring down at the bright red nail polish on her toes.

"I know vulnerability scares you, because it's connected to emotions, and in the past people haven't handled yours very well," I say quietly. "But I'm fully capable of loving all the different parts of you, Rachel. Even the broken ones. And I'll choose you, and your messy, tragic and even occasionally remorseful chaos every day of the week because nothing is more beautiful."

"You're saying my messy vulnerability is beautiful?" She asks. "Because you should know, that in *my* world, vulnerability is a liability. That shit is dangerous."

She leans against the counter and wraps her arms tightly around her body, biting her trembling lip. Almost impulsively, I am drawn to her, pulling up the chair in the bathroom and taking a seat. Her eyes find mine, a timid sadness reflected in them.

I place my hands on her hips, and pull her so that she's standing in front of me.

"Look, I know this is terrifying for you. I know it's been a

505

lot of vulnerable conversations, and I know that you are actively tearing down walls to let me inside," I say softly. "I know you've been hurt before, and I know your go-to method of protection when you feel scared is to downplay your feelings. You think that if you don't *feel* anything, then there's no risk of you getting hurt or burned. But I'm not here to burn you. I have no ulterior motive other than to love you, as best as I can, for as long as you will allow me. Part of that involves helping you feel safe, and realizing that I don't need you to hide your feelings from me. Because being a cold-hearted bitch won't protect you."

"Why do you say that?" She stammers.

"Because even hearts made of ice can *shatter*."

"Adam, I—" she starts to say, but I pull her into my lap, and cup her face with my hand, kissing her deeply, running my fingers through her hair.

"And knowing what I know of you, Rachel Valentine," I say softly, running my thumb along her cheek. "I know for a fact that your heart would never be made of something as *weak* as ice."

"*Weak*?" She asks softly.

"Yes, weak. That's what hearts made of ice are—weak and easily fractured."

I hear her breath trembling, as her eyes fall from mine.

"And maybe that was you once, but it's not anymore," I say tenderly. "So you can swear up and down that you're heartless, remorseless, and all kinds of bad, but I know the truth. I know the real strength you possess. You had every reason in the world to become angry or bitter and perpetuate the vicious depravity your family has ingrained in you. But you *didn't*."

"But Adam," she chokes out, "You don't understand. I'm the reason my brother is wreaking havoc on this city, Adam. I helped him come to power. It's my fault."

"What do you mean?"

She takes a deep breath and bites her bottom lip.

"When I left Chicago, I thought that was going to be it," she says quietly. "I kept in contact with Ethan, just for updates on my daughter, but I knew that I wasn't coming back. Not to Chicago or to Jaxon. I was done. I even started seeing someone else. And yeah, Jaxon tried to call, tried to plead with me to take him back, but I didn't want it."

"Let me guess, I assume Mr. Always-Gets-What-He-Wants

didn't take that well," I say sarcastically.

"No, not really," she says, eyes falling to her hands in my lap. "Jaxon wasn't getting the picture, even after months and months of me living in Texas and not talking to him. So I called Ethan. He told me that he would handle it, but wouldn't tell me how, saying it was best that I didn't know."

"Ethan is either; the coolest person in the Mafia," I say snort. "Or the scariest person in the Mafia. The jury is still out."

"Well, turns out he wrote Jaxon a letter, and pretended it was from me. He even went as far as to get some postage from the town where Jaxon's house was in Texas."

"*Jaxon's house?*" I ask, confused.

She blushes and purses her lips together.

"Yeah, I guess I skipped that part," she says, clicking her tongue inside her mouth. "When I fled, the only place I could think to go was to Jaxon's house in Texas. One because I knew he hated it there, and two because I knew it was vacant."

"I don't understand, how did you get in?" I ask. "If it was his?"

"Well technically, it was *mine*," she shrugs. "He'd given it to me after one of our fights. Well, not so much a fight as it was another apology gift after I caught him in one of his many affairs. But *legally* it was still his house."

This makes me laugh.

"What?" She asks.

"Nothing, I just hope to be so rich one day that I can give out properties like they are Halloween candy."

"Anyway," Rachel continues. "I knew to break the cycle, I needed to stay in plain sight."

"What do you mean?" I ask "About being in plain sight?"

"I needed to wean Jaxon off of me like a drug. If I was really going to find a way to be on my own, I needed him to get used to me being gone, while still feeling like he *knew* where I was. Like knowing the drug is there, within reach while still not trying to use it."

"Okay…"

"If I disappeared completely or tried to run away from him too quickly he'd seize up, and snatch me back. So instead I wanted to give him a false sense of security by thinking that I was only just a plane ride away, and that I wasn't hiding from him, I just wasn't taking his calls."

"Good lord," I sigh. "Are Mafia Don's that...fragile?"

She rolls her eyes.

"Oh Baby, you have no idea," she chuckles. "My thought was that once Jaxon got used to life without me, then he might start dating again, and then who knows, maybe my life would just go on too. And it worked for a while, but then things spiraled out of control."

"How so?

"Well, I didn't know that Ethan had typed up a letter, and I think Ethan just assumed it would work, but it pushed Jaxon a bit too far, too quickly. He apparently decided he didn't want to hear me say my final goodbye in a letter and decided at the last second to fly out to Texas and confront me," she says, swallowing hard. "Ethan tried to warn me, by sending me a text, but I had left my phone at home that day. However, someone else had decided to pay me a little visit that day with a much worse agenda."

"Who?"

"*Michael.*"

"Holy shit," I gasp.

"Yeah, that was the first time he escaped from the mental institution," she sighs, shaking her head. "Obviously after failing The Trials, Michael was banned from the Pace Mafia. That's when he started working as an enforcer for Victor Black, who was plugging him full of all kinds of different meds. Some to keep him alert, others to mellow him out, and some that were a combination of both meant to keep him on edge...and angry. Well, naturally that's bound to fuck with you, and one day he just sort of snapped, and started killing people. Serial slashings."

"Jesus," I breathe.

"And, when they finally caught him, the prosecutor realized that his crimes matched several more that had spanned the previous five years."

"So basically, they realized he'd been doing this for a while and just happened to get caught this time?"

She nods.

"Well, he was definitely guilty, and at that time, the death penalty was legal in Illinois, so I did the only thing I could do and beg Jaxon to try and spare his life and get him help at a mental facility or something," she says, taking a deep breath. "Looking back I feel so stupid, and when I think about all the people who have died because of my brother…"

Her voice trails off.

"Rachel, you're not responsible for Michael's actions," I say firmly. "And even though I'm not convinced that there is anything or anyone that could help your brother, I know you were only doing it because you felt pity for him."

She looks down at her hands again.

"And, he was my only family," she whispers softly. "He had always been awful to me, but he was still all I had, and I wasn't ready to…Well, yeah, you get the idea."

I take her hands in mine.

"Continue, babe," I say gently. "I'm listening."

She nods.

"Well, anyway, Jaxon worked his magic and Michael was spared the death penalty and instead sent to this mental institution," she says softly. "But the security at places like that are used to petty criminals at best, not Mafia men. So it didn't take him very long to break out."

"Wow…"

"And even though the facility he was being kept at was one of the best in the country, he obviously hated it here, and blamed both Jaxon and I for putting him there," she shrugs. "Apparently he would have preferred death."

"Which somehow seems very on brand for Michael," I say, shaking my head.

"Now, I can't be sure about his motivations, because he's never directly said anything to me, but I assume he figured the best way to get back at Jaxon and I was to kill me, as he knew that would upset Jaxon, and obviously I'd be, ya know, dead."

I stiffen in my chair, unable to even handle the thought of anything happening to Rachel.

"But because I wasn't talking to Jaxon, I had no idea he had escaped the hospital, and even if I did, I never would have guessed he'd be in Texas, at my house, and being the one to see the text message from Ethan that they were on their way," she sighs, closes her eyes. "I guess somewhere between Michael being in Texas, and Jaxon landing at the airport, everything changed."

"What do you mean?"

"I came home from work that night, and I found my boyfriend

had been shot in the head," she says, her lip trembling. "And while I'm screaming and crying and freaking the fuck out, I hear a gunshot, and felt something graze my head and I felt something graze the side of my head. Then everything went black."

Rachel suddenly pulls back her hairline, revealing a scar on the side of her head that I have never seen before.

"Holy shit," I gasp. "Is this from…"

"From the bullet my brother fired at my head?" she says matter-of-factly. "Yes. A bullet that was intended to kill me, before Michael set fire to the house, and framed Jaxon for my murder."

"But, it didn't kill you," I say, my throat feeling dry.

She shakes her head.

"No, it did not," she says, shaking her head. "And I can only assume, this is because Victor Black decided that if I lived, I could be far more useful to their little revenge plot against the Pace's, alive."

"So, this guy Black," I say, trying to make sure I understand it correctly. "He saved your life?"

"Um if "saved my life" you mean that he decided to get me medical attention before I bled to death then kept me in a coma for a year while convincing the rest of the world I was dead? Then I guess yeah, you could say that," Rachel snorts

"Jesus Christ, Rachel," I say, shaking my head.

"But it also gave everyone time to craft the narrative they wanted," she says, nodding. "One in which it was *Jaxon* who had hired the hit man, set fire to the house, and wanted me dead. So when I woke up, this is what they told me, repeatedly, and to me, that all made sense given how I had left things with Jaxon and also Jaoxn's character. So it didn't take long for me to accept my reconditioning, and start believing that Jaxon was the bad guy."

"Meanwhile, everyone is saying you faked your own death on purpose," I say softly. "When in actuality, it's more like other people faked it, and you just believed it."

She nods.

"Good Lord," I snort. "Everyone is either cheating, stealing, killing, dying, nearly dying, or fake dying. Good God."

Rachel chuckles.

"But yeah, that's why I was so angry with Jaxon when I finally saw him again. And why I wanted to kidnap my own daughter…

and why I hated Natalie."

She winces when she says Natalie's name, and she licks her bottom lip.

"But I...I didn't *mean* to shoot her," she says quietly. "I never meant to do that."

"What?" I ask, trying not to sound as shocked as I actually am by this statement.

"Back before I knew the truth, about everything, I was going hard after Jaxon, trying to get revenge. And Natalie, well she was beautiful, and Jaxon was fawning all over her in ways he never had with me," she says, closing her eyes. "So I hated her for that. I know that's petty, but I did. So yeah, I...made her life difficult."

"Difficult?" I ask, raising a brow.

"Well, I blew up some of her stuff, chased her around, and threatened her. You know, typical jealous girl bullshit."

"That's not typical jealous girl bullshit, Rach," I snort. "But continue."

"Well, I broke into Pace Manor, to get a couple of my old things back," she sighs, her breath hitching. "And...and then there was this...*scuffle.*"

"What kind of a scuffle?" I ask.

"One in which Jaxon and I were fighting over a gun, it went off, and Natalie got shot. In the stomach."

"Oh shit..."

"It was an accident!" she sobs. "Jaxon and I were fighting and my hand was on the trigger but so was his! It was so hard to tell and I was just trying to not get shot! I swear to God, I never felt myself pull it, I never would have done that!"

She collapses to the ground, wrapping her hands around her body, her small frame wracked by her choking sobs.

Instinctively I go to her, pulling her into my arms and against my chest.

"Rachel," I whisper, holding her shaking body.

"I killed their baby, Adam! There's a *child*, dead in the ground because of me!" Rachel's sobs are violent, even her breaths sound strangled. "I was stupid, and I was jealous, but I never actually meant to shoot her! And I never meant to kill the fucking baby!"

Holy fuck.

There is nothing I can say to take this from her. It's almost as if every buried regret, every painful memory, every hateful word uttered about her, has suddenly bubbled to the surface and is now erupting from her.

I've been here. Right here, where she's at.

I hold her for what seems like an eternity, letting her completely purge herself of all of these pent up burdens she's been so unwilling to unload. Eventually, she starts to calm, and she can take full breaths.

"I've just made so many mistakes," she says, her lip quivering. "How do I ask forgiveness from people when I can't even forgive *myself* for what I've done?"

Her words strike a chord with me in such a visceral way.

"Rachel, we've all made mistakes," I say, gently touching her chin and raising it back to look at me. "It's what we do after we've realized that we've made those mistakes that truly defines who we are."

"She didn't deserve that. That poor baby was innocent."

"No, but we were all innocent once, and people hurt us," I say slowly. "Life is pain. We will all get hurt at some point, and none of us will deserve it when it happens too. But this is what I mean by you have to find a way to reconcile that. To balance your scales. It's the only way to find peace."

She stares back at me, tears streaming down her face.

"Okay, let's walk this back," I say slowly. "Yes, you hurt Natalie, and you nearly killed her. But you also saved her life, did you not?"

"Well, yes…"

"And her husband's life," I say, swallowing hard. "More than once if I'm hearing correctly?"

"Yes, that's true."

"And you saved Ethan's life and the entire Alpha Squad that night at the warehouse. As well as mine. Even knowing the depravity your brother was capable of, but you risked your own life to come back for everyone and ensured they all made it out of there. Without you, all of us would have died there. Horrifically. Now I don't know about you, but those are some pretty big positives, Miss Valentine."

I watch as her lip starts quivering.

"But… I abandoned my daughter," she whispers, the tears flowing hard down her cheeks.

I nod, sighing deeply.

"You did what you thought was best," he says quietly. "And, from what I understand, when you did that, it prompted Jaxon to actually pull his head out of his ass and get his shit together."

"Right but there was no guarantee that would happen," she says, shaking her head.

"No, there wasn't," I whisper. "It was a huge risk."

She sniffles quietly, wiping her eyes.

"But you left her with her father. Who, for all his many, and I do mean *many*, faults, was nothing like your father. It's clear he loves that little girl unconditionally, and he also happens to be the most powerful man in the city," I say, rolling my eyes. "...Even if he is an insufferable prick."

She chuckles softly, biting her lip.

"You, like all of us, have made mistakes. However, you also balanced the ledger in other ways. But you want to know what tells me that you still have a heart within that chest of yours?"

She stares up at me, looking confused.

"That even after being betrayed by their mother, in the worst of ways, you still brought Jessica's kids to their grandmother's house. Because you *cared*."

She swallows hard.

"Without you, those children, especially that teenage girl, could've certainly fallen victim to assault by any one of the many *clients* her mother left wandering around her house while she used," I say softly. "Or worse. And trust me, in all my years as a federal officer, I've seen worse."

I close my eyes and shake my head.

"Those were innocent children too. They didn't ask to be born, and they certainly deserved better than a mother who cared more about her high, than their wellbeing. You took them out of danger and gave them a shot at life. *You* did that Rachel."

She sniffles, wiping her eyes.

"Now, correct me if I'm wrong, but those don't sound like the actions of some cold-hearted bitch."

She blushes, a smile tugging at the corners of her lips.

"You might be one of the most insane, stubborn, and emotionally volatile human beings I have ever met, but you have so much more light in you than you realize. And I understand the dangers of walking through the thorns you've grown around your heart. But the reason I'm here, and doing it, is because I

513

know there is far more good in you. There is a fire in you, not ice, Rachel. And it's probably the reason you're still alive."

The air in the room between us is electric, and my words escape me as I find myself lost in her deep brown eyes.

"I've spent so much of my life, pretending to be what other people want. That, or just staying far enough in the fringes that they won't notice me at all. But you do notice me. The real me. And I like it. Because with you, for the first time I can just be *me*."

I move my hand to hers, keeping it pressed against me.

Logic would tell me that she's dangerous, and that this is an absolute mistake.

But fuck it.

I take a step toward her and pull her face to mine, kissing her hard.

I need her, immediately. I wrap my hands under the back of her thighs and pull her up. She presses her tongue into my mouth, and moans, as her hair falls around us.

I don't care what she is, or if she is dangerous, or if she is some sort of she-demon sent to torture me. I want her. All of her. And I want her right now.

But just as I'm about to take her into the bedroom, she stops me, pressing her hand to my chest.

"I have a better idea," she grins, wickedly. "But this time you'll have to trust *me*."

I grin.

"I'm listening," I say softly.

"…And I'm going to need your handcuffs."

"Women are drawn to dominant men for a lot of reasons. Power. Protection. Prestige," Rachel says, taking my cuffed hands and tying a rope around them.

"Cleopatra was the first female pharaoh of Egypt, the most powerful woman of her time, yet she pursued and seduced Caesar, bending his will to hers, all to benefit her country. Henry the Eighth, was so enamored with Anne Boleyn that he would bring all of Catholicism to its knees in an effort to possess her. And of course, perhaps the most famous folklore of all, Samson would die just to let Delilah cut his hair."

Rachel takes the rope attached to my handcuffs and loops it behind one of the massive banisters on the solid oak bed.

"Naturally there were certainly advantages to being with such powerful men," she says as she ties the rope tightly, suspending my cuffed hands above my head. "They brought protection to the women they adored, prestige too."

I try to remain calm, but I am now nearly naked, with my hands tied above my head and my heart begins pounding.

"But," she continues as she walks slowly back around the bed, trailing her hand down my bare chest. "When most people look at the stories of these women, they are content to stop there, thinking they understand their motivations. But they've missed a very important detail."

"What...what's that?" I say, breathing heavy as her hand brushes deliberately against my black boxer briefs.

"*Preference*," she grins, biting her bottom lip.

Her eyes find mine and she firmly squeezes my erection, making me moan.

"More important than power or prestige, these women were preferred. Of all the women in the world, they were the one he *chose*, and nothing felt more powerful than that."

She places her hands on either side of my chest and kisses it, slowly moving down my body.

I am absolutely powerless to her touch, goosebumps erupting on my skin and my body clenching as her hands hook inside my underwear, pulling them down.

Rachel tosses my boxers to the side and sits down on the edge of the bed between my legs. Taking my erection in her hand, she slowly begins to stroke the full length. A wicked smile spreads across her face, and she watches with enjoyment as I convulse every time she runs her fingers over the incredibly sensitive head.

"These women," she whispers, her lips pressed gently at the base of my cock. "Became the exception to men who granted no exceptions."

"Fuck," I grunt as she wraps her mouth around the tip, teasing me with her swirling tongue as her right hand grips my testicles, pulling down slowly.

"And just like the men they adored, whose brave and valiant actions solidified their immortality, these women, these *paramours,* had become immortal too. Baffling and bewitching historians for millennia."

Her sultry voice echoes in the room, as another tortured moan escapes my lips.

She is driving me crazy. The feral look in her eye as she continues teasing the head of my cock with her tongue, combined with her soft, plump, juicy lips dribbling spit down the shaft is making my head spin and my body twitch.

Suddenly she takes all of me in her mouth.

"Oh fuck…"

She repeats this motion several times, each time taking me deeper and deeper down her throat.

Just when I think I'm close to cumming, she suddenly stops.

"No, no, no," I whisper desperately. "Don't stop, that feels amazing."

But she doesn't listen, and without another word, she reaches down to the floor and picks up my leather shoe.

What the…?

Confused, I watch as her long fingers meticulously unthread the thin black shoelace from the brown leather.

"Forgive me," I chuckle sarcastically. "But this seems slightly less enjoyable than what you were just doing."

"I will forgive you," she smiles up at me smugly. "Because I believe I'm the one in charge this time around."

Well, damn.

And to my surprise, and momentary concern, she takes the black shoelace and wraps it around the base of my erection…and my testicles.

"Whoa whoa whoa," I say, using my foot to push off of the bed and try and wriggle away from her. "What the fuck are you—"

"Stop. Moving." She snaps, slapping the inside of my thigh with both words, making me wince.

"Ow!"

"Oh, quit bitching," she sighs, grabbing the string again, pulling it tightly and pinching me in the process.

"Fuck! That hurt!"

"And it's only going to hurt more if you don't stop fucking moving!"

I snort incredulously.

"Is there a reason you're playing Jacob's Ladder with my ball sack?"

"Obviously," she rolls her eyes, looping the string around in a half-knot. "If you're patient, maybe you'll find out."

But as she takes the string and individually wraps each of my testicles I start to get the idea. And when she finally ties a knot with the end of the string, the increased blood flow has elevated the sensitivity significantly.

"Oh...shit..." I shudder, as she runs her hand over them, stroking my cock with the other.

"Now do you understand?"

"Yes," I groan.

She squeezes my cock harder, working the tip in the palm of her hand.

"Are you going to shut the hell up and let me do what I want now?"

"Fuck..." I mumble.

"That's not an answer," she smiles, tapping them slowly and making me wince.

"Shit! Yes!" I whimper. "Yes."

"Good."

She gently runs her hand over the area she tapped, making me shiver before reaching into her pocket and pulling out a bottle of oil. Silently she trickles it on to my skin, using her hands to work it all over my chest and arms...before finally returning to my throbbing erection.

"As I was saying, deep down we all want to be the exception, Adam," she says darkly, stroking my length firmly.

My breathing becomes ragged as her hands work the shaft squeezing the tip with every stroke.

"Fuck..." I gasp, as I feel her rub her well-oiled hands against my swollen sensitive testicles before trailing them downwards to my taint.

But she doesn't stop there.

"Rachel," I warn, as I feel her fingers going further south, brushing against my asshole. "Don't."

She looks up at me, and bites her lip deviously. Reaching back into her pocket she produces a small key.

The handcuff key.

She kneels on the bed and presses it into my palm.

"What are you doing?"

"I'm giving you an out, Agent Westwood," she grins. "But if you want me to stop, then you'll have to get yourself out of those handcuffs, and stop me."

Holy. Shit. She's actually serious.

"You forget that I've seen and done this already with you, Adam. Far *more* than just this, actually."

"We agreed not to talk about that," I say defensively. "That was a one time thing."

"That you *enjoyed.*"

Without warning she swallows my cock, teasing me again with her tongue. As she sits up, she wipes a drop of spit off her lip with her finger and sucks on it.

"Point is, I know how this goes with you. You want to object, but you also don't want me to stop. And if you tell me I'm wrong, I'll remind you that you lied to me for months. So, I won't be listening to any of the words that mumble out of your mouth, because they can't be trusted. Got it?"

Fuck.

She suddenly grips my tied testicles, hard.

"Arggh!" I yelp.

"Got. It?"

"Yes, yes!"

"If you want out then what?"

"Then I can get myself out!" I whimper. "Oh, fuck that hurts!"

She chuckles darkly but releases me.

"I know it does. But the way I tied them will make you last longer and insure that your hypersensitive."

"Christ!"

"Now, where were we, pet? Ahh, right about here I think."

Her fingers stroke my ass, and I grunt, straining away from her, the feeling driving me insane as she completes a slow tantalizing circle on one of my most sensitive areas.

"You know, I know I gave you shit for shaving your body hair, but I think I actually like it. Your ass is so smooth, I bet that makes it more sensitive too."

"Rachel, I'm warning you," I growl.

"Go ahead and warn me," she laughs sarcastically. "I know the truth, because I heard it from your lips the first night we fucked."

Shit. She does have a point.

In truth, I have confessed a lot to Rachel over the last few months.

"I'm starting to think maybe I've told you too much."

"Nah baby, there's no such thing as too much. Especially with sex. It's kind of an advantage when it starts off as just transactional. It's more honest and raw. You weren't worried about your ego or my approval of your fetishes, because you were paying me to do things with you...and *to* you."

"Oh fuck!" I gasp, my chest heaving as I feel her press the tip of her finger inside of me.

"The lack of inhibitions made it very easy for me to figure out exactly what you like," she says, a grin spreading across her face. "And what you wish you *didn't* like."

She slides into me again, this time further.

"Rachel..." I groan, feeling her circling her finger around inside of me.

"See what I've learned with you, Agent Westwood, is that you're a man of power too."

She presses deeper inside of me, her other hand strokes the head of my cock.

"Even on suspension, if you really wanted to, you could bring the house down on all of us filthy little heathens here in Chicago. And while yes, that is inherently sexy, it's not just your power that intrigues me."

"Arrgh!" I moan, feeling her moving her finger inside of me, despite the efforts of her other hand to distract me.

"No. It's your contradiction."

"My what?" I ask, utterly exasperated.

"You're a good man, with a dark side. You balance your ledger, but that takes work. And to keep it at bay, you keep everything locked up and so tightly wound because you don't want the world to see any sign of humanity or weakness."

She stops working my cock with her other hand and suddenly presses her tongue against my tied testicles. The feeling makes me flinch, but then I feel her press deeper inside of me.

"Christ, Rachel!" I whimper. "St...stop."

"You don't want to like how this feels, but you can't help it, can you?"

Holy fucking hell!

I groan, my arms straining hard against the rope above my head.

"If you didn't, you'd already be out of those handcuffs, and punishing me," she teases, the darkness in her voice both turning me on…and terrifying me at the same time.

"I can tell how much you enjoyed this the first time we did it," she whispers just loud enough for me to hear her, rubbing my prostate with the tip of her finger. "You'd never had someone that knew how to stimulate you like this before. Especially not the way I could. It's intense, isn't it?"

I want to answer, but I can barely think, let alone utter words. I might lose my ever-loving mind.

"You looked so sexy when you came too," she grins. "And you know I love the way you *sound* when you cum."

"Ye…yes…"

"It's more common than you might think," she continues casually as beads of sweat start forming on my forehead. "Lots of men enjoy this, they just don't want to admit it. Just like you."

She continues to work my cock with one hand while probing me with the other.

"Maybe it's just the invasive nature of having something pushed inside your body, that's hard for men to get over," she says, relentlessly rubbing against me. "But I promise you will never cum harder than from an orgasm like this."

She smiles down at me, watching with devious enjoyment as I strain and groan, feeling her working her hands on and in my body.

"But somewhere, deep down in places you don't talk about, you enjoy it because it feels wrong, doesn't it."

"Fuck me…" I groan, the first drops of precum forming on the tip of my cock.

"Oh, baby," she giggles. "I intend to."

What does that mean?

"God, this is better than any drug on earth," she moans slightly. "Perhaps it's simply the parallel."

"What?"

"I mean, you're a pinnacle of goodness, Adam. And yet, here you are, enjoying the pleasure of the damned. You're so very brave, so very strong, and yet so very helpless right now."

Fuck, she's right.

I hate that she's right.

"For just one little moment in time, you've relinquished control to me. And it's so fucking hot."

I groan, the pressure building, her words igniting fire in my veins that threatens to blaze out of control at any second.

"I don't care what anyone says, there's no greater compliment on earth," she whispers, almost reverently.

Wait...what did she say?

"To have the trust of a man, especially one as good as you, trust me with his darkest desires."

"Yes..." I mumble, pulling hard at the ropes.

"And here you are, at my mercy. And no matter what you do, or what principles you live by, you can't fight your own arousal from my fingers deep in your ass."

"Rachel...." I whimper.

She stops her rhythmic violation and gently kisses my groin, rubbing my throbbing erection against her cheek, her eyes finding mine.

"Tell me, Adam," she whispers, kissing the shaft. "Do you enjoy the bad things I do to you?"

"Y...ye...yes..." I shudder, feeling her hands rub my overly sensitive swollen balls. "That's...that's..."

But I can't finish the sentence, my brain has melted into the mattress, and I am undone.

"Look at you, the saintly Agent Westwood...getting his cock milked by a common whore."

"Baby," I laugh, my voice slightly higher than normal and my arms shaking the ropes. "You're far from common."

She laughs.

"I guess that's true," she smirks, tapping on my balls and making me wince. "And I really do love watching you fall apart right. Want to know why?"

I can only nod as she works her fingers harder.

"Because I want to be your exception," she smiles darkly. "I want to be your one weakness. Your *Delilah*."

"I thought that was obvious," I breathe heavily, my cock dribbling more precum. "You already *are*."

Rachel says nothing, but the smile on her face says everything.

Without another word, she wraps her lips around my cock and pumps me hard down her throat.

This is the moment I lose all control.

"Holy shit," I groan. "I'm…I'm going to…"

"Are you going to cum for me, Adam?"

I can barely nod as she works the head of my cock relentlessly. I feel her start strumming her fingers hard inside of me, pushing me over the edge.

"Cum for me," she whispers. "Give in to it."

"Fuckkkkkk!"

I throw my head back, feeling the orgasm hit from deep inside my body. I moan loudly, my cum exploding all over her hand, dripping down the shaft.

"Very good," she says, working every last bit out as I twitch and thrash with every pump of her hand.

"Holy shit," I breathe.

Gently she unties the knot from the shoelace and very carefully pulls it from me.

I close my eyes and relax into the mattress.

Rachel climbs on top of me and straddles me, taking the handcuff key from my palm.

"Did you enjoy that?"

Perhaps it's her tone, or even her smug smile, or perhaps it's the feeling of her pussy rubbing against my cock, but something inside of me immediately snaps to attention.

It's time to remind her exactly how dominant I can be.

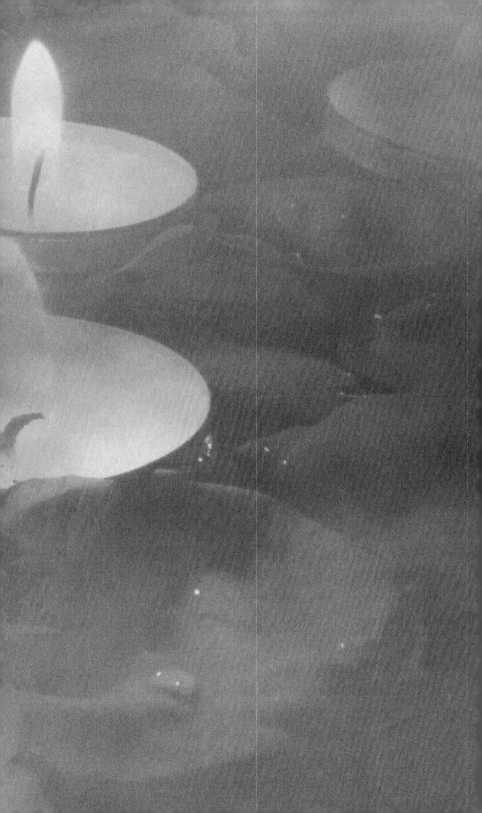

CHAPTER THIRTY-SEVEN

Rachel

The next few days at my family home are the happiest I think I've been in over a decade.

Adam and I continued to tell each other stories, but with the remaining skeletons in our closet finally removed, and the ghosts of our past finally exorcized, our storytelling becomes more relaxing as opposed to terrifying.

The only major thing we still needed to address, and figure out a way to navigate, was finding a way to tell Jaxon about the two of us.

While yes, we technically could sneak out of the Valentine Estate and go on the run, it would also pretty much guarantee that I would never get to see my daughter again. And having spent seven years away from her already, I wasn't willing to risk losing her again.

But Adam and I were going a little stir crazy, inside the house, and were also just tired of feeling like guilty teenagers sneaking around in the shadows. However, telling Jaxon that I was dating the man he likely considered to be Public Enemy number 2, second only behind Michael, would not be an easy feat. He could very easily decide to execute one or both of us, or even feed us both to those cannibalistic pigs back at his farmhouse.

However, as luck, or perhaps fate, would have it, on the day of the mayor's funeral there is an unexpected knock at the door.

"Hello Miss Valentine."

I open the door to find Ethan White, standing on my porch in the same black on black attire as he always wears when conducting Pace business.

"May I come in?"

"Of course," I say, giving him a pointed stare. "It's *just* you, correct?"

"Yes, Miss Valentine, the men are fine to wait outside like last time," Ethan says politely.

After letting him inside, and closing the door behind him, I lead him into the kitchen, where this time Adam was *waiting*.

"Mr. Westwood," Ethan says as politely as he can manage. "I'd pretend I'm shocked to see you here, but I think we're past the point in faking pleasantries, don't you?"

"God, I hope so," Adam says, clicking his tongue and offering his hand to me, pulling me beside him.

"Good. Then I'll get right down to business," Ethan says, looking at me. "Jaxon has asked me to come and fetch you. Apparently, he needs your help."

"Absolutely not," Adam growls, tightening his grip around my hand. "I think she's helped him more than enough already, don't you think?"

"Unfortunately, my opinion on the matter is irrelevant," Ethan says darkly. "As is yours, Agent Westwood. It's not up to me no more than it is up to you."

"It very much could be," Adam says, yanking the gun from the back of his pants and pointing it at Ethan.

Ethan stares at him, and then at the gun in Adam's hand looking utterly unimpressed.

"Agent Westwood," He sighs, sounding annoyed. "I have neither the time nor the patience for this today."

"So then leave," Adam growls.

"Alright boys," I say with a sigh, locking eyes with Adam and pressing my hand to the top of his gun, silently asking him to put it away. "I don't need another blood bath in the kitchen, okay? Ethan, what does Jaxon want?"

"As you may have guessed," Ethan says, still glaring at Adam suspiciously. "There was a bit of trouble at the state funeral today."

"Don't tell me Jaxon actually *attended* that," I snort. "The bomb went off in Jaxon's suite. Everyone who is anyone thinks that he did it. He'd have to be an idiot not to think that there might be some sort of scene at—"

But the way Ethan clears his throat, and purses his lips tells me that, yes, my ex-baby daddy *was* in fact that big of an idiot to attend a state funeral where the soon-to-be interred were killed by my brother's bomb…in Jaxon's suite.

"Jesus Christ," I sigh, running my hand through my hair. "What the hell was he thinking? Has he lost his mind?"

"You know," Ethan sighs, slightly rolling his eyes. "I don't know anymore. And he's becoming increasingly more stubborn."

"Well, isn't it your job?" Adam sneers bitterly. "To wrangle the Don Supreme? Clean up his messes and silence the competition?"

"Not anymore," Ethan smiles coldly. "I'm retired."

"I heard he fired you," Adam says, narrowing his eyes. "I also heard that's why your ass ended up in that warehouse a few months ago in the first place."

Jesus, Adam.

"And you say *I'm* the hothead," I say under my breath.

"Both are true," Ethan smiles in that polite yet arrogant way that tells Adam he could kill him with a pencil. "But as I recall, you yourself were in that warehouse, were you not? Were you fired too? Or are you still just *suspended?*"

"You know what—" Adam starts to say but Ethan cuts him off, turning to me directly.

"As you probably already know, I'm a very busy man so let's cut the bullshit," he snaps. "There *was* indeed a significant risk to Mr. Pace to attend that funeral today, however no one could talk him out of attending, which is pretty standard for the Don Supreme these days. And as he was leaving he witnessed a drive-by hit, orchestrated by your brother. A hit that not only killed the Chief of Police, and his wife, but also nearly killed the entire Alpha Squad and Mr. *and* Mrs. Pace."

"Holy shit, Natalie went too?!" I gasp. "Fuck me, I thought that out of all of you *Natalie* at least had her head screwed on!"

Perhaps he can't help himself, but this makes Ethan chuckle before he continues.

"Right before the shooting took place, the Chief told Jaxon in confidence that one of the men they had in the lockup downtown made mention that Michael was utilizing the old Valentine Dolor Domas again, and Jaxon seems to think that's Michael's new bolthole."

At the mere he mention of that house of horrors, my blood immediately runs cold, and I nearly stop breathing as terrifying images of torture and butchery come flooding back to me

Evidently Adam notices the shift in my demeanor and gently rubs his thumb along the top of my hand.

"I don't even know if my family *has* a Dolor Domas," I whisper, my voice strangling in my throat.

"Well, the informant says otherwise," Ethan says, his piercing eyes staring me down. "He specifically told the officers where it was, what he saw and that he remembered being *at* that location with Michael...and *you*."

"I...I...I'm sure I have no idea what you're talking about," I lie, poorly, overcome by the feeling of my heart racing.

Ethan smiles.

"Miss Valentine," he says quietly. "As I said earlier, I think we are past the point of pleasantries, and *lies*, wouldn't you say?"

"Hey, buddy," Adam suddenly snaps at Ethan. "If she says she doesn't know, then she doesn't know. And even if she did, she isn't obligated to tell you."

"She is, as it also concerns the safety of her daughter."

"You people are fucking disgusting, do you know that?" Adam snaps, glaring at Ethan.

"Adam..." I caution.

"You're using her *daughter* as leverage?! That's sick!" He shouts angrily. "And from what she's told me, even after she's risked her own neck to help you people, over and over, she's barely been able to see her fucking daughter. Without at least six fucking bodyguards present! So cut the shit, Mr. White, the only safety you fuckers are actually concerned about is that of Jaxon Pace. And it's despicable to me that you would even come here and pretend that this has anything to do with Jessica!"

"I assure you, young man," Ethan claps back. "It does."

"And I assure you, *Pops*," Adam growls. "That I'll shoot you in the face if you ever call me *young man* again."

"Maybe so, Mr. Westwood. And maybe you'd even be successful," Ethan says, narrowing his eyes at Adam. "But then one of the dozen or so men on property, who have been kept deliberately unaware of your presence by *my* orders, would be obligated to burst through that door and avenge my death. And while maybe they aren't aware of the secret tunnel to the mausoleum, I assure you that Alexei, who is part of *my* team now, *has* been made aware before I even set foot inside this house. And should I, for any reason, *not* make it out that door in one piece, Alexei would ensure that neither you, nor Miss Valentine here would either. Which I can promise you, no one, least of all I, wants this to happen. So perhaps it would be wiser for you to control your temper, or at least keep your fucking voice down and let those of us who want to act like *adults* discuss business."

Adam is momentarily shocked, but apparently having less chill than I do opens his mouth to say something but I press my hand to his chest to stop him.

"Ethan," I say calmly. "I'll ask again: What does Jaxon want?"

Ethan continues to glare at Adam for a moment before he sighs heavily, pulling back his chair and taking a seat at the table.

"I suggest you sit down for this."

Jaxon's plan was simple: sneak onto the Valentine Dolar Domas property, and see if Michael was indeed hiding there, as he expected he was.

What was not simple, however, was convincing Adam that Ethan was right, and that the security of everyone, including my daughter, would only be solidified if my brother was dead.

Adam was furious, first demanding that I refuse, and then after insisting that this was the only way I could force Jaxon to allow me to see my daughter on a more regular basis, insisted that he be allowed to join us, in order to guarantee my safety.

But as much as I wanted him to come, I knew he couldn't.

Because I couldn't guarantee his safety, and also because I knew that what would be the least simple of all, was the actual *execution* of this *simple* plan.

And I was right.

Everything that could go wrong, went wrong. Including us finding a laptop with evidence of countless tortures taking place at the dilapidated old cabin, as well as the floating corpse of Glow Bourdeaux's missing girlfriend in the ice fishing shack. But while we both had assumed my brother was both capable and responsible for these horrors, neither of us were prepared to find that my brother had chopped off the head of his bitchy ex-girlfriend, Britta...and made it into a *bomb*.

The only reason the two of us survived the explosion was because Jaxon had managed to shoot out a patch of ice, and the two of us went plummeting into the frigid depths of Lake Michigan.

And despite Adam's concerned worry that Jaxon would leave me behind if given the opportunity, he didn't.

In fact it was *Jaxon* who pulled me from the icy lake, and resuscitated me, before helping me back to the car. We drove until we found the nearest clothing store, to change out of our wet freezing clothes before starting our semi-awkward drive back into town.

That was the moment I decided to seize my opportunity for a one on one conversation with Jaxon, somehow finding the courage to initiate perhaps the most long-overdue conversation about our failed relationship.

It took some pushing, as at first Jaxon seemed determined to hold on to the anger and resentment he had over me accidentally shooting Natalie and killing their unborn child, but eventually he came around and the two of us discussed the many reasons why we didn't work.

And then Jaxon did something I never expected he would actually do: He apologized.

Of course he had superficially apologized before, but this was different. This wasn't the usual, band-aid apology he disingenuously offered when he had fucked up and just wanted to get back in my good graces. This was the real, honest, and sincere apology of a man who appeared unconvinced that *he* could ever actually be worthy of *my* forgiveness.

The conversation wasn't easy, in fact it was downright uncomfortable at points. But it was also cathartic, with the two of us finally being as brutally and bluntly honest as we should've been eight years ago. I asked him about Natalie, and why, after putting me through hell for all those years, he could suddenly give her everything he was never truly capable of giving me.

But I already knew the answer to that: He *loved* her.

And not just in the protective way he loved me, that involved him never fully trusting me, and always needing to clean up my messes. No. Jaxon loved Natalie in the same way she loved him, completely, unconditionally, and as an equal.

The same way that Adam loved me.

Speaking of Adam, Jaxon knew about us.

Apparently, Ethan at some point over the last week, *had* decided to tell Jaxon about Adam and I, and in the most shocking moment of all, Jaxon said he understood.

…And gave his blessing.

Not that I ultimately gave a flying fuck about whether Jaxon approved of my relationship, but seemed that surviving our arctic plunge combined with our little heart-to-heart in the car had softened Jaxon's heart.

Before we reached Pace Manor, Jaxon told me that the Valentine Estate was mine to do with as I pleased, and lifted the house-arrest status while promising to keep the protection detail around until Michael was officially dealt with.

However, before I let one of Jaxon's cronies take me back to Valentine Estate, I decided there was one last thing I needed to do, both to permanently cement my position with Jaxon, but also to finally clear my conscience: I needed to swear my allegiance to Natalie as the new Regina Vestra.

But I wasn't going to bend the knee and mutter some pledge.

I was going to do it *my* way.

Respect in our world isn't given, it is always earned. It's why traditions like The Trials are so important. In reality these ceremonies aren't really for Don Supreme at all, but are designed to win the hearts and loyalty of the men and women who dedicate their life in *service* to that Don Supreme.

However, when it comes to the wife of the Don Supreme, she was simply named *Regina Vestra* by default. And while yes, there technically *was* a swearing-ceremony for her as well, it definitely felt like more of a formality.

But Natalie had defied the mold from the beginning.

Unlike the beautiful but quiet wives of Don's prior, Natalie *had* actually earned the respect of Jaxon's men. She had made the benign role of Regina Vestra more than just a hollow title, but rather a position of equal pride and power. For as much as I had envied her, to her credit, the woman was courageous and bold, and she was willing to get her hands dirty, and stand up to Jaxon when she thought he was wrong...or at least being a pompous asshole. And it was clear to everyone in Jaxon's life that Natalie was the reason the Don Supreme had truly come into his own as the leader of the syndicate. She had brought him harmony and peace.

Maybe even a little badassery on occasion.

But I knew that Chicago Mafia Syndicate would need more than me just bending a knee. After all, I wasn't another grunt worker. I was Rachel Valentine, sister to Michael Valentine and mother to the current heir apparent, Jessica Pace. The entire syndicate knew my name and would be talking about this day for a long time to come, so my pledge needed to be memorable.

It would require pageantry.

It would require showmanship.

And it would require a *fight*.

...So I picked a fucking fight. With none other than the Regina Vestra herself.

Natalie, true to her nature, did not disappoint. She didn't back down, and she let me go easy on her. She got into the ring and knocked me on my ass...and then helped me to my feet.

Telling me that this was my opportunity to leave every bad memory, unresolved conflict, and a decade of pain and bitterness right there on the mat.

And you know what? I *did*

Although Jaxon and I had not succeeded in finding and killing my brother, our mission today hadn't been a total waste. Old wounds had been repaired, new alliances had been formed, and it felt like all of us now had a shot at moving forward with our lives.

So as Levi drops me off on the porch of the Valentine Estate, I feel myself overcome with an emotion that has always felt so foreign to me: *Hope.*

And I know, it was all because of Adam.

"Babe, wait til I tell you what happened today!" I say as I open the door. "You're never going to believe it."

However, as I step into the foyer, I find it dark. And quiet.

"Adam?" I call, my voice echoing upstairs.

But there's no reply.

From where I'm standing I can easily see that he's not in the study, or in the kitchen, as both rooms are dark, with the sun still setting quickly this time of year.

Is he in the shower? Maybe that's why he's not answering?

Quickly making my way upstairs to our bedroom, I find that the bed is made, but that this room too is dark and empty.

But the moment I notice that his wallet and keys are no longer on the nightstand where he left them, is the moment my heart starts racing.

Oh no...

Racing back down the steps, I feel my heart thundering in my chest, as my brain tries to come up with a rational explanation.

I *had* told him that if something happened to me, or if any of Jaxon's men gave him any problems, to use the tunnel and get out as quickly as possible.

Maybe he's hiding in there?

I run over to the painting entrance, but upon opening it and calling his name into the darkness, I hear no reply. I walk back out into the foyer, and that's when I really start to panic.

Had Ethan lied to me about Adam's being safe to stay here? Had Adam been discovered on his own by Jaxon's men? Had he been injured and taken to the hospital?

But perhaps the worst thought of all...

Had Adam been so furious and hurt over me agreeing to help Jaxon with this Michael mission that he longer wanted to be with me...and had *left*?

My body starts shaking, and I feel the tears welling in my eyes, when out of my peripheral I suddenly notice movement in the hallway. No, not movement, more like a faint subtle glow. Upon closer inspection, I see it again, except that this time I notice that it's actually *flickering*.

What the...?

Cautiously I make my way down the dark hallway, finding that the flickering glow is coming from the doorway to the ballroom, the light glowing brighter and brighter as I approach.

But the moment I step into the threshold, my heart stops entirely. Because scattered around the entire room are hundreds of candles. And in the center of the room, dressed in gray slacks and black button up shirt, holding a dozen red roses...is FBI Agent Westwood.

...And he is waiting for *me*.

EPILOGUE

ADAM

The look on Rachel's face is absolutely priceless, and worth every second of this pain-staking preparation.

"Adam," she whispers, stepping into the room and walking slowly toward me. "What is…what is all of this?"

I smile, standing here silently waiting for her to walk down the path of candles to me.

"How did you do all of this?" She gasps, looking around the room full of candles.

"Very carefully," I chuckle. "And to be honest, the store on this side of town didn't have many candles in stock so I ended up swiping a few from around the house. I hope you're not upset."

"Upset?" she chuckles. "No, I'm not upset. Impressed, and maybe slightly worried that we're going to set ourselves on fire, but, hey, I'll get over it."

"Don't worry, if we do, I grabbed a fire extinguisher just in case," I say, pointing to where it sits in the corner, and then shooting her a wink. "I figured there was a lot of dust and resin on the floor in here so I didn't want to take any chances."

Rachel smiles, though I suspect it has nothing to do with my terrible attempt at a joke.

"I thought...I thought something had happened to you," she says quietly, her voice cracking slightly. "Or that you got scared and ran off. And then I had thought that maybe you were so mad at me for going on with him, despite you not wanting me to go, that you—"

But before she can finish her sentence, I step forward, cup her face, and kiss her deeply, pausing to linger on her lips for a moment.

"I already told you, Rachel," I say quietly. "I'm not afraid of the risks of being with you. I don't care how wealthy or powerful your ex-boyfriend is, or how many burly bodyguards are posted up outside. When I told you I wouldn't leave you, I meant that. Unconditionally. Not until things get hard or scary, or until you make me mad, or don't do what I want you to do."

I stroke her cheek with my thumb.

"Because that's not who you are, Princess," I say gently. "And it's one of the many reasons I love you."

Her eyes light up and I savor the gentle blush that spreads across her face.

"I'm so happy you're here," she says softly "And this is beautiful. But Adam, why on earth would you go through all the trouble to do something like this?"

I smile, watching her looking around the room, waiting until her eyes return to mine.

"I did this, because you told me once that it's never just something, it's either nothing, or it's everything," I say, keeping my eyes locked on her as I slowly but steadily drop to one knee. "And this? This is my *everything*."

Rachel's jaw drops as I reach into my pocket and pull out a little silver box.

"Oh my God!" She breathes. "You're actually serious?!"

"Like a heart attack," I grin.

Gently I reach forward and take her hand in mine.

"Rachel Anne Valentine," I say, trying to keep my voice from trembling. "You drive me absolutely crazy. You're frustrating, and unpredictable, and it's no secret that sometimes you can be a total brat."

She breaks into a soft sob, covering her mouth with her hand as I pop open the ring box, revealing a thin white gold band, and a black diamond.

"I chose this ring for you, not only because it was as unconventional as my dark little Mafia Princess, but also because black diamonds are said to signify inner strength. And Rachel, you are hands down, the strongest, bravest, and most incredible woman I've ever known. You are one of a kind, and you deserve every ounce of happiness this world has to give. And if you will let me, I promise I will be steadfast and faithful, honest and patient, and I will love you until the end of time."

Then I take a deep breath and ask the question that is burning in my soul.

"Rachel, will you marry me?"

"Yes, Adam," she sobs without hesitation. "Of course I will marry you!"

Holy shit! She said yes!

With shaking fingers I slip the ring on her finger before immediately scooping her into my arms and spinning her around.

The moment I set her back down on her feet, I crush my lips to hers, and she wraps her arms around my neck.

She moans against my lips and suddenly I feel her hands on my body, fumbling with my zipper.

"Rachel…"

"I just said yes to marrying you, Adam Westwood," she says firmly. "The least you can do is say yes to fucking me right here on this floor. You can make love to me later."

Well damn…

"Yes ma'am," I growl.

She yanks my cock out of my pants and immediately drops to her knees, swallowing me down her throat.

"Holy Shi…" I groan, my voice trailing off as she furiously works her mouth up and down the length of me.

Just before I feel as though I am about to cum, I stop her, pulling off her sweater and hooking my thumbs inside her pants and panties and pulling them down. Wrapping my hands around the back of her thighs I bury my tongue in her pussy until I feel her legs start to shake.

And then laying her down on the floor, in a bed of our clothes, I pull her down on top of me, groaning as her tight little slit slides down onto my cock. She rips the buttons of the front of my shirt, running her hand up my bare chest.

"Fuckin hell you're sexy," I breathe as she begins to ride me, finding her rhythm. "Go on baby girl, take what's *yours*."

It's not long before Rachel moans, throwing her head back and climaxing on my cock. However, just as I feel my own orgasm building, I look up and notice that one of the two hundred candles I lit has accidentally set fire to the bottom of a set of curtains.

Whoops.

And even though I sincerely doubt Rachel would mind letting this entire house burn down to its studs, I'll still go put it out.

…After I finish fucking her that is.

Because Rachel Valentine *is* my house fire. She is exactly the right amount of chaos and the flame that has turned my world into a blazing inferno.

She might hurt me. But I don't care.

Fuck it. Let it burn.

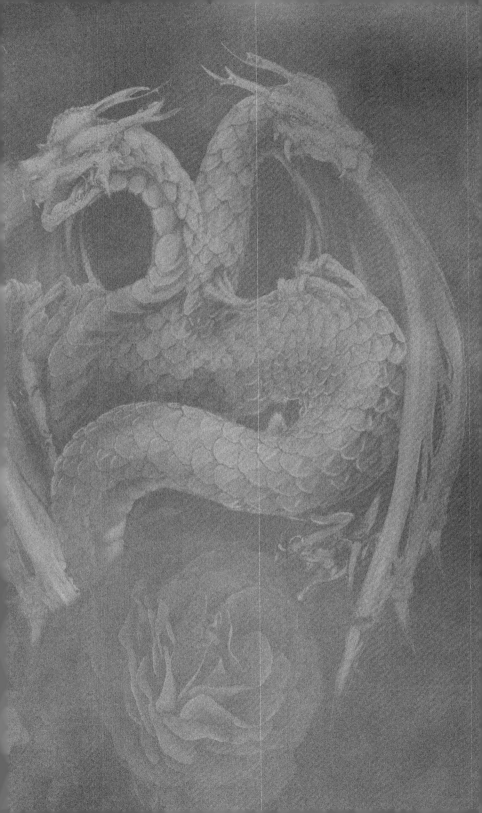

HELLO SISTER...

DID YOU REALLY
THINK I'D LET
THAT GO?

MICHAEL

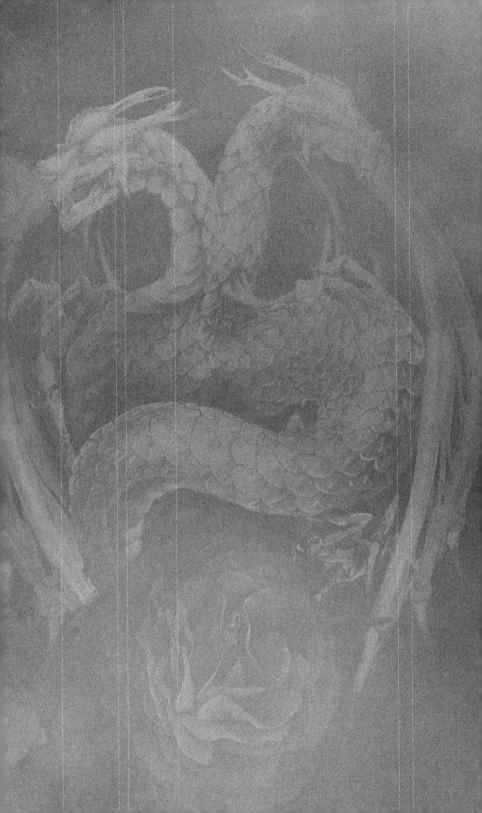